"These luminous stories—playful one minute, tragic the next—feel like the folklore of some alternate reality world. Often, they explore themes of how our identity is linked with our physicality . . . how others perceive us, and the ways in which that outside perception affects how we perceive ourselves. Yukimi Ogawa's tales are as enchanting, heartbreaking, and gorgeous as the characters they revolve around."
—**Jeffrey Thomas, Bram Stoker Award finalist and author of** *Punktown*
 and *The Unnamed Country*

"Yukimi Ogawa's first collection reveals her as a superb talent. These unsettling, sometimes harrowing journeys lead always toward grace and strange beauty."
—**C. C. Finlay, winner of the World Fantasy Award and author of the**
 Traitor to the Crown series

"Inventive, fantastical, and original; Ogawa transforms mythology, ghost stories, and the tropes of science fiction into fresh, new visions."
—**A. C. Wise, Bram Stoker, British Fantasy, Shirley Jackson, and World**
 Fantasy award-nominated author of *The Ghost Sequences*

"Ogawa's debut collection of 17 speculative shorts stuns with its delicacy. In the eponymous story, a woman is punished for her attempt to cut ties with her powerful family, sentenced to work for a man who refuses to do the same, clinging to the ghosts of his relatives. 'The Colorless Thief' introduces a sideshow performer whose act is allowing patrons to hit her and witness the brilliant beauty of the bruises. A fourteen-year-old who bleeds out a narcotic, opalescent substance in 'Taste of Opal' is sold to a protective crew of merchants who she believes only keep her safe so as not to sully the value of her blood. 'Blue Gray Blue' follows an eyewear sales-man on a tourist island whose own ultramarine eyes occasionally dull to a stormy gray. It's a fact that embarrasses him until a woman who calls her-self a 'collector of blues' helps him see the beauty he possesses. There's a gorgeous fluidity to these tales that makes them hard to pin down, as they often end somewhere very different from where they began. Harkening back to the oldest folk and fairy tales and raising pointed questions about how humans value and devalue each other, this is a showstopper."
—*Publishers Weekly,* **starred review**

Like Smoke, Like Light

Also available from Mythic Delirium Books

Novels
THE TWICE-DROWNED SAINT by C. S. E. Cooney
LATCHKEY by Nicole Kornher-Stace
THE BLACK FIRE CONCERTO by Mike Allen

Short Fiction Collections
THE COLLECTED ENCHANTMENTS by Theodora Goss
DARK BREAKERS by C. S. E. Cooney
AFTERMATH OF AN INDUSTRIAL ACCIDENT by Mike Allen
THE HISTORY OF SOUL 2065 by Barbara Krasnoff
SNOW WHITE LEARNS WITCHCRAFT by Theodora Goss
THE SPIDER TAPESTRIES by Mike Allen
BONE SWANS by C. S. E. Cooney
UNSEAMING by Mike Allen
IN THE FOREST OF FORGETTING by Theodora Goss

Anthologies
A SINISTER QUARTET by Mike Allen, C. S. E. Cooney,
Amanda J. McGee and Jessica P. Wick
CLOCKWORK PHOENIX 5 edited by Mike Allen
MYTHIC DELIRIUM Two edited by Mike and Anita Allen
MYTHIC DELIRIUM edited by Mike and Anita Allen
CLOCKWORK PHOENIX 4 edited by Mike Allen
CLOCKWORK PHOENIX 3: NEW TALES OF BEAUTY AND STRANGENESS
edited by Mike Allen
CLOCKWORK PHOENIX 2: MORE TALES OF BEAUTY AND STRANGENESS
edited by Mike Allen
CLOCKWORK PHOENIX: TALES OF BEAUTY AND STRANGENESS
edited by Mike Allen

Novelettes
THE SKY-RIDERS by Paul Dellinger and Mike Allen

Poetry Collections
HUNGRY CONSTELLATIONS by Mike Allen
SONGS FOR OPHELIA by Theodora Goss

Like Smoke, Like Light

Stories by

Yukimi Ogawa

Introduction by

Francesca Forrest

Mythic Delirium
B O O K S

mythicdelirium.com

Like Smoke, Like Light
Stories

Cover art and interior illustrations © 2023 by Paula Arwen Owen, arwendesigns.net

Cover design © 2023 by Mike Allen

Trade Paperback ISBN: 978-1-956522-00-6
E-book ISBN: 978-1-956522-01-3

Published by Mythic Delirium Books
Roanoke, Virginia
mythicdelirium.com

Library of Congress Control Number: 2023935489

"The Charity of Monsters: Introduction" © 2023 by Francesca Forrest.

Further copyright information begins on page 256.

Our gratitude goes out to the following who because of their generosity are from now on designated as supporters of Mythic Delirium Books: Saira Ali, Cora Anderson, Anonymous, Patricia M. Cryan, Steve Dempsey, Oz Drummond, Patrick Dugan, Matthew Farrer, C. R. Fowler, Mary J. Lewis, Paul T. Muse, Jr., Shyam Nunley, Finny Pendragon, Kenneth Schneyer, and Delia Sherman.

Contents

Like Smoke, Like Light

The Charity of Monsters

Introduction by

Francesca Forrest

Yukimi Ogawa is a remarkable light in the science fiction and fantasy firmament: she writes unsettling stories that are by turns horrifying and touching. She's Japanese and lives in Japan, but she writes in English, which means readers of English can experience her unique imagination without the intermediation of a translator. (Are you jealous, Haruki Murakami?)

I first met Yukimi's stories when I was doing copyediting for Mythic Delirium Books' Mike Allen: she had a story in *Clockwork Phoenix 4* and several stories in *Mythic Delirium* magazine. I had lived in Japan for several years (one of my children was born there), and the details in Yukimi's stories and her incorporation of folktale elements were very nostalgic for me, even though the stories themselves were completely fresh and new. I loved them. So I was delighted and honored when Mike asked me to write an introduction for this collection.

The majority of the stories collected here were originally published in such well-known magazines as *Clarkesworld*, *Strange Horizons*, and the *Magazine of Fantasy and Science Fiction*. There's also one new story. The tales fall into three categories: ones whose protagonists are ghosts or other types of yōkai (phantoms) out of Japanese tradition, ones set on an island where some people are born patterned and dramatically colored (indigo, plum, new-leaf green), and a handful of others that don't fall easily into those two categories.

The Yōkai Tales

A woman whose strangely long arms are covered with eyes, an animated skeleton, a woman whose head can separate from her body, and haunted dolls, plates, and umbrellas are among the cast in the yōkai stories, along with straight-up ghosts. Despite their unnerving or even terrifying looks, these yōkai are by and large a kindly lot who champion the weak and defenseless. In "Rib," Kiichi, an orphan, attaches himself to a vampiric skeleton woman, and before she knows it, she's agreed to help him:

> "I don't know why I'm doing this," I said . . . "But I'll take you to your momma tonight . . ."
>
> I woke up to something warm. It was a strange sensation; the men I slept with would have gone cold by the time I decided to leave—sometimes dead cold, sometimes almost but not quite. Some men lived. My intention wasn't to kill.
> Reflexively, I rubbed at the lump of warmth beside me. "Mmmomma?" it said.
> "Yes."
> A pause. "No, you're not."
> "No."

That combination of macabre, tender, and matter-of-fact is very Yukimi.

"Hundred Eye" goes full bore on the macabre. The protagonist's freakishly long arms are only garden-variety strange. One night, they get an upgrade:

> I woke up in the middle of the night feeling itches all over my arms . . . When I scratched, something wet and soft touched my finger . . .
> There, on my lower arm, something black gaped back at me.
> An eye . . .
> At a closer look I could see many more swellings on my arms. They looked like bug bites, but then, one by one, a slit opened on each swelling.
> Eyes. Eyes, eyes.

It turns out Hundred-Eye is able to give these arm-eyes to those who need them . . . and that's not the last strange turn the story takes. At its heart it's a story about fortitude, creating family, and forgiveness—with plenty of creepiness and a good dose of humor.

Yukimi always engages fully and entertainingly with the mechanics of the yūrei's situation, whether it's the skeleton woman who can insert herself bone by bone through a tiny hole, or the head and body in "The Flying Head at the Edge of Night," who think of themself as we, since they come in two parts. In this story Yukimi spends time on how the head and body hold together when they're together as well as on what caused their separation in the first place. Like Hundred-Eye and the skeleton woman, the flying head and body exert themself on behalf of a potential victim . . . and the end of the story is a satisfying embrace of the freedom and empowerment of yōkai status.

In "Welcome to the Haunted House" and "Like Smoke, Like Light," the phantoms are exploited—harmed and even destroyed for others' needs and gain—and the protagonists struggle against this. One is herself a phantom (a haunted doll); the other is a disgraced human who takes an interest in the ghosts in the labyrinthine house where she's employed. And this theme of exploitation and classism is a good segue to the second group of stories . . .

The Colorful-Island Tales

On this nameless island, those born colorful and patterned are high status, while people with skin, eyes, and hair such as you find in our world—referred to as colorless and patternless—are low status. In later stories there are also androids, who rate above the colorless human inhabitants but below the colorful. The colorful themselves are exploited by tourists—people from the outside world who come to gawk at them. In the earliest story, "The Colorless Thief," the protagonist is beaten regularly because her flesh bruises in rare and beautiful designs and colors, which tourists will pay to see. When a foreign artist offers respite in the form of a huge sum of money just to draw the protagonist's bruises, the protagonist agrees, but discovers that this too is a kind of violence. The conclusion is sharp and thought provoking.

Two other stories featuring colorful protagonists, "Ever Changing, Ever Turning" and "Blue Gray Blue," address other aspects of life in a place where all worth is determined by surface appearance. In "Blue Gray Blue," Tsuyu's colors weaken when he's feeling under the weather, and he wears glasses to hide his eyes in that state: "It felt good, like a wall he could carry around." Circumstances conspire to brighten his colors, but after a coworker suffers a complete draining of her own colors, she and Tsuyu have this conversation:

> "I did like your dayflower eyes. Even the way it drained. I knew it was troubling you so I never mentioned this before, but. Now that I'm gray, I'd be forgiven for saying something like this, or would I not?"
>
> Tsuyu laughed. "You would, yes." He wiped a single drop of tear at the corner of his eye. "And—thank you. I think I needed someone to mourn that color. Thanks."

Three stories feature Kiriko and her mentor, colorless craftspeople who practice a kind of color-and-pattern version of Chinese traditional medicine, creating remedies to treat their colorful patrons' ailments. These stories have a Dr. House feel to them: the clients' ailments are never as simple as they appear, and Kiriko and her mentor must find solutions. Issues of human—or android—dignity, trust, recognition, and loyalty are all important.

In "Grayer Than Lead, Heavier Than Snow," the android Mizuha, a city official, compels Kiriko to treat a wealthy addict. The island's androids are contemptuous of the colorless, but Kiriko's skill and compassion win Mizuha's respect and gratitude, and therefore she honors a sensitive request from Kiriko that she might otherwise not have. On a personal level, prejudice is deconstructed, but the power structure of society remains in place—but Kiriko imagines eventual change, and we can, too.

In "Ripen," Madam Enamel, the owner of a modest tea house, blackmails Kiriko and her mentor into providing her with a remedy to touch up the colors of her aging skin—an illegal act on the island, which has outlawed cosmetic beauty enhancements. It turns out Madam Enamel is resorting to cosmetics not out of vanity but because she fears for the fate of her teahouse—and her employees—if she's no longer beautiful enough to attract patrons.

To make matters worse, there's a foreigner involved, which causes the police to come down extra hard on Kiriko and her mentor. This particular foreigner is unusual among visitors to the island in her thoughts on beauty. She compliments Kiriko:

> "You are beautiful, too, don't forget. The way your eyes twinkle when you talk about crafts, the way your jaws are set when you are focused."

> Kiriko swallowed loudly. "Do you say that to everyone?"
>
> "Mm? Maybe. But everyone I like is beautiful in their own way, and I think it's important to tell them so."

This is a theme throughout Yukimi's stories: that to a loving eye, everyone is beautiful in their own way, and that it's important to give them the gift of telling them so.

"The Shroud for the Mourners" stresses the dignity and worth of all beings. The covert attempts of an android, Ash, to honor the memory of her terminated android friend have been causing unexpected illness in the island's elite patterned and colorful population. Kiriko must make her mentor look beyond the ill effects of Ash's actions to the devaluation of android life and death:

> "Sensei." She patted his arm and made him look at her. "If it were me dead in the fridge, would you be happy throwing my body secretly, bits by bits, never having the proper moments of mourning?" She swallowed. "Because if it were you, I wouldn't."
>
> At that, he averted his eyes and then closed them for one moment. "No," he said, "No, I wouldn't."

The Other Tales

In "Nini," humans' habit of categorizing and ranking things—and shunning some—eventually drives the titular Nini, an AI caregiver, to exclaim:

> "I don't understand . . . Uncles drink sake, Aunties tea. The medics drink data and Koma here drinks lubricant. You like differentiating yourselves so much, and yet, there are differences you can embrace, and differences you cannot. Where does the border lie? What draws the line? I do not understand."

By the story's end, Nini has drawn some decidedly negative conclusions about human nature.

"Taste of Opal" is another story that deals with exploitation: the protagonist's opal blood can be used as a narcotic—but she would like to see it used for healing medicine instead. Lush and creepy imagery combine with themes of trust, families of choice, and promises:

"You're leaving me," she said again. "You're breaking the promise you made." She didn't sound like she was accusing me. More like she was double-checking the fact that was laid out in front of her.

"In Her Head, in Her Eyes" is a sort of alternate-timeline story of the colorful island (though the action takes place away from the island) that simultaneously retells the Japanese fairytale of hachikazuki hime, the princess with a pot or bowl on her head. In the traditional story, the princess suffers at the hands of a cruel stepmother, runs away and works as a servant, but is rescued, Cinderella-like, when a prince catches a glimpse of her beautiful face under the bowl. They eventually marry and the bowl showers the couple with treasure. In Yukimi's version, the "prince" courts pot-wearing Hase solely because he's obsessed with the colorful island, and a glimpse beneath Hase's pot is enough to drive one of her tormentors mad.

The story "Perfect" further explores the pursuit of beauty: in it, a narcissistic aging beauty desperate to preserve her good looks steals cheeks, eyes, hands and more from others, patching the damage she leaves with precious gems and other treasures. And then she meets Perfect, a young sex worker. Perfect admires an old magnolia-flower dress belonging to the protagonist. It once was fresh and white; now it's withered, crumbly, and brown:

> She could see how it used to shine. And yet she liked it brown better, because it made you wonder what time could do to you. That there were things you could do nothing about. And then she said, she also could see the beauty that I truly had been, behind all the things I had stolen.

Out of love, the protagonist endows Perfect with gold-lacquer thighs and genitals—which delights Perfect's clients. The protagonist is mystified:

> Perfect was perfect, and everything else in her was just as beautiful as the gold-lacquer sex, right?

A surprising betrayal is yet to come, but the story doesn't end there: Yukimi always has at least one more twist in store.

"Town's End," the earliest of Yukimi's stories in the collection, is a gently humorous story in which a young woman working at a marriage agency ends up arranging assignations between celestial beings and humans. The mix of modern technology with divinities and magical beings is fun, and the resolution for the protagonist made me wonder if this story provided a seed of inspiration for the Kiriko tales.

"The Tree, and the Center of the World" is original with this collection and contains many of the themes and motifs of the earlier stories: there's a protagonist who facilitates exchanges from petitioners from all corners of the multiverse who come to this tree, at the center, and the facilitation involves self-mutilation: cutting off a finger or an eye (these grow back). It's not entirely voluntary, but not involuntary either: it calls to mind the situation of the protagonists in "Taste of Opal" and "Welcome to the Haunted House." And then NuNu, a potential friend, arrives, and there's a birth/creation of sorts that recalls an analogous birth/creation in "Hundred Eye." The conclusion offers freedom and a happy family of choice. The entire tale, unsettling, creepy, funny, and warm, is a good capstone for a collection that is all those things.

Good science fiction and fantasy stories remind us that other worlds are possible—better ones . . . and worse ones. They give us space and time to think about how we really feel about tricky questions—like what makes a monster. Yukimi shows us over and over that true monstrosity has nothing to do with appearance and everything to do with one's treatment of others. Her stories are full of monsters—but the monsters are not skeletons, severed heads, or creatures with eyes on their arms. Similarly, she presents us with a beautiful palette of types of love and family: we have only to accept them in the forms they choose to wear.

Like Smoke, Like Light

"**H**ere." Thick, hard paper was handed to me. "There is no other copy, but for the original in his head. Please take good care of it."

My employer slid the door shut with a soft thud as soon as I nodded, but then I heard her footsteps breaking into almost a run outside; she'd seemed eager to leave ever since she'd slid the door to their annex building open for me. I placed the paper at an angle on the corner of the tray I was carrying, so that I could see it with my hands occupied. Then I looked up.

So many candles and lanterns, lamps and torches in shapes I'd never seen adorned the annex building that extended before me, and yet, the entire space seemed too dim. No light reached the ceiling, which wasn't particularly high. Shelves and tables, or very tall candlesticks, blocked the view to the center of the building, which was my destination. Something flickered over one of the thick beams, where it wasn't as dark as the ceiling, but still too high for my own shadow to reach.

I breathed in, and out.

I set out.

Take five steps to stand right in front of the first lantern—and don't look at the beautifully painted one just beside it for too long; that would only end up disastrous. Face straight to the simple one and clap your hands two times. I couldn't do this, not with the tray, so I had to make do with stomping my foot on the recently-cemented floor; they'd given me a pair of sandals that'd generate a sound that carried when it struck the floor, and I had the impression that the cement patch underfoot had been installed specifically for this purpose.

Now turn forty-five degrees to the right.

This time, let the fanciness speak to you. Take exactly five steps again, to be close enough to the ornately carved candle holder to feel its warmth. Exhale just enough breath to stir the flame, never—*never*—enough to put it out.

Instructions after instructions like these forever, scribbled over the paper, with the rough layout of the lanterns, candle dishes and incense bowls, et cetera, et cetera. With my short legs, and the robe I'd chosen to wear for my first day of this new job restricting my movement, I had to measure my strides carefully. The soup on the tray had gone long cold, and every joint in my no-longer-young body was numb, I finally found the first son of the family in the middle of the annex. The burn scars on my palms—marks of my betrayal—felt raw where I gripped the wooden tray too tight for too long, and I had trouble letting go of it as I set the meal down.

When he heard me, he looked up a little. "You're new."

"Yes, sir." I stifled a sigh of exhaustion.

He looked around. "You managed. Good." Then up at me again. "You don't look much younger than I."

Of course, younger people were always much better with memories and tasks that involved a lot of fiddling around with precision. But another part of me said this was not a task for a young person, not for someone with a future that still looked bright. "I am only two years younger than you. My father sent me here."

"Ah," he said, as if that explained. "So. First you shall witness *it*, to understand why and how the procedures you've just undergone are important."

I nodded.

He lifted a corner of the cloth covering his meal. "Well. Lunch can wait. Take a seat."

There was no seat as far as I could see, so I sat down on the corner of his pallet. His pallet was lit by a lantern placed beside his low, small desk, an ordinary light, whereas the candle burning on the other side of the desk whispered magic, the way it sizzled. I looked up and around: from here, in the safety of the ordinary flame of his lantern, all the lighting equipment seemed to cast both light and dimness. Each device confined one monster, which was trapped to play a role in the greater sealing magic that bound the whole annex. I couldn't feel the monsters, not any longer, but I could see the flames and lights flicker unnaturally, which made me careful enough but not too frightened. And that had been the problem with the younger people who had stronger magic in them, who had previously worked in this position—they saw and felt too much, got frightened too easily or acted too boldly, with their quicker minds.

In front of us gaped a void.

Roughly the size of a six-tatami room, the space was dark, too dark, despite everything around us. The first son looked into this darkness for a moment as if bracing himself, then put a leaf or two into his mouth and chewed. He said a few words I couldn't make out, and blew on the candle. The flame went out for a few seconds before coming back to life in a slightly different color. And then—

I felt the air shift, as if all the monsters trapped in the building had now ceased to breathe, nervous and fearful and expectant. The faint line of vapor from the candle flowed into the void. About one human-length away, something emerged, like a waft of smoke, at first, condensing slowly into a shape of . . .

. . . A woman.

I swallowed. This was not the first time I had seen a ghost of course, but the first time in quite a long while I had seen a ghost *summoned* this way, and surely the first time I saw someone other than my father do the summoning. A beautiful woman, maybe ten or fifteen years younger than me, if she were alive.

I couldn't help but stand for a better look.

Beside her, as if lit by the ghost's presence, a small table appeared. On it a simple black incense holder sat. My breath caught as the ghost struck a match. The flame seemed to carve her outlines deeper against the dark, and I could see her eyes shine as she took an incense stick out of the pile on the table and touched the flame to its tip.

The ghost blew on the match and the flame went out, making her sink into dimness again.

Smoke rose from the incense, just a thin line of gray at first, then curling and furling around the stick as if the smoke couldn't quite get away from it. And then . . .

In the smoke, as it got thicker and thicker around the stick, I started to see the image: a woman and a small boy. Mother and son. The boy waved, but to whom, I had no idea. I knew the first son—the man beside me—wanted to believe the child was waving at him, that the mother was smiling at him. But the gestures, their expressions, everything about the image seemed distant, hollow. Which made it all the sadder, all the more horrifying.

I was not going to keep watching these sad shadows for the time it took an incense stick to burn out. "I . . . " My mouth felt stupidly dry. "I should not be intruding a single minute more in your precious moments of reunion," I managed to say, slowly turning away. "Now I understand the nature of all this, what those procedures mean. If you'd excuse me."

The man nodded without looking at me. "You're dismissed. Don't forget you have to reverse all the procedures to go back out of this place."

Oh. Oh no.

REVERSING THE STEPS I'D GONE THROUGH was the hardest part, in fact. By the time I was safely out of the annex building I was exhausted, my eyes aching, shoulders too stiff even to sit straight.

I came awake out of my half-sleep on the main building's porch, with the sound of a cup placed near me. My employer, the first son's younger sister, knelt beside me with a tray to her chest, both of us now facing the garden as if afraid to meet each other's eyes.

"Thank you," I said as I took the cup with one hand and massaged my eyebrow with the other. The tea was a bit too thick, which was good, and she probably knew that well. There was also a very nice looking piece of confection, shaped like a simplified flower, its color soft pink. "Peony?" I asked without thinking. The family's crest.

She nodded. "I hope you're not considering quitting already."

I laughed a little, too tired to pretend. "I don't have a choice."

"You only think you don't."

"Debts are debts. Damage done to reputation cannot ever be repaired, but I'm lucky you let me try anyway." More than half of this, I was literally repeating my father.

My palms tingled, where burn scars reminded me what nuisance I was to my family. Our family had a magic to tie someone's soul to a place, or to another person, and they used this magic to keep servants, or sometimes even mistreated wives, from running away. And I had been bound by the same magic, once. Trivial as I was, a daughter related to this family being under the magic was bad enough; but I managed to cast away that bond, in the wrong way, which was blasphemous to this family, to say the least.

Her expression shaded a little, and something about it reminded me of the child I'd seen in that smoke. She was the child's aunt, after all. "As if all that had been done is your fault? I might've done the same if I knew how."

I blinked. I had thought everyone, every member of this family, blamed me for the damage. I didn't know what to say, but then I heard a child burst into crying somewhere in the house; I tensed.

She laughed, just a little. "It's my daughter. Quite alive. If you'd excuse me."

I watched her back as she shuffled along the corridor, around a corner and disappeared. Looking around to make sure no one was watching, I put my tea down and slid closer to the peony confection. At home, no one would hire me, let alone give me something sweet, because of the mistake I'd made. But my father had found this job for me, too lowly for the member of the head family itself, but one they didn't want to assign to a total stranger. I was a perfect fit here.

I cut it into pieces and put one into my mouth. Delicately sweet and fragrant. Silky to the tongue.

DAY AFTER DAY, THE FIRST SON stared into the nothingness, and I carried his meals. After a week or so my pilgrimage, as it were, became a sort of pattern, and I could perform it without too much thinking. I asked no questions to him or to his sister, and I knew only a handful of truths about all this: that his wife and son were very dead, and the image in the smoke was the only thing keeping the first son alive; that the first son had sealed the annex, and the procedures I followed every day now were required to keep that seal in place. I'd seen a device like this annex, though much, much smaller in scale, in my home village. It was shaped like a simple house the size of a home altar, and my father had trapped a monster in it which was around that time messing with the village's harvest. My father, the head of one of the far-spread branches of this family I worked for, set a few complex traps to prevent other monsters from breaking the seal. If someone, something, failed in the undoing, the altar would collapse and the trapped monster would be confined forever in the ruins, together with the thing which had tried to break in.

If this annex worked on the same theory, should I ever fail, the ghosts, the first son, and I would be trapped here forever. And it was likely other monsters were bound against their will, even if they didn't deserve this treatment, to lamps and lanterns as a means to complicate and strengthen the magical seal. Something this family—and my father—did all the time.

I'd shudder at the flickering of the shadows sometimes, with this thought in mind. I didn't have much magic left in me, but it wasn't like I could drain my blood completely and unsee and unlearn everything.

IT HAD BEEN A FEW WEEKS since I started working here, when, one day, a servant accidentally slammed the door shut, which was discouraged.

Not because closing the door gently was part of the procedures, but because a wind too strong might cause some kind of reaction inside the annex, like put out some of the bare flames—no one but the first son was sure how magical these flames were. I stood there for a few heartbeats, waiting for something to happen.

Nothing did.

I let out a faint sigh and looked down at the tray. The instruction paper was not there.

It had landed an arm's-length away from me, in the opposite direction of my usual course. I crouched, set the tray down, and reached out. I had a feeling that once I stood in this position, my procedures were as good as started. But my shoulders were stiff and my arms were short, and an arm's length felt like an entire annex away for me. Just a few more finger-widths . . . if I could hook my pinky around that curl . . .

I almost yelped: in my desperation my foot had moved, though just a little. I listened; nothing again. I managed to catch the paper. Stood up.

Silence.

I looked up, ready to set out, ready to forget what'd just happened. But to my dismay, I realized something was wrong; the lights from the equipment connected to the floor seemed to have changed hues. Maybe just my eyes getting older? But then the circles on the floor from these lights—where they didn't overlap with the lights from the ceiling or on the wall—seemed to waver, just a little. Like water rippling as an insect glided over it. Was this, too, some kind of trick that my aging eyes were doing?

Or—

I almost cried out, managed to stop myself with a miracle I really didn't deserve. In the shadows made with the hanging lights, there she was, beautiful as ever. The match-lighting ghost.

"You could have screamed," she said.

I blinked. "What?"

"For help, you know. I could try to drag you away to the world beyond."

Surprisingly—I laughed. "No one would hear me. Or no one would come if they did. I'm dispensable."

"Oh. Dispensable. So am I." She smiled as if happy to finally find the right word. "We all are—all the things in this place. Anyway. I think you just broke one of those meticulously woven lines of his sealing magic." *Oh no.* "Just one, and I cannot move around much, but this is far better than nothing. So." She bowed. "I must thank you."

"Oh please." I hugged myself and tried to rub the chill out of me. "That feels weird."

She laughed. "You must be related to him? Otherwise you wouldn't be able to change a thing here like this, without making the entire building tumble down."

I frowned. "I am related to him, yes, but I shouldn't have enough power left in me to do that. We all are sure of this, and that is part of how I ended up here."

"Then you all misjudged."

But I should be a power-less. I had been *made* power-less, in fact, months ago. "How did you come to work for him?" I asked her, still a little confused.

"I was one of the servants here, and was getting a bit old for the work assigned to me, and surely too old to be married off. Died falling off a ladder. That was, what, a hundred years ago?" She crossed her arms. "I've been one of their monsters-for-use ever since, but this is the first time they locked me up this tightly."

I shuddered at the implication—there was no telling if that had indeed been an accident. And they kept the master-servant tie even after the servant was *dead*? "I'm sorry," was the only thing I could say.

"Don't be, it's not your fault. Do you know how the incense works?"

I shook my head.

"It's a crazy mixture of dark secrets, that incense. His ancestors first made the recipe long ago at an emperor's request. They did succeed, but it requires a certain price."

"And that is?" Did I want to know?

Her smile flickered again, as if she'd heard my silent question. "It takes a small chunk of life that's close enough to it every time it burns. Just like an ordinary flame takes the air around it to burn."

I didn't understand.

"So." She giggled at my stare. "If a flower is too close to the incense when it burns, the flower withers. If a human is near the incense to light it—and surely they have to be—it sucks a little bit of life out of them, so that in the end they'd die, at least sooner than they were supposed to."

"Oh." I licked my lips. "So they locked you up here, to make you light that incense every day for him, because you're a ghost and already very dead and the incense cannot kill you."

"That's right."

"But that's not right!"

She laughed again, quite heartily despite everything. "You are a strange thing. I am a dispensable ghost, I've always been dispensable ever since I was sold to this family, and there's really no right or wrong for the way you treat me. If I may, I'd say the way this family treats *you* is less right."

"That's not the same! You're not even related to these people by blood." But before she could say anything for an answer to that, she flickered out. After a moment I realized the first son must have summoned her.

I took time deliberately, and arrived at his pallet just when the smoke image was going out. Good for me. The ghost was looking at the smoke as it slowly dispersed. Her profile was a silhouette, but for some reason, I sensed that she did something—maybe smile. Something she'd probably never done in that void before. A flicker of something like a shade of life, in that lifeless space.

The first son sucked in a sharp breath. I wasn't sure if he saw what I saw, or if he simply wanted to draw the smoke into him.

THE FIRST SON GREW MORE AND more unstable after that. I'd sometimes arrive at his pallet as he muttered to himself, his eyes fixed on the dimness of the void, or scribbled fiercely on a notebook. One day he asked me to bring a new notebook along with the meal, which was mostly left untouched every time I retrieved the tray these days. A few days later, he asked for another. I could see black circles under his eyes. "Sir," I said one day, though I knew I shouldn't. "You should take a rest."

He looked up, and his expression said *What the hell is a rest?* Then he blinked. "Something is changing in there." His voice sounded much older than he actually was. "If I can grasp that change correctly . . . direct it the right way I may . . . "

No, I wanted to say. *The dead will never come back. The past can never be undone.* "I'll bring some amazake," I said instead.

He blinked again, but said nothing in reply and stared on at me as if he didn't quite understand what'd just happened. I bowed and started my backward procedures.

WHEN I CAME BACK WITH A slightly-steaming cup of amazake (I had wrapped it in cloths to keep it as warm as it could be), he was asleep. This was the first time I saw him sleeping—I hadn't even seen him eat or drink before for that matter, anything that indicated he was human, not a ghost.

I looked to the void. The last of the steam from the cup looked a little like smoke, but when she appeared behind it, I jumped all the same.

"You know, people of this house don't do that," she said, laughing.

I sighed. "Of course they aren't afraid of ghosts or monsters—" I frowned. "No. Sorry, I didn't mean you're a monster."

She shook her head, and slid my way as close as she'd dare, to the edge of the void, of the ordinary light of his lantern. "You should, though. Ghost is a category of Monster, and the difference is a thin, unstable line."

I sighed again, and when the steam drifted away I saw her robe, laden with flower printing, or maybe even embroidery. "That's beautiful," I said, forgetting about the man asleep at my feet. "I wasn't aware your robe was patterned." Peony flowers, the crest of this family.

Something crossed her face: surprise? fear, even? "It wasn't," she said. "I never could afford such luxury."

Could a ghost fear?

* * *

I TRIED TO ASK AROUND, WHAT it meant if a ghost changed its appearance. This was a house full of ghost experts, after all. I'd intended to ask my employer first, but she was out for the day. So after doing a small chore for one of the younger husbands, I ventured and asked him, because for that moment he seemed friendly enough.

His mouth twisted into one of those don't-you-dare sneering curves, though, the next moment. "But you don't see ghosts anymore?"

"It depends," I said, already resigned. "I do see the ghost in the annex."

"Huh. Well. That's probably because the first son's making you see it. You're a power-less, you better not try to understand our doings."

I looked somewhere around his chin. "Yes, sir." He wasn't even as old as the match-lighting ghost, and yet to this man in front of me, I mattered no more than a ghost-in-use. To him, I was an "it."

But then: "Is he . . . well?"

I looked up and accidentally met his eye. At least he was concerned about his relative's well-being. This pleased me more than I liked; I shouldn't care about the first son, really. "Yes, sir, he is well, I believe. Though he looks rather tired these days."

The young man looked away. "You know. If he were older and weaker we could use a counterspell stronger than his seal and drag him out of that damned annex. If he were younger nobody would have allowed him to use our monsters-for-use that way in the first place. Either way we'd have been able to force him to reveal where he hid the family deed of property, so we can change heads." He eyed down at me, sighing a little. "He hasn't mentioned the deed?"

"No, sir." My chest ached. "He doesn't talk to me."

"Oh, of course. All right, then."

Without another word the young man left me. I looked at the frontground of the house and the annex at the end of it. Maybe the first son was an "it," just like me. Just like every ghost and monster confined in that building.

WHEN I ARRIVED THE NEXT DAY, the first son was awake, and the amazake cup had been emptied. As I took the cup, he said without looking up, "You stay."

I jumped—this surprised me more than a ghost could. "Excuse me, sir?"

"You watch this time."

Something prickled at the small of my neck. The circles under his eyes were now so bad that it looked as though he had huge, sagged eyes that were half his face. "But—"

He didn't wait for me to say anything further. Before I could decide whether or not to ignore his order, he went on to summon the match-lighting ghost.

Her robe's patterns now seemed even clearer against the dark, the flowers more colorful. I could see thin lines of golden threads at the edges of some of the petals, which I was sure hadn't been there before. She looked very uncomfortable in it.

He looked up at me. "Do you see it?" he said. "Do you see—obviously, there's more *life* there. I can feel it. Can't you feel it?" For a moment he seemed unsure, remembering who I was. "Well if—if *it* could change, my wife and son can, too, can't they?"

Probably he had realized she was changing not because of her robe, but because of something only a powerful person could sense. Did I do this? Had my small misstep carried this all along, this far? That felt wrong, all wrong. I was a power-less. An idiot who'd let go of the precious family inheritance, ruining the family's privilege. It was possible that I still had a thin trickle of magic left somewhere in me, enough to just trigger the change, perhaps—but this? And the flowers. They just didn't make sense; what did a peony have to do with life?

The first son, as if irritated by my dumbness, turned sharply to the ghost woman. "What are you waiting for!" he yelled. "Bring up the smoke!"

Her robe was overflowing with flowers, its beauty mesmerizing. She was a flower, the flower that illuminated that lightless void.

That lifeless void.

The ghost reached for the match.

"No!"

The ghost, and the first son, both looked at me.

I said, "Sir, look. As you say, she is changing—changing into something more corporeal, because you bind her here." The first son looked at me blankly. "I mean—she was a mere ghost before, yes, but now—" *Oh, how can I put this into words—* "She is becoming a monster of another sort. Because by binding her here, you are giving her a purpose, a new characteristic—you are making her into something more than just 'a dead woman.' Look at her. And look around!"

And, surprisingly, he did. He looked around. It took a few moments, it seemed, for him to really take in the surroundings. I wasn't sure if he had intended it that way, but many of the devices that were hanging from the ceiling or on the walls bore the crest of this family: peony. And their colors had started to change, responding to her changes. This whole annex was changing, unlike us two humans, who couldn't find a way to change but age and wither. It wasn't me who had made all of this happen.

It was the first son; he had started it all long ago, when he'd built this place. Mine had been a feeble—even if necessary in retrospect—push that added just a little bit of momentum.

"Sir." I knelt down, eyes level with his. "Soon, she'll be a proper corporeal monster, and your incense will start hurting her. And if you keep doing this, sooner or later, your wife and son will be corporeal just like her, too. Not to be back alive. Your wife and son will be *monsters*, too." He didn't respond, but something in his eye shifted. "And the incense will start hurting them, too. Do you want that? Do you want your wife and son to be monsters—are you sure you want to bind them to this family like your monsters-for-use?" His eyes started to spin, it seemed: misty. From lack of blinking, or from the realization of what he was doing, there was no telling. "Sir. Sir, do you want to be a monster yourself, who creates monster after monster?"

I'd never spoken this much at a time since I left home, and I was panting, throat sore. He looked away from me, now his eyes on the void, where the match-lighting ghost—half monster—stood looking worried, unlit match in her hand.

.   I was about to place my hand on his shoulder, when he stood, involuntarily brushing me away. This was the first time I saw him on his feet, and I wondered how people could be so terrified of such a small man. He walked over to the void, though his steps were unsteady, after a long time of disuse.

He took the match out of her hand. I thought he, impatient now, was going to light the incense himself. But he turned on his heels, and came back to his pallet.

"The paper," he said, to me.

I blinked, but then realized what he meant and gave him the wax paper with the instructions written.

"I hid the final seal of the binding spell in this paper," he whispered, as he touched the match to the candle beside his desk. The match came to life. "To get to the center of this annex in order to kill me, you'd need this paper. People would take good care of this paper that way, see? I'm a very wise, knowledgeable, powerful family head."

I said, "Yes, sir." It was the only thing I could say right there, right then.

The paper caught fire.

THE FAMILY TRUSTED ME NOW, BECAUSE I was the person who led the first son out of the cursed annex. Burning the paper, and the walls and the furniture that the building had housed along with it, freed the match-lighting ghost, and broke the seal on the annex itself so that people could now access the center of the building without going through the painstaking procedures. But the fire didn't burn the lamps and lanterns (magically warded against fire for good measure, apparently,) to set free the other things bound in the annex. People upturned his pallet but couldn't find the deed of property; they suspected one of the lanterns hid it, but the family was afraid to touch those traps still with the angry monsters inside.

So they allowed me access, though begrudgingly, to their books and records, along with their magical artifacts. And slowly, I learned how to deactivate the first son's trapping spells. Why had no one done this? Had no one been willing enough to use their own energy on this? By the time I was sure I could free every monster in a way safe to both the monsters themselves and also the humans around the building, the first son was dead. He'd already been too weak when he'd got out. At least, some of the family were around his death bed and he didn't go alone.

I started to work on actually unbinding the trapped monsters. After the first son left it, the building started decomposing, and no one knew when it'd collapse, so I declined my employer's offer of help and went in alone. It was a strange feeling, seeing the familiar lights go out one by one. Were some of the trapped things ghosts, too, before they'd become trap-monsters? Maybe. I saw some human forms, which flickered out or faded away instead of scuttling out of the annex. Some even bowed to me, I think.

It took me almost a week, but finally, I was standing at his pallet, every light gone out around it. His pallet was charred but otherwise absurdly well-preserved, though I saw strange colors marking it that seemed to have nothing to do with the fire that had licked it; in my imagination the freed monsters had left their marks there, of hatred, of unforgivingness. I peered down and saw the colors went down to the earthen floor, and likely, deeper under. This kind of mark would never go away, no matter how hard we tried.

I looked to the void, and squinted. Could I see some residue of smoke there, or was it the fine ashes of the incense from the bowl? With all the lights gone the void was so dark, even though there were windows near the ceiling. I didn't have a source of light, as I'd thought freeing the monsters would bring ordinary sunlight back into the annex. But the void remained the void, so I had to walk in with nothing, nothing to protect me from the hatred that filled that place.

And the hatred found its mark.

MEMORIES DID STRANGE THINGS, AS YOU got older. Farther ones shone with clear-cut edges, while closer ones blurred and bled. Somewhere in-between, I saw the two figures standing side by side near a cliff. They were mere silhouettes against the night sky, which was brighter than the ground under them, and brighter, probably, than the invisible sea below that cliff.

I know how to nullify magic, the girl was saying, with a voice that carried, so that I could hear her even from in the shadows where I hid, a few human lengths away. She was too young for my husband to be seen with, but the glint in her eye was too cunning for her age. *I can set you free from those monsters—your wife, your father-in-law.*

And then—*Why did you let them?* These, my father's words, as he struck me, with his bony, weak hand and arm that I should have had no trouble flicking away. *Why did you let him do it, why did you let him get away with it?*

And now and here, I looked down at my hands, which were marked with strange symbols near the fate lines on my palms.

My father had made me and my husband share a cup of enchanted sake at our wedding so that some magic went inside us both, binding my husband to me; I had already long been tied to my father, so that would prevent both of us wandering away from him. Any branch of this family used that same magic to secure a master-servant bond, or sometimes a marriage, a business connection, depending on the client's demand. That too-young girl had probably been a member of one of the families secured by this magical enforcement in one way or another. I do not know how she'd come up with these marks on my palms; did she think our magic wasn't real and we were all just being superstitious, and that she could persuade my husband with this kind of show?

The truth was, the only way to drain the magic my father had made us swallow at our wedding out of our bodies was through a ritual that had to be performed at a great cost on the performer's side, if the magic had not been cast by the performer in the first place. I'd thought the ritual would simply kill me, the chain taking me down with it beyond reach of my father's spell. And really, what is a woman to the world, without a man, a child, binding her to it? I ended up surviving it, though, losing my magic instead of life. This way I cut the link between me and my husband, the chain that had tethered him to my father. My father, and everyone related to this family, were furious that I'd exposed the fact that there had been a way to defy the magic they possessed.

But my husband and his lover weren't sure what had happened to me, so they sneaked in to my bedroom anyway, where I lay trying to recover from the aftermath of the ritual. I could have shouted for help, but I never did, and just let them burn those meaningless marks on my palms.

Compared to all of that? The hatred that plagued the void wasn't even toward me. It made the scars on my palms tingle, but only a little, and never followed me as I walked out.

It was already long after dark when I went out of the annex. My employer was waiting for me with a torch just outside the door. "I didn't know if I could come in to fetch you," she said.

I smiled at her. "Sorry. All over now. You can tear it down and build something new, though I think you should be careful what to build. And maybe some purifying ritual is required."

My employer nodded. "They just found the deed of property in the main building. They believe you made the final push to uncover it." She smiled weakly. "Would you stay? Even the stone-headed men of this family would be happy to take you into the family, after all this."

I looked back at the annex over my shoulder. That would promise me a life without worrying about food and shelter till I die. Best choice I'd ever get, probably.

" . . . Oh, what is that?" she said, looking down at my hand.

I raised the thing I was holding. "Found this inside—it's not haunted," I hastily added. "Beautiful, isn't it?" It was a small, simply shaped lantern, with a small peony flower carved at one point. The first son's lantern—the only lantern in that annex which was truly a lantern. The fire and the following chaos must have knocked it off into the void.

She seemed unsure, but nodded anyway. "Let me know what you decide, when you decide."

I smiled again, an ambiguous answer, and walked back to the room allotted to me. There, I struck an ordinary match, lit an ordinary candle and put it into the lantern I'd brought back from the void. And watched, as the flame steadied, as the shadow stretched out of the lantern, onto the wall of my room.

"It took a lot out of me, you know, to smuggle all of these," she said, when the flame was stable enough. Beautiful as ever. "Now I can only reside in the lantern's shadow, but so much of these dark materials I managed to spare. You can do anything with these. Maybe kill your ex-husband, or your father."

I let out a weak laugh. "And be a monster myself?" I said. I'd known she was in there, in the lantern left in the dark void, the lantern I had had to go fetch from that hatred-ridden, dangerous darkness. "*You* could have gone anywhere," I said. "You should have. What are you doing?"

She chuckled, with her peony robe mostly black-and-white now. "It's good to have someone to talk to."

"Just that?"

"Just that, or maybe not."

I sighed. As she said, though broken into many pieces, the magical incense filled the lantern's bottom, around the raised candle holder. "What am I supposed to do with these?" I said, truly at a loss but finding the situation laughable, for some reason.

"Like I said, anything. You know how to use these magical things, you have as good as got your magic back—I know this family spent a fortune preparing the ingredients for these."

I heaved a sigh again. At least no child, no husband bound me to any place in the world. "Anything" really meant *anything*.

Which reminded me of the ghosts, monsters, bound by my father's doings. Just like in that annex, like by the first son. There were plenty of them, I knew, trapped in perpetual discomfort, endless pain, if my father hadn't felt like fixing the situation.

Maybe I could right the wrongs of my father, now that he was weak, and I had these dark secrets. And the knowledge I acquired through this family's records.

"You'll help me, if I ask?" I ventured.

She laughed. "Of course. Many of the things that you set free would work for you to return the favor, I'm sure."

Huh. "That sounds like I'd be using you just like my father, and I don't like it," I said, and saw her raise her brows and regard me. "But I could do with a friend for a start."

In response, the ghost in the peony lantern grinned.

Perfect

Look! My magnolia dress!

Do you see the skirt is all made of countless magnolia flowers? All white, custard-tinted, except for this one . . . yes, the tailor made a stupid mistake and only this one here is purple. But it was near the back, and really low down, so I decided to overlook the mistake. And it seems mysterious, doesn't it? As if some secret were hidden here! Just one flower out of hundreds of its own kin, so different!

My husband? Never mind my husband! Now look, my fabulous headdress!

And of course, I got what I got because I didn't pay enough attention to things around me.

But my husband only loved my beauty in the first place, and how could I guess that he'd have to go away—how would I guess anything at all—while I had to be so self-centered and focused on my own beauty? And no, he didn't *leave* my side! I sent him away, almost.

Because after a while he started to take my beauty for granted. But no beauty is just given to you like water in a river that flows from mountain to plain. It was just natural that I started to see men who appropriately adored my beauty.

But then, other beauty-admiring men went away, too, when my beauty came to be harder and harder to polish and rub the shine back into. One day I suddenly—really suddenly, damnation forgetfulness from old age—realized I was alone. There was no one around me, in this huge, gorgeous house I had inherited from my husband, who died of poison from the flowers in the huge, ever-thriving garden. I opened my closet and saw years, years, years on my own face, reflected not on the mirror which was fashioned to deceive yourself but in thousands of facets of the jewels my husband had bought for me.

I wanted to scream, but somehow, I just snorted and closed the closet door.

RIGHT AFTER I CLOSED THE DOOR, I heard the bell at the house's entrance. It was a house cleaning service girl, who smiled brightly as soon as she saw me.

Such a young smile.

I reached a hand out and touched her cheek. The girl looked stunned and then confused, and made faint traces of wrinkles that never reached the end of her eye. Such smoothness, and I couldn't even remember when I had lost it. I tore at the skin.

It came off surprisingly easily. I squeaked in delight, and attached her skin onto my own cheeks.

The cleaner girl sobbed, her cheeks red and raw and horrible, and I felt pity. I offered my emerald from my closet to her, right onto her skin.

Her cheeks became rose-cut emerald. When she saw herself in the mirror I passed to her she sobbed harder, but it looked beautiful in its own way; her tears just added to the shines!

So perhaps I could just get beauty from others and give them different beauty in exchange, hmm?

I OPENED ANOTHER CLOSET TO FIND the dress withered and browned. I had told the tailor to care for it so that it'd be beautiful forever. But I'd forgot, he ceased to come and tend the magnolia dress when he was caught twitching under me by my husband. I could no longer tell apart that mysterious purple flower; so time fell equally on everything, I guessed. I wondered what had happened between now and then, to me and the dress, other than losing the love that hadn't been there in the first place. As I tried to wear it a few flowers crushed into brown powder and smeared the uncleaned floor.

I fetched my headdress spangled with diamonds and lead glass, my shoes and gloves of embroidered silk, and put on all the jewelry I owned. I found myself unable to detach from the dresses and all the beautiful clothes, either, so I put them all into a bag. And I set out, to regain the beauty I'd lost.

PEOPLE STARED AT THE MIDDLE-AGED woman in her withered wedding costumes. I realized I no longer enjoyed the attention, it was the beauty I wanted their eyes on, not strangeness. I spotted a young woman with black gloves on, even under the hot sun. I asked her why and she told me, looking a little scared, that she modeled for hand-cream and ring ads, because she had such beautiful hands.

I asked her if I could have a look, and she hesitantly took the black gloves off.

And yes, they were such beautiful hands. No spots, no wrinkles no scars. Fingers so slender, so straight that I wanted to suck at them. I tore her hands off her, and gave her my silk gloves instead. Her hands became smooth, pure white, embroidered in silver thread and studded with crystal. I skipped away from the screaming woman.

A little away from her I found a man with smoky-quartz eyes. I wasn't particularly drawn to the eyes, but he was beautiful, and it struck me that he might look better with pink spinel eyes. Incidentally, I had a pair of spinel earrings. Coincidence!

So I scooped his eyes out with my gold spoon and replaced them.

IT WAS SO MUCH FUN! It was best when I could find a beautiful person that I could steal from, but it was also nice to find someone I could *improve*. Most people fled, but some bold enough visited to get their details changed, those who wanted bi-color hair or mother-of-pearl teeth. I enjoyed it so much when two furries came to have their skins replaced. I lost my comfy fur coat to them, but it was well worth it. My bag was now full of eyeballs, nails, hairs, skins, but less and less accessories and furs and silks. But at least it was really nice that my skin was as smooth and shiny as a twenty-year-old's, that my hair no longer grayed.

One night it rained.

It rained, the half of the night sky cloud-padded, but the other half intact. It rained, but still, the moon shone.

I watched thousands, millions of moon-ridden rain drops. I would have watched them much longer but for my withered dress being spoiled. I wished it could absorb all the moon-water so it could shine again, like it did that day, that day my husband was still there, that day my husband still loved my beauty.

I needed shelter so I went into a shop nearest to me. I had no idea what shop it was, and I didn't care. I squeezed my fabulous crow-feather colored hair that I had stolen a few days back to get some water out of it. And I heard someone clear their throat.

It was a shop assistant there, I vaguely guessed, and I didn't care. She said something about her having just finished cleaning the floor. I still didn't care whatever she said. She. The young woman in front of me was the most beautiful person I'd ever seen. She was perfect. Her glossy hair shaded her eyes which looked like a cross between onyx and smoky-quartz, just about enough light to make sparks dance in them. I could see she wore no makeup and yet, her cheeks bloomed like moss pink. There was nothing I could offer, no gold, no jewel, no flower to *improve* her. While I gazed at her open-mouthed Perfect smiled her perfect smile, and asked me if I knew what she was selling there.

I stared on at her and said nothing.

Perfect let out a laugh that sounded like a bed giving under two people's weights, warm and inviting.

And yes. It was herself that she sold there.

WE WENT UP THE STAIRS AT the back of the shop (at this point I finally realized it was a sex-toy shop.) Her room was tiny, the only furniture the mattress on which a thin futon set lay crumpled. I asked her if she could lie down on the futon and spread out for me, so I could examine her more thoroughly. I'd pay with my leftover golds, I promised. She let out that same laugh and went over to her futon, peeling her clothes and underwear on the way.

The curtains were open and I could see the moon-ridden drops stuck on the window pane. The light danced on her black, black hair.

Oh, Perfect.

I walked over, the hem of my withered dress catching things on the floor, some of the flowers crumbling. I didn't care. I knelt and looked at every square centimeter of her. I sometimes touched things on her, to feel their perfect shape, perfect texture. Sometimes she moaned. The moan made everything only more perfect.

I wanted the perfectness for myself, but it was impossible, I knew, because no matter how careful I was to be, deep down the structure was just me and I couldn't fully be her.

I sobbed there, above her, and my tears fell on her naked, wrinkle-free belly. Perfect shifted and rested her head on her hand, the elbow pressing into the thin, weak futon. Why was I crying, she asked.

All I could say was, there was nothing I could do.

She sat up and stroked my hair. Then she scooped a tear drop off her belly with a finger and tasted it. She kissed my cheeks and licked at the rolling tears as if one tiny drop wasn't quite enough. Her teeth grazed my cheek, and I wondered if she'd do the same if my skin had been wrinkled as it used to be.

Beautiful dress, she whispered.

But withered, I told her.

Perfect shook her head. She could see the beauty when it was young. She could see how it used to shine. And yet she liked it brown better, because it made you wonder what time could do to you. That there were things you could do nothing about. And then she said, she also could see the beauty that I truly had been, behind all the things I had stolen.

I guessed she couldn't see that one flower used to have a different color, but before I could point it out she gave me a full, perfect kiss on my lips.

Oh. Oh, Perfect.

She peeled my dress off me and hung it near the window. In the moonlight perhaps I could see it as it used to be, yes, the illusion of it. But I still couldn't tell the purple one from the others. Then every thought, every memory-tracing drowned in kisses and moans and amazed cries.

LATER, TOGETHER WE LOOKED OVER MY collection. She giggled at my eyes-skins-hairs bag, but then sobered and took a meticulous look at the left-over jewels.

Perfect seemed especially drawn to my husband's gold-lacquer cigar box.

That was something I'd put aside, not because it used to belong to my husband. No. I had no idea why.

Perfect traced the golden patterns on the box and smiled.

So I transferred the gold lacquer onto her thighs and deeper places, because I couldn't bear to detach anything from her. I was careful not to spoil anything, her skin or the patterns from the cigar box, and she kept on moaning and twitching, making everything harder, only making me want to try even harder.

At the end I was so tired. Just before falling asleep I saw her perfect, satisfied grin, from behind my long lashes as they fluttered shut.

WHILE PERFECT ENTERTAINED HER CUSTOMERS I'D have to wait for them to finish off, curled in a storage space behind curtains. I was not a child, I protested, but she said no, she was the one who was the child. She needed me there, she needed to know I was there, while she worked. I could tell when she was mocking her moans and cries, and then I wanted to rush off out of the curtains and tell the customer how to truly please her. Or perhaps not.

One day it rained again.

Perfect had a new customer. It was a rare she. She's didn't happen often enough but not never, Perfect had told me. Curiosity tugged and opened my curtains a crack and I looked out. Perfect's eyes met mine and they watered, as the she customer kissed her lower and lower. When the she customer stopped short Perfect looked away from me for the first time.

The customer slowly and tenderly spread Perfect's perfect legs even wider, and told her how beautiful she was down there.

But Perfect was perfect, and everything else in her was just as beautiful as the gold-lacquer sex, right?

Perfect let out that laugh. As if taking it as signal, the customer resumed her kissing. Perfect never looked in my way again. I watched them the entire time, during which Perfect never mocked a moan, every single one genuine.

A FEW MORNINGS LATER, I WOKE to the sounds of footsteps.

I was still half asleep and had no idea why those men were here. Well, you wouldn't imagine you had a bounty on your head, right? It took me moments to realize they were all in uniforms.

Behind them all, Perfect was smiling her perfect smile.

She was grateful, she said and laughed that laugh. The gold-lacquer sex would attract more customers, and she was grateful. That laugh like creaking wood. Only it no longer sounded warm or inviting.

There was nothing funny in the situation, but suddenly *everything* felt funny to me. I tried and let out my first laugh. It sounded like someone clawing at a pane of glass. The men in uniform winced at my laugh, and it was so funny! I let out the second laugh, and when the third followed, I didn't know how to stop laughing.

They told me to stop laughing, but I couldn't, I couldn't even stop to say that I couldn't. I looked to Perfect. My precious Perfect, love that I thought I found for the first time in many, many years. Perfect smiled her lovely smile, and bowed as if in sincere appreciation.

A lot of the magnolia flowers crumpled and crumbled between me and the uniformed men, and I looked more and more like a heap of dead leaves the gardener had left behind.

I WOULDN'T, COULDN'T STOP LAUGHING AND so they gave me a shot and let me sleep. When I was half-awake again they made me sit up on a chair.

They said the bounty wasn't on my head, in fact. It was on the woman whose hands I had stolen. She now didn't have proper fingerprints, her hand being silk, and she obviously killed a person but they couldn't get the evidence of her crime, and while they hesitated the woman left the country. I asked them, so the money wouldn't go to Perfect? They said no it wouldn't, not to worry, misunderstanding my question. And then they said they were really disturbed because they didn't have a proper article in the law about what I was doing, stealing people's beauty and leaving something different behind. Some of the "victims" even liked their new colors, and it was making things more difficult.

I looked at my hands. The man in front of me said I had to stop doing this. And I had to return everything I had, including the ones I had in my bag, to the original owners. They didn't know how to do it, so I had to be willing to cooperate and undo everything for them.

But that meant I had to be back to that middle-aged, withered woman that I had been, didn't it? And I wasn't sure if Perfect would recognize me, once that happened. I yelled, no! and once I said no! I couldn't stop saying no! Because the men, customers, husbands tailors gardeners wedding-planners teachers classmates parents everything was no! Everything that had pretended they cared, when they never did.

They gave me another shot. That was another no! but I couldn't.

WHEN I CAME TO I WAS ALONE. I looked around, and my bag was at the foot of the bed; I wasn't exactly committing a "crime," so they couldn't confiscate my belongings. I opened my left-over valuables and stuff onto the bed. Without thinking, I started to attach them all to me and my withered dress.

Then I had more eyes than necessary, more hair than my jeweled headdress could handle, skins that had nothing to cover, and a crazy dress with too much silk and fur. I coated redundant skin with precious metals and stones. Of all the things I had, I had nothing from Perfect, or nothing from my husband, to tether me to this world, no matter how frail the connection. I hopped to stand in front of the mirror, a mirror that had no light-bending effect, and in it found a crazy-looking creature.

Look! The beast that I have become!

I shrieked in amazement, started dancing and twirling, kicking tables and chairs out of the way. People noticed and came to check on me, and the first person who peered in screamed and ran away.

Don't run! Look!

I tried to say, but my mouth was too busy shrieking and screaming and laughing. Most people ran away, someone tried to shoot me, but the bullet went into an unessential part of my layers of skins so it didn't hurt me. The person who shot me misunderstood that I was bullet-proof or something, and ran away, eventually.

Outside the building I found a pond in which carps swam, whose scales I stole and attached to my dress. The carps tried to escape me and splashed water, and it looked like the rain drops that night, the moon-ridden ones.

I attached them to me, too.

Autumn leaves were ablaze, and I replaced the crumpled remains of the magnolia flowers with them. I chuckled at the smoothness of crape myrtle trunk and made my feet like them. I looked up and I wanted my eyes to turn to the color of the starry sky. When I arrived at a beach I wanted the star-shaped dead coral grains to sprinkle my shoulders. I wanted the color of the sea at dawn, but where could I put them in?

Look! Too many colors to have!

* * *

By the time I decided to set out into the sea, I could no longer bear to see what I was.

I couldn't feel the water on my feet, damn my tree-skin feet. People watched as I went deeper and deeper into the sea. Did I look like a monster to them? But a monster was supposed to come out of the sea to attack them, right? I had only wanted to be beautiful, and thought I was only helping others when I was changing them. And now, what was I?

I went deeper and deeper, attaching more things on the way, colorful fishes and sea anemones. Now, I just couldn't stop myself.

At some point I made my feet sea water. At first it seemed like a good idea, but soon I got carried away with the waves. I didn't find getting carried away against my will particularly appealing, and so changed my feet into the soil of the sea bed.

When my feet became solid again, I suddenly realized I was so, so very tired.

Of course, I'd come such a long way. The surface of the sea, the surfaces of the waves, almost never stopped and here I didn't have to worry about seeing the reflection of the creature I had become. No one screamed at me here, no one tried to steal anything from me. I could sleep here a little. Or as long as I wanted to.

And so I became an island.

It took many years for people to realize there was a new island far from any shore. But then, once they found it, they soon knew that it was me; the island was too strange. Impossible trees for the climate, jeweled cliffs and carps swimming in the salty water.

Those few who liked my doings—changing their physical details— made homage visits, bringing in more beautiful things, things they themselves had acquired over time, adding to my landscapes.

And Perfect came.

She looked old, withered, but her gold-lacquer sex still shiny as ever. I felt it as she dipped naked into my water, the secret pond of moon-color water that people threw their offerings onto. Did she not know? Or was she offering herself to me? Oh, whatever. Because, her smile. Hesitant at first, taking time as if she hadn't made that face for a long while, but then, finally, perfect.

She laughed that warm, inviting laugh.

Perfect lived happily ever after, on the crazy island that was me.

Welcome to the Haunted House

I chi tries not to stare at the children as they scream, squeak or hide behind the body of their parent, bigger sibling or friend. "Behind them" is no safer than in front of them; Mirror creeps up from behind them all, so that when they turn they still find Ichi's hollow smile right there.

Most of the time, it's the sense of *We did it!* as she exchanges quick glances with Mirror, that gives joy to her, rather than the screams they win.

She doesn't know how she knows that this is her job. She remembers waking up in twilight, and the next thing she knew, the master was saying to the curious humans who gathered around them: "Come and experience the extraordinary Haunted House! Monsters, ghosts, every kind of horror you can dream of, and all *real*! We'll open at nightfall; come back with all the courage you can pluck up."

And she cannot help but get the feeling that she has gone through this before. The children, the adults, their temperature surging and dropping in crazy patterns; their sweat-ridden breath filling the space. The cooperation, the shared feeling of achievement, with all these trinket monsters that surround her.

After midnight, when the children have gone to bed and only a few adults dare come into the Haunted House from time to time, the monsters of the House have enough time to chat with each other. "We are looking for our former owners," Lute says, all considerate, fidgeting with one of its strings to put out a note that's obviously out of tune. "That's why we need to see many humans like this. It must be that."

"Oh, I hope our former owner does recognize us, though?" One of the Dishes rattles. "Surely we are no longer what we were before we came

39

here—and when was it? Why is it that none of us remembers how or why we ended up here?" Everyone falls silent for a moment, none of them having an answer to offer to that.

Again, Ichi thinks she's heard a conversation just like this before—or maybe two. When? Where? And another strange feeling nudges something, somewhere inside her wooden skull. She counts the Dishes, there are three. The number feels wrong, somehow.

When the nudge in her head feels too much, she goes to see the master. The master looks down at her, in a form roughly passable as human, just in case a guest unexpectedly comes in to talk to them. Under their heavy coat and the large hood, the master is a flock of small feathery things, like starlings, like moths. "Have I forgotten something?" Ichi asks, and even as she says this, comes another nudge: *I have asked this question before.*

The master smiles, with eyes and mouth made of down and rachises. "Ichi doll, you are older than others and made of more flexible materials, that should be why you remember better than the others." The master of the House touches Ichi's white cheek with their fluttery edges. "Don't worry, you'll forget all of this in the morning. You always do."

Ichi nods, unable to find anything to say to this. Why would she have to worry if she remembers? Why should she forget? She heads back into the chatter of her fellow monsters. Without humans around to scare right now, Lute strums its stupid tune, to the rhythm Cracked Pot and Weaving Loom make. Umbrella pirouettes to this crazy music, opening its canopy to full and bumping into everything around; everything laughs.

The Dishes trot over to Ichi. "We were saying," Dish One tings. "If we stand in a line, the drawings on us look like they make up one big picture." As they demonstrate, Ichi sees the point, too. A landscape done in blue. "But then, don't you think here, something is missing?" One points at the space between Two and Three. Yes—a pond abruptly ends at the end of Two, and on Three she can only see a rock that might be standing over a pond.

"Don't worry," Ichi says, despite herself. "Everything will be fine in the morning."

Dish One stares at her, as Two and Three exchange looks. "Good to hear. Thanks." One says after a moment, though what it's thanking her for, it has no idea.

THE HAUNTED HOUSE CLOSES AT ONE in the morning, because it's not safe for humans to be around monsters at the Darkest Hour—two a.m.— even with these trinket monsters. Just when the monsters start to wonder how much time they have left before their own bedtime, right outside the front door to the House, the master appears, without their coat.

"It's a moonless night tonight, my little monsters! Let's have a party!" the master exclaims.

The monsters cheer, and they all go outside to join it. Even Ichi's sawdust-filled chest swells with joy. Under the distant stars, her fellow monsters start singing—the songs they don't know where they learned. And dance: Umbrella its favorite, obtrusive dance, while others get more space and spin around each other. Even Ichi trots around, her steps unsteady on her wooden sandals that make a funny noise.

And then—

At the corner of her eye, she sees a strange movement. By the time she fully looks at it, the master is in a form like a huge, black mouth gaping, a ghastly emptiness against the starry sky. While she wonders what that means, a part in their fluttery mass, at the bottom-most edge near the ground, start wriggling out like a tentacle, before the master grabs Umbrella around its torn canopy with that tentacle-like arm, pops Ichi's little friend into their hollow. And crunches, crunches, crunches.

Ichi screams as she realizes what just happened, and others look her way and then the master's way, following her gaze. One by one others start screaming, too, as they see Umbrella's hands and foot sticking out of the horrible mouth and then disappearing into the blackness. "Umbrella! *Umbrella!*" The sawdust almost rises to her throat. "Umbrella!"

The master crunches on a little longer, before their shape curves into a thin crescent, sealing the hollow over Umbrella, making a content, smiley mouth. "Don't worry, Ichi. I told you. You all will just forget everything in the morning. Don't you worry."

But she screams on, even as the master melts back to their usual fluttery mass and slithers away. She is somehow aware, though vaguely, that while she screams, other monsters can concentrate on trying to console her, and don't have to think about something that's just too horrifying to think.

By THE TIME ICHI IS TOO tired to scream on, others seem exhausted, too, from trying too hard not to let their thoughts drift in the wrong direction. They all *look* exhausted, Ichi notes—Mosquito Net looks even more threadbare than usual, Lute is splintered just a little around its neck. Dish Three's edges are slightly ragged, chipped. They all sit in silence. The sky slowly grays; morning is coming.

Ichi shudders, as something almost irresistible tries to drag her eastward. She looks around, bewildered by her own self, only to find others stand and start walking towards east. As the light gets stronger, so does the urge. And again, something inside her sawdust chest says: she's been through this before, too.

It's like when sleep pulls down your eyelid; it'd be so much easier, if you just let it be. Ichi shudders again, but when the urge is doubled by the exhaustion from a long time of screaming, she lets it carry her. Almost. As the morning gray hits the ground ahead of her, beside her Weaving Loom sways its unbalanced body, and its shoulder hits Ichi's arm. She yelps and falls sideways.

Her white, wooden hand pops out of the socket at the end of her fabric arm and skitters away, back into the House through the open door. Someone careless must have forgotten to close it behind. A little light-headed, Ichi goes back into the House, after her hand. She wishes Lantern was still here, to help her find the hand by casting its weirdly wobbly ghost-flame. It's really dark inside. The master doesn't allow any kind of light inside the House, except for Lantern. The master hates lights, their body with too many surfaces, too exposed.

The master.

She feels the unpleasant taste of sawdust surging up to her throat again. *Umbrella*. Did that just happen? Or was she dreaming? *Is* she dreaming?

Disheveled, Ichi looks around, and finds something small and white glimmer in a corner, behind a fake tombstone. She stretches, but it's a little out of reach, and she wishes she had Umbrella to help her here with its long shaft. It's always willing to help. Was. Somewhere, around the back of her torso, she hears a thread snap. No. There is no Umbrella.

She coaxes her robe into a kind of rope, and manages to catch the hand with it. She'll have to ask Sewing Kit to help her mend her where the snapping just happened, and also strengthen the hand-socket.

Her hand back in place, she straightens her robe and looks back at the door. The sun is almost up. "Hurry Ichi!" she hears Dishes call her in chorus. Why should she, though? And where to?

She trots back towards the door—

—But before she reaches it, she sees the burst of morning light over the horizon. The door is closed—she'd shut it, just out of habit—and she peers out through the glass pane on the upper side of the door. Dish Three looks back at her.

And the sun sweeps her fellow monsters off the surface of the earth.

No, that's not exactly what happens. The bodies of the monsters, all the trinkets, are still there on the ground, but she can feel that their souls have evaporated out of them. They stand there in their mid-movements: walking, running or about to leap into the air. Three is still looking her way with its hollow eyes.

Ichi is unable to move. Not even a twitch of her hand.

* * *

THE DIRTY PANE ON THE DOOR protects her from the first light, but after a half hour or so the sun starts scathing her black hair and eyes, so she slumps away into the dimness behind the fake tomb. She doesn't know how long she's stayed there. When she looks up for no reason, she sees the sun has inclined into west, from the color of the sky visible through the pane on the door. She crawls up, peers out. Three is still looking her way, seeing nothing.

Ichi slowly opens the door and walks to her unmoving fellow monsters. The sun goes down, completely, behind the hill. She is about to poke Lantern's accordion face when she hears a sound. Reflexively she faces east and freezes.

The House's master comes gliding over the ground, all wings and feathers. With their numerous claws the master picks up the trinkets one by one. Ichi wants to scream—is the master going to do the same to all others, after Umbrella? But the master only tucks her into their fuzzy body, where she settles among the others.

Upon reaching Dish Three, though, the master stops. And looks at Three and then at the closed door of the House. Frowns a little.

Ichi holds her breath inside their downy body.

Then the master shakes their own mass a little and collects Three, too. From the back door they reenter the House, into the master's own quarters. There, the master places the monsters' bodies on the floor, and flutters their own body like a small night over each monster one at a time, rustling out their own strange feather language.

Something soft like butterfly scales fall silently on the monster over which the master hovers. And the monster stirs awake.

Ichi tries her best to look hollow like she does in humans' presence, while she watches other monsters. When her turn comes, the powdery stuff feels so tickling and tingly that she has trouble staying calm, but she fakes coming half-awake just the way others do.

"Okay, all. Come awake!"

At the master's words everyone yawns and stretches. Ichi does the same. When Dish Three leaps onto its feet opposite her, the master looks at it.

"How do you feel?" the master asks it.

Three blinks its twinkling small eyes at the master. "What? I don't know!"

"Okay." The master nods. "Now everyone, help me prepare for our guests."

* * *

WHEN THE HUMAN GUESTS HAVE COME and gone, and the monsters have some time among themselves, the conversation about why they are traveling, or why they are here in the first place, springs up from nowhere in particular.

"I think a woman looked at me as though she *knew* me!" Mirror clinks. "And Ichi! A girl looked at you in a strange way! She must be your former owner!"

"Yes!" agreed Sewing Kit, going through Ichi's seams. "I saw that, too! You must go say hi to that girl, Ichi!"

Ichi only smiles. The conversation chatters on, but now nothing about it has that sheen of hope it used to have, to Ichi.

They don't remember. When the master does that resurrecting, re-souling, whatever they do—and they do that every night, probably—none of the monsters remember a thing. Even that horrifying image of their fellow monster's body *crunch*ed, *crunch*ed and *crunch*ed.

You'll forget all of this in the morning. You always do.

EVERY MORNING AFTER THAT, ICHI ESCAPES the evaporation. Thankfully, it is not like the master eats one of them every night—if they do, the Haunted House will be empty soon. Still. She feels the weight of the memory now pressing heavily into her: sawdust inside her chest is damp and clogged, and her wooden face, hands and feet are scratched all over; her hair feels dry, unkempt strands gone wild here and there. Her fellow monsters seem unchanged, untroubled, since that last moonless night.

One night there is an addition of Parasol to the House. Parasol is brightly colored, and its canopy is not torn like Umbrella's. Ichi tries to determine if the soul in Parasol is the same one as Umbrella, concentrates on its conversation with others. But the mere effort makes a strand of her hair come off.

Parasol is not Umbrella.

Maybe the evaporating, and going through the ritual of the master's re-souling and forgetting everything along the way, is just something necessary for the monsters to keep being what they are. Without memories that dampen them, the fear that weighs them down.

Ichi looks up, as the master comes into the monsters' side of the House, just before opening up for the humans. "Ichi," the master says, their voice somewhere between perturbed foliage and shrieking starling flock. "You look ill."

Ichi cannot answer this.

"Well. I have news that may cheer you up, Ichi," the master says, buzzing a little around the edges. Excited. "Last night a human child misplaced something on the way back to town from here. It's a doll." Ichi stares at the master. "Not quite like you, but you can play sisters, perhaps. The mismatch might give the guests a more terrifying image."

And then a fear is too much in her chest such that every joint of her body cracks, as she realizes: it's a moonless night again, tonight.

"Are you cold, Ichi doll?"

She looks up and meets Mosquito Net's eye, as it dangles from the beam just above her. It did this—the dangling—when the human children were still only recovering from the shock of being between Ichi and her reflection on Mirror, and their frantic movement pleased the monsters quite a bit. And Ichi realizes she's been shaking, amidst those cheerful fellow monsters. They have no idea. How can she tell them why she is shaking so hard? How can she share this horrible truth with her fellows, when she knows knowing it will only hurt them?

Ichi looks around and finds everybody looking at her, worried. They have no idea. She feels the distance expand, that unfillable gap between herself and everything around her. Back when she kept almost no memory, she was just like them. Now, a horrible thought tightens her chest: what if they don't even believe it when she tells them?

But if she goes tonight, the master will just keep on consuming her trinket friends, and there will be no end to all of this.

She looks around, and takes a deep breath.

Night deepens, and a little after midnight the master closes the gate. "Anything wrong, my dear monsters?" the master asks. "Some of the humans said you came too close to them. You never did that before, did you?" The monsters say nothing, because of course, there has never been a before for them. The master is probably too excited, because . . . "Well. Since it's a moonless night, let's just forget everything, and dance, dance and dance!"

The monsters cheer. They all go out into the night, following the master, who has left their protective coat behind in their quarters. The monsters loosely circle around the master as they go spreading over the ground in front of the House. Ichi comes out last, taking the space between the master and the House, on the other side of her fellow monsters.

The monsters dance, celebrating the light-less night. Lantern slowly comes near Ichi, as Broom sidles up and holds Ichi as if being playful. From behind them comes Sewing Kit trotting, swinging its hand of scissors above it. The master looks up at the dark sky, their rachises spiking in endearment.

Now's the time.

Of course they've all been quite preoccupied during the night. They needed to steal one thing from one of the human guests. One thing that the master would never tolerate in the House.

Broom holds Ichi higher up, and she is now a little higher in the air than anyone else—even the master. With its hand Sewing Kit opens Ichi's chest; there is a swirl of sawdust. Lantern blows the oil it found left in itself, just a little bit, but enough for the already flammable sawdust. Ichi holds the lighter—that one thing they had to go through a lot of trouble to get—in front of her open torso. And her chest ignites.

The light is simply too much for the master. The master falters, yelling, shrieking, utterly confused. On the other side Mirror reflects the light and brightness doubles. At the moment's impulse Ichi takes off from Broom and dives into the sea of feathers which is the panicking master. Their downy claws catch fire first, and the firmer feathers and rachises follow. The two, Ichi and the master, burn and burn, bright and hot, her sawdust and their down bursting into flame here and there from time to time. But then she feels she is running low on fuel. "More!" she cries. "More!"

"But . . ." Mosquito Net looks horrified. "But Ichi, I don't know what'll happen to you!"

"No no Net, you back away! Just give me—"

"But Ichi!"

"*Umbrella!*"

They have no idea what this word should mean to them. But somewhere deep, very deep inside them, something stirs. *Umbrella.*

And then without thinking, Broom snaps its bristles and throws them into the flame. Mosquito Net absorbs what little oil is left in Lantern with its ends, rips them off and adds them to the fire. Parasol does its best to send air by flapping its large, untorn canopy fabric over the burning two. *Snap, bang, ping. Boom.* Strange sounds echo, as everything tries to help with everything they can spare.

Blast.

Mosquito Net tries to throw more in, but the Dishes stop it. Non-flammable things are now doing their best to not let go of the flammables. Without knowing, they know they cannot bear another loss. At the corner of her eye Ichi sees them, and finds herself relieved because her friends are safe, more or less. She feels something in her slipping away, and she does not wish for others to experience this. Is this what Umbrella might have felt as it was consumed by the master? The master is burning all around her, together with the bits from other monsters. Ichi is aware that her wooden parts will hold longer than the master, but how long, no way knowing that.

And then from within the fuzzy darkness around her comes the master's temporary face, zooming, twisted and warped. Ichi flinches, just like the human guests of the House. "Do you even know what you're doing?" the master's voice is almost ashes now, and Ichi has to strain to hear them—even now, she has to hear them; it's their master, after all. "Without me they cannot go on. They'll turn into dust in the end, without my making them anew, letting them lift the weight of their memories off their bodies. Eating them once a month is just an inevitable sacrifice for their futures. Do you know what you're doing?"

Ichi grinds her teeth. But through them she says, "All I know is we trinket monsters love each other, master." Her own voice echoes as if from a long distance. "Even if you regard us as nothing but trinkets. And I don't want to lose another one to you. This is all I know. All we know."

At that, the remnants of her master shudder, and back away, just a little.

And with her wooden hands slowly burning on, Ichi embraces the last of the master.

"EXPERIENCE THE HORROR," SHE CALLS TO the human guests, with her voice a little cracked, a little like starlings' cries. "The extraordinary monsters, all real." But the guests are already experiencing the horror, they think—the master of the House looks more terrifying than the things the House's flyer promises. She is bald, her skin strangely charred, marred, and inside her oversized robe, in her chest, something seems to perpetually buzz, giving the humans an image of a half-dead entity, maggots eating their way in and out of her body.

The master goes back into the House and looks around at the monsters. She is not yet quite used to the new structure of her body: her torso made from a part of Mosquito Net and Parasol, stuffed with the former master's remnants; her legs and arms consist of bits of Broom, Lute and Loom; her eyes are glistening fragments from chipped Dishes and Mirror, her jaw formerly the curving edge of Cracked Pot. All sewn together clumsily with the hands and limbs of Sewing Kit.

"Master." Broom comes to her. "I just heard one of the humans laugh at me as they peeped in, and they said I was too short for a broom. I think I need more bristles. I used to have more, didn't I?" Then it frowns. "But when was that?"

The new master sighs. "Well. Okay. Let's do something about it later. Tonight, can you just bear with it the way it is?"

"Of course I can. But master, why am I so short? Why so scarce? What happened to this ragged end of me?"

The master of the House smiles and touches that ragged end of it. Of course, after letting them offer these bits, in order to let them stay, the only thing she could do was to use the remnants of the master's feathers and remake them all. Let them let go of the weight of the memory of that horrible fire—even if the remaking made her weaker by day. Now she wonders what happens if she goes on like this, without consuming another monster for nutrients. But of course she cannot bring herself to even think of that deed. "It means you are a sweet, kind trinket, and I'm really proud of you." And then Broom beams. "But our job here is to scare the guests, so it won't do if they laugh at you. I'll think of something to do about it, I promise."

Broom nods and scurries away to its post. Tomorrow, Broom will not remember the promise she just made. Even so the promise will be kept, every promise ever made will be kept here, at least till the day she falls.

She looks across the room to see Lantern and Lighter snuggling. She wonders, maybe, there used to be a Flint Stone to pair with Lantern. Before the former master forbade any light source from the House. Lighter's oil has been thoroughly drained for safety. She wonders, maybe, if the former owner forbade fire for the monsters' safety, as well as the master's own. She'll never know.

That night. That last night that she was one of them, and was feeling weak and didn't know if her fellow monsters would believe her, they all said: "Ichi, we are not going to let you go alone. We stay us forever. We'll do anything to keep us *us* forever." The memory is warm, and bitter, too, in her feathery chest. Now she realizes the former master was playing their role in their own way; she has her own role to play, in her own way.

For one last moment, she looks back at her monsters. Their eyes are a mixture of love and respect, and fear. She smiles at them all, and wonders what her smile means to them.

She opens up the House, to welcome the guests.

The Colorless Thief

I really hated snakes, and the snakes themselves weren't the worst part. The snake-woman would, every time she saw me, show me her stained, cracked teeth, which she used to bite the heads off snakes, as if they were foreign, tube-shaped pieces of some sort of meat a rich merchant once brought in.

As if *that* was the worst part.

Now Dai loomed above me, huge and tall, just true to his name. He had a name that was related to none of his colors. His skin was brown, one of the common colors. And he had his head and face all shaved and always wore a long robe even when it was too hot, but I knew, from a few occasions when he let us see his body hairs, that it was the bright, reddish pink of a peach flower. I'd once heard that his father had been a warrior, so I guess his parents didn't want to name him Peach or something of the sort. His eyes were the color of pomegranate, only another choice of fruit/flower name.

And really, none of this was important, except that he was huge like his name. He raised his meaty hand, and I stood there rigid, a cloth between my teeth, trying, but never managing, to be prepared for the blow.

It landed in full, and the next thing I knew the ground hit my other cheek. Both cheeks burnt and I curled up whimpering, like a puppy. And this was only the first blow this month yet.

"Pick up your cloth and stand," Dai demanded.

I swore many times, loudly, and the only reason I could stand all this about Dai was that he didn't mind my swearing. I said something about hoping he would die, and I meant it, and he didn't seem to care. He motioned for me to hurry and get ready for the next blow. I stuffed the dirty cloth into my mouth and stood in front of him.

Again and again.

Half an hour later Dai was satisfied with hitting me; or more accurately, he was happy with the results of his hitting me, showing on my face and arms. My original skin color was one of the commonest ones, pale and vulnerable to any sort of damage including strong sunlight. But when it was hit, it showed the craziest color spectra. Blue to green, yellow to pink to purple, all weaving pointless patterns all over my skin. Later, when they were half-way healed, the bruises would look like golden needles. Caramelized frost crystals.

I sighed, my face and lips about to swell. "I'll be in my booth, get ready for the visitors."

"Yes." Dai rubbed at his jaw, probably checking for his peach-flower stubbles. "Wear the silver dress. This time the colors are a little weak."

"Okay."

I went back to one of the staff's tents. Everything on me hurt, but I didn't know how to live without being hit by Dai and showing my stupid bruises to stupid visitors. From the closet I pulled a foreign-style dress, one of the things Dai the Freak-Show Hut owner had bought for me a few years ago.

And I never seemed to outgrow it.

BEING AN ORPHAN, AND ONE WITH the commonest of the common colors, had never been easy. Many of my old friends found decent jobs in the end, most of them companions for sight-seers from abroad, or some of them, at the very least, shop assistants. Moe with her hair the green of early summer greens, too bright and too rich for the eye, worked at a wig shop, the last time I heard. Tsuyu, his eyes the color of Asiatic dayflower, attracted customers to his eyewear shop. Shino's skin was the color of pre-dawn sky, and she stood in a kimono shop like a mannequin for simple, no-pattern, no-embroidery garments, for her skin was a little too complicated for more exquisite ones.

And, really, me. My skin pale-pink at first sight, hair and eyes dull brownish gray. True, if you were careful, you might notice my eyes emit blue-green schiller, but that was like only when you looked from one and only one perfect angle, which was close to *never*. When I was twelve and kicked out from the temple which cared for smaller children, I knew the only ways for me to survive were to become a thief, or to sell my body.

Almost naturally I chose to become a thief, but I'd always been clumsy, and so just as naturally, one night got caught. It was a lean, tall man with bulging moon-gold eyes, and that was all I could remember about the man. He hit me once, twice, across my face. The pain dimmed the world. I was somewhere between conscious and unconscious. The man grabbed at my collars and tore them apart, muttering, "You filthy dog—"

Funny how he wanted to touch a filthy dog.

I was conscious and unconscious, too weak to do anything. But I knew, if I let him have his way into me, I would shatter to the point where I would never recover. In many ways. I was thirteen, and even a lean man like him was too big for me. I wouldn't survive this, even if I survived just this one minute.

But then something much, much bigger came into the scene. The thing hauled the man away from me. I looked up, into those pomegranate eyes.

The huge, huge guy grinned, as the lean man yelped away from us. He produced a small mirror from his bosom—it was so strange, a huge man like him carrying a woman's mirror.

What I saw in the mirror was my cheeks blooming in crazy gradations.

"Come with me," the huge man said, and of course, that was why I'd never run away from him.

THE SILVER DRESS'S HEM WAS JUST a little above my knees. My legs had been whipped a few weeks back, and the scars were now golden needles. I went into the Freak Show Hut, this month stopping at a shrine near a relatively large town, and let myself into one of the small booths, thinking of how to exhibit myself.

Baba the three-limbed woman talked to me from the next booth. She wasn't actually three-limbed, just one leg was too deformed to work properly as a limb. "You should shackle yourself," she said, chuckling. "Will look sexy."

I sighed. I was seventeen by now, and though I couldn't seem to grow much (probably from too much hitting) my body curved like a woman, at least much more so than Baba herself. "Do we *have* shackles?" I asked her.

She chuckled some more, disappeared into the back. Baba had black-diamond eyes, sterling-silver hair and seven-color skin that shimmered like rainbow. People wanted to experiment with her colors on a genetic level, and what they got was those extraordinary ones she had, as well as her deformity. Funny how they didn't like the latter result they themselves had created, so much so that they had to drop her at a dump.

Baba came back with a thick rope. She tied me to one of the bars of the cage-like wall of the booth. "Look sexy," she said between her chuckles, and went back into her own booth, dragging her useless leg.

I leant onto the bar, trying to look weak, look helpless, making sure my face, arms and legs showed well. I wondered if this was any different from the way I so much hated to live, when I'd got kicked out to live on my own.

* * *

"SNAKE BLOOD FOR YOUR MEDICINE?" THE snake woman grinned wide as she asked. Her features were something you'd call beautiful, but she had black hair, black eyes without whites, as well as black lips and nails, and some said she looked like the worst ghost. Some said she first bit into a snake to avoid men who wanted to have her.

I grunted. "Some ice would do. And I don't want my bruises to fade so quickly, anyway."

"At least people come to see you for your beauty, no matter how swollen your face is!"

"True." I grunt-laughed, popped some rice into my mouth and chewed. "Do you know how long we will stay in this region? I have to control my healing speed, if I can," I added, my mouth still half-full.

Our dining area was set in the store-room tent, the low table placed amongst jars of jewel-colored eyeballs, and a skeleton of transparent bones. Stuffed foreign animals were stacked in the corner, because they didn't attract the sight-seers.

"Better be more than a few weeks. My back still hurts from the last travelling." The crow-speaker joined the table. Like Snake, Crow's colors were mostly black, and his skin was gray with patterns like a crack crawling all over. His shoulder blades protruded, just deformity like Baba's and not "growing wings," and his bird wasn't a crow. It was some speaking sort of bird from abroad, he only *insisted* it was a crow that could speak.

After that, we ate in silence. Until Dai came in to find me. "Hai," my name almost drowned in his sigh. "We have to talk."

"Yeah?"

When he saw I wasn't going to leave the table, he sighed but came to sit beside me. "We have a customer who wants to have a look at you personally."

I put a piece of pickled radish into my mouth and munched noisily. When I had swallowed, I said, "You know I wouldn't take 'personal' customers."

"I know, and I told her that. She says she just wants to examine you more closely, and thoroughly. She says she's a jewelry designer and wants inspiration."

I laughed at the word; it seemed like the last thing we had to offer an artist: inspiration.

"She'll pay us a lot if you accept this. Perhaps we could have a season off."

"That much?"

"Or at least we could afford a more comfortable van?" Crow cut in, but his grin faded as soon as Dai cast a glance at him.

"She said she wouldn't do anything to hurt you, though I'm not sure how far promises go with artists."

"Well, if she's a designer what she'd do wouldn't hurt me as bad as what you do to me every month." I meant it to be a joke, but Dai didn't seem to find it funny at all. He stared at me for some time, and looked at my dish of pickles. I quickly scooped them up, into my mouth. "Perhaps I should talk to her and figure out what she is," I said, mouth full.

"Yeah. Okay." Dai stood up, and without looking at any of us, left us behind.

DAI BROUGHT THE WOMAN TO ME a few days later. At first sight I knew she was a foreigner, with her unfamiliar features, and her colors all common ones yet suiting her well. Her eyes were the same honey of her hair, but they didn't seem to have any schiller effect. I should have known; an artist who'd be interested in our colors, with such a big amount of money to spend on it, was always a foreigner.

I bowed low to her. She smiled, tilted her head, her wavy hair moving slightly. I saw strange, sesame-oil gold streaks in her hair, and suspected she might have dyed it that way.

"Hai, your name, I heard." Her pronunciation of our language was pretty good, though the intonation still had that strange, song-like rhythm to it. "Nice to see you again."

I didn't remember seeing her. "You, too, ma'am," I said anyway.

After that, the artist talked like a profuse river that had been stopped at a bank and then suddenly released. She did give me her name, but I couldn't pronounce it, and I settled with "ma'am." She chattered on how she liked this country, the people with their *beautiful* colors, how everything inspired her, without stammering once. I didn't like her particularly, but the way she talked on made me smile sometimes. I decided she was an okay person.

So later I talked to Dai, said, "Let's take her offer and get the vacation, or the nicer van, or whatever."

"Are you sure?"

"Yeah. She just needs sketches of the process of my healing, right? What's there to lose for that?"

Dai shook his enormous head. "I've heard people doing nasty things to learn the secret of our colors."

"Like they done to Baba?"

"Right."

I shook my own head and tapped his upper arm with my knuckle. "Baba was a helpless egg when they tampered with her. I'll just run at first hint of nastiness."

He still seemed uncertain, but after a moment, nodded.

SO THE NEXT MORNING, I FOUND myself at the lobby of the finest hotel in the region. A young man wearing a strange cap—which didn't seem to serve any other purpose than looking ridiculous—volunteered to take me to the artist's room. He had a foreign accent and all his colors were very common ones, but his features looked like ours, and when I commented on it he smiled and said, "My parents were from this island, taken to a country afar from here, where I was born. Seems like the magic can't cross the border, for some reason."

I frowned, not knowing what to say. But then we were standing in front of a door, and he was knocking on it.

The artist herself came to answer. "Hai, come in. How would you like some tea?"

The tea had a different color than our usual one, and I couldn't decide if I liked its bitterness or not. The confections she let me have were good, and when I was discussing in my head whether to sneak a few pieces for the Hut's members, she looked up and said, "You can take the rest home with you, of course."

I felt my cheeks burn.

The artist muttered something in her own tongue, set down her cup and walked round to my side. "You blush and the colors get even more beautiful!"

"D-do they?"

"You didn't know? You should spend more time looking at yourself, really."

She produced a small sketch pad and started sketching fiercely. I stole a glance, and could just see a rough outline of my face and many words in her language. I stiffened, not knowing how to react to this, but relaxed as soon as I realized she didn't mind whatever pose I was in as long as she could see the colors on my face.

Fifteen minutes or so later she moved on to other parts of me. "You want to see me naked?" I asked.

"You don't mind?"

"Sure. What would a freak-show girl want to hide?"

"You shouldn't talk like that."

"Why not?" I stripped off my undergarment. "This whole island is a huge, huge freak show, isn't it?"

The artist didn't answer this, and went on drawing me. Today my bruises were just a little healed, the borderline of each color slightly blurring. She turned my arms around, asked me to wiggle my toes.

By the end of the daylight she looked pleased and said, "Come back in . . . two days? Do you think the bruises will have healed a little further by then?"

I said yes, and promised to come back in two days.

THE FREAK SHOW MEMBERS ASKED ME how it went, to which I answered by shrugging.

"She didn't do anything that hurt, did she? Or did she?" For the first time, Snake looked worried.

"No." I almost laughed at her unusual tone. "She just drew me. She didn't even touch me too much."

"Dai had been worried for nothing, then," Baba said. "When she pays, we'll treat you like a princess, for a few days."

"A few *days*?"

Everyone laughed. Crow chuckled on a little longer and then said, "Sure, we'll make you a crown with flowers of colors that suit you when your skin is healed. And we'll bow and sing for you."

I shook my head, grinning.

When I went back to the artist's hotel room two days later, my cheeks and forearms already had the golden needles. The artist asked me if I made them by scratching, and I said no, they just came out this way.

"Wonderful," she said, cupping my cheeks with her jeweled hands. All the fingers had at least one ring on, and all shimmered like a distant river.

"Aren't they heavy?"

"Oh, of course they are. But we aren't fortunate like you and we have to wear them to shine."

"What do you mean, fortunate?"

She slowly released my cheeks. Then said, "Rutile."

"What?"

"The needles. I'll use rutile quartz for them."

I frowned, but she took my hand and led me to a sofa beside the window. There she even tried seeing if my arms were translucent, holding them over in the sunlight. Silly; who could see through a solid human?

Two days later I went back to her, and another two days after that, and on and on. By the time my bruises had mostly healed, she seemed to have got some idea of her new design, so on the final day of our meeting we just chatted over her strange tea.

"I'm almost done with my new design. Would you like to see it?"

I wasn't sure if I did, but nodded, just to be polite.

The artist woman retrieved a large, heavy-looking sketchbook from a shelf and opened it in front of me.

At first I wasn't quite sure what I was seeing. The page in front of me was all a blurry gradation of colors. But when the first shock passed I could see, at the center of it all, a model, who looked a lot like me. I was sure, at that moment, my cheeks turned very red.

"Don't you think this is beautiful?" the artist said when I looked up at her. I nodded, using the gesture to look back down on it. Yes, the colors were beautiful. The stones were very deliberately arranged, and what had looked crazy on my skin was now, on this sketchbook, a mass of colors that was alive, that had purposes. But . . .

The model had a sort of head-gear that made colorful stones hover around the face. The eyes looked like opal, and I could guess this was one of the strange, tiny lenses some people bought at Tsuyu's eyewear shop.

Over the torso of the model, over her simple dress, was draped a cape-like thingy, densely yet delicately strung with those stones of countless colors. At the front, I could see slightly darker stones aligned as to probably indicate collars of our traditional robes. On the wrists were flowing cuff-like bracelets, made with wire and lined with stones with weaker and yellower colors. Thinner wires like vines drew upwards to just short of the elbows, writhing and winding, and there, golden stones with needles trapped inside shimmered like painful dew. I could see that every color was neatly placed in such a way that no color came next to the same color, while on the whole everything built up the gradation imagery.

"These stones are mostly fluorite; they aren't exactly what you'd call 'precious' stones, but they look just like your bruised skin, don't they?" she said, pointing at the cape costume. "And these." Her finger slid down to the model's stockings. "Will be made of gold thread, knitted and woven in many different ways to depict your half-healed skin."

I stared on at the picture. Jewelry and other luxuries as such had never been my—our—thing, but nevertheless, this whole thing looked ridiculous. This strange costume looked like "the way foreigners would think of us," exotic to them but meaningless to us; she didn't seem to even understand that we had a rule for the way collars were folded one over another.

The artist giggled and held my shoulder. "This is for becoming you."

Me? Becoming me? "But . . . is this—structure—even possible?"

"Of course! It's bound to be rather heavy, but it's a price for wanting what we don't have, isn't it?"

I felt my face flush; why would she keep saying that? "We didn't want these colors in the first place, you know?"

"Oh, but how could that be so?" She tilted her head, her eyes slanting, genuinely confused. "You are so beautiful!"

"Okay, thanks, but that beauty only comes from beating me, you see? It hurts, but that's how we get by. If I could help it, I would've chosen a life without bruises."

"Well . . . but . . . " She looked down on her own sketch. "Sorry, I'm just an artist, I understand only beauty."

"But even that!" I knew, probably, I should have stopped here, or before. But I couldn't. "Before you foreigners came, we didn't even know our colors were different from others'. Before you came, no one had trouble finding a job without worrying about our colors. Before you came, no one put anyone above anyone only because of the colors!"

The last few words came out much louder and hoarser than I intended, and it made her—the older, taller, and of course, higher one—flinch. I thought she might cry, but she didn't. "I'm sorry," she said. "I didn't mean any offense."

I shook my head, suddenly really, really weary. "No, sorry. Like I said, this is a country-size freak show. We feed on you, and you feed on us. There's nothing wrong with it. *I'm* sorry."

She seemed at a loss what to do for one moment, but then, touched my almost-healed forearm and said, "I have something for you."

Embarrassed but unable to avert my eyes, I said, "You do?"

"Yes. Give me one moment."

She went to the small chest beside the bed, and came back to me with a glass vial in her hand. "You see, obviously, we know magic you don't," she said, but flinched when she saw me frown. "Uh. Sorry. Anyway. I asked around among wizards and witches. And finally reached a conclusion about this."

"And this is?"

She flashed the same, radiating smile that she had when she saw me with my bruises still very vivid. "Fixative!"

"Fix . . . ?"

"Fixative. A magical one, of course. It's used to stabilize the colors on artwork. We usually spray these magical ones on something we want to paint, because it preserves the real colors better than photographs. But after some research, we believe that, by drinking it, you can have your extraordinary skin colors preserved!"

"W-what?" I stammered out, but didn't protest when she made me hold the vial. "Just . . . like that?"

"Yes, I talked to high-rank wizards and witches, so it's bound to be true!"

Could it be true? If it could . . . "I don't have to be beaten again?"

"Well, you have to, once. To get the colors onto the surface that you want to preserve. But after that, no, you will never have to bear with that guy's beating anymore!"

I looked up at her honey eyes, and back down at the vial. The vial itself, and the liquid inside, both were plain clear, with no color, no tinge to it. Might as well be just water.

"Keep it." The artist closed my fingers around the vial, holding my hand as if it—my hand—were something very special. "Use it well. It's my personal thank-you. The payment has been already made this morning. Thank you."

I nodded and bowed low, clutching the vial tight to my chest.

I RAN BACK TO THE HUT. Dai was leaning on the shrine's gate when I found him, waiting for me.

"We got the money." He smiled down at me. "You can have a month of no pain."

But I shook my head. "Give me the bruises, just one last time!"

"What?"

I shook the vial in front of his face and explained what it was. When he'd heard me out, he said, "But I've never heard of anything like that."

"It doesn't necessarily have to be something we know of. They even pray to different gods, you see? Perhaps they know things we don't. They must! And they even spray this onto animals to bring home the colors, so it must be safe to humans, too."

Dai still seemed uncertain.

"Besides," I said, impatient, "what's there to lose even if it doesn't work? I'd only get extra pains, not you."

He grunted. I knew his hand hurt when he struck me as well, and he hated beating me as much as I hated him beating me, but for now, I decided to take advantage.

Dai rubbed at his peach stubbles on his brow. "At least, you should wait till you are fully healed of the last bruises."

"It's almost fully healed." I nearly begged. "Please!"

He sighed. But then led me to the back of the shrine, and told me to put my biting cloth into my mouth.

THE NEXT FEW MINUTES WERE ALL a blur. Like Dai had been concerned, it was the first time I ever got struck while there were still more than a few golden needles. It hurt like hell, and I had to lie down for a few hours afterwards.

Meanwhile, my co-workers came to visit the makeshift medical ward of the van. Baba and Snake came and placed a flower crown beside my head. Crow came with his bird, and the bird repeatedly tweeted "Hail Hai! Hail Hai!"

I laughed weakly. They smiled back at me.

When I was just a little more recovered, I went to kneel in front of the mirror. Yes, it hurt like hell, but it was worth it; my bruises were the most vivid and beautiful ever. I sighed with joy and excitement at my own reflection. The needles were still there, along with other colors and patterns. I looked like the best mosaic I'd ever seen.

Perhaps I could be the highlight of the Hut. Perhaps I could even find a better job.

As if a better job than at a freak show even existed on this island.

I pulled the vial out of my bosom, and drained the content in one go.

It tasted slightly bitter and weird, and I almost coughed out some, before forcing my mouth shut. Only after I had swallowed it all I let myself cough, again and again. My chest still weary, I looked at myself in the mirror.

The faint lines between colors seemed to shimmer. Oh, would I even get glows? Feeling almost drunk—perhaps the liquid did contain some alcohol—I giggled at the new pattern woven by the light-ish thing. The shimmer seemed to come from within me; how could I have held something so glorious hidden within me?

But then—

I found something new happening on my skin, and squinted. From where the light seeped out, something—something very much like cracks—ran, over all the colors. I looked away from the mirror and then down at my own skin, only to find the cracks getting worse and worse.

And then—

Without a sound, all the cracks exploded. Like paint on an old oil painting, or bark on a dry, dead branch, the colors peeled off me. Beneath my colorful skin, a black appeared. A black of wet feather of the crow. Darker, deeper, more hopeless black than anyone's. Even through my gray hair the same color ran down, making me wholly wet-feather black.

I screamed. When my lungs could no longer give me enough air, I looked down at my skin, up at my reflection in the mirror, in turns, so many times. Nothing changed.

Nothing further happened.

AT SOME POINT, HEARING MY SCREAMS, the Hut's members came into the van. Crow and Snake. Baba wasn't fast enough. I shrunk into a shadowed corner, unable to face my co-workers in this state.

Crow hunched down over my peeled skin. "What happened here?"

"Look." Snake pointed at my crumpled futon. "Someone must have been sleeping here. But who?"

What did she just say?

"I don't know. Baba was with us at the back. I saw Dai go out, to get some painkillers, he said. The drug must be for the same person who was sleeping here. But . . . who?"

As it turned out, even Dai didn't remember who had needed the painkiller. He came back empty-handed. They cleaned the van, of the peeled skin, of the sweat-drenched futon, of the beautiful flower crown that no one remembered making.

Only the black bird repeated, "Hail Hai, Hail Hai," to everyone's confusion. The words that meant nothing now.

I SAW THE NEW, NICE VAN off, just before it left town. A few drops of liquid fell off my face, landed on the soil, before they singed blue and green and then went out. It took me moments to realize they were my tears, rolling out of my labradorite eyes, the only thing that didn't turn wet-feather.

I erased the traces in the soil with my foot.

Someone bumped into me, swore, but then looked around, utterly perplexed. Now my colors blended too well into the night, and no one could see me in the dimly lit corridors between rows of houses, shops.

Well, perfect for a thief, right? The path that I'd chosen a long, long time ago.

I made my first step as a thief, towards the artist's hotel. I'm going to steal the jeweled gear. It was being made for becoming *me*. I'm going to steal it, to be me again.

The Flying Head at the Edge of Night

"**N**ow now," I called out, arms spread. Closest to us, right across the cloth we'd laid out, were two very young persons, small and plump, standing hand in hand and staring expectantly at us. Too small, perhaps. Grown-up ones crowded a little distance away—some of them held even smaller persons in their arms. It wasn't the best possible situation, probably, but I had to try. "You!" I said to the closest two. "Are you ready to witness the horror with your own little black eyes?"

The two giggled. Not so bad, perhaps? I smiled, curving my lips just a fraction too slowly to be friendly.

One hand hovering near my jawline, fingers slightly waving. The other hand held out in front, palm up—no, wait, not that far forward . . . good. I wanted to swallow, but instead, ran my tongue along my lips. "Behold—" Fighting to keep smiling, I hopped off, and landed on the palm, with a thump. "A flying head! For real!"

I opened my eyes wider for good measure, bouncing a little there. Waiting for applause to come, for the clinking sound of coins flying in. But for a moment, nothing happened.

Then there were screams—first from the two closest small ones, and then the very small ones in the bigger ones' arms, who weren't even looking our way; and *then* the grown-ups started staggering away.

Oh well.

In a matter of seconds there were no people around us. No coin on our cloth. My body put me back on its neck, stomach rumbling. "Sorry," I said. I couldn't help it. Scaring the audience too much never got us too many coins.

* * *

I VAGUELY REMEMBERED HAVING BEEN THROWN into the back of a van by a horrified housekeeper at the end of the night, in those in-between hours; and later, being thrown out of the van by its terrified owner.

Not much of my memory was left of the night, like most of the time. Every night, it was like I became something I wasn't, almost no me left inside this skull.

We'd agreed long ago that my body should rest during the night, while I freaked out unconscious, leaping and flying around as if I never ever needed a body at all. It had to rest while it could. Sometimes it broke this promise and kept trying to run after me, making us both groggy and weak for the rest of the day. Sometimes, it stood by the promise and slept, while I unexpectedly travelled far away like this morning, and it would have to search for me for a long time, all day, even. Making us both groggy and weak for the rest of the day.

As we walked away from the clearing, my body put our choker back on around the line our stumps touched. The accessory was a beautiful piece, something woven with silvery thread, with black and blue twinkling things here and there, though we weren't sure where we'd got it from. Perhaps a gift, from either of us, to either of us.

We stopped at the end of the town, under a small tree at the edge of a copse. Night would fall again in a couple hours. "I'm sorry," I said, again, and it crouched down and took me off it, and placed me on its lap, stroking my cheeks and brushing my hair.

Why would I want to hop away from *this*?

But then, we both started. Something moved behind the bush some paces away. *Did you hear that*, I asked the body silently. An affirmative wave came through.

Cautiously it lifted itself off the sodden ground, and started to sneak away with me cradled in its arms. We hoped it was a rogue cat or something, but also knew it'd sounded too heavy. We had nothing to be robbed of, but we didn't know what'd happen to us, like, if we were severed permanently.

A few moments later, we heard a yelp, and a loud thud. "What was that?" My mouth slipped, and my body turned a little, allowing me a peep behind.

It was nearing dusk, and under the shadowy trees it was hard to see anything properly. We could just see a large lump beside the bush. It took me a while to make out that the thing sticking upwards was a leg, and a sandaled foot at the end of it.

I frowned, matching the body's confusion. "What is that?"

The lump wriggled, straightened, coughing and muttering something obscene. A grown-up person? My body and I exchanged a silent agreement and turned away to go.

Then the thing cried out: "Please! Wait! Hear me out!"

We turned back to it again, and it flinched and yelped again. But after taking a long moment of hesitation, the thing stepped into a circle of light where the foliage was scarce above, with an obvious effort. Yes, it was a grown-up person, thin and shaky. I frowned even harder to see it better.

"Oh please! Please don't bite!" The person flailed.

"You said wait. We're waiting."

"What?" The person looked around a little. "We? Um. So." It swallowed very loudly. "Um. I . . . " It coughed. "I wish you be our . . . tutor."

I thought I heard it wrong, and we stepped a little closer to it; it backed away double the distance we'd closed, emitting a feeble shriek. "What tutor?" I asked.

"I . . . " Its eyes were brimming with tears, I could see now. "I want to know how you do it."

I finally realized what this thing was talking about. "Oh!" I said, and my body held me out with two hands in front of it, letting me ever closer to the person. "But there's no secret to it that we can teach you."

For a long moment the person did nothing but let out a whining sound, but then finally said, "I-I-I understand, you cannot let go of such precious knowledge and skill so easily. That is how you make living, right? Don't worry, we will not be your competitor. We only need to perform it once, or maybe twice, if needs be. And we plan to go away when it's all over." It said all this very fast.

I widened my eyes, and the person made a choking sound. I said, "That is not what we meant. We—"

But then a voice came from elsewhere: "Who's there? What are you doing there?"

The person in front of us gasped, and ducked into deeper shadow. "It's right in the middle of festival period for our shrine on the hill, and the highlight is coming near and people are becoming kind of prickly these days," the person whispered, as if it just fully remembered itself. "Come to my house. I can at least offer shelter tonight, and can feed you, too, of course."

I heard my body's stomach growl again.

The person smiled, chuckled a little. "Yes, you're human, of course. Silly me."

"But what makes you think monsters don't get hungry?"

"Please, we have no time, hurry!"

So we trotted after the person, away from the lights of searchers, people that the one we followed wanted to avoid. It felt strange to be *this* cautious, even in the time of a ritual. My body was slow as usual, still cradling me like a precious thing made of some fragile material, and the person kept looking out for us over its shoulder, thus stumbling a lot. After some time we cleared out of the woods, and then were led up along a winding path. Finally we found a hut at the edge of another copse.

Sensing another entity in the house, my body's hands placed me gently onto its stump as a precaution. As the person went in, it called, "Hana. Hana, we have help!"

We hadn't said we'd help, I thought, I was sure *we* thought, as we took in the interior of the house. There wasn't much—a stove at the end of the earthen floor, just a small low table and a few sitting rags on the raised floor. A small person knelt beside the table, and it straightened and then bowed when it saw us. "Thank goodness," this new person said when it sat back up. As it did tiny bells around its ankle jingled. "Thank you."

And when this new person looked up—it was like watching a flower bloom right in front of our eye. This thing was *beautiful*, but not the kind of pretty we got to see from time to time. Perhaps divine might be the word, and how blasphemous of me to use this one? But I knew nothing that could describe the way it seemed to glow from within, the way the stars in its eyes shifted meaningfully. I swallowed, and felt my body react, a little bit like when we were slightly drunk.

I did my best with what resembled a few kicks to our touching stumps. My body faltered and sent an apologetic shiver, and I bounced a little there. The two persons in front of us intoned in harmony, helplessly.

"Oh, we—I—" I pursed my lips once. The priority here was feeding my body. "Sorry. Well. Nice house?"

Eating was a strange habit, but we managed it. The two people stared at us, intrigued by the way I swallowed the food, bouncing there on its stump from time to time in the effort; maybe the smaller one was trying to make out how the food went down between us—it didn't, the food I took somehow appeared in the body's stomach, and we ourselves had no idea how that happened. I knew the body wanted to gobble, but I took enough time to not upset the empty stomach and also not appear too bad in front of these two persons.

When my body was sensibly sated, the new person gave us tea. "So," I said, in between careful sips. "Why would you want to do—what we do?"

The first person straightened. "My daughter Hana here—" Oh, so this new person was female! "—was chosen as the Bride, for the ritual performed in accordance with the festival."

I frowned as the body's bewilderment filled my skull. "Huh? What's that to do with us?"

"Mother, this honorable guest is not from around here, obviously." Okay, so they were both female. "Every seven years, a girl is chosen as the Bride. That's another word for sacrifice."

Oh. "So that's why persons were all so careful out there? So as not to let in any intruder during this ritual?"

The first person, Mother, nodded. "Also not to let Hana here escape. People are watching this house as we speak, though not too closely for the moment. See the bells attached to Hana?" We did—bound around her ankle, some of them were made of porcelain and others metal, letting the sound carry farther. "If they don't ring for too long someone comes to check in. And the rope is woven with holy material the shrine provided, so if we try to cut it the priest would send a terrible curse through it."

I looked at the rope. It seemed ordinary enough. "Are you sure?"

"Some of the men said they saw the priest make a flower from the cemetery wither in the water with a piece of the rope in it. Because the flower was haunted and the rope made the water sacred. And we don't want to risk drawing them closer, anyway."

My body's sadness crept up. I downed a hot, large gulp of the tea, making the body jump the jump it deserved. Though it was always me who ended up coughing. "What exactly do they do to the Bride?" I said hoarsely.

"They'll dress the child in white and then prick a finger with a needle, and stain the robe with the blood. To indicate this child is offered to a god as a gift. I've seen a few Brides before Hana, of course, and from what I heard those girls only had to spend one night in the shrine building after the blood. But this time . . . something seems off." She shook her head. "Once in several rounds, the Bride never returns. They're taking extra care this year not to let Hana go, and the way they talk about this god somehow implies . . . I cannot . . . she . . . " Mother swallowed. "Hana is way too young."

"You mean—" I felt heat rise up in both of us. "Really, as a *bride*? That's ridiculous!"

Hana didn't seem to understand much about it. "Everyone congratulated me, on being chosen," she said at length. "But I don't want to be separated from Mother. Not yet."

My head hurt, and my body's hand shook. I wanted its fists to smash those tiny bells around Hana's ankle. "So you want to scare these persons away from Hana."

"They might reconsider, I thought, if they find out she is . . . misbegotten, in some way."

Misbegotten. Of course. But then, before any of us could say another word, we heard the large bell of a temple toll somewhere. Declaring night.

Night.

"Oh dear," I said, and then everything fell silent, pitch black.

I CAME TO SLOWLY, MY EYES still closed.

It was warm, for a change. I could hear the fire. We didn't get fire in the morning too often. And I could feel the hands. Two hands holding me, and another hand wiping me gently.

Another hand?

I opened my eyes with a start. Hana shrieked, making the bells jingle and jingle. But then with an obvious effort she said "Sorry," and resumed wiping at me. I was in my body's lap, Mother was stirring something over the stove, chuckling a little. "You seem to have a very strange habit," Mother said and Hana giggled, too.

Outside I could hear teeny birds tweeting. So it really was morning. "You saw it all?"

"Yes," Mother said, and came carrying bowls of soup. "There was a lot of screaming, of course." I felt somehow disappointed that I missed it all. "And we're still a bit—a *lot*—shaken. But it was also, so funny! The way you got upset! I could tell from your gestures that we needn't worry, but you yourself flailing around so hard!"

"You were there, and saw it *all*? I do not remember a thing."

"Oh, I kind of supposed that," Hana said, tending to my lip that I'd apparently cut. "You didn't seem to hear us. Were you drunk or something?"

My body was now doing my hair. "I don't know." I was irrationally scared to say this aloud. "We aren't one person, if you aren't aware of it yet. When night falls I lose consciousness and try to run away. My body is slow and never manages to catch me. In the morning, when I'm me again, it has to come look for me. Where did you find me this morning?"

Hana stood, and started laying the food on the table with Mother. "We were here to catch you, you know?" she said, apparently shivering once at the memory. "It was very hard, of course. The three of us were barely enough to hold you back. But when you almost tore through the door, we *had* to catch you. We cannot afford a new door."

"We got you in a wrapping cloth and held you all night." Mother shook herself, too, but more for a theatrical effect. "You—your body got settled down then."

So for the first time in our relationship it didn't have to come after me. It was still stroking my hair, and I could feel more energy within us.

I was tired, probably from trying to get away all night, but that was just half our energy wasted. "Thank you, Mother, Hana. But now you really know we cannot teach you how to do this."

Mother sighed. "We have to think of another way. The ritual will be held tonight. I'll do whatever it takes to get her out of this." Then she knelt straight, formally. "Also, I'm sorry about calling you 'misbegotten' last night. I didn't mean it that way, but still."

I smiled, felt my body amused. "It's okay. We are so. Look, maybe there's still something my body and I can do, to help you two. At least we want to repay for the food and shelter you are giving us."

Mother frowned as she considered this. "We cannot drag you that deep in, there might be danger," she said after a while. "In my original plan, you'd have been long gone at the time we'd actually be doing the performance. We'd never be able to pay back if something goes terribly wrong."

"I don't think they would be able to hurt us bad enough, me and my body. Let us help. We are much too deep in already, Mother."

She looked at us. Then she nodded. "Thank you," she said.

"If everything goes well, we'll meet two towns away along the highway," I told them. "Wishing you luck. Wish us luck."

Hana squeezed my body's arm, and touched my cheek with the other hand. She must have wanted to say something, but her lips were trembling.

I let my body take our neck piece off our stumps. "Here," I said and my body handed the thing to Hana. "Keep it for us."

The small person beamed as she took it. The smile was enough to freshen our resolution all over. "Ooh, I like fancy," she said and wrapped it around her own neck. It was a bit loose for her, and dangled there like a short necklace.

Mother stroked her daughter's head. "Good luck to us all."

I could feel the night creeping towards us, pulling darkness over us slowly. We had only one chance. Right before the dark took me, in that final sliver of my consciousness, I saw my body cut the rope of Hana's bells, and took the rope between my teeth.

And let darkness engulf. After that, there was no catching me.

Pains woke me, and I groaned. Felt the chill of the mist. Morning.

"You're awake," something said. I felt for my teeth with my tongue; no rope, no bells. Oh no. "I didn't think I'd meet you again like this." What felt like a sandaled foot prodded me. I opened my eyes.

I was on a hard floor. When I sniffed, there was something in the air that smelled kind of familiar. I'd been here before? I didn't care much about places—it was long since places became "somewhere my body was" and "somewhere not." I squinted, found a person staring down at me. Okay, perhaps this person did look familiar a little, too. Though I didn't care much about persons, either.

Where were the bells? I tried to shake myself around best as I could but didn't see or hear them. Maybe dropped it somewhere, drawing the watches only just a little way away from the house, making them realize it was all fake too soon, only to send them back to the house before Hana could get away. What a failure.

That remotely-familiar person grabbed my hair, lifted me up to its eye-level. That hurt, but I sensed more pains than I could possibly count in my own skull. Perhaps my body was injured, too, and the thought made me sick. I let it down again. I let them all down.

Mid-air, I could finally size up my surroundings: we were on a stone stage on the hilltop; off the stage, on my right, I could barely see a winding path leading to this place below the small cliff, and far off below that, a small building that looked like a shrine. On the other side there was an altar at the end of this stone stage. Persons wouldn't come all the way up here, probably, as they all usually stopped at the shrine and never climbed any farther. So this must be some kind of hidden sacred area, for secret rituals. Five or six watch persons stood blocking the steps that led off this stage downhill—the only possible escape.

Before I could properly assess those faces, that remotely-familiar person tossed me away, making me land with a loud thud and a disgraceful yelp. "You were saying?" I heard it hiss at the watch persons.

"We—we heard the bells and thought the girl ran away," one of them replied. "Then after some time, the bells suddenly stopped sounding, and then they started ringing again, far away, from an entirely different direction. We searched and searched for them, all night." Then this person narrowed its eyes a little and cast a glance my way. "That filthy monster tricked us all, Priest Great. All is its fault."

That remotely-familiar person, Priest Great, nodded gravely. "We'll find her, sooner or later. It is the fate. Do not fret, my power protects this region. Monsters have no place here."

"Monsters have no place here?" I furrowed my brow. "But didn't you just say we've met before? You do seem familiar to me. Why didn't you slay me immediately last time?"

All the persons looked at me. Priest Great said nothing for a moment, its lips trembling a little. Then one of the watches started casting its glances around, nervously.

"You haven't found Hana, did you just say? What about those bells with that rope which should have been enchanted by Priest Great? I held it in my mouth, but I'm still alive." Well, as alive as I could be. "How's that?"

The nervous watch person pursed its lips, looking ill. "Priest Great, you said . . . you need her blood to bring peace and prosperity to our region. The monster sneaking in is bad enough as it is, and . . . "

Now, the persons around all stared at Priest Great. "What?" Priest spat. "I've worked with this region for ages. Are you taking more seriously the words from such a filthy mouth as this monster's?"

"But the rope—"

As more morning light came through the trees, I was returning more properly to my self—my body's head. I felt a tug somewhere, in my throat. I thought I was going to cough, but then—vomited, over Priest Great's sandals, my body's fluid and the bells still attached to the "holy" rope.

"Uh-oh," I said and coughed and spat.

Priest Great screamed, and the watch persons backed away, one of them almost falling off the stone stage.

"It's been inside my body but never killed us, the rope." I rolled around a little, messing my hair and dirtying my skin. "The rope didn't protect your beloved village from a monster." I gave out a laugh as hysterical as I could manage. "Now, Priest Great can protect you all just with Hana's blood? Are you sure?"

Priest Great cried something incomprehensible, and kicked me against the rock behind me. It hurt like hell, but I found myself enjoying the situation immensely. While jumping around during the night, I must have swallowed the bells, sending them to my body. It'd worked after all. Hana was safe.

"Priest Great," said one of the village persons, "what exactly does your—our—god do to the Bride? What," it swallowed loudly, "what exactly happened, to my mother's cousin, who disappeared after the ritual thirty-five years ago?"

"What the—"

"What *would* you do if *your* own daughter is chosen as the Bride?" I raised my voice as much as I could, ignoring every muscle in me—and in my body—complaining. I turned my glare at the person who got nervous first, probably the youngest of them all. "Seven years from now, right? Imagine your little girl sliced open by a god, or Priest Great on this hard cold stone, still too small in your arms!"

Realization diluted the person's pupils. "My daughter," it muttered. "No!"

And then this person was gone, running down the winding path, through the trees.

Others looked horrified or at least disconcerted as understanding dawned equally on them, and eventually they all stepped off the stone stage, climbed down the hill. "Come back now!" Priest Great yelled. "Come back, or I'll curse you to the last drop of the blood of your descendants!"

But no one even looked back.

I laughed. "How lovely, your loyal villagers!" I exclaimed. "So we've really met before? I do have some very obscure slivers of memories of that ugly face of yours. Not that I wanted to keep them."

Priest's muscles twitched right below its eye. "I didn't know you'd lose your memory, but maybe you two discarded it intentionally."

"What do you—"

But then, we heard voices. Priest craned its neck and I turned as much as I could, and we saw three figures climbing uphill. A small person leading, another one some distance behind the first who kept tripping on nothing but gravel, *and* another without a head trying to catch up and of course, failing. Now that I could see it, I realized pains could be sensed mostly on its front, especially around the lower parts like shin and calf, as if a small person had inflicted the damage; I could even feel a bite on its lower arm. "Hana!" Mother cried, stumbling a few more times in that one breath. "Don't go!"

In no time at all Hana hopped onto the stone stage. I sent irritation to my body. What was it doing, letting Hana run into the arms of her very enemy? My body shuddered as it helped Mother to her feet. Hana glared at Priest Great, not even panting. "I cannot leave you behind so that I can reach my own safety," she said, glancing at me. "I don't want to be that kind of person."

Oh, Hana. Sweet Hana. She had every right to see to her safety. Out of the corner of my eye I saw Priest cast its dirty eye towards the small person. "Someone here has sense, at least. Come here, girl. Let me lay my hands on your—"

"Oh, if you are so sure." Hana took a step closer. My body and Mother finally made it to the edge of the stage, but . . . it and Mother seemed uncertain about something. What were they waiting for? My body should drag the small person away from here, whatever it cost it . . .

The small person in question lifted her head high, as if showing her chin clearly to Priest. Oh no, not chin. "Hana!" I exclaimed, I couldn't help it. "Your neck!"

She craned her neck farther, balancing her head with one hand. Almost one-third of her neck was severed, just like between me and my body. Priest's eyes snapped to the choker we'd given her. It screamed.

"Where did you find that thing around your neck?" Priest almost sounded like it was wailing.

Hana snorted. "I got it from Flying Head and Body. So *you* made this thing, right? Made them Head and Body with this thing, too." I could see Priest shaking, but Hana continued, pointing at the altar. "Just as I thought! This is a pattern from here. I like fancy, and I once tried to copy it, even."

We grown-ups all looked, though Priest should have already known it was there. As the morning mist crept away, as more columns of sunlight slid uphill, it became clearer and clearer. The same curves and lines as our choker were drawn across the upper part of the altar's front. Also, there were vines that looked a lot like the same pattern, twining themselves around the holy structure, dew shimmering like those twinkling things on our accessory.

"Of course Mother wanted me to run, but when I remembered about this altar and realized that Head must be here, and something nasty, like this," she pointed at her own neck, "is going to be done to Head, I came running here. Body sensed that and tried to stop me, it just wasn't deft enough or fast enough. Head, don't be mad at Body, please."

I wanted to *shake my head*, but to do that I'd need that stupid useless lump of limbs.

Priest slumped down. My body finally made itself useful and removed the choker from Hana's neck.

"Oh, but I like it," she protested.

"Hana," Mother had just regained steady enough breathing. "We can craft something similar later. Just not this one." She carefully held her daughter's face between her hands, as though she couldn't decide if it was safe to touch it.

Hana pouted.

"Girl," Priest's voice was still shaking—how weak could this person be? "Girl, I'm working on the antidote. That neck isn't just the way I want . . . "

"An antidote?" Mother and I said in unison. "Priest," I said, "tell us exactly what this is all about."

PRIEST HADN'T STARTED OUT AS A priest. It was first a very religious chemist. After some experiments it learned that this particular vine, with the pure water from the hilltop and an appropriate amount of prayer, could produce a potion that would sever parts of a person's body without killing or hurting it—at least, not too much. With enough practice and more experiments, Priest realized, it might even find a way to sever its own mind from body, move that severed mind to another body that it liked.

Once upon a time when it first started the experiments, Priest caught me and tried to use me, but I had a lover who did everything to prevent that. Though the lover was a bit too slow, and we ended up . . . like this.

"I never, ever liked my face and body," Priest sobbed. *It sobbed.* It had no right! "Look at her, she's perfect! Is it so bad, really, wanting something and doing one's best to obtain it?"

"It's not wanting something or striving towards it that's wrong," I said, through my gritted teeth, "it's stealing it from someone else that's totally, madly *wrong.*"

Priest wailed. I almost pouted. I'd wanted to wail for a long time, preferably in my body's arms. Hana was still pouting, eyeing our choker. Mother nudged her, but then embraced her with those clumsy yet warm arms.

"So this choker has been keeping us . . . separate? It's been immersed in your poison, right? Did you do the same with the rope for Hana's bells?"

Priest sniffed. "The rope, no, I just bluffed to keep folks under control. Your choker, yes. I lied and told you it was a gift, and you accepted it happily at that time. Then your lover got jealous and things went wrong." It threw its hands up in resignation. "You cannot merge into one without my antidote—when it's complete. But I think, if you keep being incomplete body parts for too long, then your minds start to be fogged, the borders blur until the two mingle into one eventually. So the poison—oh how I hate to call it that—"

"*Priest.*"

"So, so, wearing it must have kept your *minds* separate, so you're still two lovers in one set, instead of one completely memory-less person. But the p-p-poison is poison, after all. You need to wear it out sometimes. That's why you have to bounce away every night, as far as I can tell."

I sighed. "So we were the first. How many bodies have you wasted since?"

"It takes seven years to prepare a portion enough for one body, and I had to wait for a nice looking girl to come by, so I haven't been able to do a lot. Three, including you. Or four if we count your lover."

Of course we'd count it. "Are they both dead, those other two?"

"They refused me, both body and mind. So I made them into monsters and kicked them out, they were useless to me. One with a skull gaping open, the other with her mouth split from ear to ear."

I saw Hana dig deeper into Mother's arms. "You need to cure them," her voice came muffled.

"I'm working on it, I need the antidote before I can use the potion on myself—"

"Not so that you can have those faces and bodies back ready for you to use," I said, "but to give their life back to them."

Priest—or Chemist—sobbed some more. It had no right, really. "Do you want yourself cured?" At one point, Mother asked us.

I looked at her. The answer came easily: "No."

She nodded, but her expression stiffened as we all heard voices from downhill. Persons were climbing, making their way to the stone stage. Those watch persons in the lead, but there were more. Very small things, too, in the arms of some larger ones. If they were here to kill us all, we were completely outnumbered. But . . . planning an assault with those small persons among them seemed absurd, even to my monster's eyes.

All those persons hesitated just before the steps leading onto the stage. Then the young person who had left the priest first climbed the final slope and stood before us.

This young person bowed its head to Mother. "I'm sorry," it said. "So very sorry. We shouldn't have forgotten she is our fellow villager. Forgive me. Forgive us."

"Not to me, really." Her eyes were cold, but I could hear some tears behind her voice.

The young one nodded and crouched to fully face Hana. But before it could speak she said, "You're the dye farmer's first son! I'll forgive you if you give me some pretty threads with which I can—"

"*Hana*," Mother and I said at the same time.

She giggled and hid behind Mother.

All the persons climbed onto the stage one by one, or in twos and threes in case of those with the very small ones, and bowed to Mother and Hana in turns. The larger ones tied Chemist's hands behind its back and took it down the hill. My body took me gently off the hard floor and cradled me in its arms. Finally.

I sighed. From relief and fatigue both. "You need to wait for the antidote, Hana. Until then maybe you really should ask for some fancy scarf of the dye farmer, to cover your neck."

"It's not that bad, really. And it will keep evil men at bay, don't you think?" She grinned, playing with her own head that lolled unnaturally.

"I'm not sure about that—it might keep away very good persons, too."

"I only need people who would like me for my mind, not just my outer shape."

I laughed. "Mind also lives in your face and body. Never underestimate it."

WE SAID GOODBYE TO MOTHER AND Hana, but promised to come back. Now we had a place to go—a place we could find Cracked Skull and Split

Mouth, wherever they might be. The antidote should be ready by the time we got back with them.

"You'll still have to search for me every morning," I said. "Go through all those troubles, even before breakfast. And wipe mud off me. Every. Single. Morning."

It stroked my hair with its fingers. Warm, gentle fingers.

"I know," I said in reply.

In Her Head, In Her Eyes

Trills of silver, trills of blue.

She wanted to watch on. She wanted to remember them, wanted to make them her own. But soon, too soon, she was pulled up, back into the air, where she had to fight for breath, fight to be on her feet.

SHE HIT THE HARD WORKSHOP FLOOR, heavy head first. Though her head was protected, she cried out anyway. Slowly, she raised herself up and tried to glare at them, all of them standing around the stale pot of unused indigo dye in which they had just tried to drown her. Most of them kept laughing at her, but a few seemed to sense her unseen glare, and backed off warily.

Then, a voice from the entrance to the workshop. "What is going on in here?"

The bullies scattered instantly at the voice's calm authority. Everyone knew who commanded that voice, just as everyone knew he was the only person who would dare stand up for the strange new servant. Drenched in old dye, the servant girl shifted and dipped her heavy head, and busied herself squeezing her sleeves. Slowly the owner of the voice walked in, frowning. "Hase. I told you to come or call for me when in trouble. Are you all right?"

Hase bowed as low as she could, unbalanced with the substantial weight atop her head. "Yes. I appreciate our young master's concern."

The young man—the third noble son of the family of artisan dyers— knelt before her. "Hase," he said. "You must tell them they'll be in trouble if they do anything to you. Use my name. Who were they?" He was the only person in the entire house who called her by her real name and not Pot Head.

"Again, I appreciate my master's concern," Hase said, "but in truth, I am fine. And here, my robe—now it's dyed in indigo and looks pretty!"

Still kneeling, the young man grinned. "You smiled. At last!"

Hase hurriedly composed herself and looked down. Suddenly she was aware of how her robe was clinging to her skin, how the blue-black pungent water was running down her dark hair, down her torso, how quickly the warm dye was starting to cool off. "Young master, this is not a place for a noble. I must tidy myself up now."

"Yes. Be sure to keep yourself warm."

Hase bowed again, watching the young man leave before standing and rushing abruptly to the servants quarters in search of solitude and warmth.

No one knew why Hase wore a pot on her head. No one in the noble house, in the region, had even seen the materials from which the pot was made. *It must be some sort of iron*, people would whisper marveling at the reflective surface shining brightly as a mirror in the space where her eyes should be. No one had ever seen Hase's eyes, or anything behind the pot's smooth countenance—only her nose and mouth were visible below its cold protective edge.

Since her arrival at the house, of course many had tried to rip the pot form her head, but to no avail. The pot, so closely fitted to Hase's skull, would not, could not come off. Yet others tried to crack it open to reveal the girl beneath, but no tool could do it any damage. Eventually, they all gave up.

The only thing anyone knew about Hase for certain was that she came from the Island—a fabled place, far away from their shores. Even nobles, such as the ones who owned this fine home, were not rich enough to travel to the Island. How pot-covered Hase ended up here, people could only speculate.

Beyond the metallic pot concealing her head, Hase appeared perfectly plain, which only added to the mystery surrounding her. The people of Hase's Island were rumored to be great beauties, with skin and hair and eyes of all colors: hues of flowers and jewels, of stars and sunsets. Some, it was rumored, even bore patterns on their skin—not tattooed or painted on, but opalescent designs born from the womb. It was common knowledge that everyone from the Island was beautiful, inspiring poetry and art, stories and dreams.

Only look at Hase. She had ordinary skin just like everyone else, without a single shocking color or pattern to be seen. Her hair was thick, beautiful and dark as a crow's wing, but perfectly ordinary. So no one in the household, neither noble nor servant, believed her claim as to her birthplace—no one, that is, save the family's third son.

A FEW NIGHTS AFTER HER ARRIVAL at the house, Sai visited Hase's makeshift cot inside the storehouse. At first she shied away, thinking he had come to take advantage of her. But he waved his hand dismissively and sat down by the door, leaving it fully open. There was no light inside, for no fire was allowed in the storehouse; only moonlight illuminated the room, spilling through the door and reflecting off her potted head.

Sai gestured towards the moon. "Look at how beautiful the moon is here, without all the lights of the house. Don't be greedy and keep it all to yourself!"

Slowly, Hase closed the distance to the door where he was, her thin blanket wrapped tightly around her body. She peered at him cautiously, the starry night reflecting in the cool metal of her gaze. "We have a pond of the color of moonlight," she said quietly.

"On your island? Where they say everyone is beautiful?"

"There is no such place where everyone is beautiful. People always try to find the flaws and imperfections in all things. On my island, there are other plain things. As plain as Hase appears here." She bowed her spherical heavy head and clutched her blanket tighter around her.

"And the pot . . . "

"It has nothing to do with Hase's island, master." Hase gave her heavy head a little shake.

The young man nodded. He looked as though he had more things he wanted to ask, but said nothing and looked on at the moon.

UNLIKE THE YOUNGER SERVANTS, THE ADULTS didn't quite bully Hase, though no one seemed to like her much. They knew a certain amount of money had been exchanged for her service, enough of a sum to make them believe that she must be from the Island and that she genuinely must want to work under the dye masters. Still, among any of the servants, any kindness towards Hase remained to be seen. For when Hase, dripping with old indigo dye and shivering, finally made her way to the servants' quarters to ask for towels, she found little sympathy. The elder dye master, Hase's superior, simply wrinkled her nose and dropped the towels at Hase's feet. "For once, just have a bath. I can't let you serve at the meeting tonight in that state, and we can't spare a hand."

"What meeting?"

"You don't notice anything, do you?" The woman sighed. "The eldest and the middle brothers' wives and other relatives are coming to visit."

Hase tilted her heavy head to one side in question. "What about the third brother's wife?"

"You know he doesn't have a wife yet," the dye master snorted. "If he did we'd all have stopped him before he went into that storehouse your first night to have you."

Hase stared blankly at the dye master, smooth impassive metal reflecting the older woman's sneer, until the dye master shooed her away.

HASE DIDN'T HAVE MUCH TIME TO enjoy the bath. Soon the relatives started to arrive, and she was herded along with the other servants, bustling tea and refreshments to the family. All the relatives openly stared at Hase and the smooth pot covering her head, mouths agape at her strangeness. *Pot Head*, they whispered behind her back, quickly picking up the servants' name for her. The wives of the first and second brothers took great delight in her peculiar appearance, laughing at her gleaming helmet of metal. The elder wife quickly tired of the game and Hase's calm, and exclaimed, "Why, I hate her face!"

"But she doesn't have a face!" The younger wife laughed even harder than before.

"I hate that she doesn't. We are laughing at her and she should be angry, or embarrassed at the very least! Look at her, with her stupid mouth, her tiny nose." The elder wife gestured rudely at Hase, trying to engage the servant. "The only parts of her face you can see, and she has no reaction."

Hase bowed as gracefully as she could in the style of her fellow servants, the movement awkward in many ways. The angle of her neck and back were tilted just wrong, the speed with which she retreated to the more comfortable, upright position to alleviate the weight of her head a little too fast. The jerky movements only fueled the younger wife's amusement, her laughter renewed with malicious glee.

"Oh Pot Head, heavy-head, just try not to get in our way!" The younger wife pushed Hase by the pot on her head, cackling harder still when Hase fell to the wooden floor with a dull thud, potted-head first.

Slowly, slowly, Hase dragged herself up onto her feet, as she heard the two wives walk away, laughing and laughing.

BOTH WIVES AND THEIR HUSBANDS WERE young and relatively newly-wed, and the two women measured themselves against each other in every regard. They compared their wedding gifts and the favor of their new parents-in-law; they compared their best robes, their skills in music and poetry. Every day and every night, the wives would compare their positions, while their men drank sake, the women tea, and a steady barrage of refreshments flew from the kitchens into their mouths.

All the while, Hase lurked in the background, her domed, impassive head missing not a single detail. From the hallways and the corners of each room, Hase stole glimpses of the fine embroidery of the women's robes, fascinated by the expensive, exquisite artifacts that shimmered in the wives' hands.

One day, the elder wife caught Hase staring at her robe and sneered, her venomous glare focused on Hase's reflective helmet. Hase shivered, transfixed by the wife's disdain, unable to look or move away.

"HERE." SAI HANDED HER A BUNDLE. "Of all the gifts the women brought, these were the only things my relatives weren't much keen on. I'm sure you can have it."

Hase opened the bundle, and found two spindles of fine gold and silver threads. She turned the spools in her hands, feeling the fine filigree of each thread, and sighed. "These must be expensive enough that someone may like to save for later use. Is it certain that Hase can have it?"

"We are dye masters here, not for embroidery or even weaving." Sai smiled at Hase encouragingly. "But you like patterns, I've heard? That's why you've come all the way here, isn't it?"

"Yes." She nodded, a slow, languid inclination of her heavy, masked head. "On my island, we need more colors, more patterns. Patterns, especially, to be reflected on the beloved children of the Island. I must study."

"You mean you can decide what colors and patterns your babies will bear?" Sai leaned forward eagerly.

"No, sir. We create new patterns, we discover more colors, but our goddess alone can decide. We all wish to please our goddess."

Sai frowned, confused. Hase almost smiled at that.

After a moment of silence, she said quietly, "These look as though they represent the young wives themselves. They are so different and yet, they go so well with each other."

Sai, leaning in closer to hear her better, laughed. "Are you being sarcastic?"

"No, sir! They are lovely, those two."

She had said this a little louder, but still, the third son did not lean back. She knew what that meant. And though everything was awkward with her heavy pot, the hard wooden ground, the thin futon, this time Hase smiled. The pot weighed her down, pinned her to the floor, as if Sai's eyes intent on her covered face weren't enough to affix her there already.

When she was alone again, Hase pulled the spindles Sai had given her out from the folds of her sleeves. She placed them on the ground beside her futon, then changed her mind and put them on the pillow and carefully laid her heavy head beside them. The two colors filled her reflected sight, shimmering and twining in cruel beauty, fueling rather than smothering her desire.

THE NEXT DAY, HASE WALKED DREAMILY through the dyed cloths fluttering in the wind, being dried. Some bore glue for patterns to be washed away later, and some still had strings marking the fabric for simpler patterns. A few plain cloths with no patterns at all fluttered alongside these elaborate designs, forming a small sea of color and texture upon which Hase and her metal potted head were afloat. Her heavy head swiveled in wonder, slowly, taking in all of the colors and styles. She had to memorize all these patterns, for the dye masters would never teach her how to make them. The blues. The whites. Everything in between. But just then she heard a voice, interrupting her quiet study. "You seem to have had a very good time last night."

Startled, Hase spun around, searching for the source of the voice though she already knew its owner. She walked on in between the waves of cloths, currents and bubbles, seaweeds of patterns, towards the voice. At the end of the last row, she found her.

Hase bowed as well as she could, and asked: "Was that statement aimed at me, mistress?"

Trills of blue, a line of silver. For a moment, the older of the two wives — the one Hase called in her mind Silver — looked away from her. "Why did you come here? What is it you want from us?"

"I come to learn about dyeing . . . "

"Oh do you? So seducing our brother-in-law was part of your plan?"

Hase shook her head; that was all she could do.

"With a face like yours it must be really easy to lie, isn't it? Are you even really from that Island everybody's talking about? Does it even exist? Did you think looking ordinary would make us feel you're one of us, or did you think we'd be too easy to deceive, so you didn't bother coloring or decorating your face?" The elder wife's anger and spite burned in her eyes.

Involuntarily, Hase raised her hand through Silver's tirade, resting it gently over a nearby cloth and marveling at its fine knots and textures. She tried to imagine the pattern the knots might make eventually, and failed. "My patterns, I guess, are in my head."

Silver frowned. "In your head? What are you talking about?"

Hase stroked the cloth again, trying to coax the pattern into life. "Yes. I'm the head pattern designer of my clan, as I have told the great mistress here." She recalled Sai's mother in her finest robes, her eyes cold as she assessed Hase and her claims. "I have to extract the patterns from my head, and to do that, I need to know more ways to express the patterns, of course!"

Hase's voice rose in pitch, in eagerness and fervor. Her potted head glittered in the sunlight. "But, but the people in this region, especially the dye masters wouldn't allow the dye or dyeing methods out of the region. We — my aunts and other guardians and I, of course, of course — had to promise I wouldn't take any—*any!*—indigo out of this place when we arranged my apprenticeship here! But nobody can prevent me from taking these blues and whites and everything else with me inside my head! And . . . what is the matter?"

Silver had backed away from Hase, the hate in her eyes faded into wariness and fear at Hase's rambling outburst.

At Silver's discomfort, Hase immediately reverted to her usual quiet demeanor. "Forgive me, I shouldn't have kept our young mistress standing here, listening to Hase's useless babblings! Did I answer the question well enough?"

Silver shook her head. "I . . . no. Not at all. Now, there are only more questions than before."

"Forgive me, mistress. Please, pardon my rudeness!"

"Don't." Silver raised a hand towards Hase, who had just taken one step closer to her. "Come no closer. And don't you dare look at me like that."

"Like what, mistress?"

But Silver just waved her hand and walked away in a flutter of silk, leaving Hase standing amid the sea of patterned cloth, her face as smooth and impassive as ever.

SAI'S WORDS WERE ALWAYS GENTLE. HASE felt as though she could fall asleep listening to him.

"Is it true," the young man asked, waking her up out from her reverie, "that on the Island, some people change their colors as they grow old? I heard that from one of the relatives; they'd heard that somewhere along the trip here."

Hase inclined her potted head. "Some do, yes. I know a person whose eyes changed from light green to viridian, yellow, and eventually brown, like leaves. They crumbled in the end, and the person went blind."

"Oh. I'm sorry to hear that."

"That person knew what was going to happen and worked hard to prepare for it. It's not that bad, when things are predictable like that."

After a while he sighed. "I cannot imagine the life of your people."

"There is no need, sir."

"But I want to. I want to know more about you."

Hase turned from Sai and remained silent, playing with the twines of silver and gold spindles he had given her.

* * *

IN HER EYES SHE WOVE HER patterns of gold and silver. With occasional blue that punctuated the new design, it shaped hearts and veins.

But then, just before she could wholly grasp the new pattern, her heavy head was yanked back as another pair of hands held onto her shoulders. Her shoulders ached under the hands' vice-like grip, pain blossoming in sharp edges and radiating from her chest. And yet, despite the ache, Hase felt the most bitter edge of frustration at losing the pattern she had been imagining, weaving in her eyes.

Below her, Hase could see a large basin of water as the pair of hands holding her shoulders yanked backwards further and the other hands pulling at the pot on her head went the other direction. She coughed, and heard a young servant's voice: "Mistress, if we go any further she might be sick, or even, she might die. I wouldn't be able to explain to our masters what happened, if asked."

"Simple, tell them you punished her because she had stolen the gold and silver threads." Silver's calm voice. "If she dies, it's an accident."

She'd have preferred drowning in the dye pot, especially now with the new indigo being brewed, the bubbles from fermentation slowly blooming like a nebula over the dark liquid. But that would spoil the new dye. Through the pain she imagined the dye's warmth, the smell, explosion of stars as the liquid rushed into her head. Hase shivered.

Behind her, the younger of the wives burst out laughing, her voice full of gold dust. "Then let me do it! I want to choke her with my own hands!"

Silver glowered at Gold. "Are you stupid? We cannot do it ourselves. We are going to say that the servant did it to impress us, of their own will. Be careful not to get your robe wet or touch anything that could prove we were here."

At that, the servant boy's hands loosened a little from Hase's shoulders. Hase whimpered, as she heard Gold make a frustrated noise.

"Anyway." Silver came around to where Hase could see her, and crouched down to flash the two spindles of thread. "These are confiscated. You don't need them, anyway, do you? Because the patterns are all in your head, like you said."

"No! Please, I need them! They are my inspiration!"

Silver smiled her cold, cold smile. Hase tried to reach out for the spindles, but the servant boy pulled her back. She heard Gold laughing again, saw Silver tuck the spindles into her sleeve.

HASE COULD FEEL HER AUNTS' FRUSTRATION. She wasn't making enough progress. Seeing the color of indigo change in impossible gradation, learning simple knots that revealed unexpected patterns weren't enough yet for her to create new, satisfying designs. She needed inspiration, and it seemed as though the people here were determined to snatch away that inspiration just when she thought she had found it.

Until one night, at the far end of the house, where she found the three young nobles.

She watched as they tangled and disentangled, making new patterns for her every second. The unreliable screen of organdy, which they must have chosen so that they *would* be seen, provided her with even more inspirations, as it swayed and added a sheen to their passion. Patterns, patterns, patterns.

"What is it that we don't have and the pot girl does?" Silver's cool voice carried through the night as she gracefully moved to ride the man.

"The pot hides her face and let me see my own lovely self on it," Sai said breezily. Gold sighed with pleasure behind them.

"And also," he said, pushing up a little to grab at Silver's buttocks, "she is from an island full of treasures. Why not make her a slave of mine, let her serve as a liaison between us and the Island?"

"Did you say 'us'?" Gold crawled up from behind Sai and kissed him upside down.

"Besides." Sai lay fully down again and reached out to touch Gold now. "She looks ordinary, I mean, apart from that pot, but who knows what her children will look like? I know her aunts have the colors, because she told just to me, because she trusts me, so why not her children?"

"So then you can sell them?"

"Or we could give them to the high generals or perhaps even the Emperor!"

The three all laughed. Then Silver said, while Gold's laughing voice was still trilling in the air: "How did you make her trust you? She doesn't have a face, it's hard to tell what she thinks. Even if you're good at putting up with your own face staring back at you."

"Oh, that was easy. Just being kind to her is more than enough. Treat her as a woman, as no one else does around here. And she's yours."

Gold laughed. Sai chuckled. Silver grinned and licked her lips as she cast her glance upward. "Really? If that's true, you must be a very, very undemanding person, aren't you, Pot Head?"

Sai followed Silver's eyes. Hase, previously hidden in the dimness of the corridor behind the screen, stepped into the light and moaned softly, her sigh swaying the cotton organdy in front of her. Sai bolted upright, pushing Silver off him. "Hase!"

Silver let out a laugh, a trilling of cold, cruel bells. "Oh, Sai, didn't you know she uses this path to get to that stupid cot of hers in the storehouse? You should have paid more attention! If you intended to fool her long enough so that she would take you to that stupid Island, that is!"

Sai looked embarrassed, seemed to be searching for the right words. But soon he gave up, knowing there were no right words to save face with Hase. He looked at her mouth, her smooth, potted head and spoke. "Yes, I was using you, but you had to know this. Why else would I, a man with a rank, place special favor upon an odd girl like you if it weren't to use you?"

None of the three could read Hase's face, of course, with that mirrored helmet of hers. But they could see her shaking. Silver and Gold looked pleased. Sai still looked a little embarrassed, a little uncertain, despite his declaration.

"So why don't we make a child here?" Gold said.

Taking that as invitation, Hase stepped over the threshold, pushing the organdy out of the way. "But why? Why are you so interested in me?" she asked.

Sai frowned. "No, I told you, I'm more interested in your . . . "

But Hase wasn't listening to him. She crouched down, not to face him, but to face Silver beside him. "You are like a cold fire that seeks to burn me out."

Silver's grin became wider. "Of course, I hate you, your pot, your behavior, your strangeness—"

"Am I? Am I strange enough? Everybody says I'm plain, with my ordinary hair, my ordinary skin, my plain colors. Everybody's disappointed!"

"What?"

She turned to Sai. "And to you, yes, I don't mind having your genes. We always need more variations."

"We . . . what?"

Hase moved on her hands and knees, scampering towards Gold. "Oh, I love the way you laugh. Like gold dust exploding and filling the space. Laugh! Laugh, laugh, laugh at me!"

By then, even Gold was frowning with discomfort, and the silence drew out between the four.

"You are disgusting," Silver spat, breaking the quiet.

"Yes!" Hase turned around to her. "Yes, I'm disgusting! I love being bullied! I love being punished! Bully me! Punish me! You like it too, don't you!"

The three young people slowly backed away from Hase. She swiveled her heavy smooth head back and forth between Silver and Gold—Sai was no use now for her, not paying enough attention to her and therefore, misunderstanding her. Of course, in retrospect, all the questions he had asked her were about the Island, not Hase herself. Gold was nicely cruel, but she was more like a small child, always looking for a new toy. She'd probably tire of Hase sooner or later. So she looked at Silver, whose hateful stare almost choked Hase, like a flood of warm indigo dye.

Trills of silver, quiver of gold.

"Aunts," Hase whispered, grinning impossibly wide, resembling a huge-headed, one-eye monster. "I finally found what I needed. My offering to our goddess!"

Silver backed further away on her hands and buttocks, eyes shining with fear. Her terror made a sharp pang run through Hase, a shiver that wove new patterns, a shiver that pierced colorful stitches over her bright darkness, her white-out canvas.

Silver winced at her own reflection on the mirror of Hase's helmet; what she didn't, couldn't know was that it was a mirror both outside and inside alike. The inner mirror was always connected to the server, where her aunts received and observed every pattern Hase formed. The outer mirror projected and transferred information from the outside world onto Hase's brain, in the place of her long-crumbled eyes. Pains and hurts, both physical and psychological, inspired her more than anything; they had known that much through years of observation. That was why her aunts had sent her to this strangely feudal place—as much for the pain, as for the rare colors and dyes that weren't allowed to be exported.

"I'm the head designer of the clan, you see," Hase said, smiling her eye-less, reflective smile. "We need more patterns, colors shapes to satisfy our goddess. Favor of our goddess means wealth, and wealth means we will be able to afford a more expensive, lighter-smaller-better helmet for me. But if you prefer me in this heavy old thing, if you'd bully me more in this thing, I want to keep wearing it forever!"

Hase's breath came in quick pants of arousal and excitement, while Silver's breathing turned ragged with terror. Hase could hear Gold making strange noises, like choking, like gagging, like she was about to vomit. No noise, no move could be heard from Sai. *Has he fainted?* Hase queried halfheartedly. *Useless youngest boy.*

"What do you want?" Silver choked out.

Hase shifted into a seiza position. "I want you inside my helmet." She thought for a split second, and then, waved her hands in excited denial. "Not you, but the copy of your mental map, so that you'd keep on inspiring me." She stopped her hands and placed them on her chest, and crooned, "Yes, those eyes. I want your eyes, spiteful, hateful, always on me. Don't worry, it won't hurt you!"

"I don't understand." Silver backed away further, frantically looking for an exit. ""If I let you do that, you will leave us alone?"

Hase's cheeks and lips were enough to tell Silver that the pot headed girl was disappointed. "I thought you wanted to keep me around, to hate me, to laugh at me. But yes, if you let me have your copy, I'd simply go home with it. And I'll send you treasures with the patterns you inspired, if you'd like that."

Quietly, slowly, as to not startle Hase into excitement again, Silver shifted to sit cross-legged. "Do send them, then. You are going to be rich, right? Why not us, too?" Silver's eyes turned calculating, momentarily forgetting her fear.

Hase grinned wide again. Behind them Gold started to sob. "Sister, no! What if she's lying about not hurting you?"

"I am *not*!" Hase whipped her large head back, wobbling slightly, making Gold jump. "It's just like . . . drawing a picture of her! Surely you've been drawn a portrait before? A beautiful person like you? Did it hurt you, ever?"

"N-no, but . . . "

"I'm all right," Silver said. "She looks much more interested in being hurt, rather than hurting people, anyway."

Hase nodded eagerly.

Silver said, "All the beautiful things sent from her are mine, then."

HASE SLOWLY LIFTED THE HELMET, THE mirror in front of her eyes.

Gold couldn't see what her sister-in-law saw, but she saw Silver's incomprehension as she took in whatever lay beyond the girl's helmet, and began to scream. Silver screamed on, and on, until she lost all her breath, until her throat started to bleed.

Until her sanity was lost.

APATHY SEIZED SAI AFTER POT HEAD disappeared, people concluded. As for the two young wives, no one could determine what caused their sad turn of situation. The older one, Silver, kept her eyes open unseeing, her lips slightly parted but always unspeaking—and when she saw something beautiful, anything remotely beautiful, she'd start to scream anew. The family decided to keep her in a white-walled room with plain white doors, where she was always dressed in coarse linen robes without design, color or pattern. The younger wife, whom Hase had named Gold, fared a little better than her sister-in-law, but not by much. She wouldn't leave Silver's side, sometimes crying loudly like a small girl, sometimes giggling hysterically, especially when anyone ever tried to detach her from her sister. But she took care of Silver and of herself without problem, so people decided to keep her in the white room, too.

People laughed at Sai and despised him for his laziness. They treated the women as if they didn't exist, and the first and the second brothers of the house remarried. The white room became a small fish bone stuck in the household's throat; it hurts and you want to get rid of it, but it might hurt even worse if you try to force it out.

THERE ARE THINGS PEOPLE DON'T FORGET. Things like the way the people of the house mistreated the strange woman from the Island with her heavy, potted head. Things like how, eventually, the hired woman disappeared, and all those close to her were driven to madness. No one wanted to go near the family after that.

Slowly, the once prosperous house decayed.

IT HAPPENED ON A CRISP AUTUMN day, the clouds high, the air thin, the cold enfolding the quiet, decaying house. It arrived, alone, bearing nothing. It walked through the people who gazed, who gaped. Without searching or asking or even hesitating, it walked into the house, towards the white room. And it opened the white doors.

It was a child.

Its hair was indigo, its eyes the color of young leaves. Its face—every surface of its skin—bore intricate patterns, woven with silver, gold, and every shade of indigo. It was a thing of beauty framed in the whiteness of the room.

No one had to ask; the two women recognized it as soon as they saw it. It was Hase's creation.

"I have come, to be yours," the child said.

The women started to scream.

Town's End

A t the counter of a marriage agency at the end of the town, I felt my lip twitch in spite of myself. "Pardon me, ma'am?"

"I need a male," the woman in front of me repeated. "I badly need to bear a child."

I looked down at the PC and tapped the corner of my mouth, hoping it would stop twitching. It didn't help. "Well, I see you're a very straightforward person. But perhaps that sort of statement could wait until you are emotionally closer to the man."

"But why?"

"It'd scare the man."

"Really? I didn't know."

The woman looked nervous and tucked a strand of hair behind her ear, behind the string that was holding her mask in place. The mask looked old-fashioned, made of cotton not unwoven cloth. "Do you have a cold? Or is that for an allergy?" I asked.

She shook her head, her thick, long black hair almost unmoving.

Below this old-fashioned hairstyle and mask, she wore a long, one-piece dress that was almost stark-white, which didn't help her pale skin. I wondered if I would have to advise her on what to wear. "I think that would scare them, too. Never taking a mask off for some secret reason."

"Oh, really? Oh my . . . "

This woman, Saeko Kimura, claimed to be from a faraway region, which she had said was why she wouldn't give me the name of the high school she'd graduated from. She gave me no information that would tell me about her life, not even her age, but she looked to be about the same age as I, mid-thirties or so. She was the first client since I started working here four months ago. I had come back from the city to this small town last year after I had split up with my boyfriend, and for a half year I couldn't find a job. When I finally found the position at this marriage agency at the end of my hometown, I had no other choice but to take it.

The firm stood adjacent to a house the boss had said he lived in but never seemed to be using. I had never seen the boss, except for the one time when I saw a shadow of a tall, lean figure reflected on the screen door of the house a few weeks back. Our communication had been solely through e-mails. Not even phone calls.

"But me taking off the mask would scare them away, too," Kimura was saying. Wrinkles forming between her downward-slanting brows, which gave her an atmosphere of an unlucky woman. "I really need a man's seed."

For five years in the city I worked as a receptionist at an English language school, where I had to deal with countless, groundless complaints and had developed a Noh-mask on my face devoid of any real expression. But even that was nothing to fight against this. "You just want to sleep with someone?"

"Yes," the answer came quick. "Without a condom."

I actually chuckled. "In that case you shouldn't be here. This is where people who want to find a husband or wife come. You should sign up for an SNS that is famous for that sort of community."

"What's an SNS?"

"You know condom and don't know SNS?"

"I've seen couples using a condom and discarding the thing in the woods."

"Huh. You have a mobile, right?"

"No."

"No?" I asked, incredulous. "What about a PC?"

"No way."

I considered this. It would be easier if I just told her to find a mobile and Google for a service that suited her purposes. But she was my first client here, and after four months of having nothing but cleaning to do at this very small firm, it was nice to have someone to talk to.

"I have to ask my boss first," I said, "but I could let you use this PC and teach you how to use these SNS sites. For, perhaps—one third of the fee you'd usually have to pay here. If my boss says yes, would you like that?"

Kimura's eyes shone brightly. She nodded so eagerly that I feared her head might drop off her neck.

* * *

THE BOSS SAID YES VIA E-MAIL. I phoned Kimura on the fixed line (she had warned me that it would take a long time before she could answer, and asked me not to give up) and she said she'd come back next day. And she did. We chose a service that seemed to be favored by older people, sent out a few messages which wouldn't give away too much of her but weren't lies, either. A message came back. I let her use my firm as the meeting point. I told her to tell the guy that she took pills. What pills, don't mention.

A few days later Kimura came trotting up to the firm and hugged me over the counter. "Thank you," she said and I could even feel her smile behind my shoulder. "He even liked my mask and gave me a thing that would cover my entire face to wear when I was naked!"

"O-okay, good. But you don't know if you got the seed you needed yet," I said, patting her back a few times.

"Oh, I know I have. We always know."

"Who we?"

"My kin."

"Uh-huh."

When she finally pulled back she was frowning. "What?" I asked.

"You don't ask too many questions, do you? I know I've been a little . . . queer."

That made me smile. "Not my business, you're a grown woman."

"Well, thank you. You've been great."

"Glad I helped."

She had already paid, but as her personal thank-you she gave me an envelope. It contained a few partially used prepaid cards. They amounted to about thirty thousand yen. "This is too much." I shook my head and tried to give them back to her.

Kimura shook her own head and closed my fingers around the cards. "They were all we could gather. This has been a very important step for us, and it's not enough to show our gratitude, but cash doesn't come in very handy, you know?"

"Mmm?" I intoned. I understood nothing of what she had just said.

Kimura smiled and squeezed my hand. "Thank you," she said again and left.

I e-mailed my boss about what had just happened, stupidly including everything about the prepaid cards. His reply was only one word: "Good."

AND WHAT HAD I JUST DONE? A few days later I had twin brothers across my counter. "We heard a lot about you," the one on my left said. "That you helped them."

"I helped Kimura-san, yes. But you look a lot younger." I had already given up my Noh-mask.

"We have a lady that we protect," the left one said. "We need someone to come for her." The one on my right said nothing.

"Where to?"

"The shrine in the woods."

I very vaguely remembered the place. "The one with the sun-goddess?"

"That's the place."

"And she 'needs the seed'?"

"Yep."

I wasn't sure if I wanted to laugh or scream. "Can you at least bring her to some hotel? It's not easy to bring in a stranger into your own place, you know."

The twins looked at each other and then back at me. "She's too weak."

"She's too weak but can have sex?"

"Within her own place it's okay."

"You mean she's the priestess?"

The left one glanced at his brother. His brother shrugged, saying nothing. "Something like that," the speaking one said. For the first time he didn't meet my eyes.

" . . . You're not going to do any harm to the guy, are you?"

"No! Did Sae do anything to hurt the man?"

I considered this. And also the fact that I hadn't heard anything really bad happening around here, anyway. "Well. Okay, then. But we have to make up some excuse for luring the guy into this shrine of yours."

"Do you have any suggestions?" The left one looked relieved and nervous at the same time.

I looked into my PC screen, thinking hard. "Perhaps you could just say your lady is a priestess."

"Huh?"

"Some people get more aroused by abnormal situations," I said. "In this case, you tell him your lady is a priestess locked up in a shrine. When the guy goes in she tells him she shouldn't be doing it there because it's a holy place, and the concept itself makes him want to do it there more and he wants to tear her robes away from her . . . "

The twins blushed. "Ah, well, it sounds—okay. Could you make an ad calling for that?" His speech faltered from time to time, and his not-speaking brother was even looking down at his feet.

I grinned. "Yeah, no problem. Tell the plan to your lady and come back tomorrow. I'll have her profile and message ready."

"Okay, thanks."

After they left I realized I hadn't asked for my boss's permission. I e-mailed him, to which he replied with "OK."

The twins came back the next day, saying they had even prepared a nice set of robes for the occasion. I let out a laugh and started searching for an appropriate service.

"What does she look like?"

"Beautiful," the left one said and blushed. "Slender. A bit sharp-featured, but beautiful."

"'Cool beauty'?"

"Yeah."

I frowned. "You really okay with her sleeping with another guy?"

"What do you mean?"

"You don't want to do that yourself?"

The twins both went deep, deep red in the face. "Oh, no. We aren't her kin. We can't."

"Oh."

I wanted to ask what "kin" meant in their context, and Kimura's. But somehow it didn't seem very wise a thing to ask. I shrugged it off and Googled a few services.

A few days later we got a message from a guy who seemed to be really thrilled about the idea of making it in the tiny shrine building. I let them use the firm's phone number in case the guy couldn't find the place. But it turned out it wasn't necessary.

The day after their meeting the twins came hopping into the office. "She was really, really pleased. The man seemed pleased, too."

"Did you watch them?"

"N-no! Oh, no!"

I laughed.

The boys hesitated a few moments before handing me a tiny, purple crepe sachet. Inside it I found a small piece of wood with a strange character written on it; it didn't mean anything to me.

"It's a token," the speaker-boy said, his expression grave. "It would protect you no matter what. You won't even have to worry about earthquakes again."

"I've heard something very similar from a woman who tried to sell me a 'spiritual' painting."

I meant it to be a joke but the boys didn't even smile. "It's really powerful and I've never seen her give it to one of your kind. Don't show it off, okay? There are some clans who would be really jealous."

I closed my fingers tight around the sachet. "Okay. Thanks."

They smiled and nodded. "Thanks to *you*. We won't forget. There are some things that won't fade."

I cocked my head, not fully understanding. But the next moment they had turned on their heels and were out of the door.

PERHAPS I SHOULD HAVE ASKED THEM what they meant. Kimura and the boys. Because more, some of them acting queerer than the previous clients, followed. A woman came, paler even than Kimura, and she brought a very fine kimono and said she wanted to pay with it. It was made of some fabric I had never seen or felt, and the boss said okay so I accepted it. Another woman, dressed all in black, asked me to teach her how to get to a mountain at the far end of Tokyo. For this I couldn't let her pay and so she touched my forehead and said, "May the good wind always be at your back."

Then one day a girl came, obviously too young for all this, so I just gave her a chocolate from my drawer.

The girl ate the chocolate and smiled widely. "What can I give you for this?"

"You don't have to. Just eat it up and leave, and never even think of doing this until you're five years older."

"But I'm of age, according to our kin's standard. I'm ready to have children."

Kin again. "Well, why don't you have them with a boy of your own kin, then?"

She licked her fingers and frowned. "They said you wouldn't ask questions."

"You don't have to answer it if you won't make me find your mate."

The girl giggled. "I like you, I think," she said. "I almost never liked a human."

"Oh, I'm honored."

The girl suddenly sobered. "You should come with me. I'll show you how I'm old enough."

"How will you show me?"

"Oh, I'll show you. But not here."

The girl stared at me. Her brown eyes had a strange quality I couldn't name. It felt as though they were boring into my brain through my eyes. I tried to look away but somehow failed.

I shook my head. "I can't leave this place. I work here."

"But after?"

"I need to do some grocery shopping."

The girl smiled. "Sooner or later I'll come. You'll come."

She left. I sensed a waft of strange odor under the chocolate, so I stood and opened the windows. But it lingered for a long time.

I e-mailed my mysterious boss about the girl. As usual the message contained only one word: "Don't." I wondered if he meant don't give a chocolate to a stranger, don't open the windows, or don't bother letting in a young girl in the first place.

Or don't go after the girl.

THE NEXT DAY I HAD OFF. I spent the day sluggishly, doing some laundry and browsing through the internet. When at dusk I thought of cooking dinner, I realized I had run out of soy sauce.

Which was weird. I had thought I had at least one meal's worth left in the bottle. How had I been mistaken?

I sighed and got into my car. Perhaps my aunt in the next town had a stock bottle. I didn't want to go into a shop because I had been dressed lightly and had no makeup, and my hair was a mess.

I started the engine. By that time dusk had turned into night. After a few minutes I was running on a narrow road which cut through corn fields. There were no street lights along the path, and it was just so dark . . .

Then I felt something collide with my bumper.

I hit the brake. I didn't see anyone running across the path, so it must have been a cat or something. Something very small. But it was the first time I ever hit anything. My hands started trembling. With the engine on and the lights gleaming, I stepped out of my car to check.

The bumper showed no sign of collision. I looked around. It was just so dark. The headlights lit the path in front of the car, but it was all that was visible.

At the corner of my eye something moved.

I spun around and squinted into darkness. Something was trying to go into the corn field. And it whined. I gasped.

"It's you, isn't it?" I said. I didn't remember asking for her name. "You . . . I gave you a chocolate . . . "

The girl whined again and went through the high corn plants. "Wait! Are you hurt?" I said and went after her.

Don't.

Something pulsed. Not my heartbeat. I felt for my breast pocket of my polo-shirt.

The token the twins had given me.

But the girl whined once more. Her movement sounded as if she was limping.

I hurried after her.

ROWS AFTER ROWS OF CORN PLANTS. I'd lost count, but at the back of my head I knew it was summing up to too many. Ripe corns. Young ones. All weaving a strange pattern, the one which invaded your brain just before you fell asleep. I ran. My breaths sang a rhythm that was nonsense. And why was I running?

AT THE END OF THE CORN field was a stream.

Fireflies danced everywhere. When their lights touched the long-faded hydrangeas the flowers sprung to life, their blues, purples and pinks so vivid in this dim place. I looked up and saw the Milky Way. The stream reflected the stars, becoming the Milky Way itself, only on the ground.

On the other side, a man stood, hands in his pockets. He smiled.

"Why?" I heard myself say. "Why are you here?"

"I came for you."

"You're lying."

He shook his head, smiling sadly. "I've been wrong. I shouldn't have gone to her. I shouldn't have let you go. I'm sorry. You're the one I love."

"You—you're lying . . . aren't you?"

My ex-boyfriend pulled his hands out of his pockets and jumped across the Milky Way, and stood in front of me. He took my hands. "I'm sorry. Will you forgive me?"

Another pulse, not my heartbeat.

"But . . . "

Don't.

"Please." He said and kissed me.

And why did it feel the same way as it always had? We had never kissed under the Milky Way, or beside it. It made no sense; I felt my desire, the one that I had pushed away so deep within me, coming back to the surface. Or perhaps it was the way I had wanted it to feel, not the way I really remembered. It didn't matter. The world spun, leaving us motionless at its center. I felt his tongue seek mine. Soon my legs would cease to support me. His hand slowly extended downwards . . .

"I said *don't*!"

I gasped and pushed him away from me. It wasn't his voice; we'd been kissing. The lady's token pulsed again, the strongest I had felt, and then swashed through the space with its hot, white light. My ex-boyfriend—someone who looked like him—stumbled and splashed into the stream.

And the space dissolved into nothing—

Just before my consciousness faltered, I felt someone else's arms under me.

I OPENED MY EYES AND FOUND Kimura looking down at me. She smiled and I felt a hand squeeze mine. "She's awake," she said.

At her word there was a commotion around me. More faces appeared into my sight. The twins, the woman with the kimono and other former clients.

I was lying on a thin futon, and though I couldn't see very much of my surroundings, from the way the ceiling looked I was probably in the main building of a shrine. I looked to the twins. "Your place?"

They nodded. A face came into my view from my head's side, upside down. A very beautiful face. "Hello, human."

I grinned. "Hi, goddess." With an effort I sat up; Kimura helped me. "So what's all this about?" I asked her.

Kimura sighed and looked down. Then she looked up again and said, "We don't mean any harm to you, okay?"

"If you did you'd already have done it, right?"

She nodded, and unhooked her mask from behind her ears. Under the mask was a huge mouth, from ear to ear, and I almost choked at the sight.

The twins sprung up, did loops in the air and came back onto the floor as two guardian dogs of a shrine; one of them had a mouth that was forever closed, that was why this one wouldn't speak. The woman with the kimono spun around on the spot, and when she stopped she was a beautiful crane.

Others followed. The woman in black smiled and showed me her magnificent wings. A snow-woman blew some diamond dust. I shook my head, grinning helplessly. "But why did you want to have sex with humans?"

Kimura put her mask back on, probably just for my sake. "We are running short in number. Soon our kinds will extinguish. To stop that, we decided, we needed to mate and have children, but we couldn't find enough male ones of our kind. We decided mating with humans would do, for the time being. Our genes are dominant, you know."

No, I didn't. "I see," I said anyway.

"I'm sorry, I shouldn't have spread the word so widely. I didn't imagine the tanuki would try to do the same."

"Tanuki? You mean . . . raccoon dogs that metamorphose to deceive humans?"

"Right. The ones you just met."

I nodded. So it wasn't him. Of course, my ex-boyfriend had dumped me and went to a prettier, richer woman. "They were trying to make me pregnant?"

"We just can't believe it." One of the guardian-dogs frowned with his already ancient-and-wrinkled brows. "We animal-shaped ones know we cannot mate with human-shaped ones. And borrowing a few seeds from a man and taking the earth from a woman are really different things."

Other creatures around me murmured agreement.

I sat straight facing the lady of the shrine. "Thank you, I think your token helped me."

The lady nodded. "Yes. But you have to say thanks to the man who brought you here, too."

"Who brought me here?"

"Well, who was it?"

The lady looked around. No one answered. Kimura shook her head and said, "We didn't know him. He was probably a human."

I felt a pang of hope. "Was he about my age? Tanned and big?"

She shook her head. "He didn't look like it at all. Lean, tall and pale. Did he wear glasses?"

Some said yes, some said no to this. I felt my hope shrink to nothing. So it wasn't my ex-boyfriend.

Then we heard a car. It stopped in front of the shrine and the engine died. The twins volunteered to go check. When they came back they both cocked their heads. "Someone left the car at the foot of the gate, and placed this on my pedestal," the twin said and held up a pair of keys bound by a chain.

"It's my keys."

"The driver was already gone."

I took the keys and turned them around on my palm. They were slightly warm. And I remembered the voice, "I said *don't*!"

I smiled at Kimura and others. "I'm going home now. I promise not to go after a tanuki again."

The lady nodded gravely. "If you get into trouble you come here, okay?" she said. "At least the twins are always at the gate."

"Thanks. And you all tell me when your babies are due, okay?"

Kimura looked amazed at that. "I'd thought you would never want anything to do with us again."

I grinned. "Who wouldn't want to see her client being happy because of the service she had offered?"

ON THE WAY HOME I DROPPED by at the firm and e-mailed my boss. I said, "Thank you."

A few minutes later a message came back.

"You're welcome," it said.

Taste of Opal

I was fourteen, old enough to be given away as a bride, and probably I looked like one at the shrine in the village that had been my home. I wore a simple yet beautiful robe that I hadn't known my parents could afford, something that made my glowing veins look like fine accessories. The difference from a wedding ceremony here, though, was that I wasn't the one saying prayers. With a feeling of floating and watching everything looking down from an odd angle, I waited as the strangers went through the short ritual.

"We'll protect her value," one of the strangers was saying, "no matter what, no matter how."

My value.

The priest beckoned and I walked over, right into the middle of the ritual. I was then handed a shallow cup of sake, in which floated a small piece of paper with an unfamiliar rune written on it. "Drink it up: everything in it." Which I did, with a hard swallow.

The stranger, who had said the prayer, held before my face a mirror which bore on its reverse a paint-filled carving of the same rune as I'd just swallowed. "Look." I did as I was told, and something flickered in my reflection's eyes. After a moment, the flicker was gone.

"Good," the stranger said and nodded.

I turned around to find my parents watching. My parents, whom I had trusted more than anyone else in the world, right until a few weeks ago. They had their best robes on, too. And their best smiles. "Farewell, our dearest child," Mother said. "Our paths part here, leading us to different goals of happiness."

She said it as if it were a blessing.

They had the grace not to let me see the actual exchange of money, so how much I had been bartered for, I'd never find out. But perhaps seeing the money these strangers handed to my parents would have given me a better sense of being sold. Finally, I was ushered into a palanquin, and I looked up at them all, all these grown-ups, and wondered how small, how ignorant I'd been all this time, as they pulled the screen down between me and the world.

THE FIRST JEWELER WAS AN ELDERLY woman.

Her place was only a few villages away from where I had lived, and as they carried me through the relatively short first trip, the merchants who had bought me didn't even bother introducing themselves. Which was good, because if we talked, they'd have heard my voice shaking, or seen my teary eyes. They just told me from outside the litter that this first jeweler was a veteran. "You'll stay with her for ten days, during which period you will let her draw your blood from time to time," one of them was saying, though her voice was muffled by the fabric of the palanquin. "Later we'll come retrieve you." At this point, though, there was no knowing what having a veteran as the first jeweler meant. I was only horrified. So damn afraid.

The jeweler wasn't kind, though she was not unkind, either. She said no reassuring words, and as soon as I was alone with her, she shut all the screens over the windows except one, through which we could see an oddly thin line of the Moon.

"New Moon is always good for the beginning of things," she muttered. To me, to herself, or to the Moon, I was never sure. Something glistened in her hand—a needle. "It may hurt," she said. "I've never had this done to me, of course, so I don't know how it feels. But one thing I know is that if you fuss and make it go wrong, it will hurt *a lot*. Clear?"

I nodded. I had already been determined not to look away, and to stay calm; at least on the surface.

She took my arm. Could she see well enough in this dimness? The question proved meaningless, because as she rubbed my arm, my veins started to glow stronger than usual, and then there was no mistaking where the needle had to go. The sting surprised me more than hurt, but I managed not to yelp. I watched as my blood filled the cylinder, this strange, milky liquid that shone green and blue. The only thing that made me bear it, the only idea that had kept my tears away when I had been sitting alone in the dim palanquin, was that they would be making an effective medicine out of my blood. That I was valuable, more than the money that had gone to my parents.

"Done," my first jeweler said, when the cylinder was full. It didn't take as long as I had expected, and it didn't hurt at all after she placed a pad where I had been stung. Later I'd learn through experience that some were better or poorer with needles than others, and for all I knew, she was among the best. While I was with her, I didn't have to fear the needles again. And that was probably why I didn't hate my merchants as much as I should have by the end of those ten days.

There were four of them, the merchants. The tallest one did most of the talking when dealing with a buyer. The shortest of the four, slightly taller than I, had deft fingers for cooking and brewing. The nimble one often disappeared, and I came to realize that she probably carried messages and watched out for us, climbing trees or running under bushes. And then there was the strong one, who was strong, of course.

The merchants took turns in pairs bearing the palanquin that carried me, though most of the time the strong one took the rear end. "You don't have to carry me, you know. I don't mind walking," I told them. "I walked a lot, ran a lot, before—" *Before I was sold to you.* I closed my mouth over these words.

"No," the tall one said, her lips twisted. "We don't want you bleeding outside, Kei. Not even a drop."

"But what's a drop worth, anyway? Like, one copper coin?" I had no idea of my blood's price.

She shook her head. "Your value is one of the reasons, but not the only one. Now stop talking and eat."

Just as she said that, the short one appeared and handed me a few pieces of smoked pheasant meat.

As I chewed obediently, the nimble one returned from her short disappearance and whispered something into the tall one's ear. The tall one nodded and whispered back, and soon the nimble one sprinted away, back into the woods. It looked like a deal settled.

After a few hours of walking, we entered a farmhouse complex. We stopped in front of the annex as the nimble one reappeared and joined the tall one, and the two went into the main building. This was the fourth or fifth place I was leased out to, and I sighed audibly as I looked up through the raised screen of the palanquin at the two merchants who remained with me. "What do you all do when you're rid of me?"

The strong one looked down at me. "Enjoy ourselves, without a child to mind."

The short one laughed. I glared at them; the two merchants chuckled on.

The other two came back. "Let's go into the annex," the tall one said, and the two beside me lifted the litter with my head still stuck out and set it down again on the earthen floor of the annex. I crawled out, stood and looked around.

Low shelves were moved to line the walls, to make space in the middle of the ground floor. In that space was a pallet, on which a cot and a brazier were set.

"Am I supposed to sleep *here*?" My voice echoed throughout the wide and mostly empty building.

"Looks like it." The tall one patted my shoulder as she whispered back. Then she glanced up. "Probably can't use fire in the loft."

Then a voice from behind us said, "Sorry, that's right." We all turned around to find a man standing there, arms folded in the sleeves of his robe. "I'm usually all alone in this house, except for the servant who's only here during the day, and I thought you'd feel a lot more comfortable if you had a place of your own."

The man, the jeweler, was thin, with an air of sadness to his smile. He looked young for a blood-jeweler—thirty something, I guessed—and his robes bore subtle, intricate patterns. I didn't know the requirements for a "good" jeweler, but he must have been one to afford such luxury.

The nimble one laughed. "The opal here isn't as vulnerable as she looks. We've taught her how to protect herself, because we swore to protect her." Nobody called me by name when it was business.

The jeweler only smiled at her. And then to me: "This building didn't have proper windows on the upper level so we had to shield the openings with glass." He pulled one arm out of a sleeve and gestured toward the floor. "So I had to set the cot down here, where the air circulation is better. Please let me or my servant know if you need anything."

I bowed as gracefully as a country girl could. The strong one stroked my hair once, and then lifted the empty palanquin off the floor alone.

"We're watching out for you," the tall one said over her shoulder as they left.

I nodded; then stopped myself just before saying, "Have a great, grown-up time!"

THAT FIRST EVENING, THE JEWELER LED me to his porch at dusk, where I could see the annex on the left and the fields encompassing the west of the house on the right; once, the former owner of this house must have owned the fields, too. I sat on the porch, my feet dangling, while he sat cross-legged near me.

"Look," he said. "The night is coming."

I glanced up.

Yes. The crows slid over the sky, as if they were the first drops of darkness, leading more of their color in tow. Shadows of mulberry trees that lined the fields grew longer and longer until they overlapped and blended completely with each other. Night was coming; I shivered, having the illusion of the black physically covering the world.

"There." His voice reminded me where I was. "Done for today."

I looked at him to find he already had a full cylinder of my blood, shimmering green in the last light of the day. "When?" I asked, stupidly.

He laughed. "While you were distracted, of course. Did it hurt?"

I shook my head. "Thanks."

"What for?" He laughed some more. "Now I'll have the servant bring you dinner. You can stay here looking agape at the sky as long as you'd like"—I snapped my mouth shut—"but please try not to startle the servant, because you look too otherworldly in the dusk with your beautiful skin."

With that, he left me there.

ONE OF THE PREVIOUS JEWELERS, a petite woman with large, pretty eyes, had let me see the opals from other people's blood. They were stored in a specimen case, each with a tag that told the name of the opal-blood person, and the part of the body from which the blood had been drawn. All were cabochon with smooth, domed surfaces, some on white pillows, some black, for the colors to show better.

"These are just samples," she said, "so a customer can decide which one they like best. Before-polish roughs are put away in a safe, so that I can polish them exactly how the customer wants!"

I frowned at her then. Me innocently thinking I was being shuffled around for a good cause. "I heard you just powder them after solidifying them, to make them into a painkiller or antidepressant. I thought that's why you are called apothecaries as well as jewelers."

Her large eyes twinkled. "Of course—I have put away the lower-quality ones to be ground up for medicines. But these pretties are for narcotics, naturally!" She then touched my cheek. "I see not a drop of jet element in your blood—which is so unusual. I'm sure your blood, with that purity, would attract the richest people of the world, if I succeed in rendering it the right way!"

I stared at her.

"Didn't you know?" Her brows furrowed, though her eyes were still as large. "The way they're polished decides what dreams they bring, what effect they have on the taker's mind and body. I thought this was an open secret."

I looked down at the samples. The jeweler woman hastily put the lid back on the case and bade the servant put it away.

INSIDE THE ANNEX ALLOTTED TO ME, I'd wait for the panes of the high, fixed windows to change colors one by one as the sun moved lower to the west. It was beautiful. I wondered if the jeweler had chosen these coarse panes, with various thicknesses and different refractivity, exactly for this effect. When the third pane from the right turned amber, I'd hear him call, "Opal?" And then I'd jump off the pallet and trot to his porch. Maybe I'd come to look forward to this ritual. Or at least, it didn't feel as though I was forced to go to him.

But today I felt somehow reluctant about everything as I trod to his porch. I frowned at him for no reason at all and said, "What if I said I don't want my blood taken today?"

He raised his brows. "Just today?"

I shrugged, unable to meet his eye.

And I heard him move, slide the doors open, and walk away. He might send word to the merchants: *Breach of contract.* After all, he was a buyer and I was merchandise. What use was I if I didn't give him my blood?

What use was I to anyone, if my blood wasn't valuable?

But just when I was about to walk miserably back to the annex, he returned to the porch with a tray. He set the tray down on the porch and sat down beside it. And beckoned.

On the tray was a teapot and two cups. He poured tea into the cups and slid one of them toward me.

"Where is the servant?" I wondered aloud.

"Took leave for the day—her child is ill." He sipped at his own cup.

I tried my own cup, carefully. It was a good brew, thick but not too strong even on my young tongue. The fragrance had a strange tang to it that I could not place.

"I've seen only one person ever, before you, who had such pure blood as yours," he said over his cup. "That blood made very good opals and I secretly kept the best piece."

I choked on the tea a little. "Why didn't you sell it?"

"Because it felt so precious, so dear to me. Would you like to see it?"

Did I? I wasn't sure. But I nodded anyway.

"Then come." He smiled and reached his hand out to me. "I'll show you."

I hesitated a moment. The servant had taken leave. We were alone. How did I know this man meant no harm to me, even though the nimble one and the strong one had taught me how to protect myself?

But the hesitation only lasted for a very short moment. I took his hand and climbed the porch, oblivious of my dirty feet.

I WAS STILL HOLDING HIS HAND when we entered the room at the far end of the farmhouse. My head was on the verge of exploding, full of anticipation about the best opal, and the worry that my hand might be too sweaty.

He led me to a chest, gently pulled out a drawer, and removed a wooden box: carved and varnished, the size of my hand. "You can open it," he whispered and passed the box to me.

And I did.

A large opal piece, rough and unpolished but with the most delicate play-of-color I'd ever seen nonetheless. It sat there without a cushion, a little smaller than the round made with my thumb and index finger. In it I could see a sky, looked up at from a clearing in an early-summer forest.

"Beautiful, isn't it?" He gazed into the opal and then at me. "Your blood might be even better."

My cheeks burned opal.

He carefully took the stone out of the box and held it in front of my face. In the air now, it looked as though half the sky had turned to dusk inside the stone. The windows in my annex. I swallowed.

"Go on, kiss it," he said. "See how it feels."

My mouth watered. The bitterness of the tea returned at the back of my throat.

I kissed the opal between his fingers—

—And then an explosion. Where I'd touched, it was soon as warm as my lips, and an impact rippled, as if the opal was kissing me back. *This is how the best opal feels*, I thought, and didn't want to open my eyes ever again—but when had I closed them?

Slowly, he slid the opal between my lips, into my mouth. My tongue accepted it, and it filled my mouth, my nostrils, and my closed eyes. It no longer felt like a stone. Oh, how it *tasted*. I had to have it inside me, deep, deep in—

"Enough." A familiar voice, and my eyes flew open. I coughed the stone out and it landed on the floor surprisingly loudly.

I realized I was shaking. I looked up, found the merchants glaring at me—or rather at the jeweler beside me.

"We assumed," the tall one said, in a tone I'd never heard her speak, "jewelers well knew the stakes for this sort of transaction. Or do we have to repeat ourselves every time we make a deal?" She put away a mirror into her sleeve, deliberately slowly as if making sure the jeweler saw it: the mirror they'd used at the shrine, where we'd first met.

The jeweler said nothing, but took a step away from me.

"What's wrong with you all?" I demanded, my voice ridiculously unsteady.

The tall one turned her eyes to me for only one moment. "You come with us, now."

"But—what did he do?"

"He violated the contract. He cannot have your blood. Furthermore, every blood merchant will refuse to deal with him in the future. You come with us, Opal."

I felt the surge of blood all the way up to my dizzy head. "Whatever you're trying to hide, I have a name, Merchant." I shifted a little closer to the jeweler. "I came here of my own free will, and—"

"Wake up, child!" she snapped. "Don't forget, when a jeweler calls you important, there's always *value in money* behind it."

I inhaled sharply. "That's exactly what you're doing, right? Selling me around. What's the difference, anyway?"

But just then, the jeweler beside me took another step back, away from me, and shrugged. I looked at him, and then back at the tall one, who nodded to the opal on the floor. "I assume he's been using that piece to corrupt others and have his way with them. Am I right, Jeweler?"

When the jeweler finally spoke, his tone, too, was quite different from what I was used to hearing from him. "Send any authorities you like." He took another step back and leaned on the wall. "But what you are making her do is illegal, too. Does she even know that?"

The tall one didn't answer this. She said nothing, just nodded at the strong one.

The jeweler stood there, expertly avoiding my eyes in a very grown-up way. Had I made yet another mistake, to think maybe he cared for me, maybe he treated me as something more than merchandise? To think there might be someone, anyone at all, who'd think of me as *me*, not just a body carrying the blood?

I let the strong one carry me to the palanquin without a word.

BACK ON THE ROAD, I COULD tell from the way the litter rocked that the merchants were still angry. At me, or at him? The taste of the opal returned from time to time, and, with it, his sad smile. I shook my head and tried my best to suppress the urge to scream.

The screen often swayed out of the way, allowing me peeks at the outside, which mercifully offered distraction: the sun, so *warm, so* bright. What colors *were* they; the trees, flowers, birds and bugs? And everyone talking, walking, working, all so *joyous*. How could I have forgotten that the world was so beautiful? That I used to run, squeak, and laugh for no particular reason back in the village? I wanted to do that again. I needed to do that again. Why would anyone stop me?

Why wouldn't they understand? I was so irritated, felt so ridiculed. I clawed at the walls, called the merchants names. What did he do, to make them not listen to me? Wait, what "he" was I thinking about?

What was I so angry about?

At one point, the merchants put the litter down, and as soon as the screen was lifted, the nimble one's hand was on my mouth.

The tall one examined my eyes. "Shit, we must have been too late. Sorry, Kei."

I tried to frown, failed, with her fingers still holding my eyelids open. How could she say sorry and mean it, forcing my eyes open and my mouth closed?

"We still have some time before we get to the next place," the short one said behind them. "Maybe we should medicate her."

What?

The tall one looked at the short one, and then back at me. "Maybe that's better than this."

What?

"Listen," the tall one said. "We don't mind whatever names you call us, but you might start hurting yourself at some point. We didn't know a piece so strong even existed—but it's too late to worry about that now. This is to protect you, okay? And bear in mind that you'll have to go through this again if you let someone do stupid things to you."

The strong one flashed a sorry face before pinning me on the ground, totally unmovable. The nimble one forced my mouth open as the short one poured something bitter into me.

FIRST MY SIGHT DIMINISHED INTO BLURRY dots, and then sounds got farther and farther away. Something started to burn in my veins—slowly at first, and then suddenly explosions, so many, all at once. My chest ached in a way I'd never experienced. I believe I cried out. But I couldn't even hear that. Blast, blast, blast. The explosions went on and on, and the pain swept over me the way the blood ran.

And then—

—And then a fire that was also a complete darkness, darkness that swallowed me. Embraced me. It felt so comfortable; maybe this was *home* —not the home where people had all just pretended, but the real home, made and kept for me. Maybe this was where I should be, even if it meant being trapped in darkness for good.

But then—

—But then I remembered the opal, the jeweler, and with a cry that wasn't a cry, I tore through an opalescent blast. I could hear a river. An opal river—my veins and arteries. Dot by dot, the world came back.

The world came back and I was looking into a starry sky against the silhouette of a forest. I was shaking.

A hand landed on my forehead. "The other three are pretending to be asleep." The tall one. "I don't think anyone could sleep after forcing you through that."

And then I fell into a calm, true sleep.

THEY TOLD ME I HAD BEEN unconscious for two days, which left one or two days till we reached the next buyer's place.

"How did you know I was letting him 'do stupid things' to me?" I asked them, sulkily, when I had recovered enough to speak. "Were you watching me all the while?"

The tall one shook her head. "We watch your blood pressure, hormones, and other things, and the combinations thereof." She touched a lump in her sleeve, where that mirror must have rested; I shivered a little at the memory of my reflection in it, at my old village's shrine. "We knew your breathing rhythm was strange, but it didn't look like you were scared from other factors, so we got there a bit too late. Sorry."

I said nothing.

"Such a powerful opal, it'd have been sold for a fortune," the short one said as he rummaged around inside his bag. Then he found what he had been looking for: a bundle of smoked meat. Of course. "Eat as much as you can. Pump around some blood."

Of course. Always the blood first. Me second.

THE MEDICINE HAD WASHED AWAY THE taste of the opal, it seemed. I no longer craved to be let out, or to be free. But instead of the taste, now something different lingered. Something I might call a flavor, maybe, not as thick as the opal, but which somehow persisted. At first, I tried to wash it away with water, but when that didn't work, I thought maybe I should chase it down, see exactly what it was, and why it was there at all. I stared into the darkness, trying to locate the flavor.

Then it came back. The memory of the flash, the home I had for a split second and lost, before I came back into the opal.

A flash a bit like this complete darkness.

Jet.

Of course. Everybody knew that we opal-bloods all had an element of jet to some extent. That was the balance of the world. And yet, until just then, I had never thought about my own jet. I had never felt its existence. *Not a drop of jet*, that jeweler woman with the large eyes had said. Where was my jet, then?

Once I started, my mind wouldn't waver off the jet. The strong one had a way of rocking the litter when trying to put me to sleep, but now it had stopped and all I could feel were the usual, steady steps of the merchants. It probably meant an hour or so had passed since I said good night to them.

Then the screen swayed, just once, in a strange way that seemed to have nothing do with the bearers' steps, and I thought I saw some glimmer at the corner of my eye. The next moment, another set of hands was over my mouth.

"Shh." A whisper. "Don't worry, you know I won't hurt you."

Did I?

"I've been looking for you for such a long time," the voice continued. "*Such* a long time. Finally. Thank you so much for searching for me—it needed to be two-way, of course." The owner of the voice moved one hand and stroked my hair with it. I slowly reached for the hand that was still over my mouth, tried to push it out of the way. To my surprise, it simply let me.

I swallowed; my throat burned. "Who are you?" I managed to ask.

A faint noise. A sigh? Or a laugh? "Do you not know about Ko here, Kei?"

The palanquin jolted to a stop. "Kei?" I heard the nimble one say. "Something is wrong—if I'm not mistaken, the litter feels too heavy—"

"What?" The tall one. "Kei, are you all right?"

But then the darkness lifted me off the floor and yanked the screen away. The next moment, I was standing on the soil, barefoot, in the darkness's arms.

The thing holding me felt person-shaped. Almost as tall as I, arms around my shoulders so warm. The merchants lowered their lanterns, getting the intruder out of the circles of their lights, so that they could see better. I could only see her as a contrast against the starry sky. *Her.* A girl's voice, distantly familiar.

"Ko?" I whispered into the darkness beside me.

"Yes," she answered.

The jet.

"How did you—" the tall one was saying. "Why? What did you . . . ." I'd never heard her so confused.

Ko grinned; I knew this only because a tiny tooth glimmered at the mouth's height. "Why don't you come rescue her, Merchants? You promised to protect her, didn't you? Didn't they, Kei?"

They had. They'd promised to protect my value. But now, for some reason, no one came even half a step closer. No one tried to grab me back from this girl, who was half the size of the tall one.

"Ko," I said again.

"Yes," she answered, again, and then we ran, away from the merchants, into the night.

* * *

WE RAN WITHOUT SAYING A WORD. She wasn't out of breath like me, moving so quietly, so smoothly, and without the warmth of her hand in mine I wouldn't have been able to follow her. At one point, I winced as some thorny plant cut my foot, but I was so worried about losing her that I didn't say anything for a while.

Then she gradually came to a halt and said, "Kei, are you bleeding?"

"Maybe. How can you tell?" I squinted but still couldn't see her in the dark.

"Look behind you."

I did. In the moonlight, where we had trodden, grasses, vines, undergrowth—everything we had passed along the way—had shot crazily up toward the sky, making for triple, even quintuple, their usual height. If the landscape had been like this when I first arrived, it would have been impossible for me to run through it. I gasped and squeezed her hand.

"Ha! You didn't know what your blood can do?" She laughed, and the blurry darkness lowered her head. "Let me have a look."

I stared back the way we'd just come. Did my blood really do this? Absentminded, I waited as she bandaged my foot and slipped on a pair of sandals.

"Oh." I looked down. "I can walk with the bandages, you don't have to give me your sandals."

"My house is not far now. Let's just get there faster."

I nodded and we started off again, slowly this time. Soon in front of us loomed a forest, a true forest, forbidding and merciless. I staggered and pulled at the hand I was holding. "Do we have to . . . "

"It's just looking scary to protect me. My house is in it. Don't worry."

Her outline wavered as she slithered in through the undergrowth. I don't know how this happened, but I, too, flowed into the forest.

It was so dark, not even the moonlight reached the forest floor. But where my bleeding foot touched—the blood had almost seeped through the bandages—the ground started to glow faintly. There, for the first time, I saw her face; for the first time, her features didn't elude me. The darkness of the forest was now cutting her into a relief.

"Ko," I said, looking into the mirror image of myself in front of me. "Are we sisters?"

She laughed. "We're twins, you silly." Then she looked down at my foot. "She's reacting to you."

"Who?"

"Sei. Another opal-blood concentrate—an opal without jet, like you. My guardian who abandoned her duty." She frowned and unfrowned with what looked like a great deal of effort. "Come. People can't find us here—Sei's presence will confuse our shadows."

"Even the merchants?"

"Even the merchants."

The house stood in a small clearing, and though the clearing itself looked oppressed by the dense forest, the one-story residence felt comfortable enough. Just the right size for two people, perhaps. A bit too large for a small girl like Ko by herself.

"How long have you been here alone?" I asked her.

"A year, almost. I had to let her flesh rot, then blend the flesh with the soil of this place."

I tried hard to not change my expression too much. "And . . . that grew this forest in less than a year?"

"It used to be nice and friendly woods at first, when Sei was still around," she said with a sigh. "Grew to be a forest with her as fertilizer. You saw what a mere drop of your blood can do, didn't you?"

I nodded. I was thinking about what the tall one had said, when she told me she didn't want me to bleed outside. My value not being the only reason.

"I put her opalized bones aside. The conc's blood crystallizes in their bones, becoming even more concentrated, but that kills the conc. Such bones sell so well, for a lot of money."

This time, I couldn't help but wince. "Do you know what crystallized opal blood is used for?"

"Of course. It drives folks crazy. Sei was crazy toward the end. I don't care." She frowned again. Couldn't seem to unfrown, this time.

"Was she your—our—relative or something?"

"No. Our parents sold me to her. Let me redo your bandages now."

She made me sit on the porch, brought a basin there, and started washing my feet.

"So our parents sold you to Sei. Sold me to the merchants, who in turn sell me to the jewelers."

Ko said nothing.

"Did Sei do this for you when you were tired or injured?" I asked, meaning the washing.

After a moment's pause, she said, "Yes."

No one had ever done this for me. Not even the merchants. Not even our parents.

WHEN I WOKE THE NEXT MORNING, Ko wasn't in the cot we had shared.

Feeling a little lost, I walked around the house; the previous night had been all blurred in the dark and I hadn't seen much. In the morning sun, I saw that this was a half-foreign, half-traditional style house, with every wall being mostly window, making the best of what little sunlight came through the foliage. Curtains and screens were open, and I found Ko working in the garden to the east. At the entrance I found a pair of sandals, and in them I walked around a corner of the house to join her.

"Do you like them?" she said without looking up.

"The sandals? Yes. Thanks. The merchants didn't give me any sort of shoes, to prevent me from running, I guess."

She then looked up. Surrounded by the trees, standing on the soil fertilized by an opal-blood's corpse, she looked almost like a normal girl, not a jet conc extracted from me. She smiled. "Soon we'll be harvesting sweet potatoes."

"You grew them?"

"I grew them alone!" She looked proud. "But first, let me show you around."

Hand in hand we walked, around the house first, then through the forest. To the north of the house there was another clearing, with flowers crazily abloom. Sei's grave. We shoved through them to find a small structure, one that could be used for storing food stock.

Ko let me open the door. Cautiously I peered in, expecting the inside to be very dark. Instead, it was lit by a glowing pile of opal shards. Sei's bones.

"I get on by selling them piece by piece. She protects me with the forest, she nurtures me with the bones. And now I want to protect you. Will you let me?"

That tickled, and I smiled shyly. "Of course."

"You'd never leave me alone?"

"Of course, never. You wouldn't leave me, either, would you?"

She smiled back. Our two-way need led us to each other, and now it was strengthening our bond.

THE SWEET POTATOES LOOKED NORMAL, UNLIKE every other plant in her forest. They were really sweet, comfortably heavy in my stomach. But I secretly missed the short one's smoked pheasant. "Do you ever eat any meat?" I asked at one point.

She shook her head. "Trust me, Kei. I know how to deal with blood opalescence. You'll be much better off without all the animal protein."

"Will I?"

"I'll get you some beans. Here, eat the things I grow, please? You don't mind that?"

"No, I love these potatoes."

She smiled as if self-conscious.

And so I did as she told me, eating things she gave me, but day by day, the small house felt just more and more like the merchants' palanquin. I wanted to help her, as her twin, as her family; but she wouldn't let me, not with farming or cooking, or anything to do with food preparation which was just "too important and sensitive" for me, the way she put it. When I had insisted long enough, even my sandals were gone. I grew anxious; I had read fairy tales where a witch confined a child only to try and eat them after the child had been fed to her liking. And I didn't really know what Ko was feeding me with . . . .

I shook my head. What was I thinking? Ko would never hurt me.

Something was wrong with me. Perhaps my blood circulation was sluggish and my brain wasn't working as it should. I walked to the kitchen in the hopes of finding something to nibble, maybe some beans or nuts. Ko wasn't there, but the back door was open a crack. From outside came the sound of a knife rasping against a whetstone. But the way she was doing it—nothing she cooked was that hard to cut, and I didn't see the need for honing it so meticulously. Unless she was planning on preparing some meat or bone that I couldn't eat . . . .

No. What was I even thinking?

I shook my head again, harder this time. I peered through the gap and was about to push the door open all the way and call her when she lowered the knife to her arm.

My hand twitched, never actually reaching the door.

The knife opened a black cut on her flesh. Blood spilled out, but she didn't waste it; she had done the cutting over a pot. Her jet blood pooled in the small vessel, and when she looked satisfied by the quantity, she bandaged her arm quite methodically, as if she had done it so many times she could do it without thinking.

Without a word, I crept away from the kitchen.

IT WAS A SMALL HOUSE, AND there was nowhere I could hide in it. At dinnertime she called me to the dining room, which was just the small space between the kitchen and the bedroom. I could only hope she didn't see me shaking.

Dinner was a bowl of thick soup, with steamed potatoes and other vegetables on a large plate which we would share. And the tea was already there in a black cup. "I . . . I'm not hungry, Ko," I managed to say at last.

She looked up. "Are you sick or something?"

Maybe I was. "No, just not hungry."

"But you have to eat *something*. Maybe the soup? That's easiest to swallow."

I choked; the soup, which was thick and could easily hide the black. "Sorry."

"But . . . " She frowned. "Kei, is there anything that you are not telling me?"

"N-no. Why?"

Her brows furrowed further. "Kei."

I could feel my face turning opal as tears threatened to fall. There was nowhere to hide. "Why won't you let me help you cook?"

She didn't change her expression by a muscle, but blinked once, very slowly. "I like cooking."

"Why can't I even work in the field?" My lips trembled. "Everything in this place grows crazily because of Sei, so why are the veggies normal? What do you fertilize the garden with? What do you put into my dinner?"

She looked down at the dishes.

"Why, Ko, my Ko." I walked around the table, grabbed her arm, and slid her sleeve up. "What is this?"

Scars anew, scars half-healed. The bandages covered only the most recent, fresh cut, and I winced at a closer look. Ko pulled her arm away, back into her sleeve, as if disgusted by the ugly look of her own arm.

"She refused to drink my blood," she said.

"What? Sei?"

"You opal-bloods need jet blood!" She turned to me, but soon looked away, seeing me flinch. "If . . . if you don't either draw your own blood periodically or take jet blood, your bones will opalize and you'll die."

Silence. Outside, a wind blew, two winds, three, and the forest grew loud. Was Sei trying to stick up for Ko?

Or was she on my side?

"She wouldn't drink my blood," she said. "For years, she did. She bought me from our parents because she needed my blood. But one day she said she didn't want any more, my blood was my own, no one else's. And she died."

I took her arm again; she didn't protest. "I think I understand her. If she saw this, she wouldn't be able to take your blood, Ko. You don't even have proper needles, or real antibiotics if you ever need them."

"I've never had any infections! I've been very careful, and the cutting doesn't hurt anymore!"

"It hurts me. I'm sure it hurt Sei."

"Doesn't she . . . don't you know leaving me behind hurts me? I don't mind how much blood it takes to keep you here! I don't want to be alone, not again!"

"Ko—"

"Or maybe I can do the same as Sei—I can kill myself and prepare meds for you that will last for your entire life. Just like Sei did for me!"

"Ko, listen, the merchants might know a way—"

"Merchants!" she shrieked. "What do they know? They only feast on you! Filthy merchants!"

"Ko!"

She sprang to her feet and ran for the kitchen. She was quick, but I knew this was the time when I needed to be quicker. I ran after her, and just as she snatched up the knife, I reached out from behind her, grabbed at the knife's keen blade.

At the sight of opal blood spilling from my fingers, Ko froze for a split second. I took advantage of that—still behind her, I pushed my bleeding fingers to her mouth.

She took my blood, my blood that was both narcotic and medicine at the same time.

And sank to the kitchen floor.

I SOMEHOW MANAGED TO TAKE HER to the bedroom, and she soon started to snore softly. Carrying her made my fingers bleed worse. I bandaged my hand as well as I could; the knife was well whetted and the initial cutting hadn't hurt much, just as Ko had said, but loss of blood, which had been thinning in the first place, wasn't helping me much.

I looked at the untouched dinner. I could tell what the merchants had given me when they "medicated" me was much, much stronger than the raw blood she had probably been adding to my food. And I couldn't imagine my merchants cutting into a jet-blood's skin.

The tall one might help me explain to my twin there were easier, safer ways of doing things. Only she wouldn't, because I left her, left them, slipped away from under their protection.

Still, I couldn't eat the dinner, which would be the last thing Ko would cook for me.

ON SHE SLEPT.

So soundly, so peacefully, that I had to check on her now and then to make sure she was breathing. She was, every time, of course.

This was the first opportunity I'd had to see for myself what my blood could do to people.

On she slept.

I WAS DOZING IN AND OUT beside the bed, as nausea took me on and off. Somewhere at the back of my mind I knew the forest was too quiet.

And then there they were: the four looming shadows.

"About time," I said, too tired to be angry, or even embarrassed.

They hadn't entered the house beyond the earthen floor of the entrance. "First, Kei, let us tend to your hand," the tall one said.

"So you found me because of blood loss? Were you still monitoring?" Some kind of fail-safe attached to me, I could easily imagine. "You didn't bother coming after me that night, and now that my blood is thinning, only now, you're—"

My voice was rising and Ko stirred just a little. I closed my mouth.

When her breaths were even again, I said, "I thought the forest would hide us forever."

"Of course, ordinary people wouldn't dare enter such an intimidating forest. But we needed to reach you, and then nothing could hinder us."

Were they pretending again? But then, whatever they thought of me, they'd been looking for me and had never given up. Whatever had been behind anything, even now, they still weren't trying to take me against my will. The tall one was holding that mirror, clutching it so tight her knuckles were almost white; the paint in the carved lines of the rune on the back of it had almost completely worn away—had she been clutching that thing all the time? The short one looked so eager, with his bandages ready for me. The nimble one crouched, about to leap to me at any time, while the strong one, behind everyone else, seemed to be contemplating a way to enlarge the entrance space.

I sighed. No word followed, but something reached them. They stepped up onto the floor, and the tall one finally put away the mirror and stroked my head gently.

USING A COARSE OPAL PIECE (WHICH wasn't mine), the short one burned some very slow fire for Ko. "After your raw blood, a sudden pull back into reality wouldn't help her," he said.

And slowly she woke, around noon the next day, in the small house full of the merchants' presence.

"Why are they here?" Ko growled as soon as she could sit up. The smoke still wafted, and maybe that was the only thing that kept her from lunging at them.

"They found me because of my blood loss," I told her.

Her eyes snapped back to my hand. "Oh no, Kei. I'm sorry. Does it hurt?" But then she realized my hand, and her arms, too, were expertly bandaged, and she got back to glowering at the merchants.

The tall one took that as a chance to start talking. She bowed low first. "Our sincere apologies for intruding, Ko-san. We hope you'll allow us to deal with your blood condensation now."

"I spent enough time with Sei! I know all about blood condensation!"

"We do not doubt your knowledge, or your good intensions. But we specialize in keeping the balance of things, Ko-san. We know you, too, have been suffering from having too much jet in you, just like Kei here or Sei-san, with too much opal. The jet blood isn't as influential as opal, with its color's stable quality and all, but still. Just as Sei-san needed you, you needed her, too, in a way she didn't realize."

"What are you talking about? I never made Sei let me taste her blood! I never even asked her to bleed for me!"

"Probably not. But if she was a conc like Kei, and if her jet counterpart was already dead—which must have been the reason she needed you in the first place—without her jet shadow in the world, her opalescence must have been too strong." The tall one turned to me. "Kei, we believe the opal that jeweler made you taste was Sei-san's, and you must remember what just having it in your mouth for a short time could do. And you are an opal conc, who shouldn't be affected by opal that way." She turned back to my twin. "Just being with her had a strong enough effect on you, Ko-san, I daresay."

Ko said nothing for a while. When she finally spoke, as she did so, she took my injured hand in hers. "Sometimes I feel like I'm crazy, though I don't know how or why. I go to her grave and being with her bones soothes me."

The tall one nodded. "I can imagine, yes."

Ko looked down, her lips trembling. I looked out the window, at the forest, which was swaying gently in a breeze, as if wanting to stroke a small girl's head. My eyes on the forest, I cradled Ko's head into my arms, trying to somehow respond to the forest.

THAT NIGHT, WE LET THE MERCHANTS take the house (which, I had to admit, must have been too small for the four of them) and decided to sleep ourselves in the palanquin, using it as a tent out in the forest.

"So they'd teach me how to draw blood with a needle?" Ko said as she crawled into a corner. "And how to use my blood more efficiently? They're not as bad as I thought, Kei."

I chuckled.

"I can cure you, Kei. You won't be like Sei. We will live together forever."

I smiled. Outside, the forest was singing. "Sei wants to say something, maybe."

"'Thank you,' perhaps." She giggled, curling fetus-like beside me; perhaps the opal incense was still working on her.

"Did you have a sweet dream?" I asked her.

"Maybe. I don't even remember. To me, a jet, your raw blood only had a beneficial effect. To others—maybe the merchants were about right all along."

I lay down beside her. "Just before you woke, the tall one told me something."

"Huh?"

I propped my head on one hand, looking down at my twin. "Many parents of opal twins choose to raise them just as they are, because two opal-bloods are more likely to survive than one, even though their opalescence is thinner. Some very rich people choose to get the twins made into one opal conc and one jet conc, for thicker blood. But the technology isn't stable enough yet; most of the time, this experiment fails and the conc twins are born dead. Or they die before they grow old enough to be sold—sometimes just the opal, who is weaker. Sometimes both."

Ko's eyes were fixed on my free, injured hand. "I don't understand," she said. "Our parents, I never heard they were rich."

"They still have a huge debt because of this experiment, even after selling us."

"Ha! Stupid people."

"The tall one said our parents wanted us as concs because one of us might be spared some trouble from being an opal. They fostered you out because a child without opal in the blood might be easier to raise, hence a better chance of surviving, rather than staying with our broke parents."

"They were wrong."

"They were. They weren't merchants or jewelers, after all. And it's not like the world is full of conc twins."

The tall one's words out of my own mouth had a strange impact; the previous night, when I had heard it from her, I'd only snorted. Now I wasn't so sure.

Ko snorted for me. But then she said, "If Sei had known how to make things easier for both of us, she'd have done that."

"Yes."

Outside, the forest started to glow. I cried out, amused, as Ko laughed happily. Amber, wisteria, sky blue and young leaves. That huge, strong opal. The windows of that annex. What had happened to Sei? What had happened to the jeweler, back when he was with her? No one knew, not even the merchants, and there was only so much we twins could guess; we were too young, too small.

"Stupid grown-ups," she said, her face now in shadows.

The forest glowed on.

* * *

IN THE MORNING, THE SHORT ONE taught Ko how to use needles. Ko made a face. "My blood doesn't glow, harder to find than opal." She sighed. "But I must be very good before you leave, so I won't waste the needles you gave me."

The words—the ones I'd been practicing in my head hundreds of times during the night—faded and were replaced with some others, which came out surprisingly easily: "I'll send you enough needles, Ko. Take your time getting better."

Everyone looked at me. The merchants were truly surprised, but Ko's gentle, almost resigned kind of stare made me skip my breath. "Are you leaving me?" she said quietly.

Now for those practiced words. "I still have debts to pay, for our parents, Ko. And you—we—will need to eat more as we get bigger, older."

"You're leaving me," she said again. "You're breaking the promise you made." She didn't sound like she was accusing me. More like she was double-checking the fact that was laid out in front of her.

The tall one cut in. "Ko-san. If you like, you can travel with us, too. That way it would be easier for us to keep jet medicines for Kei, and we are strong enough to carry you both."

I shook my head. "She won't."

"I won't," Ko confirmed. "I can't. Sei sleeps here. This forest, her grave, protects me. And I'll protect her, no matter what."

"And I can't quit traveling now, now that I've seen for myself what my blood can do." I was thinking of how Ko had slept so soundly, even after the quarrel. "I don't like it that people want to use it as narcotic, but as medicine, I see how useful it can be."

"You don't have to send me needles, Kei. Sei's bones are enough to get by on. But do send words, will you? I don't want to be—"

Alone. Left behind. I didn't have to make her finish the sentence. "I will."

Our paths parted here. Now I knew what our mother had meant. It was indeed a blessing, not for them, but for me, for us.

"WHEN KO-SAN APPEARED," THE TALL ONE told me when we had started traveling again, "we really wanted to rescue you, but I thought, what if she had a contaminated needle or something that we couldn't see—a mismove might make its tip graze your skin, accidentally or intentionally. We'd imagined all jet-bloods to be envious of opal-bloods and if they'd come, they'd want to destroy the opal. But it didn't look like that at all, the way she embraced you. We were so confused, torn between possibilities. I'm sorry we couldn't keep our promise right away."

"Don't be. Now I understand some promises cannot be kept. Not always." I felt tears creeping back into my eyes.

The tall one smiled. "Sleep now, Kei. When you're up again, a huge meal will be waiting. This is a sure promise."

The other three laughed. Maybe my parents had even chosen these merchants carefully, so that things would be easier for me. Maybe not. But I knew for sure that the nimble one would be watching out, that the short one would be thinking really hard what to cook for me next morning, and the strong one would be very careful to rock the palanquin comfortably. And the tall one would be looking for the best possible buyers, while I slept.

"Good night," I said to all of them, and pulled the screen down between us.

Hundred Eye

Eyes, eyes, eyes. So many eyes on my long arms.

If someone gave me these eyes to punish me, they made a huge mistake.

I could peep into people's baskets and sacks, while my face was turned completely away, looking innocent. Still, the rumors of a woman with long arms always present when there was a lot of pick-pocketing incidents served as a collective eye, always watchful. So I traveled a lot.

It was okay. Honestly.

Because of course, I didn't even know what it was that shook inside me like a tiny bell and made my eyes wobbly and uneasy. Later, when I learned the word lonely, I thought perhaps that was it, but I was never sure because there was no one to ask.

Even when I met him, while I was with him, I never asked.

He let me use his hunting hut as my flat and our meeting place. He didn't question me when I didn't take my robe off completely, only pulling the collars apart, never revealing my arms. He said it was okay. He said everybody had a secret.

Later I finally let him inspect my arms, my eyes, and even then, he didn't cower away. He looked into each eye for a few seconds at a time, which made me shiver, which made the eyes under his stare flutter in uneasy blinks. "Did you know they are all different shades of brown?" he asked.

And that'd make me forget how to steal, just a little.

* * *

WHEN I WAS A CHILD, PEOPLE often made fun of my long arms.

I don't even remember the first time I picked someone's pocket. At first it was small things like a marble, a doll, things people would dismiss as being lost, rather than stolen.

When people started to realize purses and money sacks were missing, I left my home. Everywhere there was a certain number of people who weren't wary enough, and always, my long arms helped. Stolen coins were enough for me alone to get by. I never learned to work. To cooperate. I was always alone.

And one day, it just happened.

I woke up in the middle of the night feeling itches all over my arms. At first I didn't pay much attention, but then, when I scratched, something wet and soft touched my finger. I jumped awake, crawled out of the make-shift cot of grasses and leaves, out into the moonlight, to inspect myself.

There, on my lower arm, something black gaped back at me.

An eye.

Was I dreaming?

At a closer look I could see many more swellings on my arms. They looked like bug bites, but then, one by one, a slit opened on each swelling.

Eyes. Eyes, eyes.

I wanted to scream, but how could I? That would draw bandits and stray dogs. I muffled my voice as well as I could, but couldn't stop myself from vomiting.

SOMETIMES ILLUSIONS WERE JUST TOO COMFORTABLE, like a lukewarm dream brought by mild drink. A shallow dream, which was bound to end soon.

I thought perhaps I'd stay here, at his hunting hut, by his side. Perhaps I'd change. But no, oh no, I was a monster, a thieving monster. How could I forget that?

"I finally got it," he said one day, as soon as he opened the door to the hut.

"Got what?"

From his sleeve, he produced thin incense sticks wrapped in wax paper. Even through the paper, I could feel its pungent, unpleasant perfume. "What is this thing?" I asked.

"I bought these from a traveling merchant," he said. "The smoke of this incense will make one of your eyes come off its socket."

"What?"

"One stick's worth of smoke will make one eye come off—"

Make an eye come off? "Oh, but." I placed a hand on his shoulder and leant in, my heart thudding at the prospect. "There are only . . . one, two . . . five sticks? I have too many eyes for that—"

"No, just one is enough. My son only hurt one."

I froze too long a moment to pretend, before I said: "Your son?"

For the first time, he didn't meet any of my eyes. For the first time, he started sobbing. "Sorry," he said. "Please. His eye will go blind soon if we don't do something. To be a man of rank as my oldest son, he mustn't have any bodily defect. Sorry."

"I didn't even know you were married."

"Sorry," he said again.

I let out a laugh. Of course. How could I expect this man to truly care for me? Always, ever since he'd seen the eyes on my arms, he was waiting for this moment. Or perhaps he'd even approached me knowing I was a hundred-eye monster. I chuckled on for some time, and then heaved a theatrical sigh. "Well. Why don't you start now, then?"

It didn't hurt. All my eyes went watery from the smoke, but the one which got wateriest wobbled and floated in its socket, and in no time at all, dropped off my arm, into his hand.

That eye left a dark, unfillable hollow on my arm. The man gave me the expensive incense sticks, bowed to me again and again and ran off, to replace his son's eye.

It didn't hurt.

LATER THAT NIGHT, I SNUCK INTO the man's house. I touched the hollow on my arm and set to work.

With my long arms I opened far doors and high drawers. I peered in a room, around a corner, with the eyes on my arms. Soon I found the chest where they hid their fortunes.

I took what looked like half of their year's worth of earnings.

For me alone, it would last forever.

THE IMAGE BURNT IN MY EYES, so hot that it woke me in the middle of the night. Because every eye, except for the ones on my face, had seen the boy with his two eyes, one of them a shade too brown. The father who was always careful not to get me pregnant. The mother who chose not to ask where her husband had got the eye.

The boy who smiled from inside the hollow on my arm.

Before, I'd always looked for abandoned houses which were rumored among local people to be haunted, because people avoided them. I'd never understood the feeling, of being haunted, and every one of these houses felt comfortable enough for me. But now my shaky hands, my floppy stomach, told me I was scared, was confused, was panicking.

Was haunted.

* * *

THAT COULDN'T CHANGE THE WAY OF life for me though, right? I was haunted, yes, but I was a haunted thief. I travelled more after I was haunted, not stopping in one place more than a week, because stopping long enough to know a certain child, their name, their favorite play, was unbearable for me now. But that was the only change I made. I travelled. Stole. That was it.

When the haunting was too sharp, too cold in my slim body alone, I'd go up a mountain, and imagined those feelings dissipating into the thin air. Didn't work too well most of the time, but it was one of those nights, that I found a strange tree.

Under the moon, at first I thought it was just an ordinary tree, with huge flowers all over its boughs and branches. Flowers? Oh no, they were the fruit . . . Then again I realized no, they weren't the fruit, they were faces. Human faces, like children.

Face-tree monster, then.

It was the first time I'd come across one of those, so I got curious. I went closer to a face, which was the lowest and nearest to me. Out of sheer curiosity, I poked it with my finger. "Hey."

Just as I'd heard—the face started giggling voicelessly. As though just seeing me could make it happy to no end.

And suddenly I was horrified of what would happen next.

The face like a child's giggled and giggled, and then, as if invisible scissors had cut its stem, fell off the branch, onto the ground. "Oh no," I said and crouched down. "I'm sorry. I am so sorry."

I scooped up the face, no longer giggling, half-crushed from the fall. One eye was crumpled and gone. "Sorry," I said again, rubbing at its forehead. "It's my fault."

Then with almost no thinking at all, I took the wax-paper bundle out of my pack and pulled one incense stick out of it. I lit the incense, and brought the stick near an eye on my lower arm, just beside the hollow for the man's son. And the eye popped off.

"Here," I offered it to the face. "Take it."

With my thumb I pushed a hole into its soft skin, on the other side of the remaining eye. After a while the eye seemed to settle in the make-shift socket, but I couldn't be sure. I found a grassy patch under a tree, where I could sit comfortably and also have something to lean on.

There, I lit another stick, hoping the smoke would help. I named the face Nin, because it came off from the nin-men tree. I sang, "Nin, sweet little Nin, go to sleep," all the while the incense gave off its pungent smoke around us, and then, fell asleep with the face cradled in my arms.

* * *

WHEN I WOKE NIN HAD A little body. So the incense had worked, more than I had hoped for.

It smiled when it saw I was awake. I smiled back and it giggled. I was afraid the face might come off its small body, but it didn't.

I started traveling with Nin.

IT DIDN'T SPEAK, BUT I COULD tell what it was thinking. It ate just about anything that I gave to it, but decidedly avoided apples, and those were the rare occasions where it cried angrily. Probably because they looked too much like itself.

Despite its healthy eating, its little body never got taller or plumper. I wondered if it was lacking a certain sort of nutrient that nin-men trees needed, or if it was never meant to grow in the first place. The incense sticks might do something, I suspected, but I decided to save them for now, until I knew exactly what the perfume could do.

I looked into my purse. There was still enough, but with Nin under my care, more money wouldn't hurt at all. And it'd be nice if I had saved enough, should I ever have a chance to purchase more of the incense. I'd been avoiding stealing these days because I didn't know where I should put Nin while I worked. But I suspected it could understand what I was saying—perhaps I could make it wait in the woods.

So I let it sit under a bush behind a fallen tree trunk. "Nin, listen," I said. "I'm going to work. You stay here. Understand? You. Stay. Here." I punctuated each of the last three words with a pat on its shoulder. "I will come back soon. Soon, okay? Don't worry. Soon."

It nodded without smiling. I rubbed its smooth forehead and left it there.

I'D ALMOST FORGOTTEN HOW EASY IT was to pick pockets and baskets. And the thrill that it gave me. By the time I had stolen from three people, I was feeling high. Oh, just one more. Just one more wallet and I'd quit for the day.

I snuck into a crowd that had formed in front of a traveling performer. There was a wealthy-looking man, and I shuffled quietly towards him. With the eyes on my face I watched the performer, while I examined with my arm-eyes the man's sleeve for a lump that indicated his wallet there.

There. There it was—

—But then, just as I was about to reach out my small knife to open a slit in his sleeve, I felt someone's eyes. I slowly looked around, and my eyes on my face met with those of a small boy.

His left hand was tightly clutching at his mother's right hand, and his right was fidgeting with his own lips. His eyes were wide open, staring at me.

He was about the same size as Nin.

He probably wouldn't understand if I took the man's wallet in front of his eyes. He might not even remember anything once he looked back at the performance. But my hand refused to make a move. My eyes refused to look away.

Nin.

Just then someone nearby breathed sharply. "Monster!" At first the word didn't quite register. "She has eyes on her arm!"

I snapped awake. I had forgotten to tuck my sleeve back down over my lowest eyes. People looked at me, and started screaming. That child was crying.

Nin.

After a moment of hesitation, I turned on my heels and started running. The crowd was roaring. I twisted my arm to peer back on the crowd; I couldn't help it.

All the people's eyes were turned to me, black and wide and glistening, some from fear, some from disgust. They pierced, stabbed, gnawed at my eyes, every one of them, sending a shiver like cold thread through my sockets. I ran and ran, unable to tuck my eyes in, while like always, my eyes on my face were looking only in the direction I was going.

I STUMBLED INTO THE WOODS. STILL panting and coughing, eyes cold and wobbly, I searched for the place I had left Nin. It wasn't there.

"Nin!"

No answer. Of course not, I'd never heard its voice. Without voice it wasn't able to call for help when it needed it—

"Nin!" My voice came out as a shriek that I had never heard myself utter. "*Nin!*"

After a moment of panic, though, I saw Nin trot out of a different bush. It smiled its usual smile and tugged at my sleeve, pointing. I wanted to collapse onto my knees, sweep Nin off the ground, into my arms. But then the image horrified me. Me, a thief, this disgusting thief, embracing this beautiful little thing.

So I stopped myself and frowned with an effort, and said, "Anything you want to show me?"

Nin pulled me deeper into the woods. After a little walk we reached a cave, invisible at a casual glance, in the shadow of a huge cedar tree.

"Nice hiding place!" I said to Nin. "Good thing, you."

Nin smiled again.

I carried my belongings that I had hidden with Nin into the cave, and struck a fire. I could see remains of some sort of shelf, probably something hunters had left long ago. Apart from that there was nothing in the cave, and I didn't find any trace of dangerous animals.

So we decided to sleep the night in there. In the morning, we'd flee this region.

BUT IN THE MORNING I COULDN'T get up.

First, sickness woke me. My head was on fire, my arm felt numb. With shaking hands I lit my lantern in the dim cave and examined my arms. When I inspected the eye closest to my right shoulder, I found something in the socket, something that wriggled.

Worm!

I gasped, and then vomited. I couldn't help but cry out as the bile rose. That woke Nin.

It came crawling to my side. What if this thing was contagious? I gestured to it to keep away from me, but it wouldn't. It wiped my dirty face with its own sleeve and, just like I had done when we first encountered each other, rubbed at my creased forehead.

It stroked me, this miserable thief.

I cried, and held Nin tight with my left arm.

EYES, EYES EYES. BLACK EYES ACCUSING me. All piercing my eyes on my arms. Voice, voice, voices. *Ugly monster!* Above me a huge sun glared down on me. Below me the snow tried to bury me alive. Where was I?

I opened my eyes on my face, my head drenched, cradled in our blanket. Nin was there staring down at me. It smiled weakly when I tried and failed to smile at it.

I slowly got up on my left arm. My right arm still hurt too much. Cautiously, I lifted the hurting arm, and examined it in the lantern's light. The eye closest to shoulder looked okay now. Just a little down, in the second eye's socket, I found that wriggly thing and winced.

It had somehow moved on to another.

But there seemed to be just one worm, and that relieved me. If there was only one, it'd be easier to protect Nin from it. I took the tweezers out of my pouch, held them in the fire for a few moments, and then tried to pick the worm off the eye. But when the tips of the tweezers touched the black of the eye a sharp pain shot through me. I cried out, sending Nin into a fearful panic. When the pain subsided and I looked back at the eye, I could see the tail of the worm at the corner, that it had burrowed deeper in.

I slumped down, resigned. Swore a lot under my breath.

Nin sat looking horrified beside me. "Hey, I'll be okay," I said, not sure of a single word I was saying. "I'm a grown up. I'll soon be well."

But not so soon. Because of course, I had so many eyes, so many of them for the worm to wriggle through. I'd never been this sick, not even when I transformed into this monster. Nin helped me, collecting twigs for fire, bringing in water and edible plants. It helped me a lot.

How did I deserve such sweetness? Just how?

Now, I was not only haunted by the man's son, but by the eyes of the boy who had spotted me in the town, by those accusing eyes of the adults back there. And by the fact that I had coaxed Nin into life, to be in possession of this stupid thief.

"Sorry, Nin. Sorry." I kept on muttering forever, in the darkness strewn with horrible eyes.

I HAD SOMEHOW GOT USED TO the fever when I saw the worm in the hollow in my arm, the second one counted from the wrist. The hollow that I had made for Nin.

"Heh," I said, trying my best to grin at the worm. "No more eyes. The end of you. Eh?"

The worm wriggled around in the hollow for a few seconds, and then, disappeared.

I frowned and sat up to see the hollow better. I still felt weak, but I realized the fever was gone, just as the worm was. So I had won, I thought. It was all over.

I looked at Nin, surprised but hopeful. It came trotting towards me, its short arms spread, and then—

—Collapsed.

I screamed. I didn't care what the scream might attract. I couldn't. Its face had been smooth and pink the moment before, now it was so red like a fallen apple. "Nin! Nin!" I scooped it off the floor; it felt so hot.

I looked into its eye, the one I had given it.

Yes, it was there. The worm. With some kind of silly magic the worm had somehow moved into Nin's eye. Or my eye, on Nin's face.

I had got over the fever and sickness after all, though barely. I was a grown-up monster. But what would it do to Nin, who was so small, so fragile? If something, someone, whatever, wanted to punish me, why wouldn't they be satisfied with hurting me? Or was this an entirely different sort of punishment, for my wanting to keep something so lovely? I shouldn't have given Nin an eye in the first place. Then I'd have suffered just like I should've, alone and helpless, knowing I'd survive and wake up whole, alone and helpless.

Nin.

It was shivering. The eye it'd originally had was glistening with fear. Perhaps with disgust, too? I shook my head, trying to get rid of the image of the eyes of the people in town. Without much thinking, I placed Nin on my lap, took the incense stick and lit it. Nin wasn't even strong enough to be scared of the smoke. I held its eyelids with two fingers and forced the eye to absorb the smoke. "Sorry, Nin." How many times did I have to repeat this? "Sorry. Being one-eye is better than being nothing, right?"

Right?

Maybe I should let it go? Was I going to punish myself even further by keeping the thing I could lose again?

My eye on Nin's face started to wobble in the fake socket I had made, and soon, the eye dropped off its face like an apple. I held the eye with my fingers, together with the worm, and put it back into the second hollow from my wrist, because an eye always needed a socket.

I collapsed, as Nin got up.

ANOTHER FEW DAYS OF FEVER WAS nothing, as long as Nin was healthy. It seemed more frightened, now that it knew what the fever and sickness felt like. It moved around looking upset, trying to find a way to comfort me. Once it brought back a fallen apple, something it wouldn't have touched before, and its face creased with agony as it handed the fruit to me. I laughed and bit into it. It tasted foul, but I was grateful.

A few days later, the worm was gone. Through the hollow closest to the wrist.

I knew what was happening. Of course I did. Grimly I looked at the hollow, as Nin climbed into my lap. The worm was gone. I had nothing to worry about.

Nothing.

Yes, Nin now had only one eye. I took a closer look at its empty socket. Then I looked at that one remaining incense stick. I could use it to get one of my eyes out of my skin again, to give that eye to Nin again. Nin was just as pretty one-eyed, but with two eyes things would be much easier. People would more readily accept that it was my child, an ordinary child with two eyes, and let us get by.

My eyes went teary, the ones on my face. So much so that I feared they might go wobbly and pop off my face. They didn't. Of course they didn't.

Somewhere, a child would start suffering soon. As beautiful as Nin here, no matter what the adults surrounding him had done. Just like Nin was too precious and beautiful for me, the man's son wasn't responsible for what his father had done to me.

Only one stick left.

I rubbed at Nin's smooth forehead. "Nin," I said. "You don't want your eye-brother to suffer, do you? You're a sweet, sweet thing like a ripe apple, I know."

Nin smiled its lopsided smile. Like I said, I could tell what it was thinking. "Yeah," I said, choking a little on the word. "Well then, can you help me gather my things? We should get going soon. I'm not sure if I can remember the way back soon enough."

Nin nodded and started throwing things onto my wrapping cloth. I carefully wrapped the wax paper with the incense in it with a garment, placed that on top of everything, and tied the cloth to close the baggage. I was still a bit weak from the fever, but I was a monster, after all. I'd soon regain my sure footsteps. I'd soon recall where that place was, where I had thought I'd lost everything about love, but I hadn't.

I started walking, with Nin by my side.

Grayer Than Lead, Heavier Than Snow

A chain of patterns, drawn on opaque glass in subtle colors, framed the front door of the Hotel, the most luxurious accommodation in this country. The huge chandelier above the main lobby sprinkled uneven light over the plush carpet, that danced and made you feel slightly mesmerized. The carpet was a riot of colors, only if you had the eye for such things—all of them mingled perfectly so that to a casual eye it looked somewhere between gray and beige, a soothing tone that only left impressions of colors to your subconscious.

The ceiling was so high your neck might snap when your eyes trailed the cord above the chandelier. From the niches on the walls, indirect lights illuminated the whole place; some of them were flickery, some steady, the overall rhythm weaving an entirely different pattern that buzzed the air in the lobby and the lounge right beside it. And the lounge—there were peculiarly arranged flowers every few blocks of tables and chairs, and you could not help but stop to stare at those. Before you knew you were escorted by the staff, winding over the floor in a pattern that made your legs absurdly weary, and by the time you reach your seat, you'd never want to lift your bottom once you sank onto one of the softest cushions. The tall wall at the back was covered with colored tiles, some of them even with holographic effects that worked on your neuro-system to slow the ingestion of caffeine and alcohol, so that you could maybe have *just one more* drink before leaving.

Every line, every curve, inviting folks into the comfort.

I might want to look over the whole lounge from the mezzanine, she thought, dreaming for just one sip of their extraordinarily expensive tea, until the moment she saw the displeased expression on the face of the person she would soon have to deal with.

She almost cowered away, but then forcibly braced herself. Maybe, *maybe*, this was the chance for her, and her mentor's, skills to come out, for them to stop lurking in shadows as if they were worthless.

The other person stood up, most of her features typical of islanders, though she was oddly tall for a local. Her hair was very dark, a black that almost glistened, and other surfaces visible on her were all evenly spread with a pale, pale indigo. Too perfect: just enough to sate the curiosity of the foreign tourists who came to this island for the exoticism of the islanders' skin, but not too explicit to steal spotlight from the human locals.

The city official android smiled her perfect smile, which had no warmth meant for the plain-skinned craftsperson. "Craftsperson Kiriko, glad you are here," the half-human said, as she placed a sum of money that was worth two days' meals for the craftsperson on the table, beside the apparently untouched cup of coffee. "Sorry to have to move you as soon as you have arrived, but let us go up to one of the rooms in the tower wing. I cannot discuss business with a colorless citizen here, obviously." She looked around, as if emphasizing the point. "To see our guest, Doctor Planet."

"Obviously," was the only reply Kiriko offered as they both wound their way out of the lounge, climbed the stairs to the mezzanine, where they could take the lift up the tower wing.

"As we already communicated in the letter sent to you, Doctor Planet is having an issue with his health, and we . . . cannot talk to the clinic about this." The ando pressed the button for one of the topmost floors.

Kiriko wanted to ask why, but also knew she was in no position asking whys. "What do you require of us?" she said instead, into the official's back, eyeing the gold-gilded mirrors on the wall and the ceiling of the lift.

"Alleviate Doctor's discomfort. He takes some . . . doses regularly. But the aftermath of the recent storm is keeping the next ferry away, and his supplies are running out."

A bell *ting*ed somewhere above, and the doors slid open. "What about the Aeros?" Kiriko asked, frowning. She knew the government used aircrafts in case of emergency, though they rarely carried people. They'd fly over, drop supplies and then be gone without even touching down. The storm itself had gone a few days ago, and the winds weren't that bad at the moment.

"For the same reason we cannot talk to the clinic, we cannot open the Aero line for this. Hope you'd understand." From the way she said it,

Kiriko knew this android—Mizuha, as the letter demanding the craftsperson's presence had stated the attending official's name was—didn't care if Kiriko understood or not in the slightest. "Just until he gets his supplies. It is not that much to ask, is it?"

Kiriko knew her mentor at her pattern atelier hated talking to the andos, but he probably wasn't alone. The andos were an open secret of the city, not because they weren't fully human beings, but because they were *manufactured*, with their calculated colors and patterns, in this place where you must be born with special complexions to be considered colored or patterned, where everything created or tampered by the hands of humans was regarded as lowly, fake. In a city where coloring your nails or your eyelids was deemed illegal.

And that their general attitude towards humans was for some reason disdainful—even hostile in cases with colorless and patternless humans—only added to the discomfort of the human islanders. For Kiriko, it was easier, though; many colorful and patterned folks looked down upon people like her, those who had no special colors or patterns on their skin to entertain foreign tourists, and to Kiriko it was just another pack of people disrespecting her. To the colorful and patterned who didn't have much experience with disrespect, the andos must have been almost unbearable.

"No, it is not," Kiriko replied. "As long as you pay enough for the service." That Mizuha looked younger than her helped her keep calm, even though how old the andos looked didn't really matter.

They seemed to have finally arrived at their destination. Mizuha knocked on the door, and then there was a click. After a few words exchanged, they were invited into one of the most luxurious rooms of the most expensive hotel in this country.

And what was there to do, but to gasp, gape and stare around?

The curtains, of a material that Kiriko had never seen! Was it woven with threads of all the colors existent and imaginable, one for each thread? And the window behind them—at a glance the glass was plain, the most transparent thing she had ever looked through, but no, oh no, there were lines etched onto the surface, shallow and deep, deep and shallow, twining and stretching to provide the best possible light-filter for the scenery outside. And the lampshades. And the bed canopy. Furniture. If she strained her ears, she could hear the water running through the pipes under the floor; the way it sounded . . . maybe even the inside of the pipes was patterned, to play music that soothed your . . .

"Ms. Craftsperson," Mizuha called, sighing. "Stop looking stupid and get to work."

Flushing, Kiriko closed her mouth and swallowed. "Yes. Of course."

Doctor Planet was seated on the long sofa, beside which Mizuha stood straight, very much likely looking down her nose at Kiriko on purpose. The man looked ill at ease on that fancy sofa, fidgeting with a pouch in his hands. An old man, very pale tan color, eyes the color of the sky just before snow fall. He muttered something quietly, as if . . . sulking. Mizuha said something in the official language in reply.

Kiriko swallowed again. "First—can we have a sample of the dose that he needs?" she asked the half-human.

"Of course." Mizuha smiled. Doctor Planet made a weak sound when the attending ando gestured for the pouch in his hand, as if parting with the precious portion of the dose was too much for him. "Doctor Planet." Mizuha repeated gently, pried the small pouch out of his hand. And gave it to Kiriko.

"Thank you," said the craftsperson as she took it. "Now, can you ask him if I can get sketches of patterns from his body parts?"

Mizuha's smile vanished at an impossible speed. "I don't know what you mean at all. He is a foreigner, he is not patterned, as you can well see. Oh, of course." The half-human's lips curved just a fraction at the corner. "I knew you colorless folks see the world differently than us. But not *that* differently."

Kiriko let out a sound that was a perfect cross between sigh and laugh. She hated this kind of dance, really, but a long time working in the city had trained her somewhat well. "You are quite right about that," she said, over another sigh. "For the remedy to actually work on Doctor, we need to see the pattern woven by his blood flows, skin firmness and refractivity of elements over his parts and his body, and combinations thereof. We call these silent patterns, and everything—even you—have many of these all over. We will control the efficiency of this dose of his using these. Oh of course." She forced a smile on her face. "We see the world differently, this is what only the colorless, experienced craftspersons can do. It might be too much for you to understand?"

Mizuha's lower lip stiffened, ever so slightly. Then she said, "Perhaps you might want to learn the official language, so that you wouldn't have to rely on entities like us, on an occasion such as this."

"Oh great, then we can do such business as this directly with the tourists, can't we? I thought you officials deliberately took the opportunity away from us colorless laborers for learning the language, from the way things look?"

Mizuha glared at Kiriko. Even Doctor Planet seemed to realize something was wrong, and he said something to Mizuha, who replied with a reassuring smile. After a few more words exchanged, Doctor Planet nodded weakly.

"You're asking too much, and you know that," Mizuha said, her perfect mask back on. "This has got to be really, really good."

"YOU LIED," KIRIKO'S MENTOR SAID, WITHOUT looking up from his drawing.

Kiriko groaned, thumping loudly down onto her favorite flat cushion. "I didn't know what this 'dose' really was, so I had to collect every piece of information available, right? Our usual method may not work."

The atelier's dealings were mostly true to its name: putting out patterned textiles for furniture and small objects for decorations, to be used in restaurants and shops, and sometimes, rich houses. But when these two craftspersons added a few tricks to the patterns they used on these things, chairs looked more comfortable, commodities on shelves seemed more attractive, and food even tasted better under certain lampshades. They also applied the same principles on minor body discomforts—and it worked. Though not everybody believed in them.

But her mentor was right. If all they needed was enhancing the efficiency of the medication, they had a handful of generic patterns they could choose from. Customized patterns were required for more complex cases such as persisting allergic reactions with rare allergen, or maybe pregnant women. This time they could probably just pick out readymade-patterned starch paper and tell Doctor Planet to take the remaining doses—cut down to halves or thirds, or even less—wrapped in it.

Kiriko had wanted to say something, anything, that might have looked as though she was striking back. Even if there was no point in striking back at the colorful. "And I got enough time to see the interior of the Hotel's room because of that!" She sighed at the memory. "Oh, anyway. Let's just get working on this, sensei."

Her mentor frowned, put his brush down and finally looked up at her. "My dear apprentice."

"What? What are you going to scold me for now?"

"Why are you so eager this time?"

She cocked her head. "I don't know what you mean."

"You do know what I mean. You've always been quite intimidated by the andos. When you had to work with them before, you kept procrastinating forever, until I actually had to scold you like your father or something."

"You are my mentor, that's your job."

"I'm not that much older than you and it hurts my sensitive little heart when I have to do that."

Under other circumstances Kiriko would have laughed, but now, she pulled another cushion out of a pile and hugged it. "You have been to the Hotel, haven't you?"

"I have."

"Then you must know." She fidgeted with the tassel at a corner of the cushion. "That whole place. It was made by someone like *us*."

Every color, ever pattern used in the building had been very, very carefully calculated; not a single one stood out to distract the guests or the staff, not a single one jarred the view without blending with the structure of the building itself. And yet, every one of them served the purpose of the bigger picture, of making everyone there feel comfortable, making them want to come back. It couldn't have been achieved by one craftsperson alone. There must have been a team of them. Which meant that there had been a time when even the colorless people like Kiriko herself or her mentor, those regarded worthless in this island where tourism was the only means for it to survive as a nation, had been respected, had more say on the way things worked.

Her mentor fell silent for a while. Then he said, "If you think things can be like that again . . . "

"No," she cut him short, unable to hear the entire sentence. "But still. I cannot stop thinking about it. We could . . . maybe make one tiny step, impress this one ando-san, if we keep trying and some younger persons do the same, and then maybe in one hundred years' time . . . "

Her mentor only smiled weakly in reply. That smile always made her heart contract—there was too much behind it. Then he picked up another brush. "Do your best with each project. That's the only thing we can do. Right? I guess you don't need my input for that kind of simple remedy anyway, do you?"

"I'll look into the medication and then let you know."

Only minutes later, it turned out the chemical was nothing like what they had expected.

"So BASICALLY YOU TRICKED US INTO supporting a criminal," said Kiriko, doing everything to not grind her teeth loud enough for others to hear.

Mizuha shrugged like a foreigner. "You think you'd have had a choice?"

"That's just outright rude and inhumane," Kiriko's voice came out louder and shrill, no longer able to restrict herself.

Mizuha lazily looked around, and Kiriko winced; they were both seated on the stiff sofas near the reception lobby inside the National Archives, to which most of the city andos belonged. Entities like Mizuha usually worked at this site, and went out to attend foreign guests when needed, following orders from the city. Here, it was hard to tell humans from andos by looks, but Kiriko thought she could, anyway, by the way some of the people did nothing to hide their disdain towards the craftsperson.

Really—they should have guessed. It was not hard to guess. Of course, the city wouldn't have involved a colorless craftsperson in a treatment of an ordinary health-related issue. But they'd wrongly assumed that it was more about Doctor, not the thing they had to actually touch.

There was no mistaking the crazy pattern that this "medication" wove under the atelier's customized microscope, which not only enlarged the object but also helped the craftspersons' eyes take apart elements to grasp the silent pattern they needed for the particular case. General medicines had a way of spreading out overly regular waves of a pattern, which forced the pattern from an affected area to submerge and smooth out. But this . . . this thing seemed to send out lines that were so irregular that they felt regular in the end, incessant and persistent, every line holding the potential of striking others into irregularity.

Of course, she knew narcotic when she saw it.

Mizuha snorted. "For whatever reason, we cannot afford to displease Doctor at the moment. We have already paid and will pay grandly again once you turn over the remedy, Craftsperson. You took this job for the money, right?"

"No!" Kiriko forgot herself again. "We took it because you bigheaded city tengu might remember that we are not worthless!"

Mizuha blinked, and Kiriko winced again; Kiriko had had no intention of saying that. She felt heat surging up to her face. "You may not have noticed," she said, trying to cover embarrassment, "but the Hotel was full of work by craftspersons like us. When I saw the interior of that place, I thought you knew how the city used to value our patterns. But obviously, I was mistaken."

Kiriko grabbed a bundle out of her bag and slammed it on the table between them. To her surprise, Mizuha flinched.

"Take one ground moontime-primrose seed, with just a few grains of Doctor Planet's dose, wrapped in one sheet of the patterned starch paper here." She pressed her hand harder on the bundle when Mizuha reached out for it. "Apothecary-prepared moontime-primrose seed. One sheet at a time. Use water only. Alcohol or caffeine is strictly prohibited. Understand?"

After a few moments of eye-to-eye, silent fight, Mizuha seemed to concede and nodded. Kiriko withdrew her hand and Mizuha took the bundle. "How many?" Mizuha asked without opening it.

"Two weeks' worth. Certainly the tides will clear by that time?"

"Let us hope," Mizuha said as she stood, and disappeared down the stairs, without another glance spared for the craftsperson.

* * *

KIRIKO WANTED VERY MUCH TO FORGET about this incident, but it haunted her dreams. She'd helped a drug addict. On the third night, she woke crying, from a dream where she contorted every pattern on the surface of the world with mere touches; looked up into the dim morning gray to find her mentor peering down at her. On the floor beside him, beside the mattress, there was a tray with a steaming pot of tea. "Sorry, did I wake you?" She sounded like sandpaper.

"Almost morning, anyway. Have a sip."

She sat up and took the lukewarm cup from him. Fragrant and pungent at the same time, but the aftertaste was sweet. Something finer than the everyday green tea.

"It's not your fault, in case you aren't aware," he said.

Kiriko groaned. "What is this?"

"A strong-green blend with moontime-primrose leaf."

"Oh you sadistic idiot."

Slowly the sun rose, its light seeping through their window, row by row of tiles of glass. The first row, six tiles with different sand-blasted patterns, was gradually warming the two craftspersons with the blood-flow-improving effect. The second row would work more radically.

"When I moved to the city, when I came to this place and knew that I had been right about what potential these patterns held, and the people—calling me liar all my life in my old village—were wrong all along, I thought I might deserve some respect for the work I could do." With a pang, she realized it had been more than ten years since. "I was young and stupid."

"You're still young, my dear apprentice. And at least your service this time gained a lot of money."

"Can I buy some fancy inks?"

He thought about it. "Just one."

"Two."

"No way."

"One for me, and one for you."

"I'd prefer a brush in that case."

They laughed and Kiriko got out of bed. The sun had reached the bottommost row, and the patterns down there simply enhanced the light so that there was no sleeping under it.

THAT AFTERNOON SAW AN UNEXPECTED GUEST to the atelier. For a moment Kiriko didn't recognize the person standing at their door, with their hair pinned and shoved into a cap, and a pair of glasses that made it difficult for her to see the pattern of their irises. But her mentor running up the stairs and shutting the door and locking it behind him was good enough a hint. She frowned as she spotted the pale indigo skin. "Mizuha-san?" she asked, still unsure.

The ando removed her cap and showed her dark, gorgeous hair. "I just wanted to talk to you."

"Is everything all right with Doctor Planet?"

"It is. May I come in?"

Kiriko prepared tea as Mizuha climbed the raised floor of the atelier's reception space. When she returned with a tray of pot and cups Mizuha was seated at the low table in a neat kneeling position. It looked so unlike the ando that Kiriko laughed.

"What?"

"Nothing. Have our mediocre tea."

Mizuha obliged. Then she said, "Actually, I was surprised that Doctor really loved your remedy. I didn't think it would work that well."

Kiriko groaned.

"What now?"

"It means we successfully helped an addict."

Mizuha smiled, and for a moment, Kiriko wondered if she'd just seen the ando's genuine smile for the first time. "Think of it this way: you helped the nation."

"I always want to help people rather than the country."

"Would you count me as part of your people?"

Kiriko looked up from her cup. She didn't like looking straight into others' eyes, as the patterns of irises always made her uneasy for some reason. But now, she couldn't help it. "Yes," after a moment she said, "if you count us the colorless as part of your people."

To Kiriko's surprise, Mizuha looked hurt at that. "I guess you're right." She sighed into her own cup. "Can you perhaps explain what you did with that starch paper? I'm curious."

Kiriko tried to shrug, but she wasn't good at that foreign gesture. "We combined the dose's silent pattern and one of our remedy patterns for enhancing water and air flow and thus created a new pattern, and put that down on the starch paper. The seed of moontime-primrose has the property of strengthening the effect of stimulant. The leaf doesn't work that way, only the seed. The seed also somehow works on the ragged lines of the drug, making it easier for it to blend with the flow-inducing pattern."

Kiriko wondered if Mizuha was following her and paused. The ando nodded.

"Okay. So when all the things mingle perfectly with one another, Doctor can feel the effect of the drug much better as it soars through his systems with water. Also moontime-primrose seeds are relatively less soluble, so their larger particles leave their traces along the way, smearing his systems with echoes of the concoction's effect, making for a longer duration of the drug's work on him. This is working well just because he'd had less of that thing lately due to its running out, the deficiency itself working as another stimulant. When he gets to have enough of the drug again, the remedy won't give the same result."

"Oh."

Mizuha sipped her tea while the craftsperson waited for hers to cool down a little. The silence was awkward; one where you had but to wonder why you chose to be alone with the other being at all.

So when Mizuha spoke again, Kiriko jumped. "Can you make such things for any substance of choice?"

Kiriko put down her cup and held Mizuha's eyes. "What are you saying?"

Mizuha seemed to be groping for words. Kiriko realized the ando's perfect mask had been carefully made, not a default feature of the entities like her. Mizuha looked down into her tea. "I'm not asking you to help another drug addict," she said. "But there are things that *we* cannot have enough of. Have you ever thought about that?"

"The luxury of colorful folks' life is beyond my imagination." Kiriko tried her tea again—now wonderfully lukewarm. "That pattern will probably work for many things that are addictive . . . more or less. But there will be a lot of margin for . . . error, so to speak. So I would not recommend applying it for another use." She frowned to herself. "No. I would prohibit that, as the issuer."

Mizuha looked up at Kiriko with the slightest frown Kiriko had ever seen; she'd have missed it if she did not have the eye for the thin lines near Mizuha's eyes. "Do you think you are in any position of telling us what not to do?"

"I am," replied Kiriko as she grabbed a handful of rice cracker dices from a bowl. "This is my job and I know what I'm doing. You do take your own job seriously yourself, don't you?"

"Yes. But we are built so. Literally. That is different."

"Is it?" She popped a few crackers into her mouth.

"You can make yourself known for this," Mizuha pushed on. "You might be able to raise your place in the society. You might even leave your name etched onto history."

Kiriko chewed loudly. She thought about the Hotel—she couldn't help it. The ando's eyes seemed to see something deep inside Kiriko's eyes. She swallowed, purposefully loudly again. "Leave my name as a supporter of addicts? I don't think so."

"I said—"

Just then the phone rang. This time they both jumped. "Excuse me," Kiriko said to the other woman and climbed down the floor, to walk to the other side of the earthen corridor. The call was from one of the atelier's dedicated patrons, a good friend of the craftspersons. Kiriko promised to get back to them, and they suggested dropping by. Kiriko hung up, laughing; when she turned and sobered, Mizuha was nowhere to be seen.

And her fingers got sweaty on the quilt of the receiver cover, as the feeling of something missing clouded her mind like a thin yet unsweepable fog.

"So?"

Kiriko looked up, from under the workshop table, hugging her knees. "She stole it," her voice came out quite wet.

"That . . . Mizuha-san?"

"Yes."

"She stole what?"

"The bag of our industrial waste."

Her mentor frowned. "I don't see—" Then he shook his head a little. "Oh. You mean, the print panel waste."

For most of their remedy patterns, they made wooden print panels so that they could reuse them many times. With many tailor-made patterns for each client, they used thick, waterproof paper that they had made by other craftspersons who specialized in the material. But for this one project, they knew that there would be no repeat orders, and they had to make the patterned starch paper for a very speedy turnaround, so they went with a softer resin material, which was easy to handle but quick to deteriorate. They'd never had to dispose of wooden and paper print-panels before; Kiriko had cracked this soft panel into a few pieces this time and put them into a bag along with scrap cloth, broken brushes and used towels. And that bag was gone after Mizuha had left.

Kiriko's mentor sighed, knelt down and then sat cross-legged on the floor. "They probably won't be able to reproduce that pattern. Even if they do manage that, then they'll have the pigment concoction to consider. Just photocopying it won't work."

"I know. What scares me though is . . . "

"Now *are* you scared?"

Kiriko slapped his knee. "My concern is, she sounded so desperate. As if any tiny bit of help mattered, even from a colorless. Why would the ando-san need the amplifier pattern? What does she want to amplify?" She rubbed her face. "And they aren't exactly human, so we don't know what abilities they actually possess."

Her mentor sighed again. "Even if they do, miraculously, manage to replicate the pattern, get the exact concoction, apply that pattern quite the right way and get the desired result, after all of those efforts, by then you cannot and should not count it as your doing, *your* fault. They decided to go with whatever they needed."

"But I dropped the seed of it all at their foot."

"*Doctor Planet* dropped the seed, not you."

Kiriko rested her forehead on her knees, covered her head with her arms. "Or maybe the government who decided to be *so* nice to foreigners." Her voice came out muffled.

"That's more like it, yes. Now come on, we have to discuss the updates on Hama-san's pattern, he is complaining new symptoms."

"Okay." Kiriko sniffed. "I'm sorry, sensei."

"Stop being sorry, my dear apprentice, and get to work. Just as always."

SOON THE FERRIES AND CARGO SHIPS started to crowd the island's not-so-large port. Doctor Planet was probably gone, or at least, he wasn't having trouble with his daily doses. As she hung the dyed cloths to dry in their small courtyard, Kiriko thought maybe she would never have to hear from Mizuha again. And for a long time, she didn't.

That afternoon, the early-winter air was crisp and silvery. Kiriko hurried along the High Street near the port, bundles of deliveries for a restaurant on her hands and in her backpack. She didn't particularly enjoy walking along the tourist-crowded High Street—just as no colorless laborer usually did—and kept her eyes low, eager to get to the client's place.

When she was almost past the park enclosing the port, something tugged her mind at the corner of her eye.

The park was crammed with colors and patterns—dancers welcoming incoming tourists, stalls selling last-minute souvenirs to departing ones. Kiriko looked around and sighed; perhaps too many colors and patterns jarring her tired brain. That happened sometimes. She shook her head and was ready to resume walking.

Then something, again. She turned sharply, the momentum making her whirl with the heavy bundles. But this time she caught it. At the end of the park, quietly overlooking the scene was a tall, pale figure—her expression weary on her young face. Mizuha. Kiriko strained her eyes at the ando.

Something seemed to buzz over Mizuha's pale skin. Static cracks and holographic flashes here and there. A shiver ran through Kiriko; she had never seen anything like it. She had no idea what it was, but she was sure it was not good. Kiriko readjusted her bundles and backpack, and trotted through the crowd.

"Mizuha-san," she called, when she was close enough to the ando.

Mizuha blinked, as if she had been forcibly plucked out of a dream. "Miss Craftsperson," Mizuha said, slowly and quietly. "Good day to you."

"Mizuha-san, is this common with entities like you?"

"What is?"

Kiriko gestured vaguely at Mizuha. "These cracks. Buzzes. I . . . I think something in your systems isn't working quite right. Do you *feel* okay?"

And then in front of the craftsperson's eyes, Mizuha's perfect mask crushed so suddenly, so fast. "Can you see it? None of our caregiver human workers seem to see this."

Kiriko's heart gave a painful thud. "Maybe not all human eyes can see such a thing. When did this start? Do you know how it started?"

"Not exactly when or what, but I have an idea. Look." Mizuha reached out, trying to touch Kiriko's arm, maybe, but stopped short as if remembering herself. "Can you perhaps meet me at the National Archives? After office hours?"

"Sure. If you tell me more about how it feels, perhaps I can bring around something that might help?"

Mizuha shook her head. "Not now. I'm sorry, I'm on duty right now. You don't want to be caught occupying me."

"I see. At six, then?"

"At six."

Kiriko nodded, and wanted to leave immediately, without a glance, just like the ando had done when they had met at the Archives last time. But she could not help peering over her shoulder. Mizuha's mask was back in place, mostly, only her right eye twitched as she looked on after Kiriko, a crack appearing and then soon disappearing right beneath it.

THE SKY WAS BEAUTIFUL AT DUSK as she left the atelier, but by the time she reached the National Archives building more than half of the colors were lost beyond the black of night. There were electric lamps around the building, and near one of them, Kiriko found Mizuha standing. The ando was not alone.

"This is Sakura," Mizuha said, by way of greeting. "I guess I don't have to explain why he is here."

"No," replied the craftsperson, wincing.

Like Mizuha, this Sakura person—who looked older than Mizuha or Kiriko, with a pale, pale pink skin and gray hair and dark-purple eyes— was obviously suffering from the cracks and buzzes that ran along his skin. But it was worse on Sakura. There was always a part or two that twitched and shivered, and the flashes changed colors so rapidly that it made Kiriko dizzy, with innumerable squares and dots of many shades of pink. Kiriko counted about twenty, from the pale color of the whiter part of cherry blossom, to the eye-piercing beni red. There were tears in Sakura's eyes constantly, as if he himself could not bear the flashes.

Kiriko swallowed down her pity. "This has to do with the print panel you stole from us."

Sakura looked down at his feet, but Mizuha held her eyes with the craftsperson. "We didn't have many choices. Let me talk about the ones we did."

THERE WAS AN ABANDONED PARK a little away from the Archives. A bench, an elephant-shaped slide and not much more. Mizuha suggested Kiriko use the bench, but the craftsperson was too restless to be seated and keep still. "So." She pulled her shawl tighter about her. "You are all tasked with collecting colors?"

"Not all of us," Mizuha said. "I am not. Sakura is. We all have a color receptor here," she turned a little, held her hair away from her neck and tapped her skin there. "Only the receptors on half of us are actually activated. The government archives those rare colors, you know, that have appeared on only a handful of people. It's difficult to find those, naturally, so some of us take bits of colors from many islanders randomly and compare them with the records. We apply a kind of agent on an islander's skin, and take the color that bleeds out into our receptor. Then analyze the color and store the info in our facility. This is performed very quickly, with no pain inflicted on the islander, so they usually never even notice anything is happening. But when entities like us, ones with very pale dominant colors, conduct this, sometimes we take too much, and strip the affected islander completely of the color in question."

Kiriko had heard about the incidents, of course; no one was really sure when or how it had started, but there were cases where a colorful person's color got gradually or suddenly replaced with a gray, a complete gray which was devoid of any tinge at all. In most cases, this graying-down or graying-out robbed the affected islander of their job, or a status in the society. No cause had been quite pinned down so far. Knowing the secret behind the most-feared disease in the nation didn't make Kiriko feel any better.

"That makes me guess," Kiriko said, shifting weight on her feet, "when a pale person like Sakura-san takes too much, that topples the balance of elements on the taker's part, too. Your systems and fluids might not be entirely the same as ours, but how the flows and movements work, and how these affect the air and light around us, work in a very similar way."

"I suppose you are right. We wanted to stop Sakura from doing that. Drawing too much against his will, I mean. And I thought, maybe, your pattern could help us."

Kiriko's lips curved into a weak, exhausted smile. "Did it help?"

Mizuha echoed the smile. "No, it didn't. I should have listened to you. I apologize."

The craftsperson waved a dismissive hand. "So what exactly did you do?"

"In fact, we got your pattern quite right," Mizuha said. Sakura quietly walked over to the slide and sat down on the elephant's head, his back to the other two. "We replicated the pattern not just from what was carved on the material but by calculating the flexibility of the print panel material, the kind and the amount of substances that bled out into the ink from the panel. Ink composition, too, of course. We were very, very careful. I know how much work you put into it; we cannot create such a thing, we do not have a room for epiphany like that, but we can copy."

Kiriko wondered if this was the closest thing Mizuha would get to a compliment. "Then what happened?"

"Sakura . . . " Mizuha eyed the other ando. "Most of us are familiar with some kind of science and chemistry, to deal with human colors and the analyses for them. He is one of the best ones at that. And . . . "

"He didn't trust our judgement on the composition," Kiriko finished the sentence for her.

"Right. And the amount of the ink and the moontime-primrose seed combined with it. I didn't know that he had done that, and personally helped with transferring the pattern onto his receptor."

Kiriko sighed. "And instead of preventing his drawing too much from the islander, it only made him not able to stop taking."

Mizuha nodded. "Thankfully, he didn't do his first experiment on a human—he did it on a flower. But even now, now that he is not even touching this particular flower, he is somehow still taking, he will keep taking until every flower of the same kind loses its color—the entire species. He cannot stop."

"Okay. Not okay, but I see the situation with Sakura-san." She massaged the bridge of her nose. "But what happened to you? Your receptor isn't active, didn't you say?"

Mizuha rubbed her upper arms with her hands, as if she was suddenly cold. "We weren't aware of this, but . . . it looks like the wrong balance within one of us affects other entities like us."

"You mean, like, this is contagious?"

"Contagious. Yes." Mizuha nodded as if she finally found the right word. "I'm keeping Sakura away from others right now, telling them he is ill and confined to his cell. But the fact itself that he is not showing up is already having bad influences on them, and I cannot keep this secret forever. And I'm getting worse, too—spreading a little bit of these cracks to the ones closest to me." She hugged herself tighter. "This must sound ridiculous to you. We half-machines acting like humans."

Kiriko shook her head. "Flows, energies, elements can work the same way on you as on us, you are built to look just like us. Also—when we customize patterns by combining more than two existing patterns, no matter what the symptom of the particular patient is, there are always a few patterns that always work for similar causes. Like, two specific patterns are always used for any patient with severe allergic reactions." She frowned at herself, realizing she was derailing just a little. "I mean . . . what I'm saying here is, I have a feeling that, no matter how different each of you seems, you share certain parts in your configuration. Which makes it easier for something to affect all of you with one kind of malfunction."

"You really do see the world differently, don't you?" Mizuha cocked her head. "I've never thought of it that way."

"Your caregiver humans never told you about that?"

"No. They don't really give any care for us, in fact. Just some maintenance stuff from time to time. But even so they'll probably find out something is wrong with Sakura before long, then they'll look into his receptor. And then mine, too."

"All right, then." Kiriko puffed a thin cloud of her breath, into the air whose temperature had dropped in the last hour. "We need a pattern to revert the effect of the wrong pattern on Sakura-san, and also a pattern to prevent damage spreading over you all."

"What? Is that possible?"

Kiriko tried to shrug, winced as her shoulder gave a strange jolt instead. "I'm sure we can come up with something."

"Thank you. My pride kept me from asking for your help, I suppose. Until you came up to me and outright offered it. I apologize. For being what I am."

Kiriko snorted. "Don't be sorry for such a thing. You cannot help that. Be sorry for not acting sooner for your friend and only for that. Anyway." She rolled up her sleeves. "Let's get working."

THE RECEPTOR ITSELF COULDN'T BE SEEN, as it was embedded under the skin. Mizuha mailed the blueprint of the part, along with the leftover configuration of ink and seed, to Kiriko care of the atelier. At the park she had sketched a few patterns that seemed to indicate Sakura's vulnerability to intense colors; she'd found similar tendencies from parts of Doctor

Planet, who was an addict, and Sakura was addicted to the color, too, after all. Kiriko and her mentor made proper drawings of these patterns first, and then started discussing a new pattern that could offset the effect of the original one. Line by careful line they constructed, a pattern that could bend the way the world ran over Sakura and his affected systems.

And then there was one more thing they had to do to this offset pattern. They now looked into each line again, added new ones that could change the way *light* travelled over the first line, to build a new pattern that would only offset the first offset pattern optically. When this optical pattern was a perfect shadow to the first offset pattern, an ordinary eye could detect neither of the two when they were placed one over the other precisely.

"So we use three layers of films here," her mentor said, as he tapped his long fingers on a roll of thin, transparent film, which had come very, very expensive. "We attach a small piece of the layers of this film on Sakura's neck, just over where his receptor is located—where, supposedly, everything started. On the inside of the first layer we print the offset pattern with the ink composition altered by Sakura, concocted with a medium to prevent it from drying too fast. So that the pattern will slowly seep over to the receptor. We place another layer of the film, with no pattern on it, and then cover the two layers with one more layer with the optical pattern on the outside. Theoretically speaking, the caregiver humans, or other andos, won't be able to see something is written on Sakura's neck."

Kiriko nodded. "The most dangerous part would be when the ink on the offset pattern is completely drained. Someone with a very keen eye might be able to tell the optical pattern alone there, even though the medium left on the first layer would still work as shadow to the optical pattern more or less."

"Make sure that happens when he is off duty. Adjust the amount of the medium according to his shift timetable."

"Yes. The weather forecast, too, for the amount of moisture in the air—there's going to be a hell of a lot of calculations to make."

Kiriko handed the patterned films along with the instructions to Mizuha. The ando looked uncomfortable; as she held the bundle between her hands she said, "I told Sakura that he should be here, too. Say his thanks by himself. But . . . "

"It's okay." Kiriko laughed. "Well, how predicable."

Mizuha sighed. "I'll make him pay."

Kiriko laughed again. "You scare me."

The ando put the bundle inside her coat. "Thank you. This is my thank you. Because I won't have to lose a friend if this works."

"I'm sure it works. If you follow instructions. If *he* follows."

"I'll make sure of that." Mizuha shook her head, a smile playing at her lips. "But how can you be so certain that it will work? I mean, humans are subject to errors, always. And I can only guess what you do here leaves no room for errors."

Kiriko cocked her head, smiling. "Funny . . . you're right. I don't even remember when I stopped worrying about such a thing—our pattern not working. Those my mentor and I build together. We still worry a lot about whether or not a client *likes* our work, though." She shook her head a little, and then nodded. "I assure you that it will work. And also . . . " She pulled another bundle from her backpack and passed it to Mizuha.

Mizuha looked at the craftsperson quizzically. "This is?"

"The blueprint of the color receptor that you provided—it wasn't marked as Sakura-san's. So we assumed that you share this same module—at least more or less."

"You are correct to assume that. That part is one of the few which are identical from one another."

"Good." Kiriko nodded. "So we made a small, emergency pattern that would work for you all." She pointed at the bundle with her hand, urging the ando to open it. When Mizuha did, three small objects shaped like tiny wooden pillars came rolling out of a leather pouch. One end of each was carved with a simple pattern. "We usually customize patterns by combining conventional ones. These three patterns are what we believe would work on you if combined precisely. Do you see those tiny cuts on the other ends?" Mizuha nodded. "For ordinary clients we make a pattern with the three overlaid perfectly, but carving that combined thing onto this very hard material would have taken a long, long time. But we believe in your precision. Use the cuts as marker to inflict the stamp precisely at the same place over your receptor, in a very speedy manner. Then you can make the desired pattern on the skin right there. They are receptors there, after all—you won't need an ink, just the touch of the pattern would be enough to soothe the roused edges of your neuro signals, to stop the fractal progress of the unwanted stimulation within you."

Mizuha placed the stamps back into the pouch, and put the pouch into her breast pocket. "Thank you. I don't know how I can thank you enough."

"Do me a favor, then, would you?"

"Anything."

Kiriko let out a breath. "Thoroughly eliminate the info in your data attached to these patterns, specifically about who made them. We can't tell how much your caregiver humans know of what you know, so we cannot risk leaving any trace, for the city to hunt us down in case something goes wrong. Don't make a mistake that we made the other day—leaving a half-broken print panel like that, for you to easily take away."

Kiriko had expected Mizuha would immediately say yes to that. Instead, silence fell on them like soft snow. When Mizuha spoke, Kiriko could hear lead on the ando's tongue. "But I want to remember."

The craftsperson blinked. "What do you want to remember?"

"You. That you helped us all. That you will help us all in the future, yet again, with these patterns. I don't want to let go of it." Mizuha shook her head. "But then . . . we cannot share the information that a colorless craftsperson can be trustworthy enough for that. That memory itself would throw off the balance of elements in us."

Kiriko laughed. "See? You cannot keep my doings secret, one way or the other. Just discard it."

"We cannot attach the data of a colorless laborer to the patterns. But maybe just your name?" Mizuha looked up and met Kiriko's eyes. "Just as the brilliant person who came up with this solution. We don't have to attach data about your being colorless. We'll remember your name, we'll always relish your name. Let us remember."

The colorless craftsperson looked back at the ando, who was apparently young, so young, that her chest ached with protectiveness. But then heard herself saying, "It's too dangerous . . . "

"Then we will not *attach* your name to your patterns. Just your name? We'll all store these memories in very separate places. And make a map for them when we need to turn to you again, so that our indifferent caregiver humans would never know to connect those." Mizuha came a step closer. "I don't want to let go. I'll make sure those like Sakura understand the importance of your name. Please."

Kiriko held a hand near Mizuha's shoulder, as the ando closed another half-step. "Not only is it dangerous. You don't understand. I don't want to be remembered like that. When I'm remembered, I want it to be as a colorless craftsperson, and my mentor must be there with me, too. Just my name attached to one single work, is not the same as me being acknowledged."

For a moment, Mizuha looked at Kiriko's hand, as if she wanted to touch it with her own. But she didn't. "I don't understand," she finally said.

"It's okay." Kiriko looked up, strained her eyes at the clouds. "Not any information on us. Can you do that?"

At the corner of her eye, Kiriko saw Mizuha nod after a second of hesitation. "Can *I* remember you?"

"It's your memory. Do whatever you like with it."

The air was filled with the hint of moisture—Kiriko could see it and smell it. But it wasn't yet cold enough—it would be half-snow, half-rain when it fell, that heavy thing that made the ground smeary and ugly, and made people shiver to the core, colorful, colorless, andos all alike.

"AND YOU FORGOT TO COLLECT CASH even for the films?" Kiriko's mentor said, to his apprentice who had come back soaked and shaking.

"I'm sorry, sensei. I really am. I give up the new ink."

"Oh of course. No ink of your choice for the rest of the fiscal year."

She wrapped her blanket tighter around her, and drank warm water from a cup with a blood-circulation improving pattern drawn on the bottom. "But ink can be our asset, not just my fancy thing."

He grinned. "It's okay, we'll add an asset to our balance sheet. I'm going to get that brush for me, anyway."

Kiriko almost dropped her cup. "That's not fair!"

"It doesn't have to be. I'm the owner here."

Kiriko groaned and covered herself entirely in the blanket, head to toe. Her mentor laughed and went away into their workshop. Taking another sip of the warm water, she wondered if there was a reason that no one knew the names of the craftspersons who had worked on the interior of the Hotel. Not a reason that came from the city, or any other colorful entities, but from the old craftspersons themselves.

Rib

How convenient, this loose-fitting thing called a kimono. When the sky was not light enough to see me properly, not dark enough for people to feel too alarmed, that was the time of day I'd walk around among humans. I loved the thrill. Just waiting for the Darkest Hour, doing nothing was too boring.

"Momma?"

These days people were getting more and more stupid, not paying enough attention, even at twilight time. No one seemed to be too disturbed by the presence of a woman a little too thin, hiding her face completely in a cloth.

". . . Momma?"

I could freely walk around and sniff in the air smelling of dinners and baths. Of lives.

"Mooooooooomma?"

And who was this stupid child calling to?

I turned around, careful not to show too much of my face, careful what little skin I had be shadowed completely under my head-cloth.

There, a boy, six or seven years old the way he looked, was staring at me. I furrowed my non-existent brows and demanded, "What?"

"Momma." The boy smiled and sighed.

Stupid boy. It was time to learn a lesson. "Little apricot," I said, slowly tugging at my head-cloth. "Are you sure your momma looks like . . . this!"

I threw back my head-cloth to reveal my face, hands (previously hidden in my sleeves) and all, that were all bones, bones, bones. I had the grace to arrange a dead woman's hair on my bare skull like a wig, though.

150

The skeleton woman was supposed to scare the life out of living people she didn't like, and now, look what I got here: birds fluttering away, children standing dumbstruck; soon grownups would start to notice, start to scream. And of course, that was the way I expected the boy to react.

Amidst the chaos of scared things the boy widened his eyes, then gaped a few times. Then he said, "Sorry. You are so much more beautiful than my momma."

WE SAT ON A BENCH BY the riverside, near a bridge and in its shadow. I had bought two sticks of rice dumplings, and let him eat them all. The money had come from the sleeve of the last man I had slept with, of course.

The boy licked the sticky syrup off the sticks and his fingers. He wiped his fingers on his kimono, and sat straight, looking very happy.

"What was your name again?" I asked him.

"Kiichi. You really are forgetful, aren't you?"

"Kiichi. Whatever. And you really think I'm beautiful?"

"Have you even forgot—"

"Oh, shut it." I waved a hand and sighed. A skeleton woman was supposed to look beautiful only to those whom she had enchanted. Scaring people was only a recreation at best. What we wanted was a human's strength, and a little money to make life easier. All the while I was thinking, the boy, Kiichi, was staring at me. I turned sharply at him. "What?"

"Why are you wearing my momma's kimono?"

I looked down. "Oh . . . because . . . I stole it from your mother!" I tried scaring him again, just in case.

But Kiichi chuckled. "Oh, I thought so. Momma's been dead for almost a full year."

I touched my hair unnecessarily, not knowing what to do with my hands. I had raised them up trying to scare him. "Where's your papa?" I asked him at length.

The boy shook his head. "Long dead. I never knew him."

I looked up, and saw the sky already darkened. "Then where's your home?"

"Why are you wearing my momma's kimono?"

I turned to him again. "Don't answer a question with another question."

"But you haven't answered my question."

Oh well, he had a point. "I was hanging around just near the cemetery," I said, the first "I" more a sigh than word. "One night someone came and dumped a body. A woman. I wanted a new kimono so I just borrowed it from her. In the morning the temple took care of the body . . .

Hey." I shifted and faced the boy. "That doesn't sound like your momma had been offered a proper service, does it?"

He reached out and fidgeted with my sleeve. "Which temple is she at?"

"Well." I tugged it violently out of his hand. "I think it was the one halfway up the sloping road towards the hill in the west."

"I see. Thanks."

"Are you going to talk to them?"

"It's nice to have a place to visit and pray."

I wasn't sure about this. "Good luck," I said anyway.

"Thanks."

Without looking at my face again, he walked away.

IT WOULDN'T BE VERY WISE TO go walking round the same area again, not after I foolishly drew attention to myself because of that stupid boy. Perhaps I should have a try on a traveler.

I walked towards the place where a few inns stood in a row. It was totally a coincidence that they stood vaguely in the same area as the temple Kiichi had gone for. I asked around, pretending to be a shop assistant who wanted to deliver something to a traveler, but I could find no lonely person to seduce tonight.

So I slipped in beneath the raised floor of the temple in question, and waited for the morning.

MORNING CAME ALL RIGHT. I WAS really sleepy, but I tried my best to keep awake. As I had expected, I heard voices, a boy's and a man's, arguing.

"But it must be my momma!"

"And who told you she was here?"

"I—I heard."

"Who?"

The boy said nothing.

"Listen." The temple man sounded exasperated. "If you are so sure that your mother is here, come back with your guardian. An adult. Understand?"

Before the boy could reply, the door banged shut.

I chuckled. He heard. "You?"

"Yeah," I answered. "Come over under here. I hate to be in the sun."

Kiichi came crawling in and sat beside me.

"So who's your guardian, actually?" I asked.

The boy tried to be stubborn, it seemed, only for a moment. Then he rubbed his eyes. "Grandpa and Grandma handed me to a group of carpenters."

"They dumped you?"

"They hate me. They hate Momma."

"And you ran away?"

"Uh-huh."

I could say no more. Silence never felt this way to me—clumsy, perhaps. Needed to be filled, but there was nothing that could fill it in a proper way.

I waved my arms around frantically, like a person about to drown. Kiichi looked at me as if I had lost my mind—perhaps I had, but what was there for a skeleton woman to lose, anyway?

"I don't know why I'm doing this," I said when I had finished flailing. "But I'll take you to your momma tonight. After the temple people have gone to sleep. For now, we both sleep."

I WOKE UP TO SOMETHING WARM. It was a strange sensation; the men I slept with would have gone cold by the time I decided to leave—sometimes dead cold, sometimes almost but not quite. Some men lived. My intention wasn't to kill.

Reflexively, I rubbed at the lump of warmth beside me. "Mmmomma?" it said.

"Yes."

A pause. "No, you're not."

"No."

We dragged ourselves out from under the temple's floor. It was almost pitch dark; I didn't have trouble seeing, but I guessed Kiichi did. I took his hand and we walked slowly, until his eyes adjusted to the dark.

Finally we came to the far corner of the graveyard. There was nothing to mark the place, but I could see the subtle difference in the colors of the mud. "Here." I pointed.

Kiichi knelt down. He reached out, hesitated one moment before he lowered his hand and let it touch the ground. "Momma sleeps here." His voice shook.

"Do you . . . want me to let you alone?" I asked.

"Did you see Momma's hair stick?"

"What?"

"Her hair stick. Tortoiseshell. It was her favorite."

I thought hard. But . . . "No. If I did, I would have taken it, too."

Kiichi nodded. "I thought so."

The boy abruptly stood up, trotted towards me, and hugged me. Then he started to sob.

His sobs soon turned to wailing, and at first I worried it might wake the priests. But here, probably his momma's protection worked well again. I wrapped him in the sleeves, and they muffled the sound strangely perfectly. In the temple, no one even stirred.

"MOMMA SAID SHE'D GIVE ME THE hair stick when I grow up," Kiichi said, when he was finished with his wailing. "So that I could give it to the girl I like."

"How did you learn that your momma was dead?"

"Grandma told me just before she sold me to the carpenters. She said Momma won't come back, for good. She was smiling when she said that."

"Sounds like your grandma knows what's behind it all."

Kiichi said nothing.

In silence we walked out of the graveyard, of the temple, to that same bench beside the river. "Your grandpa is probably too old," I said when we reached the bench.

"For what?"

"For me to take his strength. But I can try, I can stop as soon as he says what I need to hear."

I could feel his eyes. I couldn't help but turn to face him.

"You are helping me?" he said when our eyes met.

I shrugged. "This is a boat I've put one foot onto; I'll row to the end."

His eyes went watery for one second, before he looked away. "Thanks."

KIICHI'S GRANDPARENTS LIVED AT THE FAR end of the village. It was a fairly big house, considering the mid-to-small scale of the village it stood in, and I could guess it belonged to a relatively wealthy family as soon as I saw it. No wonder Kiichi's mother had such a nice kimono, and a tortoiseshell hair stick.

I had left Kiichi in the bamboo woods nearby. He didn't have to see or hear what I'd do here.

There were only a few servants, most of them resting in their quarters for the night, so it was easy to slip in unnoticed. I strained to hear more voices, and realized that another couple, other than the boy's grandparents, lived in this house; well, their lovemaking didn't sound as though it was from an elderly couple, anyway.

I shuffled through the corridors, towards the opposite end of the wing from the younger couple's room. And I had guessed correctly; now I could hear voices of older people.

"The boy ran away from the carpenters," a woman was saying. Kiichi's grandma.

"Really?" a man—her husband.

"We should have killed the boy. We shouldn't have listened to the woman's last plea."

"I really don't think we have to go that far . . . killing a child who knows nothing—"

"But what if he comes back? What if he claims his rights?"

"Well, we could just . . ." I heard the man shift, his kimono rustling. "We could just say we don't know the boy. He doesn't have any proof, anyway."

The woman murmured a few things. And then, "I'm going to have a bath now."

"Okay."

I hid myself in the shadows until the woman had gone past me and turned a corner. Slowly, quietly, I went to slide the door open to the old couple's room.

Grandpa's back was to me. I almost glided to him, making no sound, and put my hands, then my cheek, onto his back. The old man jumped, but soon, as my spell seeped through his back and permeated his body, his shoulders slumped.

"Sir?" I whispered into his ear. I rubbed his back, up and down, up and down again, and then extended one hand through the gap between his collars, towards his abdomen. "Sir, I need to know something."

"Oh . . . what is it?"

It was dangerous to mention the boy at this stage—he might remember where he was and the spell might break. "Where is that beautiful hair stick?"

"What—uh—hair stick?"

"Tortoiseshell, sir."

"Tortoise . . . you mean . . ." He swallowed. "You mean my daughter's?"

Damn. "Well, maybe." I reached lower and added a delicate touch on his groin. "Whatever. The hair stick."

He moaned, back in his dreamy haze. "I . . . I gave that away . . ."

"Who?"

The old man shifted, wanting more, so I coaxed him to face me. He blinked; he was seeing his ideal woman, his favorite actress, or whatever he wanted to see. He gasped, so I formed lips and a tongue to cover his mouth. When I pulled back I asked again, "Who?"

"The temple."

"Temple?"

He inserted his hand through between the collars of my kimono, for my phony breast. "We paid the bandits with money and future favors, the temple with the accessories."

"Bandits?" I let him pull my kimono away from my thighs.

"The ones who killed my daughter . . . Killed my daughter?"

The man focused on me with fully open eyes. Oh, shit. Now there was no going back for the spell. "Yeah?" I dropped my jaw slightly, making a deadly grin. "So you killed your daughter?"

He screamed. I heard a funny noise, and soon smelled urine. "Oops, don't spoil my beautiful kimono." I backed away a little. Good thing that I had let him open the kimono, away from his cock.

He screamed and screamed, then gasped for breath. When he opened his mouth to start screaming again, I pulled him closer to give him the last, long, sucking kiss.

Then I plunged away, into the shadows, where no human could reach me.

I HAD STRAIGHTENED MY KIMONO BY the time I reached the bamboo woods. He came out into my sight as soon as I called his name.

"Hey," he said. "Find out anything?"

While walking here, I had been thinking what was the best way to tell him what I'd found. But there is no best, no worst for a skeleton woman. There is only the truth. "Your grandpa and grandma had your momma killed."

He shrugged; a very non-childlike gesture. "I knew that much."

"I didn't have enough time to hear all of it, but I guess I'm really close to the truth. You have an uncle, don't you?"

"Yeah?"

"Did he live with your parents from the start?"

Kiichi shook his head. "No. They moved in after my papa died, I heard."

I knew it. "I think your relatives—your grandpa, grandma, uncle and aunt—all want your uncle's child to inherit your grandpa's properties."

"Pro—?"

"Have his money."

"I don't want his money."

"Doesn't matter. You're the first boy of the family."

The boy looked down at his small feet. I sighed and said, "Your grandpa and grandma hired bandits."

"Bandits? Very bad people?"

"Right."

He made a choking sound at his throat. "Then . . . her hair stick . . ."

"That's where the temple pops in. I thought the corpse-carrying men simply dumped the body at the nearest temple, but it had all been planned out from the beginning. Your grandparents asked the temple to take care of it, and gave them your momma's accessories, for keeping quiet."

Kiichi said nothing.

"Your momma tried her best to keep you alive, it seems."

He still said nothing for a long time. Then finally, he took my hand and said, "Let's go back to the temple."

So we started walking.

MIDNIGHT AGAIN. MOST OF THE PRIESTS and temple staff seemed asleep. We went around to the back of the main building, and found the earthen storehouse. Valuables must have been kept there.

"It's locked," Kiichi said once he had tried the door. Of course.

I nodded and started pacing. Probably the temple master had the key with him, and a priest usually wasn't an easy prey. Perhaps the priests at this greed-blinded temple weren't so difficult to seduce, but still. . . .

I stopped and looked at the boy. He was knelt down on the ground, one side of his body in full contact with the door to the storehouse. "What are you doing?" I asked him.

"There's a hole," he said.

I crouched down beside him, and he let me inspect the door. Just as he'd said, one of the bottom corners of the door was broken, the hole a little too small for Kiichi's head to go through. "I was seeing if I could touch anything inside," he told me.

Perhaps I wouldn't have to cross the too-wobbly bridge. Only if. . . . "Kiichi." I looked at him. "You really do want your momma's thing back, do you?"

"Yeah?"

"Well. For once, I'm going to take off your momma's protection," I said. "You'll see something scary. But you cannot scream, or you'll wake the priests. Worse, you'll have to bear the horrible part and help me with your hand. Do you still want your momma's hair stick back?"

He frowned. "I'll do anything."

"Okay," I said and stood up. I pulled my kimono apart, braced myself for his reaction, then let it fall onto the ground. Kiichi stared on at me, still frowning, saying nothing.

"Well?" I spread my arms a little.

Kiichi shrugged.

"Aren't you scared?"

"Mmm. Right after you held me, just beside where Momma sleeps, I think you stopped looking beautiful."

"What?"

"Momma must have known you weren't such a bad spirit, I guess."

"And you've been with me, a skeleton woman, all the while? Holding her bony hands?"

"Yeah?"

Stupid boy. I chuckled and said, "Okay, then. Now, I'm going to dissolve myself to bones, bones, bones. You'll have to pick them up one by one, and pop them into the storehouse through the hole. Leave the skull, it's too big. When all but the head is inside the storehouse, I'll reassemble myself into a headless skeleton woman. When I've found the hair stick I'll be bones again just inside the hole, so then you'll have to pick me up again. Can you do it?"

He regarded me with those round, black-black eyes. "I'll do anything," he whispered at length.

I nodded, and inhaled.

Dark, dark. Darkness should do no harm to my eyes, but I saw nothing.

Somewhere, a voice. "Hey. You're inside the storehouse."

I remembered who I was and felt for each bone, and one by one, constructed me. My body felt so much lighter without the skull and I swung around a few times. "Yeah, thanks," I said, but the voice must have come out of the skull outside. Kiichi jumped.

I walked deeper in, spun around, felt around, and measured the amount of dust on every touchable surface, to find the latest addition to their collection.

There.

On top of a small shelf, I found a lacquered box. I took it down, lifted the lid. The box was full of exquisite accessories, like hair ornaments and obi-jewelry. At the bottom, I found what I'd come here for. Tortoiseshell.

I grinned. "Kiichi, do you want me to bring all of your momma's accessories? I don't think the box would go through the hole, though."

"Just the hair stick," Kiichi answered.

Good, because with only the hair stick gone, the temple people might not notice anything was missing at all. I put the box back onto the shelf and went back to the door. "Here." I put the hair stick through the hole.

Kiichi grabbed it. Turned it around in his hands and stroked it. "Thanks."

"You're welcome. Now, help me get back outside. And this time keep talking to me; it's easier for me to keep awake that way."

I went tumbling down onto the floor. This time, though, the bones hit the stone floor with a loud bang, instead of landing softly onto the ground of soil. The next moment we heard commotion inside the temple building, then lights started to be lit. "Oh no," Kiichi and my skull said in unison.

Kiichi quickly retrieved the bones out of the hole. People were shouting. When all my finger-bones and most of my arm-bones were outside, I said to Kiichi, "You run, my boy."

"What?"

"I'll take care of myself now. I'm a skeleton woman, humans cannot do much to me. But they'll surely beat you up if you get caught. Now run, with your momma's hair stick. Find the girl you like."

"No! You're coming with me!"

I rubbed his cheek lightly with my incomplete fingers. "Kiichi. Please. Go."

"But—"

"Go!"

Kiichi jumped once, looked me in the eyes, then stood up. "I'll see you around—right?" He sounded scared for the first time.

"If you don't get caught, yes. Now go!"

The boy ran away. I looked back at the hole and started collecting my bones by myself. Soon they'd notice someone had come for their treasures—but now, most of my bones had been reassembled—

I tried to pull out the last bone, my fourth rib, through the hole. But I was in such a hurry. Silly me. I pulled the rib at a wrong angle, and it collided with the door without coming through; cracked into two, and the half I wasn't holding flew and went spinning away, deeper into the darkness of the storehouse.

I looked up and saw fires flickering, closing in. I really had to go.

I gave up my half-rib and ran.

I NEVER IMAGINED WHAT A MISSING rib could do.

By the time I was well away from the temple, I was exhausted. Everything in me crackled, and it hurt like hell. I settled myself behind a huge cedar tree, away and invisible from the road. I waited there for the pain, the exhaustion, to pass.

But they never went away.

Whenever I tried to move, lacking the rib to suppress it, my fake heart went crazy and I had to fall unconscious for a while. I had to wait for men to pass the road by the tree, steal their strength and live on until another man came. Somewhere along the line I lost count of the men. Of the years.

I just wished death was possible for a skeleton woman. But we don't have enough life in the first place, even to lose. That's why we have to take it from humans.

ONE NIGHT I WOKE UP TO find the moon shining like the night I had met Kiichi—Kiichi? Who was that?

I snapped fully awake. Someone was walking along the road by the tree. From the way the walking sounded—a man. I slowly drew myself up into a standing position.

When the man was close enough, I said, from behind the tree, "Sir? Please, my feet hurt. Come help me."

The man stopped. I was still behind the tree and couldn't see his face. "Are you all right?" the young man asked. "Do you want me to call for a litter?"

"No, sir. Please give me a hand as I walk, is all I need. Come round."

I heard the man step out of the road, crunching on branches and cedar needles. "Here," he said. "Let me look at you."

I secretly grinned, and then, slowly turned around. I looked up at him, just with eyes, expectant and inviting. "Thank you," I said, and looked into his eyes.

Those black, black eyes. Why did they look familiar?

The man grinned. "I knew it."

"What?"

He shook his head, held my shoulders as if he were expecting me to run away at any moment. "Look at your kimono. It used to be so beautiful—look what you've done to spoil it."

My half-tumbled teeth chattered. But no words followed.

He drew me even closer. And then, pulled out something from his bosom.

A hair stick. Tortoiseshell.

"You!"

But before I could blame him—or be nostalgic, or do whatever should have been done—he opened the front of my kimono. I wondered if I should resist; I wouldn't have even thought of resisting anyone, but in my head, he was still the child who needed his mother.

He didn't strip me completely naked, though. He only opened the front seams wide, revealing my torso. Then he produced some thin strings from his sleeve. "Don't move," he said.

The man fiddled for a few minutes with his hair stick and my imperfect rib cage. He used a few more things I couldn't see, his hands and sleeves in the way. For a long time, he seemed so concentrated that I couldn't even ask what he was doing.

When he finally stepped back, looking satisfied, I was almost unconscious from using too much strength in my effort to stay put. He called me and I snapped awake. "Have a look," he said.

I did as he said. Where there had been a hollow because of the missing rib, was now the hair stick, kept in place with strings and a few obi-ornaments. "Huh?" was all I could say.

The man chuckled. It was Kiichi—my Kiichi—childish smile and un-childlike gestures all mingled. I almost choked, but I didn't know why.

Kiichi stepped close again. "I worked so hard with the carpenters," he whispered. "When I was fully grown, I was a respected man. The temple hired me for some refurbishment, and I volunteered to fix the door of their treasure-storehouse properly—after they had seen the skeleton woman run away, they had put some wood panels to fill that hole."

I couldn't help but smile.

"When they opened the door for me, they told me about the skeleton woman's rib. Sorry, they had burned it." He shook his head again. "Then I stole my mother's jewelry box. And realizing that you must be suffering somewhere, I started looking for you."

"You shouldn't have bothered," I said, still smiling.

"But it was really easy to find you, skeleton woman. Now rumors about you are everywhere, and the village council is even considering blocking this path."

"Oh. That's why I get fewer and fewer men here."

"Right. So now, take a little of my strength. And come with me, to my house."

"You own a house?"

"Of course, I'm a respected carpenter!"

We laughed together a little and I almost fainted. Then I grinned—my old, horrible grin that I hadn't had enough energy to wear for such a long time. "I can take your strength, you say?"

"N-not too much, okay?"

So I plunged into his arms.

The Shroud
for the Mourners

Kiriko frowned as she peered into her magnifying glass. "This wasn't here last time, Hama-san."

"Oh, please don't tell me I have a new symptom *again*," Mr. Hama said, wincing.

Mr. Hama was a man in his fifties, with a vine-like pattern at the edges of his membranes, and carnelian-colored eyes. He had a long history of suffering from allergic reactions, ever since he was a child. When he'd reached this pattern atelier for the first time as a social insurance consultant, he'd long given up on his perpetually teary eyes. That day, he was looking for something to hang over the wall of his new office, but before he could start talking about his interior decorations, the founder of this atelier, Kiriko's mentor, pointed at the client's eyes and said, "Let me fix that first."

"And who would have thought you'd walk out of a pattern atelier with medication?" Mr. Hama had laughed, when Kiriko had just joined the place.

Now Kiriko looked back into his ear, just to be sure. "This is weird," she said. "As we discussed many times, most of your symptoms are caused when your native pattern is distorted on your soft, flexible skin, like near your eardrums. But this distorted allergy pattern is always your native pattern gone wrong—the basic structures are the same, but they expand in different manners into different directions. This new thing here now, however, doesn't seem to have any relevance to the pattern on your other parts. Even the color is completely different."

"Hm. Can I have a look, too?"

"Sorry, you won't be able to see it. Only a pattern craftsperson can."

Mr. Hama smiled weakly, mocking disappointment. "Of course. Can you make a pattern which 'offsets' this allergy pattern? Like always?"

Kiriko was still frowning, her hand at her chin. As he suggested, that would be something she'd normally do: make a pattern whose lines could adjust the way the blood flow and water/air currents ran around the distorted pattern, to eventually smooth the ragged edges of the distortion. But . . . "I don't know," she said. "The remedy patterns for you, they need to be something that have enough affinity with your native pattern. Otherwise the remedy pattern itself can cause a different type of malfunction in some other part of your body. But to offset this new thing, which is completely out of place itself, we would need to construct a pattern that would be too . . . foreign. You may as well go see a doctor, at the clinic."

"Oh, but the clinic could do nothing for my situation!"

The door of the atelier's lab opened and Kiriko's mentor walked in. "Hama, she's saying this might not be allergy."

The client turned in his chair. "Huh." He looked at the two craftspersons of the atelier in turns. "I—I never thought I would ever have to visit them again."

"You are old enough to, don't you think?"

Kiriko sighed. "Hama-san, take sensei with you and leave him there."

Mr. Hama laughed, and then shook his head. "You two are my primary doctors, if you say I should, I will do it."

AND THREE DAYS LATER, MR. HAMA's two primary doctors found themselves in the office of a clinic doctor.

"Why do you look so ill at ease?" asked the clinic doctor, Sakata, whose eyes were the color of blurry iolite. When he moved his head the tips of his hair shone in the same color.

"We always thought the clinic didn't like us," the owner of the atelier said. "We still do."

The doctor waved his hand in a negating gesture. "It's just the city, they don't like the way you seem to utilize patterns to get what you want. But as far as we doctors and nurses can see, no one's feeling worse under your care."

"Today you have something to say to us though?"

"I just have a question." Sakata smiled. "You sent Hama-san our way. He said you saw something unusual. We discovered a polyp down his throat, nothing too bad, as diagnoses go. But . . . there's something . . . weird about this."

"Do doctors say 'weird'?" Kiriko whispered.

To her surprise Sakata laughed heartily. "*I* do, obviously. Some figures of the test results aren't matching what we see. You felt something odd about him before our diagnosis, yes? The thing is, we are having a few more patients with the same kind of polyp. Even a foreigner. Can you tell us what this thing is that you found?"

Kiriko's mentor leaned forward. "It was a silent pattern—we call it that to distinguish it from ordinary patterns that can be found on the human body, because it's the way currents of light, air, sound and other things happening there summed up as a pattern, so ordinary eyes cannot see it. The silent pattern on Hama we found was too out of place. Kiriko here sketched it, but to compare it to other patients' cases we ourselves need to have a look."

"I see." The doctor sighed. "I've heard some of our android nurses talk about how strange the way you two see the world is."

Kiriko raised her brows. "You have ando-san as nurses here?"

"Yes, a lot more than you can imagine, I guess. Many patients don't like being treated by them, so we never disclose which ones. Only a few doctors here know. I'm counting on your discretion with this information, by the way."

Many civil servants in this city were androids, as everybody knew. But the city itself never talked about them, as it didn't want to admit that there were entities with "artificial" colors and patterns on their skin, while valuing islanders with native colors and patterns in its society. And so the people of the city didn't discuss them either—nobody was quite sure how the androids should be treated. Whereas colorless and patternless laborers like the two craftspersons were the easy prey in this society.

Kiriko and her mentor could usually tell an android when they saw one—they were too perfectly *moderate*. The androids' colors and patterns were always just a little bit less flashy, probably to not stand out more than the humans. But those working at the clinic seemed indistinguishable at this point. Some rich locals didn't even like being in the care of colorless locals, so they were unlikely to tolerate being treated by andos. The city must have been very thorough about them here.

"Do you think those patients you're talking about will gladly let us peek into their ears and nostrils? You said there's a foreigner, too, right?" Kiriko said.

"You will be here as nurses in disguise. We'll lend you masks, caps and gowns, so that the patients won't have to see much of your skin."

Kiriko and her mentor looked at each other, and then both turned back to the doctor. "All right, then," the owner of the atelier said, "we're on."

AND YES, THEY FOUND ONE OUT-OF-PLACE silent pattern in each patient, and after having a very, very close look (one patient needed sedation for this,) there seemed to be an invisible yet distinct line between the polyp and this strange pattern. And the pattern around the affected spot transformed by the second, and this must have been why the test results didn't quite match the diagnoses. But this unstable pattern was only making the patients uncomfortable with mild coughs or stomach aches and such, nothing worse.

The foreign patient, though, had to know the exact cause of this to reenter their home country on the continent. At first this foreigner thought the strange vape that he'd bought at a local souvenir shop—which put out smoke that made the landscape look slightly more colorful than the reality for the inhaler, and thus was advised to be used outside the island to avoid confusion—was to blame and made the authority talk to the proprietor. But after various tests the vape was concluded to be irrelevant.

"One tourist, one colorful, two patterned. The patients' lifestyles don't seem to overlap. What did they do to get this thing?" Kiriko remarked, back at the atelier, flopping onto her back on the cushions.

Her mentor sat down beside her. "It's not doing much to the patient, so there may be many more who are suffering unaware from the same thing, or no one else at all. Too few cases so far."

There was then a beep at the door, and when Kiriko answered it was Mr. Hama. "How is it going? When can I be rid of this itch in my ear?" he said, as he climbed the raised floor of the atelier's reception space.

Kiriko grumbled and her mentor looked away without a word.

"Okay, I see," Mr. Hama said. "Here, have some sweet things. Sugar makes your brain work better, as they say."

Kiriko went off to make tea immediately.

The client laughed and placed the small box on the low table. "We got some of these from our own client, and they tasted quite good. So I went to the shop and bought a packet myself." He lifted the lid of the simple but carefully wrapped thing. "Very savory and beautiful, and the texture . . . " he trailed off when he saw the expression on the face of the owner of the atelier.

"Apprentice," he called to Kiriko, "turn off that stove now and come back here."

"What?"

"Now."

"But sensei," Kiriko came out of the kitchen almost pouting, "we always need some tea when we—"

She stopped right beside her mentor.

"What's wrong?" asked Mr. Hama.

"Hama-san," Kiriko said, "you have to tell us where you got these candied agar pieces, now."

* * *

THE CONFECTIONERY SHOP THAT MADE THE candied agar, the bar serving a glass of smoky-purple liquor, an auntie who wanted to give her nephew some inks to play with, and a florist who experimented with the color of their roses, they all had procured their pigment from the same place—the community bulletin board. The clinic pinned the exact source after a day, and a nurse got back to the atelier with some air of . . . embarrassment.

"She is . . . a mistake," said the nurse with feathery deep-blue hair, perched neatly on the edge of the raised reception floor.

"A mistake? Who is?"

Rui the nurse sipped his tea. Kiriko wondered if his real name was Ruri after his hair color, one consonant omitted for easier pronunciation for the foreigners. "We call her Ash, we don't know her real name. She is a person in charge of the crematorium's lab. She is an ando, and she is, we believe, a little bit broken."

"Rui-san, are you ando-san, too?" asked Kiriko.

"Yes. How can you tell?"

"Just the way you talk about this Ash character, I guess."

Her mentor cut in. "The city crematorium has a laboratory?"

"Of course, do you think the city would let patterns that can be found on bones just go to waste?"

"We would think you'd do just that, yes, rather than violating somebody else's body," said Kiriko, not trying one bit to hide her disgust.

Rui looked embarrassed, for a moment. "Only those with patterns are confiscated, just for a day or so. The city wants to archive any rare patterns and colors, even those found on the bones. We'd have liked to collect the colors on them, too, but we've never seen colored ones." He shook his head. "*We* haven't. But I cannot speak for Ash." As if he didn't want to count Ash as one of them.

Silence hung for a while. "Would you go see Ash," Rui said at length, "and find out where she is obtaining these weird pigments?"

"Why don't you do that yourself?"

"I—" Rui bit his lip. "We don't get along. Please."

And the two craftspersons had to say yes.

THE CRAFTSPERSONS SAW IMMEDIATELY WHAT RUI had meant by a mistake. Ash was a very mildly-colored person, her pale skin having very, very slight shimmer as she changed angles, like there were tiny crystal grains deep down. Too subtle even for an ando.

"Rui called and said I'd be interviewed by two colorless people!" Ash beamed as she opened the door to her office for them. "How can I help you?"

"About the pigments," the owner of the atelier said.

Ash clapped her hands as if this was the most surprising thing she had heard all day. "Oh yes! All the colors are confiscated now. How unfortunate." There was no remorse in her tone, apparently. Kiriko wondered if this, too, was a reason for Ash to be called a mistake by her peers.

Her mentor cleared his throat. "We are just here to see how you got those strange pigments."

"Oh, that. They are the by-product of the pattern extracting process. I wasn't sure how I should be rid of them, and also, they are lovely, aren't they? I wouldn't have liked to just drain them down the pipe and let them go to waste."

"Why didn't you ask the city what to do with them?" asked Kiriko.

"They didn't tell me to, did they? All they said was to find the patterns to archive them."

The owner of the atelier cleared his throat again, eyeing his apprentice. Then he said, "Can we have a look at your equipment? We just want to make really sure that your pigments are what is causing this fuss, and . . . that . . . nobody is tampering with them, so to say, on purpose."

"Hm." Ash didn't seem to understand what he was implying. "Okay, I'll give you a tour of this tiny room. So, let's start with this cupboard, where we put the ingredients . . . "

The procedures and the chemicals Ash used were unfamiliar to the craftspersons, but as far as they could see, there seemed to be nothing that implicated Ash's wrongdoing. She was using some kind of marker chemical, and a specially built camera to copy the marker which had sunk onto the pattern and to reproduce how it would appear if it was drawn on a flat surface instead of bones of various shapes. It seemed the chemicals were somehow washing the pigment grains off the bones when they were exposed to the camera. Kiriko picked up a piece of bone out of a tray, and Ash chuckled. When the craftsperson cocked her head inquisitively Ash said, "No human ever held a bone like that."

"Oh. When you put it like that. I'm just, well, seeing this as an object of research right now."

"I know, I know!"

Kiriko smiled and then looked at the bone again. "Sensei," she said to her mentor, "I have this feeling . . . "

He took another piece without a word. The two examined the bones for a while, from this angle and that, as round-eyed Ash silently watched. "Can we study these in our own lab?" he finally asked, "we promise we won't do any damage."

Ash shrugged. "Go ahead."

* * *

AFTER LOOKING AT THEM THROUGH THEIR own microscope, the craftspersons agreed that the submerged pigment presence through the bones was strangely uneven. If they'd come from one single person—they certainly had to—the trace of the impression of the color should have been present more or less homogeneously. But with these bones, the pigment was scattered in a few places where it was very strong, while other parts were completely devoid of them. It was as though someone had injected them, though there was no needle scar or anything of the kind.

And for that matter . . . they had been, in fact, thoroughly surprised to find any pigment in bones at all. They'd seen people with patterns on their bones and teeth, yes. But never anyone with homogeneously colored bones; they'd have seen those appear on teeth, or through thin and soft skin, if there ever were. They'd both assumed, without saying it aloud, that bones were too hard to retain enough pigment portions. Even after finding these uneven spots, they were finding it hard to believe.

The clinic obtained the medical history and other reports about the deceased in question, but they could find nothing that might be relevant.

"Meanwhile," Sakata said on the phone, "the city decided to just dispose of the colors extracted from the bones. The colors they confiscated so far don't seem to include those worth archiving, over the risk of putting them into one place and making them more harmful. As they are at the moment, the worst thing that can happen is a few people experiencing mild discomfort. And even that's only when the affected actually touch the pigments. Down the river, or deep within the soil, the strange pigments won't do much, the city reasoned."

Kiriko scowled. "But you don't know enough about these pigments to just let it pass. For once, I don't think we colorless will be affected by them. Looks like they stir the balance of elements just when they collide with colors and patterns on a human body. For that one foreign tourist, we are guessing here that the residual phantom colors from the souvenir vape reacted with Ash's pigment, and we islanders, either colorful or colorless, never take those smokes in ourselves."

There was a pause, and Sakata sighed. "I guess you're right," he said. "I'm *sure* you're right. I'll try to talk them out of it. Will you help me if they need any evidence or proofs?"

"Anytime, Doctor, though I don't think they'll listen to us colorless folks." She laughed bitterly and hung up.

The owner of the atelier was drawing something on the low table of the reception space, sipping his tea. "Sakata looks like a man who knows what he's doing," he said. "And he has very nice colors. He might be able to talk sense into those lazy city officials. Especially if the colorful and patterned are more prone to damage in this particular case."

"Hopefully." She leaned on the pillar. "Those bones. I still cannot believe these dead pigments come from the person's native color. Can you?" She saw her mentor shake his head slowly. "The extracted pigments are the *byproduct* of the lab's work, as Ash said? If the color is so easy to leak out of bone, it should also be as easy the other way round—for one to have colors in bone. But clearly things we've seen over the years indicate otherwise. Where did Ash's dead pigments come from, for real?"

Her mentor placed his elbow on the table, and rested his cheek on his knuckle. "Hm," he said. Then he said, "Hm."

FIRST THING THE NEXT MORNING, KIRIKO was heading for the crematorium's lab, to return the bones; they argued all night, but decided there was nothing more they could do with the actual bones, anyway. Now that they were no longer research subjects, it felt so wrong to be holding them. The receptionist at the crematorium waved her in to the lab annex, and when she walked through the door, Kiriko heard someone shout. Alarmed, she sprinted towards Ash's office.

Without knocking she slid the door to the full, and found Rui the nurse ready to strike Ash. "Hey!" Kiriko yelled at the top of her already exhausted lungs.

Luckily that was enough to pull Rui back to himself, it seemed. He looked more surprised than either of the other two in the room, blinked at his own hand as if he couldn't believe it was where it was, mid-air over the other ando.

"Ash, do you want me to report this?" Kiriko said, still panting.

"No no, please, let me explain," Rui's voice was shaken like he was the one who was almost hit.

"I didn't ask *you*!"

Ash raised her hand. "Craftsperson! Please, there *is* an explanation for this!" She cocked her head. "I mean, he does have one!"

Kiriko glared at Rui. "Whatever it is, I don't want a nurse in our clinic who is ready to hurt someone else!"

"Tea!" Ash screamed. "Let's talk over a cup of tea!"

Ash duly made tea and poured a cup each for the very perplexed Kiriko and tired-looking Rui. When she sat down with her own cup Ash said, "Rui says I'm violating."

"Because you are!"

Kiriko put a hand between the two andos. "Violating what?"

"Rules," replied Rui, "and a corpse."

The craftsperson hastily put her wrapping cloth with the bones in it on the table and pushed it a little towards Ash. "A corpse?"

"I'm not violating it! I'm just dividing it into chunks, so that I can give it proper cremation."

"What are you two talking about?"

The two andos looked at each other, then at the craftsperson. "Ash is hiding a body in her fridge," Rui said. "The body of an android, it's not like she's a murderer."

"Oh all right," Kiriko said through her teeth, "it is so reassuring to hear that she didn't murder anybody, thank you. But I'd appreciate if you'd elaborate just a little more."

"It's an old friend of mine." Ash didn't seem to hear Kiriko's sarcasm. "A very old model, the city terminated it a long time ago. I wanted to give it a respectful funeral, but they wouldn't let me."

"Who wouldn't let you?"

"The city, of course."

"So you made your friend into chunks and . . . ?"

Ash spread her hands. "Put them one by one into someone's coffin. That way it wouldn't cost too much energy."

Rui sighed loudly.

Kiriko's brows were starting to ache. "And you never mentioned that to the city—the owner of this crematorium? Or the family of the deceased?"

"No. Should I?"

Kiriko looked at Rui. He shrugged. But then he sobered and said, "That is very obscene, Ash. You should stop doing that immediately, as I've said many times before. I knew it would all come down to this, sooner or later. I'm sure the craftsperson here agrees." He cast a meaningful glance Kiriko's way.

"Why? How so? I don't understand."

The craftsperson pushed the bundle of bones farther towards Ash. "Okay, now I think that is how those pigments got into the bones. Been burned in, so to speak. You ando-san have a body part for collecting organic colors, right? Many of you—at least those who work for the National Archives—have color receptors hidden in your body."

Rui looked bewildered. "How do you know that?"

"I've worked with one of you before." That was how the city clandestinely collected the information on what colors and patterns the islanders bore on their skin, to know the current situation, and to store color/pattern compositions and structures in their secret database. "Ash, were you aware that your friend's chunks were contaminating the locals' bodies?"

Ash blinked a few times and looked down at her cup. "No," she finally said, "I wasn't."

Kiriko and Rui both had to believe that.

"So you've recently started putting the parts around the color receptors in, I presume?" Kiriko said at length.

"Yes." Ash was now looking at her hands.

Rui sighed again. "Ash, are you looking worried for those humans who were affected, or are you just sad because your friend might have caused something bad?"

Kiriko turned to the nurse. "Rui, you don't have to be so harsh!"

"No? Ash was just lucky that those dead pigments are not harmful enough, right?"

"Oh come on, she works here as a researcher. Surely she would have known if something went too wrong."

Rui had nothing to say to that. They sat in silence for a while, after which Ash said, "I might have missed something on purpose."

"Hmm?" Kiriko intoned, her cup to her lips.

"I mean . . . I would have liked my friend to go on. In a way, in other people's body, as the dead pigments spread over the city. If I couldn't give it a proper farewell."

Rui snickered, but Kiriko laughed, just a little. She couldn't help it. "You are talking like a very, very sentimental human being."

"They shouldn't have terminated my friend. It did go a bit insane towards the end, yes, but that was mostly due to the program the city made it install on itself. That's not fair."

Nothing was fair in this city, Kiriko thought, but kept her mouth shut.

"We have to report this," Rui said, as if grinding his teeth on the painful silence.

It was Kiriko's turn to snicker. "What, and let them realize that their damned colorful and patterned dignity has been all but tampered with, for who knows how long?"

"But we cannot let her go on like this!"

Kiriko looked at Ash, who was still staring at her own hands. "Give me and my mentor some time to consider this," she said. And extended her hand towards Ash, so that the ando would see the craftsperson's hand instead. "Ash, listen. Please stop doing what you've been doing, just for the time being. We'll come up with something."

Ash nodded. Kiriko had known andos could be sentimental, yes, but this really wasn't fair—how Ash was making Kiriko sentimental and even protective, too.

Back at the atelier, Kiriko found her mentor waiting right behind the door, looking very pleased. "How long have you been standing there like a fool, sensei?" she asked him.

"I've been talking with Sakata," he said. "We were saying, we could have a joint venture, to develop some kind of filter, to completely detoxify those dead pigments. This will be an ongoing project, which might bring us a lot of money on a regular basis, and reputation as the city's important supplier!"

Kiriko considered this, as she involuntarily made a face.

"Oh, come on. Whatever you found out today at Ash's place, this detoxification surely needs to be made, right?"

Kiriko said, "Tea?"

Her stomach was already heavy with it, but she forced herself to drink, anyway. Her mentor emptied his cup in one gulp. "We don't have to report that to the city," he said sullenly, after hearing his apprentice out. "Ash can just keep on doing what she's doing, while we sell those filters to the city and the clinic."

"Rui knows. I don't think ando-san are generally built to lie. And do you think that is what Ash wants? Burning her friend chunk by chunk?"

He glared at the dregs of his tea. "But . . . "

"Sensei." She patted his arm and made him look at her. "If it were me dead in the fridge, would you be happy throwing away my body secretly, bit by bit, never having the proper moments of mourning?" She swallowed. "Because if it were you, I wouldn't."

At that, he averted his eyes and then closed them for one moment. "No," he said. "No, I wouldn't."

AS SOON AS SAKATA GAVE THEM the name of the city's representative, the craftspersons went to the city hall, to see this person for themselves. They never talked to the person, of course, but took notes of the person's colors and patterns, which were the flashes of mosaic of many intensities of champagne. These colors appeared only when the person's skin wrinkled, around their eyes or wrists and parts like those. One of the atelier's clients overheard this person complain at an izakaya, after drinking too much, that they should be treated as more colorful persons were treated, not as a tepid civil servant.

On the big day, Sakata was frowning as he walked out of the city hall after the meeting. "I did my best," he said when he saw the two craftspersons seated on a bench on the pavement. "I was surprised to hear that the city used to dump the broken and unusable ando parts onto a landfill like some unburnable trash until quite recently. That's what would have happened if this Ash ando didn't refuse, right?" He took a breath and shook his head. "They did say they don't even terminate andos anymore, so something like Ash's friend won't happen again. Still, I couldn't help but show surprise."

"That's okay, of course. We aren't asking you to deceive them." The owner of the atelier slowly stood up. "You did tell them to choose between Ash having her way this once or taking us in as their regular, long-time supplier of the detoxifying method, right?"

Sakata nodded. "They argued they could just replace Ash and be done with it."

"Oh," Kiriko said, rising to her feet, too, "how did you retort to that?"

"I thought about how Rui and other ando nurses talked about Ash. Like she was a mistake. No other department with ando staff will be able to find another use for her, I told them. And that if they don't keep her in place and properly watched, she'll just wander about telling people of the bone violating—by her, and by the city, too." Sakata rubbed his brows. "Not that I think it's right, but I suppose it's true."

"I know." Kiriko smiled and tucked a strand of hair behind her ear. "Thank you, Doctor. We knew we could rely on you."

Sakata laughed. "I really did wish you two were there with me."

"If we were there with you the city person wouldn't have listened, not even to you."

"So you two think it all worked? That they'll let Ash do what she wants?"

Kiriko's mentor sighed. "They want to think they are so much different from us, in a much higher place. They're bound to choose an ando over us having our way."

"I hope so." Sakata sighed back. "Again, not that I think it's right."

And that was what happened of course—a few days later Ash received notification from the city, their permission for her to use one of the incinerators just for her friend. For this one time, the city ordered from the pattern atelier a solution against the leaking of the dead pigments, to be installed on the coffin, as per Sakata's recommendation. The National Archives had the blueprint of Ash's friend, and Ash remembered precisely what parts of her friend had already been consumed along with strangers. Kiriko and her mentor didn't have to look at the body in person or touch it directly—it didn't feel right to cut into the privacy of Ash and her friend, and also, it would have been quite a thing, actually seeing defrosted parts of an almost-human body.

The craftspersons made an embroidered shroud, with a pattern which would soothe and supplement the wavelength of the shadow of colors left in the body. The threads used were also absorbed in a specifically prepared concoction of inks and an agent, they would add viscosity to the leakage, making it harder to flow away and be lost in the environment.

"Would you be there?" asked Ash when she came to pick up the shroud at the atelier. She personally paid for it. "I don't want to be alone."

Kiriko could feel that her mentor wanted to say no straight away—they'd managed to evade interacting with the corpse by using the blueprint and Ash's memory, why would they want to be present at the crematorium with the mutilated body among them, after all? "Of course we would be there with you," she said, before her mentor could utter a sound, "to see your beloved friend off. After such a long time."

Her mentor didn't protest. He knew that she wanted him, or herself, to have a choice between being alone and not, when the time came for themselves.

On that day, Rui was there, too, still in his clinic clothes. He probably snuck out between shifts. "You fools," he said and placed a hand on his hip.

Kiriko had to laugh to that. "Thanks to you, too," replied the craftsperson, being sarcastic but also meaning it. "For not getting in our way. I know you could have."

Rui looked away and said, "It'd just be a waste of time, arguing over this."

To the craftspersons' relief, Ash had already wrapped the body with the shroud by the time they all gathered around the coffin lined with the filters. Kiriko and her mentor drew small patterns around the edge of the wood as finishing touches, just in case. The body was arranged there, like a specimen, with a lot of its parts missing but otherwise in perfect order of a human body. Its face was intact, and it looked as though Ash's friend was just sleeping—not the figure of speech but like really just . . . sleeping. Kiriko thought she might understand why Ash couldn't simply get rid of it, just a little.

While they waited for the incineration to finish, Ash talked ceaselessly, about her late friend. Rui rolled his eyes many times, Kiriko laughed a lot, and her mentor quietly listened and refilled their teacups. There was no ceremonial air, no real speech, no crying involved. But it was as proper a funeral as any other.

Blue Gray Blue

No one knew exactly when or how it'd all started. But there was a time he could think of specifically: it was three or four years ago, when a girl of around ten came to the shop, which sold practical eyewear for the locals. The girl said she needed a pair of glasses, because something was wrong with her eyes.

"You'd like to see a doctor first," Tsuyu had told her, crouching to meet her mosaic-like rainbow eyes, so out of place in her tanned, barley colored face.

"I did!" she had said. "And they found nothing wrong with me. But something *is* going wrong with my parrot, and Mother and Father don't see it, so it must be my eyes."

"Your parrot?"

She'd nodded defiantly. "He's got a part of his feathers just like my eyes, around his chest. That was why we got him in the first place. But that part is fading these days. As many colors, still, but they all look a bit . . . weaker."

Tsuyu never found out what happened to her, or the parrot afterward, because the girl never came back after he'd told her to watch out for a little while longer, keeping to her doctor's instructions. Much later, others started to see something similar, too. There must have been something only small children could see, in the early stage.

Now at the same shop, after an especially nasty fit of coughs, Tsuyu looked at his reflection in one of the mirrors and wondered why he was thinking this. But of course—his own eye color was so weak today that it looked as though he had no irises, and tears from the coughing made him look even more like a horrible monster of some sort.

He was about to pour himself some tea when the bell attached to the door rang. His senior, the manager of the branch who had gone for lunch, would have started talking right before the door was fully open, so the person who'd just arrived was a customer. Tsuyu hastily put the pot back down onto the desk. "Hello," he said, and forced down a cough. "Please let me know if there is anything I can assist you with."

When these automatic words had rolled out (words for the locals, of course—for foreigners the in-house manual required something much more enthusiastic) another cough threatened him, so that his eyes were brimming with tears. What did he look like right now? The customer, a woman of about his own age, stood framed in the glass door right behind her, against the backcloth of the sallow break-in-rainy-season midday. Most of her skin visible was lazurite, golden pyrite flecks punctuating her countenance here and there. Blue wasn't that uncommon of course, but gold was, and for a split second he felt a pang of jealousy.

The customer smiled at him. "I heard that an ultramarine person works for this company. And I went to the shop on High Street and they said that person can be found here at the branch."

"Ah. That is me, actually, though I'm not always ultramarine." Tsuyu wiped his eyes with a cloth. "Definitely not today. Sorry you didn't find what you came here for after all that trouble."

But as he was saying this, the woman came striding between the low shelves of glasses on display. For a moment it looked as though she was performing a fluid kind of dance, like a flower petal carried by a current and yet gracefully avoiding collision with rocks and trees, before coming to a sudden halt to stand right in front of him. He almost stepped back, not quite used to a local staring into his eyes. "That's beautiful," she said, and her eyes were the deep, deep black-blue of indigo—one of the most stable of blues. Everything he'd have wanted. "Yes, I can feel blues hiding away, but—how does that work?"

Work? "Well. When I'm ill or simply feeling down, my eyes go just— colorless. Ultramarine is only when I'm feeling really strong."

"So your eyes are basically like this? White chalcedony? Or is there anything in-between?"

"Chalcedony?" He blinked. "I never . . . well. They're Asiatic day-flower blue when I'm like, just okay and stable."

"Oh, how interesting! Oldest of blues, and quite soluble, dayflower blue is, you know!"

Tsuyu almost winced, stopped himself just in time.

The woman shifted a little, as if to have an even better look, making Tsuyu feel even more nervous. "Have you seen them actually changing colors?"

Tsuyu thought about it, using that moment to divert his eyes from her. "Not really. I don't look at myself more often than necessary."

"No?" she sounded surprised, but then took one step back. "Sorry. I'm a collector of blues. Of knowledge of them, of course." She flashed her teeth like robin eggs. "And as you can see, I'm from one of that blood line, too. But not many people have changing colors the way yours do."

Tsuyu inhaled to say something, ended up coughing again, stepping away from her.

"Oh, are you ill? Should I come back, when you're better? Are you always here at this branch?"

"I . . . it depends." He coughed some more. "When I'm ultramarine or dayflower, I'm at High Street."

"What? Why do they place you here when you're white chalcedony?"

"I asked them to. Ultramarine is quite popular with the tourists. Dayflower isn't exactly what they'd come to this island for, you know, many foreigners having blue eyes. Still, better than nothing." He pointed at his own eyes.

The woman frowned. "I don't understand."

Oh no, you *wouldn't.* "You can't watch on until they change colors, anyway."

"Do you at least know when the change is most likely to happen?"

Tsuyu gestured an ambiguous answer, smiling despite himself.

"You can't turn me away, anyway. I'm a customer."

"Are you going to buy something?"

"Yes! Recommend me a frame! . . . If you aren't too ill to do that?"

He stifled a laugh and looked around the shop. Ordinary gold was too loud for her, nor the tortoiseshell, even the brownish one, quite matched. Collector of blues. Why would anyone do that here, blue being too common and only slightly better than nothing? And he thought about his own color, how it was said to have been the root of every blue, before the strong indigo came along.

He took a green frame, green of dayflower's leaves rendered soft by morning dew, with leaf-like patterns over the temples. Just as he had hoped, the frame seemed to settle with her skin, without darkening the tone.

"The lenses . . . "

"Just leave them plano, thanks. Fashion!"

Her eyes would look much better without the lenses to veil them. He adjusted the frame to fit her small face and said, "Are you really buying this one?"

"Yes. Now I can come back, yes?"

He let out a small sound that was both sigh and laugh.

"Yes?"

"Okay."

"Say yes!"

"Yes."

She grinned her robin-egg grin again. Just as she was paying, Tsuyu saw his senior coming back, on the other side of the street; he probably couldn't see the inside of the shop, the outside so bright with all the sun. The next moment he wondered why he cared about the senior seeing this woman.

Before she could meet the senior, the woman left Tsuyu, with her name Ai ringing in his head.

Tsuyu's eyesight wasn't particularly bad. When he was thirteen, one of the priests managing the orphanage brought back a scratched-up pair of glasses from his trip to the city. "This was one of the samples they exhibited in their windows," the priest told Tsuyu. "They were about to throw this one away. I thought maybe you could use these when you don't like your own eye color."

Ever since, he had been wearing glasses. In the village there weren't many children who wore glasses, and the glasses themselves drew more of people's attention than his color-drained eyes. It felt good, like a wall he could carry around.

Up until a few decades ago, eyewear shops weren't a very strong business, as far as tourists were concerned. Glasses weren't something traditional or peculiar to this country, even though the colors and patterns of the frames manufactured here were popular enough for some peoples. It all changed when someone invented contact lenses that made you see the world in might-be colors. Almost every tourist bought a box at least, despite its ridiculous price, to take back and see their homeland or families and friends more colorful, just like the people and scenery of this island. More expensive ones even created the illusion of patterns on people's skin, too. Tsuyu wondered how the government could possibly invent such a thing, and where all these colors came from, but that was what saved the eyewear industry from ending up a miserable, only-for-locals business, which gave him this job, after all.

But then, these days, perhaps it was the locals who needed these contact lenses more. Though they were a bit too expensive for the locals . . .

"Focus."

Her voice pulled him back to here and now so forcibly that he gasped for breath. As she straddled him, a patch of shiny skin inside her knee rubbed against him, and it sent a shiver through him. There was something peculiar about this patch; it looked like a holographic image of countless blues, and if it felt soft or metallic to the touch, Tsuyu couldn't tell. Ai didn't seem to mind it when he touched it, but she didn't seem very willing to talk about it. Was it some kind of scar?

"Keep your eyes open, okay? I need to see it," she said, her voice demanding, her eyes pleading.

Tsuyu somehow managed to nod. What color was in his eyes now? As he stared up helplessly into her eyes, something changed in Ai's irises. A glint? A click? He tried to reach for the curves of her body, which felt strangely flexible, even fluid. He'd never felt anything like—

And then Ai laughed and collapsed onto him. Tsuyu coughed. "Did you see it?" His voice sounded terrible.

"Oh yes, I caught it! That was amazing."

He chuckled as he held her against him. "I wish I could see it, too. Then I might feel more . . . comfortable with myself."

She lifted her head, frowning. "What do you mean? You not comfortable with yourself? Why?"

"My colors . . . well. You wouldn't understand."

Ai sat up, slowly. The frown deepened, and it immediately made Tsuyu regret saying that; she looked bewildered and sad, rather than angry.

"Sorry," he said, though unsure what he was sorry for.

Ai unfocused from his eyes, looked down at somewhere around his chest. "Don't ever say something like that again, okay?"

"Okay."

She was beautiful, even though she looked ridiculously camouflaged in her blue gray room. She could have been anything she wanted. Maybe even a PR person for the government or something, showy *and* important for this country. Why was she working as a researcher in the field?

And that was a dangerous thought, he knew. Dangerous, which always led to him feeling sulky, and to his horrible monster-eyes.

"Ai . . . Ai?"

"Yes?"

"Does your name mean indigo? Or love, or something entirely different?"

She smiled and stroked his hair. And pushed her shiny patch hard onto him, so that he completely forgot about his own question.

"I'm so sorry again," he said to the manager of the High Street shop, just as he was about to walk out of the back door, to head for the branch. He wasn't sure if it was the rain that had got to him, or his conversation with Ai last night. Just as Ai had said, dayflower was quite soluble, and rain always affected him badly. But then, when he recalled that expression on her face, he found himself still a bit shaken.

The manager shook her head. "Don't worry, Tsuyu. We always need someone at the small shop anyway. Take care of yourself first." She smiled. "And who knows, you might even end up an urban legend of some sort—if you see the rare ultramarine guy, all your wishes will come true, or something like that."

Tsuyu smiled back. Her face full of multi-green geometric patterns, the thin wooden frame of her glasses carefully chosen so that the whole image created one of a lush tree. Was she nice because she had a lot of room in her patience having such beautiful patterns, or because she was feeling sorry for him?

He sighed as he walked out of the door. *What am I thinking?* It'd stopped raining, but the grounds were still quite wet, and he trod carefully avoiding puddles. *Boss is just such a nice woman.* And he wondered how he deserved such a nice boss and nice job. Where would he have been, if he hadn't managed to find this place?

Or did that mean, if he had more colors, or even one strong color for that matter, he deserved even better work?

"Tsuyu!"

He jumped. Looked around, embarrassed. Behind him he spotted another coworker waving at him, splashing through puddles. Sunshine fell through the gap between the clouds, and her silvery skin glinted, her hair thin honey melting over her cheeks.

When she caught up, she was quite out of breath. "Here, have my ginger tea."

He took the packet from her. "Thanks—you ran all this way just to give me this?"

"Yeah. Such a nice coworker, aren't I? Get well soon, okay?"

"Okay. Thanks again."

The coworker ran back the way she'd come.

How did he deserve all this? With his stupid, unstable color that was only in his eyes?

IN HER NAVY CHIFFON DRESS, UNDER her umbrella, Ai looked as camouflaged as she did in her own room, on her own bed. Only her glasses shone strangely as she waved and smiled. Even her teeth seemed to sink under the veil of the rain. The shiny patch at her knee was hidden under her dress.

Still beautiful. So beautiful. Tsuyu couldn't help but grin as they came near enough. "Been collecting a lot of blues today?"

"Mmm." Ai spread her arm, so that raindrops touched her hand. "I'm finding it harder to discover more these days. Maybe blue folks don't like the rain."

"Well. Blue is too common that most of us share the same shade or tint or whatever? Unless one is special like you." Then, he hastily added: "Or my eyes sometimes."

Ai cocked an eyebrow, but said, "Don't you know? Our colors and patterns are affected a lot by our life, as well as genetic information. Of course the basic ones are determined genetically, but as we grow other things get to have a lot of say. Like what we eat, what we do, what we think. No blue can be the same, really."

No, he didn't know that. How was that possible? Also, that he never heard of such a fact? He shook his head, negating many things.

"You didn't? Oh, really, this should be something everybody is taught at a very early stage." She folded her own umbrella and stepped in under his.

They had been planning to go see the Star Festival decorations in the locals' district, only, with the rain, that didn't feel like a very promising idea now. The festival wasn't tonight, but they had been hoping to have a look around while it was not too crowded. His shoulder brushing hers, they started walking, their direction uncertain. "If that is true," he said, "maybe we were one, same blue person, at some point of history? Even if we don't look like each other at all at this point. I mean, with your lazurite and my ultramarine, we have enough genetic stuff in common."

Ai fell silent, her steps even more indecisive. For a moment Tsuyu wondered if she hadn't heard him, or if he'd said something stupid again. But then, "No. It's impossible."

"No? Why?"

"Why? Because . . . because if we were, we shouldn't be here, like this."

Tsuyu laughed. "I meant Very Long Time Ago."

"I know. But still." She suddenly stopped for a second; then grinned and tugged at his hand. "This way!"

"What? Where to?"

They walked, swerving away from the festival site into a narrow alley which only the locals used as a shortcut to the High Street. It was hard with the umbrella, and Tsuyu could see that Ai was taking care not to get him too wet, while trying not to be in other pedestrians' way. *Fluid.*

When they were on the High Street, they went in line with the wave of tourists. It looked very much like they were heading for . . .

"The Festival site for the foreigners?" Tsuyu wondered aloud.

Ai smiled, without looking at him. "The site for them has a roof, you see."

"Yes, but . . . " He let out a small cough. "But there would be foreigners!"

"Of course. What do you think the roof is for?"

Before he could protest any further, Ai slipped in the dome-like site through its huge doors. Pulling Tsuyu along, who, unlike her, had to bump into others and to nod sorry so many times.

Inside, everything was bigger than the decorations in the locals' site. Paper flower-balls and paper balloons hanging near the high ceiling so large that Tsuyu wondered how many people it'd taken to make such things, with beautiful shreds dangling to almost touch the floor. The shreds were fabric, not plastic tapes like the ones prepared for the locals, obviously woven especially for this purpose. These behind-the-scene tasks were usually given to people with no prominent colors or patterns. Drowned in thoughts and density of things surrounding him, for a second Tsuyu thought he'd lost Ai in the sea of the shreds, in spite of their linked hands. But of course there she was, when the shreds parted in front of him, in the part of the dome where pinkish decorations dominated, so her color was just too striking in contrast.

The tourists noticed, and started taking photos of the blue couple. Tsuyu was torn between running away from this place and looking on at her forever.

"Look at me, Tsuyu," she whispered. "You are beautiful."

That moment, he thought he saw a flash of ultramarine reflected on Ai's glasses, over her indigo eyes, and blinked. It seemed impossible, but nevertheless he felt the surge of pride right there, and everything else around the two of them seemed to melt somehow.

And looking at her forever won. Of course it did.

HE FELT SLIGHTLY DIZZY, AND HIS head throbbed a little with every breath he took, though it wasn't as bad as he had expected when he had heard the weather forecast mentioning the center of a low air pressure hovering over the island. He forced himself to look into a mirror, and frowned. Just as he did so the manager came to stand beside him, and raised her brows. "They're blue."

Tsuyu nodded. It wasn't exactly ultramarine, but something a bit deeper. And the tinge shifted just a little at angles, as the light changed. Sometimes it even seemed to swirl—as if a distant nebula was reflected in the eye. When he had woken up this morning and felt the heaviness of his head, he hadn't even bothered looking into a mirror, assuming it looked horrible and ridiculous as usual.

"That's beautiful, too. Looks like something darker has been added to your trademark ultramarine."

Something darker. "Indigo?"

"Oh yes, that." She took out a couple of painkiller pills from the medicine box. "That'd look really good behind a lacquered frame, if you don't mind."

He looked at his boss. Today her rimless glasses had brightly colored gems on the temples. Flowers, fruit or birds in the tree. He wondered if what Ai had said was true—that who you were affected your colors and patterns. If it was, then, what had she gone through to develop these complicated yet sophisticated patterns?

"What? You don't think painkillers would do any good?"

"Oh no, sorry. I'll be fine. Thank you."

So he forced down the pills, and spent the day at the High Street shop.

A FEW TOURISTS WHO CAME IN that morning recognized Tsuyu from the festival dome, and soon, the High Street shop was crowded with foreigners who had heard the rumor. The sales that day were the highest in a long while, and of course, Tsuyu sold more than any other, both usual glasses and the special contact lenses. The silver coworker nudged at him, pretending to be jealous.

How did he deserve all this?

At the end of the day he checked his eyes again, which were still somewhere between indigo and ultramarine. The locals' street was still busy as he left the shop for the day, the sun not completely set yet. The sky was strangely colorful, the streetlights coming to life one by one, strengthening the outlines of everything he could see. He walked on, nodding to a few people he knew, and then, something caught his attention at the corner of his eye.

He looked.

There was no telling if this person was male or female, or something entirely different. This person glowed, soft silver light seeming to cool down the air around. Glowing wasn't common, but not impossible either, and Tsuyu didn't know why he was drawn to this person so.

Then a wind blew just as Tsuyu passed by them, and the person's hair swayed a little. At the small of their neck, Tsuyu saw a patch, shiny and metallic, consisting of many silvers.

Just like . . .

Tsuyu stopped, staring at the person's back, knowing somewhere in his mind that he shouldn't be doing this. Even as they were, in this island where everything was meant to be stared at, many locals hated that being done, especially by another local. But he couldn't help it.

The person was soon drowned in the sea of colors of the locals. Somewhere near the back door to the eyewear shop, he lost the glow completely.

With an effort he started walking again. Belatedly he realized it was the way the person's glow felt strangely blended into the twilight, just like Ai's blue gray, that he'd found so peculiar about this person. He couldn't help but glance back over his shoulder, but of course, there was not a hint of the person's glow in the dusk-fallen street.

That night, he called Ai. She never answered.

THE NEXT MORNING WHEN HE TURNED in there was a commotion in the main shop on the High Street. Everyone seemed to be at the center of the shop, though it was almost time to open up for the day, and some of them should be away in the backyard or running errands. At the very center of it all, was the silver coworker.

Only she wasn't silver anymore.

This was the first time Tsuyu actually saw someone completely grayed-out. He had seen people or things slowly toned down, but nothing this drastic. The silver girl had had no patterns, but different tinges of silver crammed all over her surfaces, which had looked like a pattern in a way. Some of the tinges had glowed, especially when she'd smiled, and everybody had loved that. Now, he could see the slight shade differences, but it was all dull gray instead of silver, and she looked as though she just popped out of a black-and-white photograph. The glow was gone, too, but he couldn't tell if that was because she was crying now.

The boss was touching the silver girl's shoulder, but Tsuyu could feel other employees were afraid to do the same, in case this was contagious. Researches and reasons told this was not the case—there was no logic to how and where people or things were affected—but he knew they just couldn't help it.

Tsuyu pushed on into the center. "Shiroka," he called her name, but couldn't go on.

She looked up. "Oh Tsuyu, look. I'm no longer shirokane." She tried to smile, which made everything seem even worse.

He patted on her now almost completely white hair. "Maybe I can walk her home—" he started to say to the boss.

"No." Shiroka shook her head. "I was already like this when I woke this morning, and I came in to say I wanted to work at the branch today. I'm only crying because Boss was really nice about it." She tried to smile again, and ended up sniffing. "But . . . you know, now I realize, maybe locals don't want to buy stuff from me . . . "

Tsuyu wanted to tell her it was not true, but he knew some people would react that way. Look how peripheral other workers were being right now—it was all he could do to shake his head. And then the boss cut in. "There is plenty of work to do in the backyard, if that's more comfortable for you. I know you have deft fingers, so maybe you can help with the repair team and all." The woman looked around. "Anyway. Let's get moving! The customers will be in soon!"

The workers dispersed, some awkwardly patting Shiroka's shoulder. Some still unable to make up their mind.

THAT DAY PASSED IN A BLUR, EVERYONE'S mind filled with *why*. Why was this happening? Why here, why her? Shiroka kept herself mostly to the backyard, occasionally running errands, but then covering her head with the boss's shiny silk shawl. Tsuyu caught a glimpse of her as she sneaked out of the back door, the shawl catching sunlight and shimmering as she gave him a small wave.

Tsuyu nodded back. And he realized he couldn't help, for some reason, thinking about that glowing silver person he'd seen yesterday.

And about Ai.

HE CURSED HIMSELF FOR HAVING CHOSEN the worst timing when he had left work that day, and having carelessly walked in the hard shower that had just started. And having stumbled down onto his cot, too tired from the day's work, without thoroughly drying himself and keeping warm. All of that resulted in him now feeling so weak, fever-ridden in the small hours of that night, though he had a feeling that this had nothing to do with his colors—ordinary people did catch a cold when they behaved just like he had, of course. He might be stronger than he used to be, but there was only so much that could change, really. He wanted to see Ai; or at least, hear her voice. He had tried calling her during the day, but she'd never answered. Which made him realize, in an absent-minded way, that he knew nothing of her usual work schedule, or where she would be found when she was not home.

But then—

A hand landed on his eyes. *Why*, he wanted to say, but there were too many whys that he couldn't decide which one to ask first.

So he let her speak first. "Don't open your eyes."

He sighed. "Where have you been? I tried—"

"I made a mistake. It's all my fault."

"Ai?"

Her head gently touched his, as she awkwardly slipped in beside him, her hand still over his eyes. "I take. I don't give. I'm built for taking, programmed to collect blues. If I give, that means un-becoming me. End of *me*."

Tsuyu thought about the new tinge of his eyes. How it had helped him deal with many things—if he had been still the same, unstable dayflower, he might not have felt so sympathetic for Shiroka. But then, without Ai, what were the indigo-tinted eyes any good for? "Ai. Please. If that is such a problem, take it back from me."

"It's too late." Her hand seemed to shake, or perhaps, *ripple*. "I didn't even realize what I was doing, until recently. Until another AI came to this town, until I saw it fully obliging to its duty. We only take. That one silver, me blue. When I cease to function just as I was built, then I have no right to exist—a serious bug detected. They already shut down some of the modules, I will be nothing soon. And then a new, proper blue AI will be placed."

Nothing Ai was saying made sense to Tsuyu. Except—"The contact lenses." He swallowed. "Where do all those colors come from . . . "

Ai laughed, or sighed, and stroked his hair with another hand which felt way too soft. "At least the indigo I gave you settled down well with you and you're a lot stronger. It will be fully yours once this rain is over. That much, I don't regret."

"Ai. Please—"

"Look at me, Tsuyu."

Her hand lifted and he opened his eyes. He soon understood why Ai hadn't wanted him to see her before talking. If not, he wouldn't have recognized the thing beside him as Ai. It looked like a lump of water, with a cracked holographic image projected all over its surface. Every second, Ai's face—half or quarter of it—showed on a different part of the water. Her shiny patch taking over her, with no proper control. If he hadn't heard her voice first, let her explain first, he might have screamed.

But it did have Ai's voice, so Tsuyu didn't have to scream, or to be frightened. "I'm sorry," her voice said.

"Don't go. Please. Maybe there's something—"

But then, the rain struck hard onto his windows, and he made a mistake of looking away from her for a second.

And she was gone.

A few days later when he had fully recovered from the cold, he was surprised to find Shiroka at the High Street shop, just like she'd done before graying out. "Can you believe," she said as soon as she saw Tsuyu. "The foreigners even like me this way! They make me wear a colorful frame or colored contacts and take photos. They do have strange tastes, really!"

Tsuyu smiled, relieved. "Yes, they do."

Then she looked at his eyes for a second, and tilted her head. "You know, I'm sure this sounds strange from me, but . . . " Shiroka unfolded a crazily colorful frame, which had been designed especially for her by one of the craftspeople, and placed it on her face. "I did like your dayflower eyes. Even the way they drained. I knew it was troubling you so I never mentioned this before, but. Now that I'm gray, I'd be forgiven for saying something like this, or would I not?"

Tsuyu laughed. "You would, yes." He wiped a single drop of a tear at the corner of his eye. "And—thank you. I think I needed someone to mourn that color. Thanks."

Shiroka blinked her completely gray blinks, behind the custom-made rims. "Are you . . . okay?"

"Yes."

That was all he could say as an answer to that, for now. He looked out of the front window, at sunny High Street, busy as ever with tourists and islanders. The rainy season had ended while he had slept his cold away. Summer had come.

Ripen

Kiriko was having a hard time keeping her eyes off the clutch bag the client had brought with her. The client, a woman of about forty—or maybe fifty? It was hard to tell—sat on a flat cushion placed at the lip of the raised floor of the atelier's reception space, crossing and uncrossing her legs in a sluggish manner. "I really cannot believe there's any place in this city that has no *chair*," the woman said, for the fourth or fifth time. "This is ridiculous."

"Such a beautiful bag you have," Kiriko had stopped apologizing for the lack of chairs after the second time. She herself was standing on the earthen floor that ran, right beside the wall-less reception room, across the entire length of the building. "That must be work of a very good craftsperson. I haven't seen some of the methods adopted there, though." It was too small to Kiriko's liking, of course, who wanted bags to be just as huge as they could be. But this client must have only carried a mirror, and maybe a cigarette box and a book of matches, at most. Rectangle-shaped, its lid flipped over the entire length and width of the bag, and the inside was apparently lined with silk and embroidered with natural-colored silk thread in a minute pattern; the whole lining seemed to ripple with shimmers to a casual eye. Every other surface was covered with more colored embroidery and lace, with beads threaded here and there, surrounding cabochons of enamel—which looked a lot like the client's own skin.

The client woman almost snorted. "Made abroad, of course. A gift from a foreigner. This subtle yet wild demonstration of pattern and color is nothing the craftspersons of this country can even dream of."

All right, then, go abroad and get the fix you want overseas. Kiriko downed the words with lukewarm tea, and cocked her head just a little, to hear the noise from outside better. Did she just hear him say hi to the neighbors? Yes—the sliding door burst open with a loud clang, the glass tiles on its upper half rattled badly in their grids. "No rice straw, can you believe? They burned them *all*!" Kiriko's mentor, the owner of this atelier, threw an empty cloth bag towards the reception floor. "I made them promise me their next batch—oh, hello, good day."

The bag he'd thrown had bounced off the client's shoulder and landed on her own bag. "What the—" She flicked the coarse bag off her smaller, elaborate one, as if the coarse thing could somehow contaminate her spotless possession. "I . . . " She glared at the young man who'd just assaulted her. "I heard this is the best place in the city, for crafts related to human skin! How can a *boy* like you be the best? Are you even good?"

He shrugged. "They say I am. I myself never said I am. What service do you seek here?"

For a moment the woman sat there glaring at him, and Kiriko thought she'd walk out right through the door. But then she shook her head and said, "I have heard. About those . . . surgeries."

Her mentor eyed Kiriko, who too was feeling the wrong turn coming. "Surgeries," he echoed.

"I see a lot of foreigners, you see. Part of my job." She'd introduced herself as the proprietor of one of the teahouses in the High District—the area which expanded just off the sea front to serve, entertain and accommodate tourists from abroad. This particular woman's place wasn't actually on the High Street, the spine of the High District and the center of this country's tourism, but in the western patch of the district, where things were slightly cheaper. She did seem to earn enough for her fancy one-piece dress, her soft- and warm-looking scarf, her high-heeled yet miraculously comfortable-looking shoes . . . or were they all gifts from her patrons? "They tell me and my girls and boys how rare, how beautiful we are, but very often, that talk slips towards the"—she looked around and lowered her voice—"'cosmetics' they have overseas, as they get more and more drunk. Our government discourages them to talk about things like those colors they use to hide circles under the eye, or acne spots. Or, even, just to change the color of your eyelid!" She sat back and crossed her legs. "You know, tourists do like talking about those things, they love it when we go, 'oh, how sensational!' even though we are hearing it for the hundredth time."

Kiriko's mentor retrieved the disrespected cloth bag and fidgeted with it. Of course, they had heard stories about that obscene, crazy stuff. Kiriko had recently met in a lavatory of a souvenir shop a woman who was drawing eyebrows with a soft pencil. That woman had let Kiriko have a used, very short pencil of the same kind. She and her mentor had spent days taking that thing apart. "And . . . surgeries?" he said, reluctantly.

"There are many, many, they say! Ways to alter your appearance!" the woman exclaimed, covering her mouth the next moment as if merely mentioning it was off-limits. "But the thing I'm interested in—I heard they have something to inject into human skin, so the skin stays nice and smooth, even as you age? Or the thing where you transplant healthy skin onto a different part? I need something like that."

The two young craftspersons looked at each other, then back at the client. "But your skin is impeccable, Madam."

The woman's skin was mostly the color of ripe plum, with the soft sheen of enamel thinly applied all over her surface. Here and there—like inside her eyelids or the skin beneath her nails—the mellow yellow of the fruit could be seen. People said her skin used to be fresh green when she was the age of Kiriko now, twenty years or more ago. Her entire skin had ripened, they'd say, the way a young, hard and sour meat turned to the sweet, juicy thing.

"Impeccable. That's the way it should be, of course," she said. "But the thing about age. Look."

The woman tucked her hard-bark brown hair away from her neck, and there, the two could see: a crack. Underneath it the color was one of the fruit gone foul.

"I have several more like this, in parts where I cannot show you now. And these lines are spreading, I can see. I need a way to stop it."

Kiriko was doing everything she could to not touch the cracked skin. "This looks pretty, too, though. When you're full of it, it'll be a totally new pattern!"

The woman released her hair from her grip, and looked at Kiriko side-eye. "You'd never understand."

Of course she wouldn't. Kiriko's—and her mentor's, for that matter—skin, hair, teeth and bones were all just like foreigners': plain. That was why she worked as a craftsperson in the first place. Those without a color or pattern on their skin had no place in the tourism industry of this country, where people like this client earned foreign currency for the island by showing off themselves to the sightseers. Kiriko had long been used to this kind of casual insult. But her mentor said, "No, she wouldn't. We wouldn't. Which maybe means we wouldn't feel like helping you, Madam. Thanks for your visit, sorry for the trouble."

The woman's plum deepened, to a color closer to the one inside the fissure in her skin. "I'm going to lose my teahouse if I let my color spoil!"

"And we're losing a business opportunity here just for what we are, sorry we could not come to an agreement."

A few seconds passed in an uncomfortable silence. Kiriko's mentor stood there tall, his shoulders square. But Kiriko didn't need his protection, really. She, or they, needed money. "Sensei—"

But then the enamel woman inhaled and exhaled. She was the oldest person here right now; she took back control of her emotions sooner than the atelier's young owner. "Fine. Well. Those small pieces of paper stacked right there, by the way?" She was pointing at the finished products stored temporarily in a corner of the reception space. "Those are remedy transfer-print sheets, aren't they? One of my neighbors uses it for his allergy. I saw him put one to his lower eyelid, transfer the pattern on the sheet to the membrane. He said it eases the itches and soreness he gets as allergic reactions."

This is going to be bad, Kiriko thought. She could feel her mentor having the same thought, too.

"You make things to transfer patterns onto *human* skin. How obscene, eh?"

The young man breathed in, and out. "Temporary. And just for a medical effect."

"But what if more people hear about it? Those folks like you born without colors and patterns on your skin, you can fake what you want on you, in theory. The one for my neighbor, it soon went away with enough of his tears, sure. But if you used a different kind of ink? If you applied it to some drier surface? Oh, so very appalled, I am, to imagine such a thing done to one of my girls and boys!" She placed her hands over her chest and shook herself. Kiriko almost laughed.

"Madam, are you trying to blackmail us?" he said, and Kiriko could hear his temper sliding off to something different than anger.

"No, young man, I am not. I am just trying to strike a deal."

KIRIKO'S MENTOR SAT AT THE LOW table in their reception room, drumming his finger on its surface, looking grim.

The apprentice placed a tray of teapot and cups on the floor near him and sat down herself. "She did offer a nice sum of money, at the very least. You can buy me a bottle of fancy ink if that makes you feel any better."

"Why do you think that would make *me* feel any better? What do you know about these surgeries?"

Not much, really. Changing your complexion was illegal in this country. Even if the color to be applied came from the same person's skin. That would probably end with a large fine imposed on the patient, and . . . the people who performed this surgery, putting a knife into an allegedly perfect skin? The government would never let them work as craftspersons again. Kiriko shrugged like a foreigner, making him smile a little. "You?"

He shook his head. "Even if we, like, actually get to watch those surgeries, or read about their procedure details, I'm sure they are for the clinic, not for a common folk-remedy place like ours. I know she came here because she cannot possibly ask the government-run clinic, but here we don't have adequate equipment for that. Not even injection needles!"

Of course—neither of them had any kind of certificate or license or whatever, to do anything, which would involve actually slicing into human skin. This place was called an atelier because they put out patterned artifacts like fabrics for apparel or furnishings, carved wood boards for furniture and home interior, etcetera, etcetera. But that was only one part of what these two craftspersons did. They tended to small discomforts of the human body, like minor yet persistent headaches, inefficient digestive systems, regular cases of dizziness and so on, with their only weapon—the patterns they drew.

To them, currents of fluid within human body, the way muscles flowed and the air glided over them, were just other kinds of pattern. The two craftspersons called these "silent" patterns, as opposed to plainly visible, real lines and colors; everything, including human body parts, had a pattern to it, the curls of air and swirls of energy around it, marking its place in the world. Their treatment was conducted a lot of the time by finding another silent pattern that could affect the existing one and applying it over the affected area, to adjust the currents that had gone just a little bit amiss, correcting blood flow to make the body work more efficiently, or let the patient move their muscle more freely. Some patterns worked generally, while others had to be customized to the patient and their condition.

But they couldn't treat diseases that were too severe, or perform any kind of surgical operation. And here, in this country where altering your complexion was a crime, of course they couldn't speak openly of what they did behind their shut doors and screens, as they often had to draw patterns directly on human skin, which was regarded as highly inappropriate.

"Couldn't we just make a pigment portion and fill the cracks with it? I'm sure that's what she expects, anyway."

"I think she wants something permanent, and we cannot just fill a human skin with foreign matter, even if she's an enamel." He grinned. "Even if she loves foreign stuff."

His apprentice ignored this. "If we make—even if we can—something that changes the color there forever, once we do that the city will no longer overlook what we do."

"But how long, exactly, is forever?"

"Huh?"

He took his cup up off the tray. "With the remedy transfer sheet for allergy, the pattern stays there only for a few minutes. We have those sheets with ink that remains on the skin for a few hours, for cases where slowness and steadiness are more important. Stretch that procedure time little by little, and then . . . "

"Sensei," Kiriko pointed her finger at her mentor, "that is a quibble, and a feeble one at that."

"Oh come on, a few days cannot possibly be that huge a trouble. Even though that's far longer than any we've made here."

Kiriko considered this. "A few days . . . " she whispered. "Days . . . "

"Right. Days."

She blinked. "So she'll have to reapply the pigment every few days. The cracks are small but slowly spreading? Usual transfer method won't be much convenient here. And she must be very good with brushes to do it in a way people cannot tell there's been some tampering . . . "

"Oh, I don't like that word."

"Wait. Wait, but if the pigment is manipulated in a way it will attach itself to certain places . . . "

Her mentor sighed. "Finally. How long did it take for you to get there?"

She glared at him. "We'll still have to find a way to confect this pigment—what substance can be used, to closely stick to human skin, remain there a few days, and that would do no harm to the bearer."

"Step by step, my dear apprentice," he said, touching his lips to the cup of hot tea. "One problem at a time."

AT LEAST THE CLIENT PROBABLY WASN'T as heartless as she'd seemed. She placed some ordinary orders too, a patterned cloth for a sofa cover and garlands to be installed around the ceiling light, among other smaller things. Kiriko went to deliver the crafts, and also to take sample of the proprietor's skin. While repeat tourists, who were more or less familiar with the country, dominated this area, a lot of islanders—though only colorful ones—loitered and enjoyed themselves, too. Not the cleanest or safest part of the city, but many of the places around here had a distinct taste for fancy stuff and paid the atelier well.

Kiriko entered, careful not to draw the guests' attention, into the dimly-lit hall of Madam Enamel's teahouse. "Delivery for Madam," she whispered to one of the waiters standing near the door.

"Been expecting you, Craftsperson. This way."

The higher parts of the windows in the hall were filled with cheap kinds of stained glass—not the real, super-luxurious stuff seen around the most expensive area of this country. There was only one proper chandelier, and other lights that hung from the ceiling were simple gas-mantle lamps, some with old garlands swinging around them. Still, Kiriko could see the labor and money the proprietor put into this place. After a short walk along a narrow corridor on the other side of a small door, the waiter opened another of the same size for Kiriko, behind which Madam Enamel sat at a desk with reading glasses over her nose. "Hello Craftsgirl," the woman said, slightly squinting. "Come here and let me see those best pretties of the city."

Together they spread the delivered goods. The woman did seem to care a lot about these things unlike other clients around this area, who'd just order a thing, get it delivered and then forget all about it once it got installed in their shop; she turned the goods around, checking every surface, trying the feels of every pattern to the touch.

"I don't know why, but I really like these things. How different are they, from the stuff other places put out? Maybe you really are the best."

Kiriko and her mentor did choose those patterns which would soothe people's minds, by relaxing muscles around the eye and lifting some tension off a certain area of the brain. "Thank you," Kiriko only said.

"So?" The woman sat back in her chair. "Have you figured out anything . . . for *me*?"

Just then the waiter came back with cups of tea and a plate of confectionaries. Kiriko squeaked silently at the beauty of the ridiculously small yet elaborately shaped sweet pieces, and the woman watched her eat for a while.

"You really aren't that different from my girls." To Kiriko's surprise, the woman was smiling.

Kiriko swallowed a bite, which was almost a whole of one very fragrant cake. "I am so very different from them, I am totally colorless."

"That is quite extraordinary in itself, indeed, you know?"

"Not for the tourists." Kiriko listened to check if no one was within earshot, and then said: "I need samples. Of the inside of your skin fissure."

"Does it hurt?"

"It may hurt roughly to the same extent as when you snap a rubber band against your skin. If that's too much . . . "

"No, that's fine. Anything is fine, actually, as long as there's something you can do."

Kiriko scraped bits of skin and membrane off the woman, closed the caps tight on the sample vials. The sample wasn't just for color reference. Sometimes silent patterns could be seen easily only if she strained her consciousness enough to channel through. Other times, though, they could be hard for naked craftsperson eyes to see. These could be examined with a good microscope customized over the years by the atelier. The lens helped to grasp elements of the silent pattern better by reducing the influence of the lines on one another.

When she was done, Kiriko slurped up the last of her tea. "We'll still need some time," she said, as she stood up. "We'll get back to you as soon as we can."

The woman nodded. "Take those sweets. Does your mentor eat those, too? Or prefer something that goes better with alcohol?"

"He likes sweets, thank you!"

The woman saw Kiriko off to the exit. Along the way, the proprietor exchanged a few words with each of the girls and boys she encountered, and the interaction seemed kind, or even affectionate, perhaps. "Are you sure you don't need an escort out of this part of town?" she said when they were at the door.

Kiriko nodded. "It's not so late, and I do know safer paths."

"Take care, then. Good night."

"Good night, Madam."

"I like her," Kiriko said as soon as she was inside the atelier.

Her mentor frowned, said nothing.

"Look, she gave us some sweet things."

"Oh okay, maybe she's nice."

"And I mean, she's a bitch, all right, but she does seem to care for her place and her employees. I think she needs to remain enamel that badly because she needs to keep her place nice and popular, for her employees rather than for herself."

He opened the wrapping cloth and picked up one of the tiny cakes. "You do realize that you tend to attach yourself to any kind of client, don't you?"

She almost pouted and stopped herself. "She likes our crafts!"

He popped the cake into his large mouth and chewed, and looked very happy.

"See? Nice. And anyway, every client has their own reason. We're here to help them."

He swallowed loudly and sighed contentedly. "Should have prepared some bitter tea first. Let's get working on the samples now."

Kiriko never hung around in the High District, without very good reasons. She always felt nervous around the foreigners; she'd had no education on the official language, as the government deemed it a waste of resources for the colorless folks who had no direct business with the tourists; and most of the time, she didn't get their gestures. Shrugging was one of the first few she'd understood after she first moved to the city from her village in the mountains, and sometimes she even used it, because there was no gesture native to this country that could convey what it did. Then, not all the foreigners shrugged, them coming from many different parts of the continent. She just didn't like the feeling of being at a loss.

She walked through one of the narrower avenues on the eastern side of the High District, where many inns stood between the High Street and the waterfront. Accommodation was cheaper here than the hotels along the coastline. There were a few cafes and teahouses, not the fancy kind like in the west part of the city but those which simply served just-okay coffee. On the terrace of one of these places, a foreign woman was seated, looking down at her coffee beside which the milk and sugar sat untouched.

It was a bit chilly this morning, and the woman was the only patron on the terrace. Just as Kiriko had hoped. "Nova-san," she said, tasting the unfamiliar pronunciation of the woman's name at the edge of her lips. "Good day."

The woman looked up from her cup. "Hello Craftsperson Kiriko-san!" She beamed, engaging in the local language of this island for Kiriko's sake. "How nice to see you! Come have a seat!"

Nova ordered black tea for Kiriko (this place didn't have green tea, and black was slightly better than coffee for the craftsperson). Her hair was black, just like Kiriko's, but it glowed as if there was a layer of faint light over it; Kiriko had heard foreigners took very good care of their own conditions, not quite the way the islanders did. And she was almost as deeply-tanned as Kiriko's mentor, while Kiriko herself was pale and her skin hated the sun. Something glimmered on the woman's eyelids, and her peridot earrings went very well with her skin and also with those golden shimmers around her eyes. But it wasn't these carefully aligned looks that attracted Kiriko; Nova was the first foreigner who talked to Kiriko in the local language from the start, instead of the official language.

And of course, there was that eyebrow-pencil thing. "I want to thank you again," Kiriko said, wanting to shift to more formal speech but afraid the foreigner might not understand her then. "It was such fun to take that pencil apart."

"Good to hear! You didn't get into trouble? We are told not to talk too much about cosmetics, before we depart the continent."

"Not at all. We are careful. And . . . we hate to take advantage of your kindness, but . . . hope you don't mind telling me more about how you paint your face? What you use, and how you decide the appropriate amount and such."

"You want to know more about what we do? How diligent!"

"May I see that thing on your eyelid? Is that a pencil, too?"

Nova winked. "This? No, this comes from a palette."

"Palette!" Kiriko almost squeaked.

"Yes, a tiny palette. I can show you, but is it okay to do that here? Isn't that regarded as obscene?"

Kiriko's shoulders slumped down. "Yes. That would attract a lot of unwanted attention."

"Strange people, you all. But so are we, in your eyes." The foreign woman laughed just a little. "Any place? I don't think I can afford a space at that luxurious hotel down the coastline."

Kiriko considered this. "Oh. Maybe I know a place." She considered it again. "Maybe?"

LIKE MANY OF THE TEAHOUSES IN the west, Madam Enamel's place offered a quiet space at the back for those who needed privacy. Kiriko didn't know what a reservation for the room would cost, but as she had hoped, Madam Enamel said she wouldn't charge for this particular case.

"I still don't see how a foreigner can help with this," Madam Enamel said. But Kiriko could hear excitement in her voice.

"Thank you for your cooperation, Madam. Nova-san, after you, if you please."

The foreign woman said quick thanks to the proprietor in the local language, and Kiriko saw the enamel woman blush, her ripe plum cheeks turning to a warmer color. One of the waiting boys escorted Kiriko and Nova, an adolescent with peacock smudges on his face, one of his eyes amber. "Green tea is free of charge, Craftsperson," he said to Kiriko. "What can we offer your honorable company here? We do serve alcohol, too."

Nova looked at the menu and ordered a few things, including small cakes for herself and Kiriko, too. "Can you even read our language?" Kiriko asked.

"Some. Not everything. Your colors are beautiful, you look like you come from a myth," Nova said, the latter sentence to the waiter.

His ears turned pink. "Thank you. Oh, it feels so much better when a guest compliments in our own language, if I may say so."

"Does it, now? Then please send my regards to your proprietor. Her skin is perfect. I would like to have my nails enameled in that color in her honor, if that's not an obscene thing to say."

"It is not. She would be very pleased. If you'd excuse me."

After he left Kiriko said, "You should tell that to Madam in person. And I think the enamel color would go very well with your tan color."

"Thank you, Kiriko-san. You are beautiful, too, don't forget. The way your eyes twinkle when you talk about crafts, the way your jaws are set when you are focused."

Kiriko swallowed loudly. "Do you say that to everyone?"

"Mm? Maybe. But everyone I like is beautiful in their own way, and I think it's important to tell them so. Let's get to work?"

The craftsperson nodded and started going through the cosmetics purse Nova carried with her. She touched everything, one after another, trying the various textures. Powder, paste, liquid that seeped onto the brush when you rotated the stem . . . her mentor would love this brush. These things wouldn't last a day, the bearer would even have to retouch the colors on her face from time to time! How strange, these foreign customs. Some of the things even included colorant that she had never seen—she swallowed, braced herself and bored her consciousness into these.

Her plan was to grasp how these cosmetic things were made—how the substances worked, the percentage of those substances contained, the way these things mingled—from the silent patterns those substances emitted and the way they moved around each other. She also copied the names of the chemicals, with Nova's help on the language, so that she could later look them up; once she learned the precise description of the substance's property, she'd get to combine the knowledge with the patterns she felt from these cosmetic products, and then she could start probing for other ways of using these substances.

"Thank you," she said after she scribbled everything she could as fast as possible. "Sorry to have kept you waiting."

"No problem at all. This place is lovely. Wasn't in the travel guide-book."

"Not the best part of this country that the government wants to boast about. And foreigners must be careful if they need to walk around this area late at night."

Together they left the place, and like the last time the proprietor saw them off at the door. She bowed deeper and longer than the last time, though. Maybe it was just because Nova was a foreigner. But the waiters and waitresses, too, looked sad to see Nova leave.

"I hope you'll visit us again soon," the proprietor said, as she handed a business card to the foreign woman.

"I will, thank you," replied Nova, touching Madam's hand lightly as she accepted the card.

"So this Nova person. What exactly does she do?" Kiriko's mentor asked as the two craftspersons started their work in their lab. "Is she on a mission or something? An ambassador?"

"She is a researcher. She said she's here to study our culture, but not necessarily the colorful folks."

"What is there to study at all, apart from the colors of the tourism workers?"

"She says there's always something to learn as long as people live there. And that the hierarchy of the people is very peculiar here."

Her mentor sat back and looked away from the microscope for once. "But isn't that just obvious? The colorful rule. The colorless obey."

"On the continent there are different criteria for that. Because no colorful folks."

He shook his head and looked back down the lenses. Then they started their long discussion—how could they stretch the flow of the silent pattern inside Madam's skin fissure so that it would welcome the one in the pigment portion they concocted? Was there a way to enhance the affinity of it all, or could they just draw a straight, taut line between them, so that no other thing would even *think* of intervening?

After hours of yes's and a lot of no's and but's, they agreed on a configuration. Her mentor drew the tiniest reproduction of the silent pattern found inside Madam's crack, on an impossibly thin, almost see-through piece of soft paper, which took hours of making itself. They wrapped the dried ingredients with the paper and let the colorant absorb the pattern from inside. Madam Enamel could put one wrapped potion in her bath, immerse herself in the solution and let the pigment settle in her cracks, drawn in by its pattern twin. The fibers of the paper would land around the affected areas, too, working for better smoothness. It would require a slightly-acidic bath to get rid of it.

"I love it," the enamel woman said on the phone, after the first try. "You cannot see the cracks unless you look very, very carefully. And that's only if you know what to look for. And it also improves the way my skin feels as a whole. This is perfect."

Kiriko sighed into the receiver, relieved. "Good to hear that, Madam. But please refrain from overusing it? We've been very careful, but this is the first time we made something like this, so."

"Of course. I'll call when I need the second batch."

Kiriko grinned at her mentor as she put down the receiver. He shrugged, then laughed and started humming to himself. Kiriko soon joined in the tune. A moment like this, it was one of the best things about this trade.

But when they did hear about her again, the words didn't come from the woman herself. It came in the form of an officer in uniform. "Craftspersons," they said, when Kiriko opened the door. "If you please."

* * *

MADAM ENAMEL LOOKED EXHAUSTED BEHIND THE transparent wall, but that didn't explain the cracks that had spread, covering most of her neck and invading her jawline. Kiriko had imagined the cracks to be a beautiful, tree-like pattern if and when they spread, but something was wrong with the actual thing in front of her now. The color, for instance, wasn't the bad fruit they'd seen when the woman first visited their place. It had a strange tinge of green to it. And the way it progressed . . . there were jumps and starts here and there, instead of branches going forward in the fan-form, using the momentum of its own growth; as if some unknown force tried to rip the skin randomly.

"One of the places in our area got suspended for being a site matching the locals to the tourists who need . . . special services," Madam Enamel said on the other half of the cubicle, behind the see-through wall. "Many more places got raided, and I was caught while I was having a bath with Nova-san. Not the best timing, is it?"

Kiriko raised her brows. "You were having a bath *with* Nova-san?"

"It wasn't like I was selling myself to a foreign stranger. And . . . " She rolled her eyes towards the officer who was standing behind her, who couldn't see her doing it. "She explained that we are *friends*, to the authorities, that she had brought in the bath bomb for the two of us."

"Then what happened to your skin?"

"I've no idea. It never happened before this time, the . . . thing had worked so well so far." She blinked, waiting for a question from the officer at attention; they didn't seem to have one—apparently.

"Do you know when you're getting out?" asked Kiriko.

The woman looked uneasy at this. "No. Nova is doing what she can to prove that no money was exchanged between us. The government hates us, don't they? Those of us who don't do business exclusively for rich foreigners but serve our fellow locals, too."

Kiriko massaged her brow with a finger. "We'd like to look more closely . . . at your condition. Did you put anything in your bath along with the bath bomb?" She hastily added, "I'm just curious."

"She added scented water. I think that is all."

Ordinary scented water shouldn't have been able to change anything in the composition. At least not like this. "I'll talk to Nova-san," Kiriko said after a moment.

"Please do. I—I hope I didn't get her into too much trouble." At that, her lips trembled, though just a little.

* * *

THEY COULDN'T REACH NOVA VERY SOON, though, as the foreigner was busy talking to the embassy and to authorities. Madam Enamel was released two days later. By the time she made it to the atelier, her steps were unsteady, her eyes murky and there was another thin but unbreakable layer of sweat over her enamel. Kiriko piled cushions on the reception room's raised floor while the woman's peacock subordinate and the owner of the atelier helped her up onto the makeshift cot.

"What is this?" Kiriko's mentor said, sounding bewildered. "This— this looks so much worse. The cracks are all over."

Yes; the cracks had spread even wider, to the extent that there was no smooth surface on her visible now. Nova might have said something at the embassy, but more likely this was the reason the authorities had decided to let her go. Kiriko dabbed at the woman's forehead with a cloth of a heat-absorbing pattern. "Did we do this?" It hurt to word this question.

"I don't know." His admission bit like a ragged edge of ice. "Let's just do whatever we can, for now."

The two craftspersons looked more closely at the cracks, and again, Kiriko was struck by how unnatural the way all those lines ran. It felt very abrupt—a blister that erupted, swathing the area with its nasty fluid, not a seam gradually extending. Was this just a result of aging? Unlikely, though perhaps they should have taken it into account. It had to be solely the atelier's fault.

Kiriko traced some of the cracks with her finger, and quickly started adding a new pattern that would alleviate the wrongness of the one currently there. They'd discovered Kiriko was better at this even than her mentor—he had much wider knowledge on many things, on application of those things, and his thoroughness and meticulousness of the deployment was almost impeccable; but when it came to time-critical treatment or one-shot goes, Kiriko's instinct bloomed under the pressure and she usually had control over the situation within minutes. But this . . . her hand steadied around the stem of the brush, as if she knew where the ink had to be; she had to do this, but how much would she be able to help, randomly groping for solutions as she was?

"This might hurt a little," Kiriko's mentor was saying to the woman, but there was no reply.

He spread thin acid over the woman's enamel skin, to slow the cracks going farther. Kiriko started working on the worst-looking ones, those that were thicker, with that foul, greenish tinge, applying a dusty red colorant with bold yet precise strokes. Even as she did so, thread-thin lines were spreading around the bad ones, bypassing the acid. Soon her mentor started tending to these smaller ones.

The peacock boy rubbed his face fiercely. "What the hell did she do?"

"It's us," the owner of the atelier told him. "Our doing."

"But she asked for it, didn't she? We knew she'd do something stupid to herself. She's been so obsessed with her own skin. Like that was all that there was keeping her house upright. But it was her. You know? It was she herself who bound that place in one, not just the skin—"

"Shut up, we'll apologize and hear you boast how much you love her later, but now make yourself useful and bring us washing water for the brushes." For once, Kiriko's mentor raised his voice. "The kitchen's behind that door. There are small pots and buckets lying around."

And hours afterwards ticked away like that—two craftspersons drawing patterns as fast as they could on an immobilized woman, a peacock adolescent moving to and fro over the atelier floor. When the dawn arrived, the enamel woman's breathing was finally even, and the three young people collapsed onto the reception floor around her.

THEY DIDN'T HAVE BEDS FOR PATIENTS—that, too, was for the clinic—so after a few hours' nap they wrapped up the enamel woman and let the peacock boy and his coworkers carry her via a coach. The two craftspersons prepared emergency transfer-print sheets that the workers of the teahouse could apply on the woman if and when need be. And they started trying to figure out what had gone wrong, right away.

But they couldn't see anything; they'd thoroughly examined every possibility, checked her allergic reactions and the state of the ingredients, the devices and equipment they'd used to prepare the treatment. Kiriko told him about the scented water that Nova had brought in. But with the configuration they'd made, and the fact that the foreigner herself had been in that water, too, that this scented water thing could do any harm to just Madam Enamel seemed unlikely.

"We do have to check what that water is, anyway," her mentor said over a hundredth cup of tea. "It is possible that there was something in that water, a substance that we have not heard of, that Madam can be allergic to."

Kiriko sighed. "I'll go talk to Nova-san."

THE FOREIGN WOMAN WAS ALMOST EQUALLY disconcerted, if not unwell, when Kiriko finally managed to arrange a meeting. "I was waiting for her to call me when she was released," she said as she let Kiriko into her hotel room.

Kiriko didn't like going behind a closed door alone with a foreigner, not because of Nova but of custom, but this was an emergency. "Madam was too ill to make a phone call," Kiriko replied, and took a seat near the window. "We asked Peacock to let us know of any change of state, so she must be still resting."

The foreign woman poured tea for Kiriko and herself. "How bad is it?"

"We believe we managed to stop its progress. But to eliminate it entirely—we still aren't sure if it's a disease or some other kind of disturbance—we need to know exactly what is causing it." Kiriko bit her lip for a second. "We heard you added scented water to the bath? Do you have its container with you still?"

"No, sorry, it never occurred to me—" She shook her head. "Is it my fault?"

She hesitated one moment. "*Our* fault, more likely. Me and my mentor. Do you remember its maker or seller?"

"Oh, I'll ask my sister on the continent by phone, she gave me the thing. Let me see . . . "

Nova went to the closet, came back with a datebook, sat down near the phone machine. Then she blinked hard down at the datebook, and sighed. "Kiriko-san, my old tired eyes need the light on. Can you close the curtains for me?"

"Sure." She stood and started drawing the curtains. Nova was fumbling for the light's switch. Now just one part of window was still uncovered, and Kiriko reached out to shut it there, too. But then—

"Wait," Kiriko said, "don't turn that light on."

"W-what?"

A sliver of setting sun came through between the curtains, fell on the table beside the window, and bounced off the polished surface to dimly illuminate the foreigner's face. Colors danced over her skin—green seemed to be dominant, but the sheen shifted with bronze, orange, and something that reminded of Madam's color.

Jewel-beetle.

"Nova-san, are your ancestors from this island?" Kiriko asked.

"Oh, I haven't mentioned that? Yes, but a very long time ago. That's why I'm so much into this country."

"I see," Kiriko said, her hand still hovering near the curtain. "I think now I know what caused Madam's condition."

THE LOCALS LOOKED; OF COURSE, FOREIGNERS almost never wandered out to this part of the city. But Kiriko—of all people, that introvert, entirely-colorless craftsperson—leading a foreigner to the pattern atelier in this shadowed area of the city seemed even more surreal than it should.

Kiriko moved stiffly all the way, even when she waved to a local or two she knew well. When they finally reached their destination, Kiriko almost cried out in relief. "Sensei!" she called her mentor loudly to cover that urge.

"What—oh." He went as stiff as Kiriko had been. "This . . . honorable guest here must be Nova-san?"

"Yes. Nova-san, this is my mentor, the owner of this atelier. Please take a seat; you need to take your shoes off first."

As the foreign woman did so, Kiriko went around the atelier, closing all the shutters and covering the opaque glass on the door with a cloth. Her mentor tried to catch her, failed, shifted his weight on his feet and flailed a little. Finally he almost twitched and said, "I should offer tea!"

"Sensei, stop being nervous," his apprentice scolded him, forgetting her own previous stiff walk. "And look."

She'd brought a device which emitted light that had the same characteristics as natural sunlight. Now with Nova sitting on a flat cushion, Kiriko aimed the light to the surface of the low table beside the foreigner. Immediately her mentor saw what this was all about.

"Oh," he said.

"She has an ancestor from this island. I heard that once you leave this island the colors start to fade, I didn't know it could be preserved like this."

"Me, either. But this is jewel-beetle, right? Maybe not entirely impossible."

"Okay, you two, now tell me what is going on." Nova looked as uncomfortable as the two locals here had been a few moments ago.

Kiriko put away the lighting device and switched on the ordinary bulbs. "Your ancestor must have been a jewel-beetle colored person. Jewel-beetle people have strange properties. Have you seen the insects themselves?" Nova shook her head. "Well, they wear metallic colors that change with the angle, which keep birds away. And the colors never fade even after the bug dies because they are not pigment, but come from the shell's structure. That may be the reason your colors survived. Anyway, most of the colors of the islanders only have any kind of effect—physically and mentally—on the bearer themselves. But very few colors can affect others. Jewel-beetle, and Madam's enamel, are two of these very few. Though enamel is more prone to *taking*, than giving."

Kiriko was speaking slowly, but even locals would have trouble understanding all of this instantly. But Nova was a researcher of this island; after a quick thinking, she said, "So my color, even though I never knew it existed, did some harm to her."

"Your colors are weak, but sharing a bath, with substances we composed for her, worked almost magically, I think, invading her native color." Kiriko knelt beside the woman. "If you let us take samples of your skin, we might be able to find a pattern that would cure Madam Enamel."

"Do it, then." Nova looked sharply up at the craftspersons. "Do it, by all means. Cure her. I don't care what it takes out of me."

First they had to find a silent pattern that had caused the malfunction in Madam, and then construct a new one which would offset the effect of it, considering at the same time the substances they used for the original crack-remedy bath treatment. They went through everything on Nova, and hours later, found a part of membrane deep inside her eyelid that spread an almost-invisible pattern that seemed to click. Kiriko scratched the part off and looked into it with a microscope to be sure, and then started on combinations of patterns that would counteract Nova's effect on Madam. Kiriko' mentor gave Nova eye-drop medicine, and they made her stay at their atelier while her eye cured to some extent.

And so by the morning, they had a pattern to, hopefully, heal Madam Enamel.

NOVA (AND THE CRAFTSPERSONS) HAD FORGOTTEN to inform her hotel that she was staying out, so in the morning the foreigner had to call in and then go back to the place very quickly. "Let me know how it goes. As soon as you find out," she said, as Kiriko saw her off at an intersection to the High Street.

They parted, and Kiriko started jogging towards the western quarters of the city. At the door of the teahouse Peacock was waiting for her. "Your boss is already inside."

"He's not my boss—how is Madam?"

"Resting. Not worse, not better."

The teahouse was closed. Kiriko walked through the eerily quiet place, though she soon heard commotion in the backyard. There, Kiriko's mentor was already drawing on Madam's arms. Kiriko took her coat off and dropped her bag onto the floor and started doing the same.

As soon as she spread the latest remedy-pattern over Madam's skin, Kiriko felt the current shift under her fingers. This was going to work. This was going to be okay. She almost let a sigh of relief slip, but stopped herself with an effort. And felt her mentor feeling the same relief.

She spared one split second, and smiled at the few staff who were holding their breath around the two craftspersons. They smiled and nodded back, then resumed helping them.

OF COURSE—THERE WERE OTHER ISSUES than the patient herself, to be addressed later. They'd both tried to brush that thought off, or to hold on to the possibility that maybe nothing would go into that direction this time. But the next day, the same officer who had come to notify them of Madam being held in custody, stood at their door looking almost sorry.

"We'd just pass on something like this between locals. But this time, a foreigner is involved."

"But we didn't do anything to Nova-san."

"She didn't get back to the hotel one night, came back the next morning with scratches all over and a patterned eye-patch. We cannot call that 'didn't do anything.'"

When they got to the Officers' Station, Madam Enamel was there, too, with a girl with pastel-colored cotton-candy hair they remembered accompanying her the previous day. The enamel woman looked frail, pale in her own way, but was sitting straight on the cushioned chair.

"Madam isn't properly well! How dare you drag her here?" Kiriko's mentor hissed furiously.

"Craftsperson, easy." Madam Enamel raised her hand. "I told them I wanted to be here and give accounts of the incident myself. I wanted to be in the same room as you two, so that you can do whatever you need to when something goes wrong with me." At this stage, it was no use pretending that the atelier had nothing to do with Madam's condition or its treatment. "They don't usually listen to this kind of request, but they made this exception for me. That much, I should be grateful."

He backed off, still fuming. Kiriko looked around. "Where is Nova-san?"

"She is being asked to talk in a separate room, of course."

The two craftspersons took their seats on the other side of the table from Madam. "And what are we charged for, exactly?" he asked.

"What, exactly, did you do to the foreigner? She wouldn't talk."

"That's because there's nothing to talk about. Maybe she fell off a stair or something, nothing to do with any of us," Madam said.

"Then why wouldn't she just say so?"

"Maybe she doesn't understand you."

"Madam," the officer frowned as they said, "we know she likes you. And it's good to see a foreigner liking one of us that way. But if there was a crime involving a foreigner, we must know."

"But there's no crime committed! And the foreigner herself doesn't recognize one, does she?"

The officer looked very unhappy at that. For a moment, Kiriko thought they might win—except there was no win or lose, not really—only their atelier's future poised on the officer's finger.

They said, "So she just fell off a stair. But what about your disease?"

"What about it?"

"You obviously got ill right after being caught with the foreigner. Or maybe after that bath that smelled a bit funny. We do know that you had dealings with the atelier, at around the same time. You'd had no conditions before then, we heard?"

Still crack-strewn, Madam Enamel stared at the officer. The progress had stopped entirely, malfunction of Madam's systems thoroughly eliminated, but there was no hiding the cracks now—once this kind of change happened, there was no turning back, just like her plum color itself, ripening. They held their eyes that way for some time, while the two craftspersons could do nothing but just sit there, finding even simple breathing hard, so hard. "This has nothing to do with the situation here," the enamel woman finally said, her voice even—too much so.

"We can investigate, you see. You cannot go on without knowing the cause. What if it is contagious? You may be exposing your fellow islanders to danger, even as we speak now."

"How dare you—" Her cotton candy subordinate, who had been growing impatient by the minute, was about to bang her fists on the table, but Madam Enamel stopped her with a hand.

"Candy, no," she said and shook her head. Candy breathed deep but then sprang to her feet as if to shake fume off, went to stand facing the mirrored wall.

"What is it, Madam Enamel?" the officer continued. "If you really have no idea, you should consider closing down your place, at least until we have done proper investigation and everybody knows what caused it. If it's to do with the foreign researcher, either something she did to you or she brought into our country, we must expel her from the island, never admit her any future entrance. You should never see her again. Or," they paused, just a fraction too long to be for breathing, "if that's the atelier's fault, we can just order them to discontinue their trade."

Madam lifted her head and looked to the officer. Candy turned around.

"Look, Madam Enamel," said the officer, slowly, as if Madam wasn't quite getting them. "Tell us the truth. What do you owe these colorless laborers, anyway?"

There. The two craftspersons had known it would come to this sooner or later. Yes—as long as the colorless were to blame, everything would be fine. Nova would get to stay in the island, keep on with her research, stay with Madam; Madam would be able to resume her position as proprietor as soon as she was well enough. The government would have no dispute with the continent.

Happy ending to all.

Madam Enamel looked at Kiriko and her mentor. Kiriko stared back, sending no message through that one moment of eye-contact. Because after all, what did Madam owe them, really? Just a sorry end of a lizard tail cut and discarded; there were enough colorless craftspersons in the city, to replace these two.

Madam Enamel looked back at the officer. "Sorry, I think I've been mistaken a few moments ago."

"Okay, Madam. Tell us."

"It's the foreigner. She is a descendant of islanders, and has properties that can be harmful to me."

"What?" the officer came to stand closer to her, their hands on the table. "Look, you don't have to—"

"I don't have to what? These two craftspersons did study the foreigner. They can give you the data as proofs. Or you can do it all over again, hurting her even more, and get into more trouble with the continent. And oh, I can tell there are more officers watching us behind, let me see, that mirror maybe?" She pointed at the wall and Candy jumped away from it with a small cry. "Surely you're recording this. You cannot erase my testimony here. Right?"

The officer stood back up straight. "Are you sure—"

"I am." Madam stood up. Candy came to support her. "The foreign researcher is harmful only to me, or to enamel people. But I haven't seen any other enamel than me in the city, so. I would not say this is contagious." She shrugged like a foreigner. "Can we all go home now?"

She stood tall, and nobody would have guessed she'd been down with illness only a day ago. Her eyes were hard. The officer swallowed, before they stepped back to let her pass.

"Madam," Kiriko said, when they were back in the western end of the city. "Madam." But she didn't know how she could continue.

Madam Enamel stopped there, and turned to face the craftspersons. She looked both of them in the eye, one of them after the other, and then touched Kiriko's shoulder. "I remember," she said. "I was as young as you are now, I think, when I started working in this area. A lot older than you two when I finally established my own place. I worked hard. Real hard."

A wind blew. Candy brushed a strand of Madam's tree-bark hair out of her face, and Madam smiled at her employee.

"You, too, might want to have your own place, some day," Madam said to Candy. Candy shrugged and they both giggled. Then Madam turned back to the craftspersons. "I know you are working hard. How can I take that away from you? Nova would understand. She is a foreigner, she'll have a chance to resume her research in some time. But if you lose what you have now, you'll never get it back again . . . sorry, but that's true, I think."

Kiriko's mentor nodded. "Thank you. There in the station, I thought I lost my atelier forever."

Kiriko stood there, silent. She knew she should be grateful and say it, too. But—but what? This was the best possible outcome. "But you two. You two might not see each other again." Her voice shook, embarrassing her with her own naivety.

"Again, she is a foreigner. I am a colorful. We'll find our way to each other in time."

Kiriko looked down, and couldn't lift her head back up. When she was old enough, if there ever came a time that she had to choose between someone else's future and her mentor, would she ever be able to make the same choice?

"I do everything to protect my place. You to protect your crafts. Don't let that make you feel bad, Craftsperson."

Only when Madam was well away from them, Kiriko looked up. The world was blurry. Her mentor nudged her. "Let's get home. I'm starving," he said.

Kiriko nodded. In the weeks to come, they'd hear the rumor that Madam Enamel turned into Madam Fallen Fruit. That sounded sexy, in a way foreigners and west-loitering locals liked. But Madam Enamel was lost forever, and even after years, Kiriko would mourn for that loss.

Ever Changing, Ever Turning

Shino felt the air in the shop shift as the young woman walked in. People stared—people who were used to being stared at. They just couldn't help it. The woman wore a tight dress, obviously tailor-made for her, showing off the delicate curves of her hips and the perfect downward slope that led to her long, slender legs.

Shino's boss remembered where they were first. "Ma'am!" She shuffled gracefully towards the woman. "Such an honour to welcome you here. But what brought the great Moon-White Tsukiko-sama to this mediocre robe shop?"

Today, the famous model's skin shone bronze, blue-green patina here and there. She was called Moon-White not only because her original skin color was glowing white, but because her skin was a white canvas that could change to any color, any pattern that perfectly matched what she wore at the moment. "I just spoiled a bag," Tsukiko said hurriedly to the proprietor. "Poured coffee all over it, and it's a moon-white bag! It went so well with this blue-sandstone dress. And I have an important meeting soon, at the Hotel."

Tsukiko and the proprietor both glanced in the direction of the Hotel, which was the largest and the only foreign-style place around here. In this region things mainly catered to sightseers from abroad, and High Street was clogged with shops for traditional commodities, this shop—selling traditional robes and accessories—being one of them.

"As you can see, we do not have much to offer you, to our great regret. We have drawstring purses, but I'm not sure that would suit this magnificent dress you are wearing. However . . . " Shino's boss frowned and looked around her shop. "If you do not have too much to carry, perhaps a wrapping cloth might do?"

"Wrapping cloth?"

The boss called to Shino, who nodded and took to assembling some plain crepe cloths on a tray. Then she shuffled to the two women, the tray covered with various whites: from porcelain to deutzia crenata to plum-flower. The famous woman's lips shaped a tiny O, and then she took the one tinged with faint blue-gray, the silky-mouse-fur.

Shino quickly folded and made knots in the cloth so that it would keep a shape and ensure that the famous model wouldn't have to re-fold or re-knot the thing later. The woman said, "Thanks," flashed a smile at everyone in the shop and sprinted out into the street, into a cab.

"That shapeliness of her body!" the boss exclaimed beside Shino. "How is that even possible? Her figure and countenance looking so foreign and yet, she has the colors! Colors that even change! That's no justice!"

Shino giggled. Her cheeks, swirling eastern clouds just before dawn, flushed into a deeper red of sunrise. "She's beautiful."

"She is. Oh, sir, close that mouth, for heavens' sake!" One of the customers snapped his mouth shut at that, and everyone in the shop laughed.

And everything got back to normal.

A few weeks later Shino found the model in a magazine, a photo shot during that meeting at the Hotel. The makeshift bag was out of sight, unfortunately, but the woman's nails were all white, various whites that Shino had chosen for her.

How was that even possible?

Today, off duty, Shino wore a colorful T-shirt over jeans, her usual outfit on such a day, as she walked along the street of shops for the local residents. She stopped at a place selling glasses, wanting not the color-changing contact lenses for foreigners but simple rims to frame her complicated eyelids.

"Hey," someone called. Shino shifted her gaze to look at the reflection of a woman in the window, standing right behind her. She wore sunglasses, her hair tucked in under her cap, all tourist-clad. But there was no mistaking the glowing skin, at least to Shino.

"Tsukiko-san?" Shino gaped as she spun around to face the woman. "What would you be doing here?"

Tsukiko raised an eyebrow. "Why, I'm a local here, I'd usually shop around here, not on the High Street."

"Oh. Sorry. People keep forgetting that, don't we? You look so foreign, even more so without all the colors."

Her nails were still in whites, and when she realized Shino was looking at them, Tsukiko raised a hand. "I didn't paint them, I know it's prohibited to change colors artificially. You can try some remover if you want."

"No, I just think they are pretty."

"Oh!" Tsukiko grinned. "Aren't they, though? And you look great in that shirt. A bit loud but more like you than the plain robe you were wearing the other day."

"My boss doesn't like me in loud robes. She says my skin color doesn't go along with patterns. How did the meeting go, by the way?"

"Splendid, thanks." She glanced up and down the street. "Hey. Can I buy you a coffee or something? As thanks for that cloth, and all these pretty whites?"

"Oh no, please, you don't have to—"

"Please. Let me."

Shino felt her cheeks warm up, and Tsukiko narrowed her eyes fondly. Then Shino said, "Maybe after you help me choose a pair of glasses?"

Tsukiko's smile widened. "Sure."

And soon they were friends.

"WHAT?" TSUKIKO SAID WITHOUT DETACHING HER gaze from the book she was reading.

From her chair, from behind her new black-rimmed glasses, Shino stared a boring stare at Tsukiko. "I just wonder how you do it."

They had been friends for a few weeks now, close enough that Shino had invited Tsukiko to her own place, but Shino hadn't told anyone. Perhaps on that account, Tsukiko seemed to trust her, which made her a bit bold, asking a question that seemed a bit too delicate here.

Tsukiko smirked. "The power of will."

"Just that?"

"Yes."

"Can your mother do that? Your father?"

"She could. He, no."

"Oh." Shino still wasn't sure how much detail she could go into with Tsukiko. *She could.* "When did you come to this island?" she asked after a moment of hesitation.

"Why do you think I wasn't born here?"

"You must have come here at some point, because if you've always been here, someone must've noticed you long before. You got famous like—five years ago? With that ad for tourism?"

It had been a campaign for attracting more tourists from abroad, waged by the island's government. Tsukiko had laid herself down on a huge map of the island, her limbs turned into colors characteristic of the places they were cast over: her shimmering hands over the jewelled cliff in the map; toenails the ancient trees dotting the southern coastline; her blond hair flowing along the beach of golden sand in the north. Everybody was surprised, for the islanders had never seen anyone with foreign physical features and the native colors both. The ad doubled the number of tourists that year.

Much as Shino hated the way the government cut and pasted the island into something pretty to sell to foreigners, that was what paid her. If she hadn't been hired at the shop, she might have died right after she had been kicked out of the orphanage.

Tsukiko set down Shino's book about traditional robes on the table. "You are right. My mother was from here and she crossed the sea later, had me out there. I came here when I was fifteen, when my mother died."

"Oh dear, I'm so sorry."

"Don't be." Tsukiko flashed a mesmerizing smile. "Without my colors I'd have been really lonely, but people liked them and were nice to me. So. I was okay, after all."

Shino stretched her legs and looked at her toenails, which were the pale green of the back of a leaf. "I hear they have so many tools and materials to change their colors overseas! Not just paint for nails or hair but . . . things you can put on directly over your *skin*? Have you seen that?"

"Of course I have. We were all crazy about those, us young girls. But that's obscene talk on this island, we shouldn't be talking about that at all."

"I guess I'm jealous." Shino sighed. "Why can't we change our colors just as we please? It's not fair."

"People abroad are jealous of the way you are born, that you don't have to change colors, spend money on them. They say it's not fair."

Shino made a face.

Tsukiko laughed.

Just then a soft beam of sunlight entered the room, through the sheer curtains. Tsukiko stared at Shino and said, "Did you know your hair also looks like pre-dawn clouds in the light from the setting sun? That's absurd, your hair usually being so dark. But beautiful."

Shino smiled. "Did you know your cheeks ripple like the sea in this light?"

Tsukiko put both hands over her cheeks. "No."

And Shino thought Tsukiko looked the most beautiful when she wasn't wearing any colors at all.

SHINO HAD WORKED AT THE CURRENT place for almost five years now; she was trusted quite well these days, and sometimes, when the boss had a place to go, a person to meet, she would leave the shop for Shino to close down for the day. One of those evenings, as Shino was locking the safe, the phone rang. She took it, thinking maybe it was the boss needing an urgent word. "Hello?"

"Oh! Good, there's still someone there!" A foreigner, a woman, sighed into the phone. "I need to ask a favour. This is important!"

Shino's hand stiffened over the receiver as she switched to her clumsy official language. "What's wrong?"

"I think I left my purse in one of the booths of your bathroom. Can you look? My passport is in it."

Shino inhaled sharply. "Oh dear, please hold on."

The purse was found stuck between the tank and the wall, the passport securely tucked in. As soon as Shino told the woman, the other cheered, and promised to drop by to retrieve it the next day.

Happy that she had helped someone on such an important matter, that she'd managed all of that in her second language, Shino gleefully tapped the purse with her fingers. Then she recalled the strange, small bottle she had found when she had looked into the purse to check the passport. What was that thing?

She was alone in the shop.

And it wasn't like she was trying to steal something. The owner of the purse knew Shino had opened it, anyway. Cautiously, she reopened the purse, pulled the strange bottle out with two fingers.

The bottle itself was transparent, but the liquid inside swirled in strange shimmers and glows. Shino read the label aloud: "Nail polish?"

So this was one of the things foreigners used to change their own colors. One of the things deemed extremely obscene on this island.

She had often wondered what it would be like to change her ten nails into ten different colors. She twisted the lid, and an unpleasant smell wafted out. The lid was attached to a tiny brush.

How did it work?

She looked around the empty shop again. Just a small drop wouldn't hurt? She could wipe it away soon, anyway.

With shaking fingers, she put a tiny bit of the polish onto a shaking nail.

The drop stayed at the tip of her nail for a few moments. And then, the color started to spread—a pink that looked like a cross between fuchsia and pomegranate, a color too striking for Shino's hand.

She hastily put the lid back on, and ran to the bathroom. When she opened the tap over the nail the color was already fixed, and running water could do no damage to it. She tried hot water; no good. The paint thinner from the cleaning appliance locker was no use, either. The color had so closely, smoothly spread itself out, as if it were really part of Shino's nail. So this must be a special sort of polish developed for the foreigners to take back to their homelands, which meant there must be a special remover for it.

No tourist shop was open at this time, and she couldn't go into one without making excuses, anyway, being a local. If the color was still there in the morning, the boss would know that Shino had touched a customer's belongings, and that she had committed such an obscene act as trying to change her own color.

What could she do?

She shuffled to the phone and dialled.

"Hello?" Tsukiko's voice rang in her ear, hurting and reassuring at the same time.

Shino said, "Tsuki," and she couldn't continue.

"Shino? Anything wrong?"

"I . . . I need help."

"Where are you?"

Shino blinked her tears away. "The shop."

"Okay. Be right there."

Half an hour later, Tsukiko shrugged off her jacket and hat as soon as she was inside the shop. Without a word Shino showed her the nail and the bottle of nail polish. Tsukiko's expression clouded. "I don't have a remover for this."

Shino looked down at her feet, sighing a wet sigh. "I don't mind being scolded or fined for what I've done, but I don't want the shop's, the boss's reputation hurt for my sake. A shop girl touching a foreign customer's belongings . . . "

Tsukiko was biting her own, perfect nail. "You'll be all right," she said after a while.

"But . . . "

"Hush." She moved to stand in front of a tall mirror and looked at herself in it. Her gaze settled on her back, which was barely visible under the loose shirt she was wearing. "Yeah." She tossed the shirt over her head, her torso naked now. "Here. Somewhere near the shoulder blade. It will be hidden under the bra, and if I do have to model naked, I can make up colors and some stupid story around it."

"What are you talking about?"

Tsukiko looked at Shino's reflection in the mirror. "Bring a knife from the kitchenette. Make a small cut to draw some blood."

Shino shook her head. "No! I don't see how that would make things any better, anyway."

"Come on, just a little scratch on my back, that's far better than a mark on your shop's reputation."

"But—"

"Do it! Now!"

Shino almost jumped. Without another word she went to the kitchenette and returned. She'd have said something once more, but she saw Tsukiko glaring at her in the mirror. Wincing, she touched the blade to Tsukiko's skin. Too weak, though; she had to do it once again. Tsukiko sucked air between her teeth.

A drop of blood swelled. "Spread that over the nail," Tsukiko said to Shino. And she did.

On her nail, Tsukiko's blood boiled and rippled. Shino covered her mouth with her free hand. Tsukiko came to hold her shoulders, to touch her own forehead to Shino's.

"Shh," Tsukiko said and closed her eyes.

Slowly, dot by dot, Shino's nail turned over into back-of-leaf, though a bit cloudier than the other nine nails. When the whole nail had changed, Tsukiko exhaled, and then smiled. "This will do for the moment. Until it changes back completely to your own color in coordination with your metabolic cycle."

Shino turned her hand around. "How did you do that?"

"You don't need to know that. All you need to know is that you have nothing to worry about, now. But don't you say a word about it, about what you just saw."

"I won't. I can't, obviously. But—"

Tsukiko shook her head, and pulled her shirt back down over her torso. Just before it got hidden, Shino saw the scratch in the mirror; it had already started blooming like a grotesque, yet slashingly beautiful, impossible flower.

THE NEXT MORNING THE FOREIGN CUSTOMER came and thanked Shino. "This is nothing," she said as the customer beamed at her, and wished she had something to hide the sleep-deprived redness around her eyes.

But it was an obscene thought.

The customer checked her purse just in case, confirmed that nothing had been misplaced. She had bought a few things at the shop the previous day, but today she bought a practical but expensive garment of linen before she left the shop again, the purse secure under her arm.

"Good job, Shino!" the boss said cheerfully and walked away to greet another customer.

Shino secretly touched her nail under her sleeve.

Such an obscene thought.

* * *

A few days later, after Shino had learnt from a magazine that it was Tsukiko's birthday that day, she called and told her she wanted to do whatever was suitable as celebration, and also thank her. But Tsukiko kept on saying no, Shino didn't have to. Though they were talking over the phone, Shino could almost *see* Tsukiko's frown, and for a moment she thought of retreating from the conversation. But then Tsukiko said, "Would you come to my place? Now?"

Shino sighed secretly, relieved. "Sure."

"Meet me at that eyewear shop."

Shino soon left her place and started walking towards the shop, where she had first met the "colorless" version of Tsukiko. It was dusk, and when Shino looked up, there was a flock of starlings, strangely far in the sky.

Or was it something in the eye? She rubbed at her eyes, but the flock, or ripples in her vision, followed her. In the trees, around the gaslight. When she braced herself and forced herself to focus on the ripples on a flickering neon sign, however, she saw them slowly still, staying there as if evaluating her, measuring her.

She felt a shiver down her spine, through her finger. She hid her nail under her sleeve, which pricked at the touch of another finger. The neon sign—the ripple—and her nail buzzed to the same rhythm, and her heart beat as if it were trying desperately to avoid joining them—

A hand grabbed at her shoulder, and she cried out in surprise. "Oh no, sorry." It was Tsukiko. "Didn't mean—no, Shino, don't stare at them."

Shino glanced the sign's way, but soon looked back at her friend. "What are they?"

"Not here. Let's go."

They started walking. Shino had always imagined Tsukiko's place to be in one of the buildings in the complex for foreigners—ambassadors and official guests. But as they walked they switched between locals' and foreigners' avenues, slipping into a busier region with people of various races and then out into a quieter, locals' district. Shino vaguely wondered if her friend had had to take this route before, to shake curious people off her trail.

Or those strange ripples.

Finally they were in front of a door to a very small, one-storey house. Most of the roof was covered by the huge and dense foliage of a tree, making it harder for a casual pair of eyes to notice the existence of the house.

Shino looked around the entrance as she took off her shoes. "No offense, but . . . For a famous person like you, I imagined some fancier place?"

"The landlady and her son keep an eye out, and this is such a nice hiding place, don't you think?"

"Wouldn't it be safer to be in a place with a security system?"

"I said I need a *hiding* place. Now, do sit."

Shino sat down on a small sofa in the small living room. Tsukiko passed a framed photograph to Shino. It was a black-and-white photo of a couple, and the woman had Tsukiko's eyes, while the man was obviously a foreigner.

"My parents. Right after Mother crossed the sea to marry Father."

Shino looked up.

"It took only a few years for her colors to fade. They didn't know the colors only showed on the island. Father wasn't happy, you see? He married a woman with the colors. Not a woman with common skin, even if her features were beautiful."

"What happened to her?"

"He forced her to go through surgery."

"Surgery?"

"I think he did the same to me." Tsukiko sat down and hugged herself. "I don't know what she thought of it. The only thing she said, just before she died, was 'don't exploit yourself.' But what could I do? I ran away from Father, and the best place to hide myself was this island, I thought at the time. But then people discovered me, and they wanted me to show myself off. And I had to make a living."

Somewhere an old clock struck the hour, and Shino jumped. When the air was rid of the faint residue of the note, she spoke: "He didn't let you get away just like that, did he?"

"No. He sent me a letter, telling me how he missed me."

"What? Just that?"

Tsukiko shook her head and laughed dryly. "What if he knew how to turn this thing off—how to make me completely unable to change colors? People would know I've been *using* something, not my own ability that I was born with. What names would people call me, in a land where painting a nail could stir up gossip? With a little bit of money, he'd shut up. Then why not?"

"I don't understand," Shino said. "Are you saying it's something you can turn off? Like a machine?"

Tsukiko stripped off her T-shirt and turned. The scar, which had first been just a tiny scratch, was now a scaly mosaic that covered one shoulder blade, reaching out just a little short of her left shoulder. One moment it seemed to shimmer in back-of-leaf shimmers; pre-dawn clouds the next, depending on the angle.

The scaly surface was *rippling*.

"As I see it, my skin is a mass of something that responds to my thoughts, like your legs carrying you," Tsukiko said. "But this part feels like it's no longer part of me. I never felt that way about my skin, no matter how many times I changed and unchanged it."

Shino touched her nail, and sniffed once as tears crept up her throat. "My fault . . ."

"No way," Tsukiko snapped. "Your nail or no nail, this would have come. This thing won't last forever if you use it too much. Now I know what she meant. I shouldn't have lived the way I lived. I shouldn't have come here."

Silence stretched. *Don't exploit yourself.* Was that all her mother could say, in front of her father? Or was she herself unaware and confused, of what she and her daughter had been forced to go through?

"Can I touch it?" Shino asked despite herself.

"Do you even want to?" Tsukiko said over her shoulder.

Cautiously, Shino reached out one finger, the one with the nail Tsukiko had cured. As her nail approached, the rippling grew deeper, as if excited by the approach of its sibling. Tsukiko winced; it looked as though the ripples were extending a welcoming hand . . .

"No." Shino retracted her hand almost reflexively. "I don't think so."

Tsukiko nodded and sighed.

"What can I do, Tsuki? Is there anything I can . . . or you can, do about it?"

Tsukiko looked at Shino, her huge eyes rimmed with silver tears. "Can you promise me one thing?"

"Of course!"

"I don't want to fall back into his possession, Shino. Even if I die, I don't want him to have control over the reputation I have accumulated here. I don't want him to take the money I have earned by myself and saved for my own future. I don't want him to make money talking about me, his daughter he knows nothing about—"

"Tsuki, please, stop talking like that. If that's what you really want me to promise, I'll promise. But don't you speak as if that's what's really going to happen!"

Tsukiko pursed her lips. "When the scar became un-part of me, when it started to ripple, I started to see it outside, too."

Shino's nail pricked again.

"At first it was tiny. Day by day it grew. Another mass of the same things that consist of my skin. I think my father sent them, to get at me. It was twenty years after the surgery that my mother died. And today, I turned twenty-one. If I had the surgery when I was a baby . . ."

"Oh no. No!"

Just then, as if responding to Shino, something hit the window with a loud bang. The two of them spun around to look at the curtained pane, and Shino dropped the photo frame to the floor. At almost the same moment, Tsuki cried out and fell onto the carpet.

Shino screamed—she could tell what was wrong straight away. That scaly part had grown in size, as though a blister had broken and the fluid of colors had exploded. Tsuki's back was mostly covered with the mosaic, and the rippling was so powerful, so compulsive, that how Tsukiko could keep in shape at all, Shino couldn't fathom. In the same rhythm of the rippling, the window rattled behind the curtains.

"Don't," said Tsukiko.

But Shino couldn't help it. She walked to the window, and after a moment of hesitation, drew the curtains apart.

A swarm of invisible bugs. A heat haze that buzzed and lulled. Shino tried to cry out as she fell to the floor, but her throat didn't work the way she wanted it to. The ripple outside seemed to be obsessed with moving as a mass, but how long would it take it to realize there were slight openings in the wooden windowsill, or to simply break in?

"Tsuki . . . " Shino crawled back to her friend's side.

Now, her moon-white skin and the mosaic were flashing in turns, covering Tsukiko's whole body. Her entire self was a tide that tried to push Tsukiko's—and Shino's—sanity off the shore. The worst thing was that it was *beautiful*, the most beautiful thing that Shino had ever seen. "What . . . what can I do . . . " Shino said, and sobbed, despaired by how helpless she sounded.

"Shino." Now the ripples were visibly crawling up Tsukiko's throat, towards her mouth. "Don't forget the promise."

"No! Please, don't leave me—"

Tsukiko was balancing herself on her arms, and as she moved closer to Shino, her hand smashed the photo frame on the floor under her weight. A shard cut her palm, buzzing blood spilling out.

Shino took Tsukiko's injured hand into hers. She thought she saw Tsukiko's lips curve into a smile, though now nothing was stable enough for her to even keep hold of the hand. She felt the tidal wave retreat, pulling Tsukiko away like sand on a beach. *No*, with a cry that wasn't, she thrust her hand with Tsukiko's blood into the mass.

Just then the window smashed, and the rippling swarm washed over Shino; she let it. The mass of nanobots danced and mingled, discarding the ones too weak, rewriting the genetic codes of those that were strong enough to be renewed. Shino simply let them.

When the boiling, the turning had finished, in front of her lay a mass of flesh, shaped vaguely like Tsukiko but with nothing to wrap her up beautifully. Shino vomited. As the bile rose to her mouth she realized her lips, her entire skin had changed.

She looked at the nail. With one final ripple there, the nanobots settled and became *Shino* completely. She cried, but the tears felt no longer warm enough to her cheeks.

Sooner or later people would discover this thing that used to be Tsukiko. Maybe Shino would be suspected of murder. There was no proof that she hadn't killed her—even though no one would be able to tell how Tsukiko had died.

She looked at the photo of Tsukiko's parents under the shattered glass, which was now clear of any blood. Cautiously, she picked up the photo. Under it, hidden between the photo and the frame's wooden panel at the back, was a small key. A series of numbers were written on the back of the photo.

A key to a deposit box.

Don't forget the promise.

She stood, and walked out the door.

PEOPLE SEARCHED FOR THE PSYCHOTIC MURDERER of the famous model, who must have been either fanatic or jealous, as they concluded. The police came, wanting to talk to Shino, but she had already quit the job, moved out of her place. She was already at the pier, waiting for a ferry.

The police radioed and told the ferry staff to inform them if they saw a pre-dawn cloud woman going aboard. Stop her if they could.

"You can board now, Miss," the ticket man called to the woman with the pale skin. "I hope you had a good time touring our island."

"I did. Thanks," she said as she handed him the ticket.

The man tipped his cap. "Safe journey back to your continent."

She smiled at him, but said nothing. Her skin was too pale to go with her features, but no one took much notice; with the money Tsukiko had saved over the years, it hadn't been so hard to counterfeit a foreigner's passport.

Don't exploit yourself.

She wouldn't, because she had to find the man, together with the ghost she was wearing over her own skin. Maybe another ghost awaited her somewhere—awaited her daughter's ghost to join her, in the revenge.

Shino stepped onto the ferry, onto the rippling sea.

Nini

Nini found it rather amusing that the humans regarded it as "him." To Nini, self was always "it." Its appearance didn't incline it to *feel* like a human. Even so, as it walked towards a group of women, a mere glimpse of Nini made the women cheer.

When the women were close enough, Nini bowed at the perfect angle for this specific group. Enough to show respect to the elderly, yet letting intimacy stop it from going too low. "Granny," it acknowledged one of the women, "you must go to the medical ward. One of the medic AIs says they see something unsettling about your values."

"Oh, have they been sneaking glances at my data yet again?" The Granny shook her head. "Those machines! Last time they looked into me . . . "

Nini knew she was going to repeat her story about the AIs probing into her non-health-related values and backgrounds, some time ago. Other women started to murmur agreement, so it hastily cut in: "Granny. I assure you. This is really about your conditions, and important."

The woman nodded. "Okay, Nini, if you say so. How I wish you were the doctor."

Nini just smiled, knowing any further statement carried with it the danger of a longer argument from Granny.

"Thank you, Nini dear. Now let me give you some mochi!"

"Granny, you really don't have to—"

"Don't you be so modest, young one." The woman made Nini hold the food wrapped in a cloth. "I know you like it."

Just then the transportation arrived and took Granny away. Nini bowed at the other women of the group and walked away from them to go sit under its "favorite" tree across the hill, to eat its "favorite" food—even though it didn't feel like doing any of those things. That location had been chosen because of its visibility. There, someone would notice and see it appreciating the food.

So it went to that place, and forced down a few pieces of mochi.

IT WAS ONE OF THE OLD-FASHIONED space stations, the perfect lure for these older, more stubborn people. The sky was still blue here, the grounds covered mostly with soil. The humans here told themselves that they weren't *really* being written off—they rationalized their participation as a good deed for the future of the humans. While the wholly AI-powered medical team tended to their needs, they told themselves that they had been chosen because their conditions were not *too* serious, so that being isolated wouldn't be *too* much of a problem.

They ignored the fact that they hadn't applied for the project themselves, tried not to dwell on the reality that their own children or relatives had submitted them for the mission. They certainly did not spend too long thinking about the fact that their trip to the station probably was one way.

They loved this organic space station, they told themselves, more than the others they left behind. They reminded themselves that the organic scenery would improve their health.

And so, in retrospect, it shouldn't have been so hard to imagine that they would complain about the inorganic, all-AI medical team.

Because the Program was still in the experimental stage, there were young engineers who worked with the AI team. "You should be the doctors, not these mechanical *things*," one of the Grandpas would tell the young engineers each time he saw them at the medical ward.

"We are just engineers, not doctors," the young people had to remind him each time. "We cannot heal you."

The engineers weren't bothered by the elderly people too much; in fact, they were used to that sort of absurdity, as humans.

It was the AIs who'd had enough. They hadn't been programmed to deal with endlessly repeated complaints. Let alone *absurd* endlessly repeated complaints.

And that's how Nini came to be, a ubiquitous connection, all-purpose AI.

All purpose, meaning dealing with humans.

ITS FEATURES WERE SYMMETRICAL AND NONTHREATENING, a hybrid average of every human race kneaded into one entity, so that the humans found it familiar enough to like, but too featureless to love.

Its eating habit had been added as a function to further increase humans' fondness for it. Older humans regarded sharing food as an important part of building the station community, for reasons the AIs never understood.

After consuming a few pieces of mochi, Nini rested its head against the tree and let the bugs in its digestive system work on the food. After exploring several theoretical possibilities, the research team of AIs concluded that bugs were the best way for Nini to digest food; better, even, than any chemicals that the researchers had synthesized. Chemicals had to be refilled in one way or another, causing a margin of error if a shuttle failed and supply delivery was late. Bugs, on the other hand, would reproduce themselves forever.

The bugs broke down the food and remade it into emergency provisions inside Nini's body. Rice cakes were chosen as its favorite food because the bugs' digestion capacity proved best with sticky rice starch, and also because people could carry and store rice cakes more easily than they could do so with rice in its various other forms. Also important was the fact that every year, a certain number of old people choked to death on mochi, and making Nini consume large quantities of them decreased the probability of elderly fatality by mochi.

Nini didn't particularly enjoy the stickiness of mochi. But then again, the provisions it evacuated from its body, while excellent in nutrients and efficiency, were never greeted with enthusiasm by the humans. During periodical drills Nini had distributed the provisions to the human residents, but most of them didn't eat more than one piece, and took home most of the food that had been provided.

It was some time later that Nini learned, from the information the station sent it, that the provisions were too dry, too hard to the humans' taste.

Now, there was only one piece of rice cake left in its hand, and it seriously considered throwing it away, or leaving it in the grass for other organic creatures to consume. But Nini might be seen doing that, which might be interpreted as a slight to the humans. It swallowed once, to send some moisture down its pipe. And then it bit off a large mouthful.

And that large mouthful—it stuck, blocking its windpipe. Nini knew it wouldn't die, not the way humans did, but many of its systems were organic, much to Nini's chagrin, and thus required oxygen. *Stupid humans.* It only had organic parts because humans had desired them. Nini wasn't panicking, not exactly, but its calculation on which system needed to last longer wasn't going well. And it really wasn't supposed to be wasting any more oxygen on such a useless thought process . . .

Its hearing was failing. It was aware of a faint noise, but had no idea what it was or where that noise was coming from. The next thing it knew, it was being struck on the back, hard. Its sight was mostly composed of dark dots at this stage, but it saw food dropping out of its mouth with the next whack on its back. And then, its head was yanked back and something else was shoved down its throat.

Water.

It was torn between coughing and drinking, ended up doing both and coughing more. When the worst of the cough subsided, it heard a voice: "Don't you have any sense? Choking to death on mochi is exclusively for the elderly."

It looked up, breathing hard. A quadruped robot, a very old model, was looking at it. Nini realized it still had the bottle of water in its hand, and drank more. "Thank you," Nini said. "I wouldn't have died, not exactly. But the bugs would've, and the humans would have had to wait for the next supply shipment to get the proper repair kit, and *that* would have been a lot of inconvenience."

"Bugs?" The quadruped robot frowned, in a way only robots could. "Nini, I take it? The multi-purpose AI they installed recently?"

"You are right." Nini handed the bottle back. "And you would be . . . "

"I am Koma. The last of the construction robots from the first days of this station."

"Are you that old?" Nini shifted involuntarily, sitting straight. "But why haven't I heard of you?" It searched, and found no record of Koma in the ship's records.

Koma laughed, in its own robotic way. "I am the forgotten. Take it easy. Come with me, if you will." Nini followed Koma away from its tree, over a hill dense with trees and undergrowth. It knew there was likely to be an old tomb or a shrine upon such a hill, built by the humans at some point during the station's history. But when Nini requested the details for this place, nothing came back from the station's database AI. This meant there was a lot of the station's history that had been written off, long before Nini had been installed; probably that chunk of the history had been deemed useless by both the humans and the AI.

With its four legs, Koma went much faster uphill but it waited for the biped Nini to catch up from time to time. Nini detected a lot of metals deep beneath the soil surface. "Tomb for your kind?" Nini asked, as they reached a small shrine at the top, just as it had expected.

"Exactly." Koma looked back, making a lot of creaking noises. "But the shrine isn't for them . . . "

The way up there was deserted, no sign of humans and only the trace of a trail left by four legs. Yet the shrine building looked relatively well-tended. Koma called over the polished wood door. "Lady, we have a guest."

Inside the building was dark, and Nini switched its optic nerve. It found a woman sitting in the center of the floor.

"Nini, this is the Pure Water Lady. Lady, this is Nini."

The Pure Water Lady sprang to her feet. "You have my water inside you! How interesting!"

Nini shifted, sat straight on its knees and bent its head low, according to the ancient habits data it found. "Only thanks to your pure water and your guardian's generosity I am here," it said as it sat back.

The Lady blinked. "Oh! No one does that these days." She herself knelt in a polite way. "Your pure mind has been noted." She smiled. "It feels so strange, but very nice, to have someone other than you paying proper homage, Koma."

Koma creak-creaked, clang-clanged, which was its way of grunting.

"I am not complaining!" Then she turned back to Nini. "Koma is my hero."

"It is?"

"When the humans of this station deemed me useless and abandoned me, Koma was the only thing that cared about me—which is funny since Koma itself was also deemed useless and abandoned once the construction was over. Koma's faith and care makes possible my existence as a god, and with that little bit of power that Koma helps to generate within me, I've returned the favor by preventing its late coworkers from going bad in my soil, and extracting any remaining lubricants from them in return. We're so much like each other, though we look nothing alike."

Nini nodded. And wondered if things like itself had pushed the old-fashioned entities away, out of the history and the database.

Just then, the provision food made from the mochi got ready. It was faster than usual this time. It'd have to analyze later what had caused the acceleration, but for now, it took the food out of its evacuation compartment. It was small, probably because a portion of the original mochi was still somewhere under that tree.

Losing this small piece wouldn't hurt, it thought. "Could I perhaps offer you this? If you do not mind?"

The Lady squeaked. "Food! I can have food? Are you sure?"

"Humans wouldn't like it if they saw where it comes from. But if you do not mind, sure."

"Why would I? Whatever process it's come through, food is food!"

She shuffled across the floor to the altar and placed the food there. "I'll have it later. It will last, yes? First I'll just admire it."

Nini laughed. It thought about how strictly it had been told not to let the humans know how it was producing the provisions.

* * *

NINI CHECKED ITS DIGESTIVE SYSTEM, AND soon figured out that the water from the Lady's well was the key to the efficient and fast processing of provisions. It asked the Lady if it could sample the water, and when she said yes-of-course, Koma helped it get the water. The well was located halfway down the steep hillside at the back of the building.

"I wouldn't mind stumbling down the hillside," Nini said to Koma.

"Your clothes will get muddy, and humans would mind that." Koma was already well down the slope, anyway. "Also, you don't know where my late comrades' structures are poking out of the soil, which may damage your human-like skin. It's easier for me to go alone."

Koma creak-creaked down the slope some more, until it reached a small well, hidden by a bush. In no time at all it came back with a bamboo bottle filled with the water. "Thanks." Nini took the bottle from Koma's lever. "I'll make the best use of it."

BACK IN ITS DOMICILE, NINI FOUND a certain type of bacteria in the Lady's water. The bacteria worked very well with the bugs in Nini's digestive system. Nini searched, but found no record of the bacteria throughout the entire station's data banks. The bacteria-rich water must be the reason the humans had bothered to bring the shrine with them in the first place, Nini reasoned—though, obviously, they had forgotten about the Lady and her water over time. Further examination revealed that the bacteria seemed to work quite well with a certain enzyme that most humans produced, repairing genetic defects in the human body. It would be really, really great if Nini could somehow circulate the water throughout the station so that the humans would drink it on a daily basis . . .

"No." BACK AT THE SHRINE, THE Lady looked truly sorry, embarrassed, even. "We have too little water. A few bottles a day is the most we can give away."

"Is there any way we can increase the quantity?"

"If I could have more offerings of food, perhaps . . . "

So Nini looked for more food. With the Lady's water bacteria, its bugs could incorporate far more kinds of nutrients into the resulting provision, so Nini started telling the humans that it would like food other than mochi, too. Older humans, those who relished over-feeding the young, were simply overjoyed. Nini gratefully accepted their offerings, and produced an increasing amount of nutrient-rich provisions, setting aside a small quantity for the Lady, who accepted the offerings of food gratefully.

One night, thrilled that their favorite AI could eat more than just mochi, some of the humans invited it to a small party. Nini wanted to decline the invitation, because the fact that it *could* eat didn't mean it *liked* to eat, after all. It still had to try hard to eat a lot of the time, and it didn't want humans to see it trying so hard; but it also didn't want to say no to them, especially when they seemed to be so happy.

So it went to the meeting house, where they held semi-regular parties after each supply shuttle arrived. Although it wasn't much of a feast, most of the humans in the station looked forward to it every few months. That they had invited Nini caused something to stir in the organic part of its circulation system; a tickling feeling, deep inside. Nini wondered if it was in any way similar to what the Lady must feel when Nini offered her food.

It ate a mouthful of everything, letting each bite fall into different parts of its system and recorded the process so it could refer to the data later on. As it did so, it realized that around it there were only Grandpas, Uncles and young herons—humans who identified themselves as male. "Where are Grannies and Aunties, and the young lilies?" it asked at one point.

"They're in the kitchen, can't you hear their happy laughter?" It could, but why were they in the kitchen? As if he had sensed its silent question, one of the Uncles let it hold a small, small cup, and poured some clear liquid into it, perhaps to steer it away from the complicated question.

"Is this water?" Nini asked, truly curious.

"Better than water! Now, drink it up like a man!"

Nini wanted to frown—it'd suddenly remembered that many of them regarded it as male. And the liquid before it smelled strange. But everyone present was looking at it so expectantly, and in that atmosphere, there was no saying no.

AT FIRST IT THOUGHT THE BUGS had escaped its digestive system, and they were causing Nini's sight to blur. But no, something was wrong with its brain. Although Nini didn't find itself wanting to laugh raucously or fall into a sudden slumber, like many of the Uncles around it were, there was something too strange to name right now firing somewhere in Nini's neuro system. And it couldn't locate exactly where or what was happening. This worried Nini.

And so it reached out to Koma through the communication line that they had secretly established. "It hit some of the bugs!" it said, once the connection went live. "Some of the bugs are dead!" It was aware that it didn't have to exclaim the way it was doing; the noise of the humans' dancing and singing didn't reach Koma, it well knew.

And Koma's creak-creak didn't reach through the line, of course. Nini realized it missed that noise. "You mean your digestion bugs? What hit them?" Koma sounded confused. "Are you hurt?"

"I may be," it replied. "But—the bugs!"

Koma fell silent for a while. And then, "Wait. You are at the party as you mentioned. Are you . . . drunk?"

Drunk! Nini queried the word. *Drunk!* This must be it. "The bugs cannot survive alcohol!" It knew it was repeating itself, but couldn't help it.

"Are all of them dead?"

"No. I'd divided them to study the food-specific process. But about a fifth of them were affected, the alcohol was too fluid for me to pit in precisely."

"Then it will be okay, Nini. Everything will be okay."

Maybe it would. "I cannot digest this thing. I'll have to get rid of it in some way or other . . . "

"The Lady's water might help."

"I don't want to waste your water!"

"It is not wasting. I am sure the Lady would approve."

Nini stood slowly. "I'll come to your place, anyway."

"I'll meet you at the bottom of the hill."

So Nini sneaked out of the meeting house, balancing itself so as not to let the liquid inside go slosh-slosh too much and kill more of the bugs. Nini searched the database for more information on DRUNK, and wondered if its overly careful steps right now looked like those drunken ones of the humans.

LATER, IN THE WOODS NEAR THE bottom of the hill (Nini couldn't climb with the dangerous liquid sloshing around inside it), Nini waited for the alcohol to be washed away, with its forehead on Koma's mechanical trunk, listening to its faint sighs of creak-creak, finding the sound the most soothing thing in the known universe.

"NINI! WHERE HAVE YOU BEEN?!" THREE elderly women stood waiting for Nini, looking relieved.

Belatedly it realized it had turned off the human-AI communication line when it left the party. Of course it had left the emergency line open, but this must not have occurred to the women, who now were eagerly holding its hands. "I'm sorry, Aunties, what have I missed?" Nini projected a mildly-worried look on its face.

"Oh no, no, no." The woman in the middle, who had lung problems, wheezed a little. "We heard that one of the Uncles gave you sake! And one of the young herons remembered being told that most of . . . of your . . . *your kind*—should keep clear of alcohol!"

Of course. They *did* have the users' manual, just in case. "I'm fine, Auntie. Though I have no intention of drinking it again."

The women laughed. "Of course! You should try our tea instead."

Its face muscles involuntarily stiffened. "T?"

"Oh it's nothing bad! You can check it before you drink it."

As promised, Nini was allowed to sample this "tea" first. It didn't taste as good as the Lady's water, of course, but the bugs could deal with this liquid. "This is okay," it said, and the women cheered.

The women let it try many of the tea things. Their compositions were mostly the same, with just slight differences resulting in different flavors. Nini was surprised that the humans could discern the subtle differences in taste with their incomplete receptors. The women seemed to be delighted the way Nini took one sip from each cup and mused about those differences.

And so, Nini had an idea.

OVER THE NEXT FEW WEEKS, NINI kept sampling more foods, more drinks. It made the best use of its young looks and innocent-sounding questions, and the humans indulged their favorite AI. They let it taste everything first—which gave it a chance to add some water into the liquor jug, or the tea pot. There wasn't enough of the Lady's water to circulate throughout the entire station, but adding a little bit of it every chance it could find wasn't too hard.

As it had hoped, and expected, people's health gradually began to improve. "When they are well enough to realize it," Nini said, at the shrine on the hilltop, "I'll tell them how their recovery happened. They'll be really grateful. They'll come and offer you their food."

"I do hope that will happen but . . . " the Lady looked down at her hands. "I don't know . . . maybe they'd like it better if they think the benefit comes from *you*."

"What do you mean?"

Koma walked in, with bottles of water dangling from its trunk. "We're too different from humans. They wouldn't want to attribute something good to things like us." It handed the bottles to Nini, just as it did almost every day.

Nini took it. "But . . . I am sorry to say this, but at least the Lady looks mostly like the humans."

Koma smiled, in his way. "Yes, but still, her very existence, her very nature, is too different from them to embrace her. I suspect most of them don't hear her the way you and I do."

"I don't understand."

The Lady took Nini's hand. "I appreciate your care, and you can try of course, I have no reason or way to stop you. But whatever happens, don't be hurt. We don't want to see you hurt."

Nini frowned. "I cannot be hurt. I am only an AI."

As IT HAD HOPED, THE HUMANS started to see that they were getting better. First the medical AIs noticed the improved readings, and then the young herons and lilies, the engineers with their instruments and gauges, picked up on the improvements. Some Aunties and Uncles actually *felt* better. The time was approaching, when it could finally reveal the true cause for this miracle. The humans would be happy. That would make the Lady and Koma happy.

Everything would be better.

NINI CHOSE TO REVEAL THE TRUTH at another post-supply-shipment party (this was Nini's tenth or eleventh such party). As usual, the Grannies and Aunties and young lilies were chatting in the kitchen, while the Grandpas and Uncles and young herons took the comfort of the floor. It was something Nini could never get used to—Nini was the only one that walked freely to and fro between the kitchen and the meeting room.

Nini was in the kitchen, secretly adding some water into the soup pot, when a commotion erupted in the meeting room. The women looked at one another's face for a moment and headed out of the kitchen.

There they found one of the young herons on the floor, his face red with hives, his breathing ragged and uneven.

Before anyone else could acknowledge the situation, Nini was sending the data to the AIs at the hospital: anaphylactic shock. Triggered by . . .

The organic part of Nini's brain was screaming, even as Nini automatically acted to ease the young man's suffering, appropriately positioning the young man to help his breathing. Moments later, an appropriately-prepared concoction arrived through the emergency supply line, and Nini shot it into his thigh. Nini ignored the screaming part of its brain, and there was not a moment of hesitation in its movements. The young man was breathing relatively evenly by the time the transportation to the medical ward arrived.

"I'm coming with him." Nini stood. "I need to talk to the medics."

The humans understood that there was something odd going on, and so they all followed Nini and the young man to the medical ward.

So NINI HERE, ONE OF THE core medical AIs was saying, *has been tampering with your drinks and foods.*

Nini said nothing, because it didn't sound like a question aimed at it. And one of the Aunties spoke first. "He meant well, obviously. And he's like just a child. You cannot expect him to be perfect . . . "

Unlike Nini, this AI didn't have a name. Unlike Nini it hadn't been given a human form. It was just a box, which processed a huge amount of data, and projected messages upon a screen. At first it hadn't been even given a voice; that came later, when the young ones found reading inconvenient.

This "child" almost killed one of your fellow humans.

Nini knew that the AI was exaggerating, but it couldn't say that. "This is why I don't like them machines," the Aunty muttered under her breath, though Nini knew the medic could hear that.

Nini. For the first time, the AI addressed it directly. *Why didn't you assess the possibility of contamination? You knew about the iron and lubricants of the ancient robots buried in the soil around the well. Why did you disregard that knowledge?*

"I guess my faith in the Lady's water became too strong."

The humans exchanged glances. The medical AI sighed, in its way. To the humans, it sounded no different than its normal rumblings. *Nini. Humans decided long ago that they do not need or desire gods. Your actions perfectly demonstrate why the humans made this decision.*

"Yes. But . . . have they really, truly explored every single possibility of what gods can do?"

Your god's miracle almost killed a young human.

"Yes, but can't we work together, human and AI, to figure out how we can use the Lady's water without contamination? You know perfectly well that the water *was* working miracles on most of the humans, when truly pure."

The AI rumbled again, but Nini didn't sense irritation this time. After all, just like Nini, the medical AI had been built to serve humans.

And then, one of the humans said: "Nini, Nini. Take us to this god."

THERE WASN'T A TRANSPORTATION SYSTEM that reached all the way to the hill, of course, and this fact alone made a few of the older humans decide to stay at the medical center and wait. And then there was the matter of the hill itself, and those who weren't fit enough to climb had to wait, too.

There were more than ten humans, in addition to all the young ones, who, despite their difficulties, were determined to go see the god.

Because of course it was a *god*.

Most of the Uncles and Aunties had forgotten about such things, and the young ones had only read or heard about gods in books or history class. Who wanted to miss such a chance?

Nini guided them the way Koma had done for it before. It took much longer to reach the shrine than it would have taken for Nini alone, but they all made it. The few Grannies and Grandpas were delighted at the sight of the small building—they'd left behind something similar a long time ago, when they had been very, very young.

Hearing the commotion, the Lady opened the door. Nini smiled at her and she smiled back—but for some reason, her smile looked sad. Nini looked back at the humans behind it, but there was something wrong. They all hung back with an expression on their faces that Nini did not understand.

Nini turned back towards the Lady. Just then, Koma, previously hidden in the shadows, came into view of the humans.

"What is that horrible thing? Nini, that's not the god you were talking about?" One of the Aunties pointed at Koma, her face a grimace of disgust.

Nini spun around, the way it shouldn't have done in the humans' presence—too sudden, too unnatural. All of the humans flinched—a few even jumped. "This is Koma, the wise, loyal guardian of the goddess. Don't you see her? The Lady, behind Koma?"

The humans looked uncertain. They knew Nini would never tell such a lie. But . . .

"Nini," Koma said. "I told you . . . they cannot see her."

One of the young herons covered his ears and said, "What was the sound that thing just made?" And Nini snapped around to face him. He gasped.

"Nini," Koma whispered, its voice lower. "They don't understand my speech. You can only understand my speech because you are what you are."

"So Nini, you're saying," an Uncle—the one who had made it drink alcohol—took a heavy, half-shuffling step towards the building. "That there is a god behind you, though we cannot see her, and that this old, raggedy ancient robot is the only thing that represents the god's presence to us?"

"Oh you should take over that role, Nini." A Granny chirped in. "Like you do with the medical things. Really, I don't understand those machines. They could be beautiful like our Nini! Why haven't they done their best to blend in with us, just like you do?"

"Koma has been here longer than any of us, knows this station better than any of us," Nini said, looking around at the familiar faces. "I don't understand—" Some organic membrane in its throat vibrated in a strange way, and it didn't like that one bit. "Uncles drink sake, Aunties tea. The medics drink data and Koma here drinks lubricant. You like differentiating yourselves so much, and yet, there are differences you can embrace, and differences you cannot. Where does the border lie? What draws the line? I do not understand."

In that moment, the Lady fell. Even the humans sensed it, though they could not see her, still. The building and a large part of the hill shook with the impact of her broken body.

NINI FRANTICALLY CHECKED, BUT THERE WAS no available data for helping gods. It sent a message to the medic AI, asking it to see if there was anything it could find for the goddess. Nini rushed into the building, leaving the humans crouching or kneeling on the ground outside. "Lady," Koma and Nini said in unison.

The Pure Water Lady was there, but something was wrong.

Nini winced. "If I don't concentrate really hard, I'm going to lose hold of her existence."

"I don't feel that, Nini. That's probably your organic parts." Koma shook its trunk; for the first time, it seemed to be at a loss what to do next. "I don't understand. They'd forgotten about her long ago. Why would being rude to her do any harm now?"

Koma folded its four legs and crouched beside the goddess who was becoming translucent. Nini's fingers twitched. "My fault," it said.

Koma looked up from the Lady to Nini.

"She's been okay with the humans forgetting her, because that change had been gradual, and also, she had you, and your comrades, even though she'd been weakened a lot." The medic was transmitting everything it could find to Nini, but it didn't seem enough. "Now, because recently I've been added to her worshippers, and because the food I offered her technically came from the humans, the balance was lost. And the humans were speaking ill of you, Koma. Her most devoted worshipper and guardian, the most important being in her existence."

Koma looked back down at the Lady. To Koma there was only one or zero. Nini could feel the Lady's presence getting thinner and thinner but Koma could only see it when her presence turned off completely to zero.

"I killed her," Nini said. "I killed a god."

THERE WASN'T MUCH TIME TO LINGER on that matter, though. Without the Lady, something in the hill was winding down and falling apart. "My comrades," Koma whispered, but then soon sprang onto its four legs. It ran out of the building and leapt amidst the humans who yelled or screamed. "Nini, tell them to climb onto my back."

With the choice between life and death before them, they did. But Koma's trunk wasn't large enough to accommodate all of them, and even though Nini helped one human at a time, they still had to do three rounds. Just when they had climbed the final slope down, the landslide started, somehow inwardly, taking the building into the hill itself. The Lady's remaining energy protected Koma and Nini. Here and there they could see the rusty carcasses of Koma's late comrades, fierce and intimidating to the human eye.

The well was gone.

UNSURPRISINGLY, THE RESIDENTS' HEALTH DECLINED. IT was just reverting, going back to normal as it were, but after enjoying weeks of improvement, the decline was hard for the humans to accept.

Unsurprisingly, the humans decided to leave the station, but no one told Nini where they were going. Weren't they all homeless, in a way, let go of by their families, their illnesses used as a flimsy excuse for their exile?

The humans let the medical AIs of the station choose to stay or go, because they were humans. Sensible, righteous *humans*, who always gave any sentient being the right to choose. The worthy AIs chose to go with the humans, because they knew they still could serve—even though they didn't much care to watch the Grannies and Grandpas and Uncles and Aunties sobbing and going on about how useless they were. These AIs couldn't help going with the humans—maybe there was no choice for them, after all.

Nini decided to stay, because it knew it wasn't that useful, and that the humans would rather make a new favorite android from scratch, rather than keep an AI who had made a mistake.

But Nini had Koma, and there was nothing to regret.

TIME PASSED. INCREDIBLY, THE HUMANS NEVER forgot about the station, because Aunties and Uncles, and young herons and lilies told the stories of the station. They shared tales of the cute, very likeable AI who had shared their food, to younger generations.

And so, countless years later, when their technologies had evolved sufficiently so that humans could afford to satisfy their adventurous spirit, they remembered the stories of the little station. Perhaps, they dreamed, that adorable AI still lived, though no one knew exactly how much time had passed since they abandoned it.

WHEN THE SHUTTLE ARRIVED AND DOCKED, the adventurers were quite touched by the beauty of the organic station, though it looked a bit rough with overgrowth and strange plants. And the way these plants moved towards the humans, stirring in the breeze—and here the humans had thought there wasn't enough air to generate wind on the station's surface. There must be some explanation for the breeze, some force the humans had yet to discover, and wouldn't that be *amazing*?

They walked around cautiously, looking for any remnants or hint of the legendary AI. Stories told them something about a slope, so when they found a sloping area, they climbed, to find a strangely shaped mount of soil.

When they were close enough, they realized the mount was partly made of metal, with a rusting structure made of archeological iron atop the hill. The adventurers, excited at the hint of life, entered one of the narrow openings through the ancient metal support beams.

It was dark inside, so they put on their lights. The light bounced off something metallic—iron again, most likely, but this one beam glimmered brightly in the light, unlike the rusted supports outside. Beside the shiny metallic-iron thing, there was something else—something shaped like a human head, but . . .

The iron thing made a strange noise, and the thing beside it moved, extended itself, revealing a honeycomb structure beneath its grotesque head. The human-head-like thing turned, too—and yes, it had eyes, and a nose and mouth, just like a human face.

What the adventurers had thought to be a honeycomb structure, upon closer observation, turned out to be a mass of writhing, teeming bugs. Here and there human-made materials dangled—old machinery, wires, bottles and eating utensils—but it was mostly bugs that carried the head. The face itself was pleasing—even cute, quite likeable, probably, if one could ignore everything else . . .

None of the adventurers said a word. The head looked at them, and then said, "Oh. What are these things?"

It was horrible—their own language coming out of something so foreign, so . . . alien. The iron thing made another noise, to which the head smiled. *Smiled.* "Oh these things—they are organic, whatever they are!"

How could the humans expect the AI to remember them? How could they know that when Nini—belatedly—realized that there was no one left that could repair it once its organic parts started to decompose, it had to discard relatively unused data to survive first? Just like, once, humans had had to discard the idea of gods to justify their own mecha and genetic evolution, Nini, too, had to embrace its own changes. These adventurers didn't know, would never know, how Nini had tried to get by solely on the provisions it had once made for the humans and that humans had hidden, thrown away, and left behind uneaten, at first. That later, as these excreted provisions became scarce, Nini separated itself into an organic head, and bonded itself to Koma's sturdy iron body, to minimize its dependence on organic material. How the head and the iron grew plants to have organic foodstuffs for the head to feed upon, once it had eaten up everything that had been left behind by the erstwhile humans, the lost Grannies and Grandpas, the disappeared Aunties and Uncles, the long gone herons and lilies.

How Nini felt pangs of hunger, for the first time. Not a tickle, or a fluttering, but true hunger—the kind of hunger that the humans tried to ward off with their parties, the hunger that had consumed Nini's fallen goddess.

How Nini decided to keep the station alive, maintaining its signal and appearance to the outside universe, just in case the humans ever decided to return. But of course they never returned over the years. The organic plants that Nini ate were not enough to sate its hunger. They were never enough to sustain Nini's systems, its bugs, which had colonized and spread to maintain the entire station.

NO ONE ESCAPED THIS STATION.

Not a single adventurer, or any rescuer who came after them.

And the half-organic AI and the iron AI lived happily ever after.

The Tree, and the Center of the World

I sniff at the chalky lump of an amber colored substance. "I cannot give you actual food for this, but I can maybe prepare water sweetener," I say, too quietly for most of them on the other side of the window to hear.

Their leader does, so all is well. He nods to me once. "Sounds good to me. We'll take it."

I nod back and pull down the screen over the window, and walk over to the fume hood. I start working right away: first slice a few layers off the amber lump with a small glass knife, and from the niche in the tree root right at the side of the hood pull out a jar of fine crystalline powder, and put both ingredients into an ancient plastic bottle.

I open another jar and sniff at the content; not too bad. I take a small mouthful of the pink-tinted liquid, and apply it onto my left little finger with my tongue.

Stuffing a piece of fabric woven with dead tree roots into my mouth, I cut that little finger off my left hand.

I throw my finger and the blood flooding out there into the plastic bottle, and quickly bandage the cut. I stab the lowest part of the tree root with the same knife, and pull its juice just a little, ten drops, and place the bottle on the fume hood table as fast as I can.

And then I finally allow myself to scream over it.

There is a commotion outside, of course, people shouting if I am okay and so on. The leader is telling them everything is fine, it's just the way it has to be. One minute later I grab the plastic bottle—everything inside completely liquified—out of the hood and place it on the counter.

When I release the latch of the screen, the people on the other side all look horrified, all but the leader who smiles at me, just a little. "By the way," he says, as he accepts the bottle, "where is your predecessor? Hope she is well?"

I look up at him and wonder how old he actually is, to ask me that question. "Gone," is all I offer in reply.

He looks sad, almost, just for a second.

WHEN THE PEOPLE HAVE ALL LEFT I place the latest addition to my inventory in the niche between the thinner, more complexly intertwined roots of the floor of my place. I'll find more ways to use this amber thing for others, who might come visit me, this lone existence trapped in a cage poised in the roots of a huge, huge tree at the center of the world, some time in the future. My little finger is already starting to regrow, but I can tell it's in a completely different color than the rest of me. I force myself to climb a ladder despite the dizziness to retrieve some vials from higher niches, and carefully mix the contents drop by drop. I don't add the tree's juice to this thing. I let it settle there for a while, until the concoction is perfectly blended, and then swig it as fast as I can.

This will change the texture of my blood again, even if only slightly, but I need to take something after losing a part of my body. Food and drink, I don't enjoy taking them, and I only take them when I really have to. One of the reasons the tree above me doesn't like me very much.

This cage is a crazy tangle of roots that seems to have been formed for the sole purpose of trapping me, and "outside" is a notion that I decided to forget a long time ago. I did manage to enlarge the cage as the tree grew, making the place as comfortable for me as possible, and the adventurers made the platform right outside the only opening big enough in the roots (which is now known as the window) as accessible as possible, but there's only so much I can do in the pit of a void at the center of the world.

Tired, I lie down on my cot on the other side of the fume hood. This cage doesn't have a proper roof, except for the damned tree itself, and if I stick my head into the gap between some of the thicker roots, I can see the void surrounding the tree. The void is sometimes beautiful with the vessels traveling around, but most of the time it's just a void. The adventurers typically love talking about their own adventures in and out of the void, even though I never offer them any solid response. Each of them thinks their own adventure is special, unique. The fact is they are all one thing or the other—they just want to go out or away.

"Why don't you just leave?" an adventurer once asked, "just change jobs and go explore the world. You can really go anywhere, you know, this is where all the universes and dimensions intersect. You live in a place that's most convenient for travels in the world!"

Yeah, I chose to exist here and I choose to stay here, you think? I don't even remember why or how I came to be here. Some time after I emerged here—a hundred years later or something—people started arriving at this place. Back then, everybody asked me what I was doing under the tree at the center of the world. And if I needed help. Once, I grabbed the hand of one of those who asked. And we both almost fell as the tree careened badly, and for those few seconds, the whole world had no idea which way was up, which way down or whatever. I'm sure folks got hurt. I can only hope no one died.

That's why, obviously. Why I don't, can't leave.

Another hundred years or so passed, and I realized people had started taking the leaves out of the tree's foliage. At first, I didn't care. Why should I? But then the tree began swinging at the slightest disturbance, such as a vessel going past some distance away. People (and their devices and meters) got confused again, and I got sick, really sick. I had to tell them to stop taking the leaves. They had to understand, when the swaying subsided as more leaves started shooting out.

"But that's half the reason we visit this space," one adventurer said then. "After traveling many universes that we don't inhabit, we need something fresh to eat."

"You are *eating* the leaves?"

"They taste nothing like what we ever eat in any of the universes, which is quite refreshing. They are really nice and crisp. Everybody loves them."

So I asked the adventurers to leave something behind (pun unintended) like one piece of paper or something that weighed as much as the leaf they took. For some time that worked well. But then, some folks assumed they could take all they wanted as long as they left the same weight on the tree. They took more leaves than others could, and . . . other folks complained to *me*.

"It's not my fault," of course I told them. Back then I wasn't as resigned as I am these days.

"But you need to do something! Do you know how it feels, when we find, finally out of the wormhole, the tree stripped off and no reward waiting for us?"

Hey, do you know how it feels to be stuck here forever, hearing ungrounded complaints like that?

The problem here was, the tree seemed to like them—those paper strips attached to it, in place of its leaves, and it stopped growing more leaves, at least until the paper crumbled off or simply drifted away. One of the adventurers from a tiny sphere had written their wish (for tasty food of course) on the piece of paper they tied to the branch. Others had somehow followed suit. When I asked one of the folks to remove the paper strips to make room for new leaves to grow, the tree *resisted*. By making that part of the branch go rotten. That was ridiculous.

It took all of us a lot of time; we hadn't been aware that the tree had things it wanted to say, and we didn't have many ways in which we could hear it. In the end, we reached the conclusion that the tree enjoyed attention. Very much. After a lot of discussion, we—the adventurers and I—came to an agreement: everything traded here must be appreciated in the name of the tree. The joy, or even the tears from something too sour or bitter, must be dedicated to the tree. Thus I am here, trading the substances the adventurers brought in, making things for them to take away just for their enjoyment, so that they will *want* to come back to the tree, again and over again. The leaves grew back in full and the tree no longer confused up and down. Still, for the first few centuries after the agreement, it had these unpredictable fits every once in a while. A lot of experiments later I realized that to really, *really* please the tree, I had to sacrifice a part of me, since I don't enjoy eating and thus cannot properly "taste" my appreciation. And my screams. It enjoys my screams immensely.

This ridiculous tree at the center of the world.

I examine my finger now; it's completely back, though the shape is slightly wrong. I also lost an eye the other day, and it's taking a bit longer to regenerate. I put a very shimmery substance that one adventurer brought in but could not fit in with any other stuff for food, into the socket. The weight of it feels good. It may or may not be incorporated into my tissue over time; I can never tell. This way, I keep changing, and I no longer even remember what I was like a few hundred years ago. I do remember that man, the one who asked about the previous me, but I'm not sure when I saw him last. The "predecessor" he remembers is the past configuration of me.

No one knows me anymore. Except for the tree, probably.

Except—

I look out the window, into the void. I have considered leaving and taking down everything with me. Why should I be the only one to endure this? I mean, some universes might survive and we might avoid total extinction. I have also considered the possibility of someone replacing me here, perhaps. Someone, or something . . .

Then there's a knock on the window, making me jump; I didn't hear a vessel approaching. Frowning, I release the latch of the screen. The thing shoots up to reveal a small person waving their hand at me behind the glass pane. "Hi!" they shout.

I nod, still frowning a bit, and then open the window. "What do you have?"

The person blinks. They didn't hear me?

"What do you have to barter?" I try again, a bit louder this time.

They grin, after a moment. "Me," they say.

"What?"

The person grabs the windowsill, and comes in, right foot first. "What, wait wait!" I say, the loudest I've ever been in a hundred years, "you can't come in!"

"Why not?"

Why? "No one's ever come in."

"That's not a reason though."

I look around, listening. The person in front of me is small for a person, yes, but they are far bigger than anything I've accepted from adventurers. A few places in the roots creak, and something in the far foliage buzzes. But then—nothing worse happens.

For now. "You should leave," I tell them.

"There's plenty of room here."

"This place is built around me," I want to grit my teeth but hold myself. "You're a foreign matter here."

The person cocks their head. But then they turn to look to the window. "Someone is coming."

Sure enough, I, too, hear a vessel. I stick my head out of the window exercising caution. The small person's ship is afloat on the underside of the window. It is a one-person vehicle that's many times smaller than the auxiliary craft that's coming down from above now, its mothership some distance up to the right. When the craft's window is level with mine, a man I recognize climbs out and stands on the platform, and smiles an uncertain smile. "I've never seen a . . . friend of yours inside with you," he says.

I spare a glance behind me over my shoulder. "This is not a friend. What do you have?" I say turning back.

"The usual." He drops a container on the counter and urges me to open it. When I do, it contains jelly-like plant pieces that emit dull glows. I look up and he says, "The seasoning powder you gave us last time for these, that was great. But I wonder if you might give us something more substantial this time. Something chewy."

I shake my head ever so subtly. "The substances that make up these plants cannot be regenerated into 'something chewy.' This is not magic and there is a law. I can try for some stronger spice, perhaps, but the resulting amount will be smaller than the previous powder."

He smiles weakly, as if trying to tell me *I get it*, *but*, where the *but* is what really matters. "Look, I promise to bring something really, really good next time. We're going into the gold mine soon, though of course I have no idea what gold is." He laughs. "Something shiny, they say. But the thing is, we cannot go on exploring without some kind of reward. We're all too tired."

"That's not how it works—"

"Oh, *please.*"

I want to say no again. Adventurers no longer remember what their ancestors agreed upon, and I cannot blame them; it is not a written law, after all. He is a big man and his weight is already making the platform under his feet bend a little. I start calculating: I may be able to extract slightly more than I should if I add that sticky part of the tree root juice, *and* go through some worse pain . . .

Then the small person pats my shoulder from behind, making me jump again; I totally forgot they're here. "What is a promise worth, at the center of the world?" they say. "You can go anywhere without ever keeping that promise while she's trapped here. That's not fair."

The adventurer frowns. "What are you?"

"What *am* I?" they say, their other hand on their hip. "I have a name, but since you didn't ask me for it, I'm not giving it to you. Do you or do you not want that spice?"

The man looks back up, at the mothership. As if that would give him the comfort he needs. He turns back at us and I can tell he didn't get it. "All right, then," he says.

"All right, then," they echo right behind me.

THE SMALL PERSON TELLS ME HER name is NuNu as I scream into the fume hood. She doesn't even wince, just sits on the floor and keeps on talking about her adventure alone—how it's inconvenient but gives her freedom, and what is an adventurer without freedom? Even as I hand him the spice she goes on explaining what gold is to him. I do know what gold is and she seems to know that I do.

As soon as he's gone I pull down the screen shut again, and turn to her. "Who are you?" I say.

"Weren't you listening? My name is—"

"NuNu. And you know that's not what I mean."

"Wow, you sound a lot different than when you were talking to that guy."

"You haven't offered anything yet, you are not my customer."

NuNu crosses her arms. "I'm here to offer you help."

"Help?" I blurt out, incredulous. "*Help?*"

"Why are you saying it like you've never heard of that word before?"

Because I might as well not have. "I cannot give you food in return of labor. I cannot conjure up substances out of nothing."

"I'm not here for food."

"Then what for?"

NuNu twists her lips, as if thinking hard. "For . . . knowledge. I want to know more about this place."

"What about this cage?"

"You call this a cage? How fascinating." NuNu beams. "Think about it, has anyone asked you what your life is like in this cube? Has anyone, at all, tried to understand what you do?"

I shake my head. "Not in the recent five hundred years," I say. "But I—"

"See? Research is another form of adventure. I seek knowledge. Now tell me what that device is!"

I turn to the direction NuNu points. "That . . . is . . . my fume hood." I realize nobody's ever seen it up close. "I made it out of the void debris. The tree juice makes every substance highly reactive with another, including those that I am made of, and it's not quite safe for me to touch anything once a reaction starts, so I . . . do all the food-making under the fume hood . . . "

She peers into the hood. "Where does the fume go?"

"Um, up. To be reserved among the foliage of the tree."

"So that's what we sometimes see burning and shimmering. Beautiful, isn't it?"

"I've never seen it from outside."

NuNu looks completely sorry to hear that.

Before she can tell me how unfortunate I am, I say, "Look, I'm sure you love the outside world. Why don't you just go?"

"Oh, thanks for your consideration, but I've looked at the outside plenty already."

I really shouldn't have let her in in the first place. "That's not quite—"

She trots to the wall beside my cupboard, where most of the surface is covered with thin roots of the tree, and hugs it. "How good could it be, to fall asleep, embraced by *life*?"

I scratch my nose.

NuNu frowns. "You've never thought about it that way?"

"No."

NuNu keeps dodging and bouncing the subject until I'm just too tired of simply speaking. At night she lies down next to me in her own sleeping bag. We share the view of the void. I am uncomfortable, feeling her heat raising the temperature inside the entire cage. Every time a vessel passes overhead, she claps her hands. I'm not sure what that gesture means.

* * *

And that's the problem with another being inside my place: heat. After we wake I have to explain to NuNu that the few bagfuls of the fluffy stuff in the alcove started fizzing because of her very existence, after which she shrugs and says, "Has it gone bad?"

I have to consider this. "I don't know."

"Then let's find out!"

She grabs one bag and jumps onto the table below the hood. "Hey!" I yell, at the same time as the whole cage swings. "Look, it's not safe to be in there. The tree tends to think everything under the hood that's not bottled or boxed or bagged to be its possession, and I mean *everything*!"

But the fume hood, or the tree, says nothing, for the moment. NuNu fiddles with the sealing of the bag. Her body heat, much closer to the fluff now, is making the bag inflate. She sniffs the gas that leaks out of the gap she just managed to open, and then—sticks her finger in, pokes at the fizzy foam and . . . licks.

She *licks*.

"Hey, hey hey hey!!" I'm beyond horrified. "Oh no no no, I don't think I have an appropriate stomach pumping method for you here. Do you have enough water for yourself?" I'm not even sure if the water I have here is not poisonous for her. "Just come out . . . oh no, perhaps that's not safe now that you've done that? But I . . . let me . . . "

NuNu laughs. "Easy. This tiny bit can't hurt me." But she makes a face. "Urgh. Tastes awful, though."

"You're not sick? I'd be real sick if I did that."

"You can be damaged by things from outside more easily because you only belong here," she says, still making a face. "We adventurers breathe and drink and eat a lot in other universes and dimensions than the ones we were born in. But I'm sorry I did this." She does look sorry. "Still, I'm sure there are folks who would appreciate this flavor and texture."

I'm suddenly very irritated. "You . . . " I feel my face burn. "You are wasting my precious inventory." My retort comes out very feebly.

"Come on, wear loss happens all the time. Besides, don't you want to offer adventurers the food that's better suited to them? If they get what they like better, there will be less of those like that guy who tried to talk you down."

I'm still fuming, almost literally, but she does have a point. After a breath, I pull my pen and book out of a niche in the roots. "Tell me more about how that thing tastes," I say, very, very quietly.

She hears anyway. And grins.

* * *

AND SLOWLY, EVERYTHING STARTS TO CHANGE. NuNu tries just a little bit of everything in my inventory, and describes them in weirdly accurate ways. She also tells me about the universes she visited, about the people, about their landscapes, how they decorate themselves. I take note of everything. I connect those words she offers me with the list of substances in my inventory, also attached with her words about the taste. I can see that people from the planet with the purple scenery will love the smoky concoction from a fuchsia galaxy combined with a slime from the indigo nebula, and those from the dimension where everyone wears furry clothes for special occasions will very gladly consume that one cake of sticky sparks reserved in one of the highest niches. I just can, when I hear her words. I need to rearrange the storage locations in accordance with the quality of the taste, not just the form of the substance in room temperature.

NuNu also does every kind of experiment she can think of under my hood (she is now trying to make the tree's dead bark and another substance react, a substance that's a result of another reaction of another . . . whatever). I can feel the foliage is filling up quickly with the new gas she creates with those experiments. I'm not sure what will happen when it's full, if it ever gets full. Will it burst and kill me? I may not mind that, except when that happens, I'll have to make sure NuNu is out of that mess.

Meanwhile, more adventurers arrive. NuNu always greets them at the window beside me, doing a lot of talking to them. We get to know a lot more about our customers through that.

I mean, my customers.

An especially large vessel approaches one day. I think I've seen this one before. A wired kite flies off the vessel, and a young boy drops off onto the platform. He looks startled at NuNu's presence, blinks a lot as if he were trying to bat away the bright light flooding out of the window. Then he says, "These," putting a small brown bag on the counter, eyeing NuNu and me in turns. He is probably wondering who is the one in charge.

I open the bag. There are stones. "Shiny!" NuNu jumps up and down, shaking the whole place.

The boy holds the windowsill as if he thinks that could prevent the cage from unraveling. "We've brought these things in before," he says. Apparently he cannot pronounce the name of the thing with his vocal cords. "They are fragments of very special minerals, and they can be used as metals for industrial purposes or as gems for decorations depending on which universe they are treated in. . . . Though one of you must know this of course, my grandfather personally came here to deliver them the last time. We managed to obtain a lot of these and we thought we could afford to barter some."

"Your grandfather?" I turn the stones around in my hand.

"He and I look so much alike! You must remember him, I hear you remember things well."

I shake my head. "I do remember who has visited this place. And what they brought in. But 'looking alike' doesn't mean much to me, sorry." I peer at the stones again. "I don't think I've seen these."

"You gave him very nice, crunchy slabs in exchange for them."

"Slabs?"

"About this size." He makes a rectangle with his fingers. "Mostly whitish gray, but some colors sprinkled here and there. I've seen a recording of it."

Hm. "I think I remember *that*." I turn around, walk across the cage and dig into the niche above the hood. Just as I thought, the very last, tiny piece of the mineral in question is sitting at the back in there. I come back and show it to him. "Here. This must be what your grandfather came here with."

The boy nods enthusiastically. "There you have it! We were hoping you'd make the same thing for us . . . "

I shake my head again. "They aren't the same."

"Come again?" He looks so confused, I think he didn't hear me.

"These stones. Not the same," I try a bit louder, holding one of each kind in each hand between our faces.

"But—" He licks his lips. "They look exactly the same. We checked the weight and density and ran a test, though a screening. Don't they look the same?" He holds one of his stones towards NuNu.

She takes it. "They—they might *look* the same, but . . . " she turns to me.

"Just as I said, looking the same doesn't mean anything to me. I see everything in chemical compositions. Something, perhaps a very small portion, but *something* nonetheless in the compositions is different. In that case I perceive them as completely different things. I can—" I weigh the stones the boy brought in, and almost say I can give him something similar to the slabs, by chopping my whole hand off. But NuNu's heat makes me think twice. "—Get you some squashy mass, a sweet one," I finish off the sentence.

He almost rides the windowsill. "But I must bring back the crunchy slabs! That was an order from my father."

NuNu gently pushes the boy off the sill. "Calm down! You're scaring us!"

The boy shakes his head. "You are lying!" His voice is almost a shriek. "If . . . if it's not the mineral, we went through all that for . . . "

Belatedly I realize there are many punctures on his surfaces. I wonder how much pain he and his companions had to bear to get these stones, which aren't what they wanted. "I'm sorry," I say but I don't think he hears me.

"I'm sorry," NuNu whispers beside me.

The boy shivers, holding on to the countertop. Liquid streaks down his cheeks. "Your sorry won't bring her back!" And then without warning, he smashes the closed half of the window with his fist.

For thousands of years, I always thought something like this might happen any time. What I didn't give a thought to was someone doing it with their own hand, hurting themselves in the process.

The blood flies *in.*

The fume hood clicks on detecting an anomaly. I've never seen the hood react this way; the air—not just under the hood but the whole air in the entire cage—is stirred so violently that NuNu almost loses her footing. And the boy, he is doing his best to hold on to the window and the counter, because the air is flowing in a completely different way inside and outside the cage. The hood is drawing every droplet of his blood into itself, while trying to peel the boy off the cage's only entry. As if it's intent on gathering every drop into itself, before the boy can claim the blood back into him.

Somewhere at the back of my head a phrase that I heard long, long ago rings: Blood sacrifice.

This horrible ridiculous tree at the center of the world is now demanding another form of sacrifice.

NuNu scrambles up to the countertop and grabs the boy's hand. "Call your kite," she tells the boy over the boom of the wind and the groaning of the branches, "I don't think the cube will stop treating you as foreign matter until you're physically off it."

The boy flips a switch at his belt, and his kite lurches forward. He grabs one end of the wing, his other hand still holding the window and bloody, with NuNu supporting that arm. He slides into place under the wing and holds firmly onto the handle, and then NuNu lets go.

We all exhale in relief.

But then he blinks; the next moment I realize he is looking at the stones he came here with. Whatever they are, they are not mine as of this moment, and I need to return them to him. I reach out to the bag, then find some of his blood has touched down on the stones, sizzling with minute bubbles.

Is it safe to touch it with bare hands? Or will the tree see me as part of the sacrifice?

My hesitation gives him the wrong impression, unfortunately. "What are you doing?" he yells at me. "Did you mean to steal them from us from the start?"

"No," I say, and I'm not sure if he can hear me. "I'm just—"

"Did you lie about them not being the special mineral?" He probably doesn't hear me. "Have you cheated us before? How many times have you cheated us?"

"What?"

NuNu seems to have had enough. She grabs and throws the bloody stones into the bag—luckily the blood doesn't react with her skin—and then thrusts the bag the boy's way. "Here, take it! We don't need them."

And then his face does many things. I hate it when somebody's face does many things I cannot understand. He draws his arm a little behind him. I cannot see what he has there, but I can taste the seed of fire, in the crazy flow of air polluted with his blood. "Watch out!" I call out to NuNu.

I wonder if she can hear me.

But I recall she always hears me.

By now the boy's mothership knows something is wrong here, and starts pulling his wired kite even though he hasn't tried to move his craft. The kite swings violently. I think that buys enough time, but then, that buys too much time; I try to shield her with my own body, but there's a fraction of a second that's long enough for *her* to shove me off from the line of his sight.

I scream, as the fire thing collides with NuNu's chest.

My scream startles the boy and he involuntarily lets go of his firearm. The kite is pulled away, dragging the dazed boy with it, but I cannot stop screaming. NuNu is on the floor, unmoving. Some fluid and a lot of heat is quickly coming out of her, goes into the malfunctioning hood under the crazy tree, and my scream is triggering more reactions.

The foliage will probably explode. And I don't care.

I scream on.

I touch NuNu's hand. It's not safe to touch her hand in the middle of the reaction. But I do it anyway, and feel acid peeling a layer of my skin. Her eyes are closed. Her chest is quickly corroding away with the acid of her own blood.

Corroding . . . the outmost layer of her skin . . .

. . . And deeper.

I stop screaming.

The hood finally gets a little quieter, regretfully.

I stand up without a sound and go fetch the gloves that are hanging on the side of the hood. With them on, I rip NuNu's casing away. Everything comes off, off her stomach, off her limbs, her face and head.

"Why?" I say.

NuNu, about twenty-three weight-percent smaller now, opens her eyes and looks up. And then she sits up, as if getting up out of her sleeping bag. "Why what, first?" She looks at me with ancient eyes that shine like prisms. "I'm sure you have many questions that start with that."

I sure do. I watch as she walks completely out of her organic casing, throws it onto the fume hood table. And then the stupidest question comes out from me: "Why didn't you tell me your name last time?"

NuNu laughs. "You didn't ask. In the last thousand years, while I was away and heard about you from other adventurers, I learned I needed to proactively tell you things I wanted you to know. Which in turn means I don't have to tell you things I don't want you to know just yet. Which is why I didn't tell you this wasn't the first time I came here—which should answer another question you must be having right now."

"Has it been a thousand years?"

"A little more."

I try to remember that day, so long ago—that day when some humans brought in an artificial-person body, which was all minerals and synthetic materials. This is life, I said at that time. This is still alive.

And the woman who came here with the body only shook her head with sad, sad eyes. I told her I couldn't give her food in exchange for something alive. She huffed some air and was gone the next moment.

I took the body in and set it on the table of the fume hood and massaged it with an oil blended with the tree juice. Then I turned the device on, and soon it started sucking dead parts off the artificial body, as gas and other particles. As the body became smaller and smaller its life finally kicked on, the size of the body and the life in it fitting each other, and then I snatched the body off the hood so the tree couldn't take any more. It was almost half my size by then, and one part, one vital part, was wobbling as if it were undecided whether to come completely off the body to kill it or stay and be properly functional.

I looked down at my own body. Everything in my body was outside the scope of organic/nonorganic, and the very strictly nonorganic body in my arms probably wouldn't accept any of my part as its own. But I didn't know where exactly this life was from, and so couldn't decide if any of the things in my inventory would be safe for it.

I didn't know why I cared. I still don't know.

I made myself wedge into the narrow gap between the thickest root and the back of the hood. And looked down at the part where the tender thin roots and the hood material had started interconnecting with each other. At first I thought the hood material was rusting and the root was simply invading the device. But no—the silvery, thready, slightly sticky substance was something entirely different, something even I had never seen.

It was the first thing ever born inside this cage.

Hopefully a nice fit for that life that wasn't quite life.

I reached out but stopped short. The substance looked so new, so delicate. I didn't want to waste it. I dislocated the place between my spine and legs, and extended the upper half of my body towards this new substance. The silvery thing quivered at my breath. I'd thought this might be the beginning of a change. Me, or at least this cage, moving onto a different stage. I didn't know if this new thing happened because of time passing, or of any other factor. I wouldn't be able to replicate this generation, ever.

I licked the new substance clean.

It didn't have any kind of flavor or taste. I went back out of the gap, mouth open so as not to swallow it. I grabbed a pair of scissors, and cut my tongue off.

The pain was so fierce that I could not hold my scream back for later use. Right there, bleeding and sobbing and vomiting, I screamed and screamed, and used the tongue with the new substance as temporary adhesive between the wobbly part and the mineral body on the floor.

And it worked.

WE SPENT MOST OF OUR TIME quietly staring at each other. I thought perhaps the body wanted to say something, but it didn't have a communication component (one of the things I had to let fall) and I didn't have a tongue to ask. As I'd suspected, my tongue had fallen away off the small body and the new substance was slowly spreading to cover its core system like an intricate net. Not that there was more of it there, it'd just stretched wider. I thought the body was safe now. I couldn't tell that to it, and I didn't know if it understood written language, or what kind if it did.

We stared at each other—or I stared at it, I couldn't tell. I wondered then if this thing could replace me. It was a good thing that I couldn't speak, I might have asked it if it would. I'd saved it, after all, and asking wouldn't have hurt. Except for the meager crumb of my conscience.

"AND YOU JUST LEFT ONE DAY," I say to the mineral body that has come out of NuNu's body. It is much larger than it was when it left the cage a little more than a thousand years ago, with so many sensory components and terminals grown out or acquired and added on that it looks like a smaller version of the NuNu when she told me her name, more or less.

"You can still call me NuNu," it says. She says. "I didn't know how I could tell you that I needed to leave. I smuggled into a small ship which collected space debris between universes for recycling."

I almost ask why. Why she left. But then, isn't it obvious? "You knew," I said. She knew of my selfish wish, that I was thinking of taking advantage of her. She knows. I feel my tongue tingle.

"Of course I did! I couldn't help but notice."

Of course. "But then why did you come *back*?"

Her eyes cloud. She touches her chest. "I'm sorry, I couldn't. I really, truly tried hard. And . . . I thought if you knew who I was from the start, you'd get mad and throw me out. So I made the casing to cover me up."

What? " . . . What?"

"What *what*?"

"That's not . . . " I start, but my throat is sore from the screaming.

NuNu looks at me inquisitively, and when I don't go on, she says: "Well. I knew, from the way you stared at the net protecting my heart, that the thing was very important to you. So I checked around this cube but I couldn't find any more of it. I thought I needed to find the same kind, or to find the way to cultivate it so that I could make up for your loss. In the meantime I met many people who could extend my functions. And people started to call me an adventurer in search of knowledge. I could not find anything to make up for your loss, I'm sorry, but I think I finally have something that I can give you, at least. That is why I came back."

I fumble with my processing of these words, and still say nothing.

"Are you . . . mad at me?" NuNu asks me after a moment.

Mad at her? Me? "No!" I want to scream, it's hard to focus. "NuNu, I myself had no idea what that thing was and I'm quite sure it's something as useless as anything in the world, like everything in this world is useless to me, and you have no business being sorry to this selfish food lady that's just an anchor of this stupid tree! You travelled, and then you came back, for *nothing* at all!"

I pant as she stares on at me. I'm horrified as her eyes do many things, just like that angry boy. But then—NuNu laughs.

She laughs for a long time, pointing at me or fanning at herself or flailing, while I can do nothing but stand there. After a while I cannot take any more. "NuNu," I say. "Please."

She laughs some more and shakes her head. "Not for nothing, no no!" She even hiccups a few times. "You thought I ran away from you? Oh, how shortsighted are you?"

"What?"

"Nobody would call you selfish, I don't know where you got that from. But no, I travelled, and learned many things, and one of the two most important things I learned is that there is so much to learn in this world. You cannot call this *nothing*. And the other most important thing I learned is, by the way, if you wish, you yourself can go adventuring like everyone else to see more of the world!"

That doesn't register for a long time. I involuntarily look down, thinking hard, and then up, to find NuNu patiently waiting for me to understand. "What?"

She closes the distance between us. "You thinks you're pinned here at the center of the world and cannot go away. That this cube is where everything balances out, and you need to be here to keep that balance. But for tens of thousands of years you've been offering yourself to folks from every universe and dimension. Everybody brought home a piece of you with them, everybody has eaten a piece of you through the mouths of their fathers, mothers and lovers and comrades. Now you're not *at* the world's center; you *are* the world's center.

"You still cannot get out of this cube, according to what I've learned so far. But we can expand the window so that you can look at everything more closely. All only if you do want to. You can stay. Or you can just go. To know that you have a choice, that's something, isn't it? That's what I wanted to give you."

This is insane. This is too much. "But—" Questions after questions. "If I cannot go out of this cage, how can I leave?"

"Aha!" NuNu beams. "You think I've been happy being your humble assistant all this time? Of course I've been manipulating things, every chance I had to use this hood. Namely, I synthesized a lot of new gas and pumped it up to the foliage . . . "

"Wait, what if I say I want to stay here?"

"I knew there was like an eighty-nine percent chance of you saying go."

"That's not high enough for you to just go ahead!"

NuNu just ignores me and rummages under the hood, through her discarded casing, pulls something bloody out of the leg and places that bloody object beside the casing on the table, so that I can have a better look. "If I let your tree absorb this thing, the root will be disconnected from the bottom of the void as you call it, while in the foliage it will form a film of vapor there, to make a huge balloon with all the gas you and I have accumulated there to let the tree float. Your tree and cube will be a huge airship that can go anywhere."

"But then how can the adventurers come to us?"

"Just make them find you. That's just another part of their adventures, right?"

The adventurers chasing us, no matter where we happen to be? Well, that sure will make this attention-demanding tree real happy. "All right, then," I say, and feel my lips curve upward.

NuNu grins back and crushes the bloody thing with her hand. It is a concoction of things collected from many, many places she visited, wrapped in a film made of her mineral blood, and *my* out-of-scope blood too from a thousand years ago mingled. The tree sucks it up at an unbelievable speed. I hear a boom, and feel the whole place lurch. "And how do you control it?" I ask her.

"What?"

"Control. Where it goes. Like you do your own little ship."

She twists her lips and looks up at nothing near the ceiling.

"NuNu!"

She claps her hands and starts talking about our new window. She wants one huge, huge window but I want many small ones. While we argue, our tree floats on.

Yukimi Ogawa lives in a small town in Tokyo where she writes in English but never speaks the language. She still wonders why it works that way. Her fiction can be found in such places as *Clarkesworld*, *The Magazine of Fantasy & Science Fiction*, and *Strange Horizons*. In 2021, she was finally translated into Japanese. *Like Smoke, Like Light* is her debut collecton of short fiction.

Copyright Notices

"Like Smoke, Like Light," copyright © 2018 by Yukimi Ogawa. First appeared in *Strange Horizons*, June 4, 2018.

"Perfect," copyright © 2014 by Yukimi Ogawa. First appeared in *The Dark*, Issue 4, May 2014.

"Welcome to the Haunted House," copyright © 2019 by Yukimi Ogawa. First appeared in *The Outcast Hours*, eds. Mahvesh Murad and Jared Shurin, Solaris, February 2019.

"The Colorless Thief," copyright © 2014 by Yukimi Ogawa. First appeared in *Ideomancer Speculative Fiction* #69, March 2014.

"The Flying Head at the Edge of Night," copyright © 2022 by Yukimi Ogawa. First appeared in *Interzone Digital*, Dec. 1, 2022.

"In Her Head, in Her Eyes," copyright © 2014 by Yukimi Ogawa. First appeared in *The Book Smugglers*, Oct. 21, 2014.

"Town's End," copyright © 2013 by Yukimi Ogawa. First appeared in *Strange Horizons*, March 11, 2013.

"Taste of Opal," copyright © 2018 by Yukimi Ogawa. First appeared in *The Magazine of Fantasy and Science Fiction*, September-October 2018.

"Hundred Eye," copyright © 2015 by Yukimi Ogawa. First appeared in *Strange Horizons*, 2015 Fund Drive Special, September-October 2015.

"Grayer Than Lead, Heavier Than Snow," copyright © 2020 by Yukimi Ogawa. First appeared in *Clarkesworld Science Fiction and Fantasy Magazine*, Issue 162, March 2020.

"Rib," copyright © 2014 by Yukimi Ogawa. First appeared in *Strange Horizons*, June 9, 2014.

"The Shroud for the Mourners," copyright © 2021 by Yukimi Ogawa. First appeared in *Clarkesworld Science Fiction and Fantasy Magazine*, Issue 177, June 2021.

"Blue Gray Blue," copyright © 2016 by Yukimi Ogawa. First appeared in *Clarkesworld Science Fiction and Fantasy Magazine*, Issue 123, December 2016.

"Ripen," copyright © 2019 by Yukimi Ogawa. First appeared in *Clarkesworld Science Fiction and Fantasy Magazine*, Issue 151, April 2019.

"Ever Changing, Ever Turning," copyright © 2016 by Yukimi Ogawa. First appeared in *Lackington's*, Issue 11, Summer 2016.

"Nini," copyright © 2017 by Yukimi Ogawa. First appeared in *The Book Smugglers*, Oct. 31, 2017.

"The Tree, and the Center of the World" is original to this collection. Copyright © 2023 by Yukimi Ogawa.

Printed in the USA
CPSIA information can be obtained
at www.ICGtesting.com
LVHW090217171223
766611LV00004B/453